Suddenly, the air t ... fra-
grance was overwhelmed by the sickly sweet odor of jasmine and decay.

"God!" Amber cried, pulling the doll protectively against her. "No! Get away!"

Melanie watched in horror. It looked as though Amber was fighting with herself, as if her hands and arms wanted to throw the doll, while the rest of her wanted to keep it safe.

She looked at Melanie with wide eyes. "Help me!"

Before Melanie could respond, the maniacal sound of Christabel's laughter filled the room and the doll flew from Amber's arms. The girl screamed as it crashed against the wall with a sound like breaking dishes.

"No!" Amber cried again "No!"

Melanie grabbed her. "Come on!" she ordered over the sound of Christabel's laughter. "We've got to get out of here!" The putrid odor of decay was so strong now that Melanie had to fight down the urge to retch. "Come on!"

A dark cloud swirled into existence in front of the open door, blocking it. As Melanie watched, it took shape, forming quickly into the image of a young, dark-haired woman whose face bore an expression so thoroughly evil that Melanie could barely look at her.

"Christabel," Melaine said softly.

Then, instantly, the spirit vanished.

A split second later, something slammed into Melanie like a wall of ice.

Books by Tamara Thorne

HAUNTED
MOONFALL
ETERNITY
CANDLE BAY

Published by Kensington Publishing Corporation

HAUNTED

TAMARA THORNE

PINNACLE BOOKS
Kensington Publishing Corp.
http://www.pinnaclebooks.com

For John Scognamiglio—
Nobody does it better

PINNACLE BOOKS are published by

Kensington Publishing Corp.
850 Third Avenue
New York, NY 10022

All Kensington Titles, Imprints, and Distributed Lines are available at special quantity discounts for bulk purchases for sales promotion, premiums, fund-raising, and educational or institutional use. Special book excerpts or customized printings can also be created to fit specific needs. For details, write or phone the office of the Kensington Special Sales Manager: Kensington Publishing Corp., 850 Third Avenue, New York, NY 10022, attn: Special Sales Department, Phone: 1-800-221-2647.

Pinnacle and the P logo Reg. U.S. Pat. & TM Off.

First Printing: May 1995
10 9 8 7 6 5 4 3

Printed in the United States of America

ACKNOWLEDGMENTS

An odd lot of thanks are in order here. First, thanks to my keepers, Kay and John, for moral and immoral support. It wouldn't be any fun without you two.

Much of the inspiration for certain aspects of this book came from late-night bar bitching, so cheers to bar buddies Craig, Matt, Rick, Lisa, Nancy, Ginjer, Chris, and Charlie.

Thanks to Keven Shrock, M.D., for giving me a hand and answering all my bloody questions. Leaps of logic should be blamed on the author, not the doctor.

Last but not least, thank you to the man who puts the Pismo in Pismo Beach, my darling Damian, explorer of caverns and grottos, keeper of the fire down below.

One body, two bodies,
three bodies, four
Check up in the attic,
seven bodies more
There's a dead man in the kitchen
and a blood slick in the hall,
Twenty men are hanging dead
upon the garden wall.

Verse from children's rhyme
Red Cay, California, 1916

May 15

Prologue

Byron's Finger: 6:03 P.M.

"It's haunted."
"Is not."
"Is so."
"Is not."
"Is so. Wanna bet?"
"Is not." Billy Galiano stared hard at Body House then turned to his friend. "You're full of it, Farmer."

Matty Farmer crossed his arms. "You want to go inside and see? My dad says it's haunted and it is."

"My dad says it's superstitious crap."

Billy gazed at the forbidding stone mansion, taking in the heavy pillars of the front porch and the terrace crowning it, the sharply peaked roof and the tall rounded tower that loomed above the three-story structure. The windows on the first floor were all boarded, but not those on the second and third, and he could just barely make out the colors of the stained glass fanlights that topped each one. Curious to know whether or not the glass pictures were like those in church, he cocked his head and squinted at a third floor dormer window illuminated by the setting sun.

He thought he saw something move. Startled, he squinted harder, and saw another brief flash, but then it was gone. He shivered, even though he knew it had to have been his imagination.

"Go in, I dare you," Matty whispered in his ear.

No way did Billy want to go in Body House. "Look, wiener-breath," he said, pointing at the new blue and white Pelinore Realty sign stuck in the weedy front lawn. "It's got a new For Sale sign."

"So?"

The old rusty one had been there as long as either boy could remember, so Billy figured the new one had some significance. "We can't go in. They're trying to sell it."

"They're always trying to sell it," Matty sneered. "It's empty. What's the matter? Are you scared?"

"No way!"

"Way!"

"I'm not scared because *I* don't believe in ghosts." Something shifted again behind that same dark window and, involuntarily, Billy flinched.

"What?" Matty spun around and stared at the house. "What'd you see?"

"Up there." Billy pointed.

"The ghost of Christabel," Matty whispered in awe.

"Nah. It's probably some homeless guy." His dad had told him that living people who lurked in old places like Body House were the real danger, and he believed it. "Maybe it's a serial killer," he added, half to get Matty to stop bugging him, half because he thought it might really be true.

"Look!" Matty grabbed his arm. "Look!"

Billy looked just in time to see a pale face staring out of a second floor window, all the way on the other side of the house. He couldn't tell who—or what—it was, but he could feel it watching them.

"It knows we're here," Matty said softly. "Galiano, you think somebody *alive* could go down the stairs that fast?"

"Why don't you ask your dad? He'd know." Matty was always bragging about how his dad had been one of the cops who had discovered the bodies of a bunch of hippies after the mass murder in 1968. Billy was sick of hearing about it. Matty's father never talked about it—he didn't do much of anything except drink as far as Billy knew, so he figured his friend had made most of it up. "We should tell Chief Swenson. Whoever's in there," he said as he continued to watch the windows, "is trespassing."

"Swenson can't do squat," Matty said firmly. "It's not a somebody, it's a *something.* It's the ghost of Christabel. Or maybe one of her victims. I still think we should go look. Then we'll know who's right—me or you."

"Hey, wanna go check out the lighthouse?" Billy asked hopefully. He wasn't crazy about wandering around in there either, but it seemed a whole lot safer than the house. There were less places for killers to hide.

Matty regarded Billy doubtfully before turning west to look at the old lighthouse at Widow's Peak, which was what everyone called the tip of the peninsula. It hadn't been used in years, and if you walked beyond it, you could see a modern beacon cemented into the rocky cliffs below.

"The lighthouse is haunted, too," Matty informed him.

Billy decided not to argue. "So I guess your dad saw the headless sailor, too?"

"Yeah, he did. But it's not just a headless sailor, it's a headless *sea captain.* Captain Wilder." Matty lowered his voice. "And he walks when someone's going to die."

"Let's go check it out."

"Cool."

They walked along the path toward the lighthouse. Byron's Finger—the peninsula was named for the man who built the tower and the house about a hundred years ago—was long, skinny, and very tall with steep, ragged edges jutting out of the ocean. Halfway to the lighthouse they paused to throw pebbles over the sheer cliffs into the ocean. Inland, just to the north, Billy could see the town of Red Cay nestled in the hills edging the half-moon bay. Dinky cars traveled the streets and tiny fishing boats were moored to the pier.

Before the lighthouse was built and even after, when the fog was bad, there had been lots of shipwrecks at Byron's Finger and there were always rumors that you could find sunken treasure in the deep waters below—if you didn't get smashed on the rocks first. Pretty much anyone who tried it got smashed, and according to Matty, it was because Byron's Finger was cursed. According to Billy, it was just really dangerous down there. It was dangerous up here, too, he thought, taking a step backward. Except for some old wooden railings that would probably give way if you even touched them, nothing stood between you and falling over the edge. Their parents would kill them if they knew they were out here.

They approached the splintered remains of a weathered wooden door that hung crookedly on the hinges of the lighthouse. It creaked as Matty pulled it further open. "Come on, chicken," he whispered, stepping inside.

"I'm not chicken," Billy hissed, and followed him in.

Silence. Complete, utter silence, then a slight creak from the door behind them made them both jump.

Light streamed in from above, creating a dim spotlight at the center of the room. Brighter light crisscrossed in laser-like angles, entering through the small arched windows that studded the thick walls. Plaster had fallen away in many places to reveal the stone beneath and the black iron stairs clung to the circular wall like a rickety web.

"Captain Wilder walks those stairs, top to bottom, bottom to top," Matty breathed, "looking for his head."

He likes this a lot, Billy thought as he tried to figure out if it was possible for anyone to hide on the top floor where the beacon used to be. "Come on," Matty urged. "Let's go up."

It didn't look safe, but Billy didn't want to be called chicken again, so he said okay, and took the lead. The black stairs creaked, swaying a little under his weight. A breeze ricochetted in through a window and ruffled his hair. He got goosebumps.

"What're you waiting for?"

"Nothing. Listen, Matty, go slow. Some of the fasteners are pulling out of the wall." At least the one he was looking at sure as heck was. Plaster crumbled around the bolts as he took another step.

They ascended, slowly and without incident, pausing twice when the stairs swayed perceptibly. Nearing the top, Billy got more goosebumps. He had to enter the room, climb up through the center, where the light shone from above. If someone was up there, he was in deep shit.

The sea captain . . .

Nah, he didn't believe that, but maybe Matty really did, because he'd stopped nagging him to go faster. Somehow, that made Billy feel braver. Cautiously, he poked his head through the round opening.

Welcome sunlight streamed in through the huge glassless windows that ran the circumference of the room. Still eye level with the floor, Billy checked the place out. The floor consisted of heavy wooden planks, and huge rusted metal bolts held down the skeleton of the old beacon. He wondered if there had been a foghorn here too, but he didn't know what an old one would even look like. On one side, a doorway opened to the iron widow's walk outside the building.

"Come on, Matty," he said, no longer afraid. If the floor could hold the weight of the rusty iron, it could hold theirs, too. He pushed himself into the room and turned to give Matty a hand. His friend looked a little pale. "What's the matter, Farmer, see a ghost?"

"Very funny." As Matty peered around, his cocky attitude returned. "Wanna go out on the catwalk?"

"Yeah, sure."

The floor creaked as they crossed the room, but that didn't worry Billy; he sensed it was sturdy enough. The widow's walk, however, was pretty wobbly and even Matty stayed away from the outer edge. Standing still, they gazed out to sea.

"Sun's going down," Matty said.

"Geez, what time is it?" The sun wasn't sinking into the ocean yet, but it was low enough that it was turning the thin cirrus clouds orange and purple and gold.

Matty squinted at his watch. "Shit, it's six-thirty already. I'm supposed to be home in half an hour. If I'm late again, they'll ground me for a year."

Billy didn't have to be home until seven-thirty, but he was happy to leave. "Okay, so let's go."

They reentered the beacon room and Billy paused, staring at the sunset once more. It would be extra pretty tonight, he thought, not that he'd ever admit noticing stuff like that.

"What was that?" hissed Matty.

"What?"

"That? Don't you hear it?" Matty's breathing was suddenly very loud. *"That!"*

Billy heard it now and his hackles rose. Footsteps. Heavy and dragging, they approached slowly from below.

The boys stared at each other before frantically looking around for a place to hide.

"It's the ghost," Matty whispered. He looked ready to pee his pants. "It's Captain Wilder."

"No, it's human. Probably just a kid," he added, though all he could think was *serial killer.*

Slowly, steadily, the heavy footfalls came up the stairs.

"Listen, Matty, whoever it is, we're going to surprise him" Billy whispered. "We're just gonna run down the stairs right past him and we'll be out before he can do anything, okay?"

Matty looked unsure. The footsteps sounded louder. Finally, he nodded.

"On three," Billy whispered. He held his fist out. Extended a finger. *One.* Next finger. *Two.* The last. *Three.*

And he ran, so full of adrenalin that he felt weightless. He couldn't hear the footsteps over his own feet and Matty's, just behind him.

He ran, pounding down and around and around and ar—

A dozen steps below, he saw it, a translucent darkness, vaguely man-shaped. Stunned, Billy stopped in his tracks and Matty almost ran into him. He stopped a hysterical giggle before it escaped. Farmer was right: it wasn't human. But it didn't look much like a headless sea captain either.

Time began to flow again as a footfall sounded and the shape moved closer. Behind him, Matty made a mewling sound like a newborn puppy.

The air in the stone lighthouse had been cool, but now it felt frigid. Suddenly, a rushing sound filled Billy's head and he had to order himself not to faint. He heard another footstep, so loud, so close. So cold.

"Farmer!"

Matty made a sound like a sick animal.

"Farmer, we gotta run."

"Y—yeah."

"We gotta pass it. Run like hell. *Now!"*

He didn't wait or look around, he ran straight for the dark mass, screaming as he hit, then entered it. Enveloped in cold, his whole body feeling like it was plugged into a light socket, he screamed over the pounding in his ears and emerged on the other side of the thing, running, running, vaguely aware of Matty's screams behind him.

Come on, Farmer! Go! Go! Go! He couldn't spare the breath to cry it, so he thought it as hard as he could as he pounded down the stairs.

Matty's screams sounded softer now.

"Run!" Billy yelled as he reached the bottom of the stairs. He turned and peered up into the shadows. Matty was nowhere in sight, but his cries continued. Now he could hear slow heavy footsteps again and lighter, frantic ones, slipping and running.

Running back upstairs.

"Matty!" Billy screeched, then ran for the door.

The heavy air lifted as he left the building. Quickly, he ran around the tower to the sea side of the lighthouse so he could see the doorway to the widow's walk above. An instant later, Matty appeared on the threshold, a tiny figure, but even at this distance, Billy could see the fear on his face.

"Matty! Run!"

The boy stared down at him, but didn't seem to understand his words.

"Matty! Run! Downstairs! Run through it! Hurry!"

Instead, the boy turned to look at something. Then he began to back toward the railing.

The dark doorway grew darker.

Matty backed into the railing. Billy could see it start to give, but before he could yell again, the darkness surrounded his friend. Suddenly, the boy screamed, a horrifying and desperate sound, then the railing broke away and he was falling. And falling and falling.

Without thinking, Billy backed away from the tower. After an eternity, the screams abruptly stopped as Matty smashed against a pointed boulder at the cliff's edge. His body bounced, then toppled over the rocky ledge, out of Billy's sight.

He ran to the edge, saw blood coating the sharp rocks. A lot of blood. Swallowing hard, Billy forced himself to peer over the edge, and saw a small body floating prone in the water, crashing into the rocks, over and over and over again. Matty's yellow T-shirt had turned red. A wave turned him over. His face was nothing but pulped, red meat.

Billy vomited.

Numb, he turned and looked up. The unnatural darkness had left the catwalk. He had to pass the lighthouse to get to his bike and go home. He didn't want to, but he had to, so he made himself move, walking quickly instead of running, because his head was too light and he was afraid he'd fall.

The darkness hovered at the broken door at the bottom of the tower. Billy made himself ignore it, forced himself to look straight ahead.

A moment later he passed Body House. Out of the corner of his eye, he thought he saw movement behind a second floor window, imagined he heard laughter, cruel and feminine.

He began to run as he approached the patch of junipers where they'd left their bikes. A moment later, he climbed on, looking back once more before he began to pedal. It was very pretty here, he thought crazily, a very pretty place with a house and a lighthouse backlit by a red and purple and gold sunset.

He forced his rubbery legs to pump the pedals. Gravel spewed beneath the tires, hit his legs, waking them up. *Matty was right,* he thought again. Not only were there such things as ghosts, but the one that walked the lighthouse really did foretell death.

July 10

One

Red Cay Stop 'n' Shop: 6:35 P.M.

"You're going to die in that house." The cash register chinged, underscoring the clerk's dire words.

David Masters had been watching the old man's arthritic fingers as he painstakingly punched in prices for the light bulbs, Ajax, paper towels and the rest of the things they might possibly need tonight, but hadn't brought with them in the car. Impatient to be off, to get to the real estate office and pick up the keys, and then to unlock the doors to his new home for the first time, he had paid no attention to the clerk until now, but suddenly, this was one interesting old geezer.

"What did you say?"

"You're gonna die in that house," he repeated. "Be a hell of a lot better off staying at the Cozy Crest tonight. Stay there, go back where you come from in the morning."

"You know who I am?" David asked, intrigued.

"Everybody in Red Cay knows who you are." The old man fixed him with a beetle-black stare and slowly shook his head. "You're the fool who bought Body House. You're gonna die in there."

With those nasty little eyes, the broken hawk nose and gleaming bald skull, the guy would make a great character in a book, David thought. Maybe a hellfire preacher. "How do you know about me?"

"Calla wrote about you in the paper," he answered sourly.

"You're that big time writer, you do all that Frankenstein stuff. Calla, she likes your books." *I don't* was the unspoken coda. "Been selling a lot of them since the story came out. New one's gotcher picture on the back. Had to special order copies of that old true story one you did about haunted houses. Calla and some of those lunatics up at the High Hooey Center wanted them." He snorted in disgust. "Guess you think you're some kind of expert. They all do, when they first show up."

The High Hooey Center? "I'm not unfamiliar with the paranormal—" David paused to take a deep breath. *Don't let him get you,* he cautioned himself as he realized he was trotting out his evil twin, the patronizing intellectual snob, to respond to the geezer's not-so-subtle attack. *That's not nice, Masters.* He exhaled; he could take a little criticism, especially considering the source. "I've seen some interesting things and done a little research."

"Yeah, yeah," said the man as he bagged David's purchases. "That's what they all say. Then they go in there and die. Research, my ass."

This wasn't just an old geezer, David decided. This was a certified old fart, all judgment and hot air. But fascinating. He smiled patiently. "As I understand it, the only death on the property in recent years was that of the child who fell from the lighthouse a few months ago." He handed the old fart a twenty. "Or has something happened since?"

"Wouldn't know anything about it," the clerk grunted. He laid three ones and change on the counter then pushed it toward David with his fingertips. "Don't care. Ain't none of my business."

Christ Almighty. "Have you ever been in Baudey House?" David asked, careful to pronounce the name correctly.

"Body House. Plain old Body House." He thrust the bag at David, then crossed his arms and resumed his hard stare. "Once, when I was a stupid kid, I went in on a dare. Learned my lesson. Never went back."

"Did something happen while you were inside?"

He set his mouth in a grim, uncooperative line. "I warned

you. Don't forget I warned you." An instant later, the man's gaze shifted as the market's door groaned on its hinges.

"Dad?"

Amber stood on the threshold, the afternoon sunlight forming a golden nimbus around her long, tawny hair. "Daddy, you said you'd just be a minute."

"Get in or get out, young lady," the old fart commanded. "You're letting flies in."

Unperturbed, she stepped inside and let the door slam behind her. The clerk glared but she ignored him. "Let's go. We have to check out the high school before dark. You promised." She took the paper sack from his arms and tilted her head toward the clerk. "You can come back for your local color later, Dad."

The old man grunted something that sounded like "fuggin-writer," then cleared his throat. "She yours?"

David nodded.

"You intending to take her into that house?"

"Yes."

"When it kills her, you remember Ferd Cox warned you. It's gonna be all your fault for taking her in there."

"God," moaned Amber. "Get a life."

"Amber, hush," David said softly.

Cox turned his discomfiting glare on her. "You don't believe in ghosts, is that it, little girl?"

"Of course not," she replied, her own evil twin gaining power. "Not the kind that can hurt you."

"Guess your daddy told you there was no such thing?"

She nodded. "They're just anomalies. They're simple." David cringed a little as his daughter fixed Ferd Cox with her straight-on stare and smiled condescendingly. "Only superstitious people believe in ghosts. Let's go, Daddy, please?"

"Okay, I'm coming." David followed her to the door, then glanced back at Ferd Cox. "See you later."

"Not frigging likely."

"Charming man," David said, as they got into the car.

Amber set the bag on the backseat then slid in beside him. She grinned wickedly. "That Cox, he's a sucker."

"I'm your father. Don't talk like that in front of your father." He pulled out onto the little paved road, then added, "Save it for your friends."

"All my friends are in Massachusetts, Daddy."

"You'll make more."

"I doubt it." She stared out the window at a woman in pink curlers stumping down the side of the road. "This place is full of geeks."

"Give it a chance. You know, you were really rude to that man."

"Oh, Daddy, he was really rude first. It's not like I'm a little kid anymore. I'm almost seventeen and I don't think I should have to put up with rude old far—men."

In theory, he agreed with her, but all he said was, "You're a cheeky brat."

"I know." She leaned across the seat and pecked his cheek. "You taught me everything I know."

"Maybe, but learn to exercise some self control, okay? Look, Amber, we're not in a big city anymore. Red Cay has a population of four hundred and eighty-four—"

"Four hundred and eighty-six."

"That's what I'm talking about. Don't keep correcting your elders. In the city, everything's different. Here, you give some old geezer a ration of crap and you're likely to hear your name splashed all over the place as the latest town juvie."

"That might be fun."

"Amber—"

"I'm sorry," she said as they pulled up to a stop sign. She smiled. "You know I'm just teasing you. I promise I'll try not to rile the rubes."

"Okay," David said as he made a left onto Cottage Street. "But you're making me nervous, kiddo. Look, you can call them rubes around me, but don't let them hear you do it. You do understand that, right?"

"Of course, Daddy. You're such a worrywart."

A quarter mile down Cottage, they found the high school. "Looks like they don't have summer school here, Amber. Guess you're brokenhearted."

"Oh, yeah, right. It's sure dinky. Are you sure they've got art classes?"

It was small, she was right. Low-slung, circa 1940s stucco painted babyshit yellow, and ugly as sin, it was a mini-version of the typical California public school building. "They claim to have several art classes."

"They're probably all doofus fruit-drawing classes."

"Well, Amber, consider it a challenge. You can draw bowls of rotting fruit."

"You're weird, Daddy."

He grinned at her. "If all they have are fruit drawing classes, we'll find you a private teacher."

"Here? In the middle of nowhere?"

"The hills outside of town are crawling with artistic types, remember? I'm sure we can find one."

"Do you think I could take private lessons even if there's a class at school? I'd learn a lot more."

He hesitated, unused to being able to afford things like private lessons. "Sure, why not? Now, let's go get the keys to our new palace."

"Can't we cruise around just a little more?"

"You've seen most of it already," David told her. "And you'll see more on the way to the office—Theo's place is up in the hills where all the crazy artists live. Tomorrow we'll check out the town in detail, I promise. Okay?"

"Sure, Dad. Maybe we'll meet some people just as nice as Ferd Cox."

At least she said it with a smile.

They headed into the hills west of downtown Red Cay and spent forty-five minutes attempting to find Theo's place by relying solely on David's memory. This resulted only in a number of snide inquiries from Amber about why he always refused to ask for directions, so he finally gave up, pulled over and consulted the map, an act not quite as humiliating as admitting failure to another human being. Melanie used to say he had testosterone poisoning and never let him get away with it. That was one of the things he liked about his ex-girlfriend. Actually, there were a lot of things he liked about her—chief among them, he constantly reminded himself, the fact that she was now thirty-five hundred miles away, making her own life in mid-town Manhattan instead of trying to make him feel guilty.

"Dad? Do you see it yet?"

"Oh, uh huh. I think I've got it. Take a look." After she confirmed his directions—she had a knack for reading maps—he checked his mirrors and pulled back onto the road. "Surveyors from hell designed this place."

The outskirts of town were comprised of a series of vague ovals crisscrossed by a maze of winding roads and passes, most of which they had traveled at least twice in the last thirty minutes. The outermost oval, a paved, two-lane highway, touched the coast on one side and fed from the access road to Pacific Coast Highway, farther inland, on the other.

Red Cay proper began at the coast and spread inland for several blocks. Simple to navigate with its straight streets heading in normal directions like north, south, east, and west, it contained businesses, fishing-related and otherwise, as well as older homes which ranged in style from bungalow and sea shanty to elegant Victorian.

As dusk deepened, David switched on the Bronco's headlights. The squirrely area they navigated now was not actually part of the town. Art galleries, expensive private homes, small farms, and ranches were all scattered along the twisting ovoids and switchbacks between the coast and Highway 101. This area consisted of picturesque rolling hills and pastoral meadows, and from time to time, longhorn cattle, horses, wildflowers, monarch butterflies, and any number of other scenic items which helped attract the artists and their patrons to the area. A number of colony-types who thought that Cambria, fifty miles north, had become too commercial, had relocated here and David suspected that, while the merchants in town were happy to take the artists' money, they secretly held them in contempt. Red Cay itself was a fishing town, full of real men and tired-looking women. To the townsfolk, he'd qualify as an artist too, and equally worthy of their contempt, if he wasn't careful.

He knew he'd made the correct turn when he saw The Beings of Light Church. He'd noticed it the first time he was up.

"Look, that must be the High Hooey Center," he said.

"Huh?"

He explained about Ferd Cox's term for the New Age center.

"High Hooey," Amber said. "I like it."

"Me too," he replied. "It's direct and to the point." The New Agers' buildings were beautiful constructs of redwood and glass, the central building traditionally churchlike, the rest low and nearly hidden in a plethora of pines and ferns.

A moment later, they rounded a bend, and came upon the modern split-level ranch house that Theodora Pelinore owned. Sprawling didn't begin to describe the place. He turned the truck into the circular drive, pulled up and parked.

Two

Pelinore Realty: 7:29 P.M.

"*This* is an office?" Amber asked as she got out of the car and stretched her stiff muscles. What was supposed to be a fifteen minute trip had taken almost an hour; no one could get lost like her dad. Their cross country trip, for instance, had taken twelve days instead of the planned eight, mostly because of his creative shortcuts. When he did give in and read a map, he usually read it wrong.

Not that she really minded, at least not when she wasn't in a hurry to get somewhere, because they always discovered weird places where she could acquire truly unique souvenir T-shirts. On this trip, her father's creative driving had uncovered tacky wonders (and T-shirts) like Marjoe's Alligator Farm in Ohio, The Amazing Petrified Caveman in Colorado and The Whistling Caverns of Jesus in Utah. There, the guide had told them that if they listened closely they'd hear the caverns doing "Onward Christian Soldiers." Of course, she'd never admit to her friends that she enjoyed these side trips, or that she did any more than endure her father's quirks. She wouldn't even admit it to her father, who probably knew, but had the good sense not to say so.

"Yes, this is it. It's a private home, too."

"I knew that," she said quickly.

"The office is at the far end of the house. Wait'll you meet Theo, you'll like her."

He'd said that several time during their trip here, which wasn't good. Any time her dad told her she'd like some female, it was a bad sign. He couldn't read women any better than he could read a road map. She didn't know about her mother—she'd died when Amber was only three—but ever since she could remember, he'd dated bimbo after bimbo, until he'd met Melanie. After a while, Mel had moved in with them and, for a couple of years, things were pretty great. Then they broke up, just six months ago, right before their wedding. Her dad would never say much about it, except that it had to do with business, and that sounded like major bull to Amber. As Annie, one of her girlfriends, pointed out, Melanie was a fox and knew how to flirt, big time. Maybe, suggested her friend, Melanie was screwing around on her dad and he was so hurt he couldn't talk about it. Amber thought that might be true, mostly because it made more sense than "business differences."

Old Melanie could be a lot of fun, even if she was sort of shallow; she was a literary agent and had a lot of that Teflon glitz about her that sometimes made Amber wonder if Mel would have known a deep thought if it bit her on the butt. That didn't bother Amber; what did matter was that, though she called herself an agent, it was possible that maybe she was nothing but a writer groupie. Amber guessed she probably screwed anything that could put two words together. Her dad never noticed, and no wonder: judging by the noises, old Mel was a hell of a lay. Amber liked her because she was really protective of her dad, was usually in a good mood, and she didn't treat her like a little kid.

The only time Melanie had seemed really upset was once when she tried to talk her dad into firing his agent and hiring her. But Amber knew he wouldn't dump Georgie any more than he'd dump his own daughter. Her dad was the loyal type—something Melanie couldn't understand. So, six months ago, Melanie had moved out of the condo and back to Manhattan. In retrospect, maybe her friend Annie was wrong. Maybe it really was all about business. *What a stupid reason to break up!*

"Here we are," he said as they approached a door displaying a discreet plaque that read "Pelinore Realty." He knocked, but there was no answer, so he tried the door, found it unlocked, and they walked in.

The office was a study in antiseptic monochromatics: beige carpet, cream walls, white wood blinds over the windows. Two large southwestern landscape watercolors supplied the only color with muted swipes of peach, sage, and turquoise while the furniture consisted of bleached bentwood and woven rush chairs and a low-slung white oak desk. The only things on the desk were a modern white plastic lamp-thing that looked melted, and a buzzer, also cream and white. Her father pushed the buzzer.

"Nice office, huh kiddo?"

She hated its sterility, and it reeked of rich bitch, so she just shrugged. "It's all right, I guess."

"Okay, you're the artist. What's wrong with it?"

She opened her mouth to tell him, then shut it again. For almost two weeks, they'd been together every waking moment and they were starting to get on each other's nerves. She could tell he was trying to be patient, so she decided not to be too blunt. "It looks like everything should be covered with plastic slipcovers."

He glanced around, considering. "I hate it when you're right."

"Right about what?" The door behind the desk had opened silently and a woman dressed to ornament the room stood there smiling at them.

"Nothing," her dad said, his face coloring slightly. "Nothing at all. Amber, this is Theodora Pelinore, our real estate agent. Theo, this is Amber, my daughter."

Not my realtor, Amber thought as Pelinore swept across the room in her expensive burnt-apricot Santa Fe skirt and soft western shirt. One was denim, the other, sand-washed silk. Terribly stylish, terribly elegant, terribly shallow. The outfit was belted with turquoise-encrusted silver conches that must have cost her thousands. Her dark hair was pulled away from her pale skin in a stylish twist held with a silver and turquoise comb that probably hurt like hell. *Just a little something for around the house,* Amber thought. Creativity always impressed her, but this southwest yuppie look was as magazine-like and boring as the office.

Amber noticed that her father's eyes were practically bugging out of their sockets as the woman approached. Probably the big boobs, she thought, then felt guilty. For all his faults, her dad wasn't a pig. Probably, he was taken in by the whole package, the air of success, the elegant cheekbones, the husky voice, the air of dominance. And the big boobs. Amber could imagine Theodora Pelinore in black leather underwear whipping poor, unsuspecting, drooling males into submission. Probably, she'd do a few women on the side, she had that look too. Predatory. Pelinore gave her the creeps.

Her dad, who never showed any preferences for any particular physical types, was consistently drawn to predators, to vampire women who'd suck him dry, whose expectations he couldn't possibly fulfill. The poor man never knew what was good for him. Ditzes, ballbreakers, golddiggers, and power freaks, he loved them all. Nice women didn't turn him on.

"David, how nice to see you. I expected you a little earlier." Pelinore snagged him and did the Huggy Thing. The Huggy Thing, made famous by Hollywood, was an overly familiar, insincere embrace which included meaningless mutual patting on the back. Her dad was doing it too and they looked like they were burping each other.

After about a century, Theo Pelinore released him and looked at Amber. "What a beautiful young woman you are," she said, extending her arms and stepping forward, sort of like the Bride of Frankenstein. Amber quickly moved back and stuck out her hand. Pelinore didn't falter, but took it graciously. Her hand was soft and damp. "Are you looking forward to living here, dear, with your famous father?" She smiled ingratiatingly.

Her father was watching her intently, waiting for her to say something obnoxious, like she had done to the old man in the store. She decided to surprise him and just do a little valley girl. "I guess so. Where's the mall?"

Pelinore laughed, all cultured and polite. "Well, dear, there's no mall, *per se,* but we have some magnificent shops and boutiques. And our performing arts center is just fabulous.

They host lots of concerts. It's just over the hill." She pointed toward one of the watercolors.

"Concerts?" Amber asked hopefully.

The woman smiled again, too widely. "Oh yes. They're doing an updated version of *Hair* right now. You'd really enjoy it."

Amber rolled her eyes, but before she could say something the woman really deserved to hear, her father's hand landed gently on her shoulder and squeezed, not as gently—sign language for "Be quiet."

"Theo," he said. "Is everything ready? You have the keys?"

"Certainement," she said and sailed from the room.

"Better watch out, Dad," Amber whispered. "She's bilingual and I think she wants you."

"Don't start," he whispered as Pelinore returned dangling a set of keys in one hand and clutching a manila folder in the other.

"Here you are, David," she said grandly. "The keys to your dream house." She gave them to him, letting her hand brush familiarly against his, then opened the folder and turned, standing close to him so he could see the papers within. "I just need you to sign a couple more items, then we can go. Nothing to be concerned about."

"You're going with us?" David asked, as he took the folder and sat down in one of the chairs.

"It's customary. I like to walk my clients through and make sure everything's just right. If you'd prefer I didn't . . ."

"No, no. I'd like that. I'm, ah, just surprised you're willing to come out to the house."

"Why?" she asked, fishing and flirting.

"The ghosts," Amber said, smiling sweetly.

"Oh, you aren't afraid of ghosts, are you, dear?"

"No. But I'll bet you are." The words popped out unbidden.

"Amber." Her father glared at her.

She looked meek, then tried not to flinch when Theo Pelinore's arm snaked around her. "That's all right," she said, imposing a one-armed, sideways Huggy Thing. "Amber said nothing wrong. Don't those old stories frighten you, dear?"

Don't call me dear. "They frighten most people," Amber

replied, covering nicely. "That's why I thought they'd scare you." Her dad glanced up, then went back to reading. Carefully, she pulled away from the woman. Then she heard herself add, "Of course, since you're trying to sell the house, you couldn't admit it even if you were afraid, could you?"

"That's enough." Her father sounded seriously pissed.

"Sorry."

"Nonsense," Pelinore said. "David, your daughter is refreshingly honest. Don't be angry with her. Amber, maybe some real estate agents would sell a house they didn't believe in, but I won't. If I thought there was anything dangerous in Baudey House, I'd never represent it. It wouldn't be ethical."

You lying bitch. Amber masked her evil thoughts behind a gentle smile. "So you don't believe Baudey House is haunted?" she asked, determined to end the conversation without pissing off her father any further.

The woman hesitated, fiddling with a thin silver chain around her neck. "If there *are* spirits in your new home, they won't be dangerous," she said finally. "Spirits are just poor misguided souls who need help finding their way into the light."

Amber resisted the urge to roll her eyes. She glanced at her father, but he wasn't paying any attention—he never did when she wanted him to—so he hadn't heard that darling Theo was one of *those*—a New Ager. She turned back to Pelinore and saw the polished quartz crystal dangling from the end of the chain. "What a pretty stone," she said sweetly. "What kind is it?"

The real estate agent smiled, pleased. "It's a quartz crystal. Do you know anything about the power of crystals?"

"No." Damn, her dad still wasn't picking up on this. "They have powers?"

"Oh, yes. To heal, to protect." She let the stone drop back under her shirt. "I wear it against my skin for complete protection."

Pantyliners work just as well, Amber wanted to say. Instead, she smiled again. "Does it protect you against ghosts?"

"Does what protect you from ghosts?" Her father had finally zoned back in. *Better late then never.* "All done," he added, holding up the folder.

"Oh, Daddy, Miss Pelinore has—"

"Call me Theo, dear."

"Theo has a quartz crystal," she said, doing Dorothy in the Land of Oz. "She says it can protect you and I wondered if it keeps ghosts away since we're moving into a haunted house and everything."

He stared hard at her, obviously wondering what she was up to. She tried to look innocent.

Theo broke the silence. "I think Amber's a little nervous. Have you ever seen a ghost, dear?"

Don't call me dear. "Daddy says there's no such thing."

"Enough," said her father, rising. He meant it, too. "You'll have to forgive Amber," he continued. "She's having a little fun at your expense."

"Oh, David, can't you see she's frightened? Sometimes it's hard for adults to understand children's fears, don't you think?"

"Amber has experienced a variety of ghostly phenomena," he said dryly. "She's not your average child."

Amber decided it would be best not to protest being called a child at this point.

Pelinore studied him a minute, then understanding dawned on her face. "Oh, oh yes, of course," she said nodding. "She's a teenager, an adolescent. I should have realized . . . how foolish of me."

"Realized what?"

"Why, poltergeist activity. All those hormones racing through her bloodstream, and what with her father writing all those scary books, well—"

"You don't know what the h—"

Before she could say more, her father came up behind her and clamped his hands firmly on her shoulders. "Amber," he said softly, "Hush." Surprisingly, the hands sent no warning this time, even though he had to be as pissed at her as she was at Theo Pelinore.

"My daughter," he told the woman, "is far too well adjusted to cause poltergeist activity. In the course of my research, I've explored many allegedly haunted houses and Amber has frequently accompanied me. She's—we've—seen all sorts of phenomena over the years."

"Things that would curl your hair," Amber couldn't resist throwing in. It earned her a mild be-quiet squeeze.

"Spirits?" Pelinore's eyes were huge, her breathing shallow. *Turned on by ghosts,* Amber thought as she watched the way the old bimbo did her heaving bosom thing right in her dad's face.

"Not in the sense of lost souls. These spirits are memories, sort of like the scent of old perfume on a handkerchief you might find in an attic trunk." Amber listened, as her father warmed to the subject. He was a sucker for this stuff and it showed in his every word. "Or you might think of them as imprints, loops of emotional tape. For instance, if the people in a village walk a certain path through the woods every day, year after year, to go to the well, the path gets packed down hard. But then they dig a new well on the other side of the village and stop going to the old one." He cleared his throat. "But for years after, the path remains, indelibly imprinted into the earth."

Pelinore looked like she was going to have an orgasm.

"Ghostly footsteps going up and down the hall of a haunted house are the same thing, only aural," he continued. "And apparitions floating along the hall are the visual equivalent. It's rare to have a strong enough imprint to elicit both, though some of the reports on Baudey House confirm it." He grinned. "I can hardly wait."

Boy, was that ever the truth. Her dad had been talking about this place ever since Amber could remember. He talked about anything that was haunted—Amber never quite understood his fascination with such things—but Baudey House was always his favorite. Her dad believed that most hauntings, like the Amityville Horror, were nothing but hoaxes, but he said there were so many reliable reports on Baudey House, that he believed at least some of the stories were true. He wanted to visit it, he wanted to write about it, and when he found out it was up for sale, he wanted to buy it.

Amber smiled crookedly. When she was a little kid, he'd

set her on his knee and tell her stories by the hour, just like other parents, except that he didn't retell Goldilocks and the Three Bears, or Sleeping Beauty. Instead, he told her about the Bell Witch, the Hitchhiking Ghost, the Haunted Nunnery in England, and about Christabel Baudey and her infamous collection of dolls.

To be fair, that had been her favorite story and she'd begged him to tell it over and over again. As the story went, Christabel's father had taught her voodoo and when she moved here, to the house Amber and her father were going to live in, the unhappy—and very wicked—girl spent her time making dolls that looked like real people. Christabel used voodoo to kill the people they represented, and then she'd store their souls inside the dolls, so that she'd have lots of slaves to serve her in the afterlife. As a child, sometimes Amber pretended that *she* was Christabel and she'd treat her dolls like they contained her friends and enemies. Her "friends" got to wear pretty clothes and attend tea parties, and her enemies, like her evil second grade teacher, Mrs. Mulestrap, were treated to public nudity and lying on top of ant hills in the driveway. She stifled a chuckle as she wondered if Christabel, assuming her spirit was still hanging around Baudey House, could arrange for her to have Luke Perry as her love slave in her afterlife.

"David," Pelinore was saying, "You're not asking me to believe that all hauntings are just the results of repetitive acts, are you?"

"No, no. Intense emotions cause the really interesting hauntings, like some reported at Baudey House. The most powerful are rage and fear. We pick up on those very easily. If we don't recognize them for what they are—simple residue—then anyone at all sensitive to others' emotions will become uncomfortable if it's a mild haunting or terrified if it's intense, especially if it's capable of producing phenomena. It's all electricity, Theo, charges in the walls, in the air, and the stone walls in Baudey House are perfect repositories. The emotion from a living human produces energy too, and when you combine the energy of a person's fear with the charge already present in the house, you can get some pretty spectacular stuff." He shook his head appreciatively. "The combination is quite powerful."

"You're saying ghosts don't walk if there's no one there to watch them?"

"Depends on the strength—if it's a heavy imprint, I think activation takes virtually nothing. I could be wrong. That's one of the things I'm going to research in Baudey House."

Amber realized he'd go on like this all night, if she didn't stop him. "Dad, it's getting late."

Pelinore licked her lips and smiled patronizingly. "You believe in ghosts, but you don't believe in ghosts, is that what you're saying, David?"

"I believe in certain phenomena, because I've seen them. Since I've never seen any proof of souls tied to the earth, I don't believe that. If I do, well, I'll be happy to reconsider."

"And you, dear, do you agree with your father?"

"About hauntings, yeah." She looked Pelinore straight in the eye. "If you've seen one faucet dripping blood, you've seen them all."

"Amber, knock it off. She's a little cocky about her nerves of steel," he explained.

Pelinore was still stuck on the faucet remark. "You've actually seen that?"

"Sure," Amber replied nonchalantly.

"A garden-variety haunting combined with rusted-out pipes and iron deposits," her dad explained. "The minerals turned the water red."

Pelinore nodded and smiled a big false smile. The woman wanted ghosts, not rational explanations. "David, you surprise me. How do you write believable ghost stories when you're such a skeptic?"

"A skeptic doesn't disbelieve any more than he believes. He merely questions and investigates." He smiled. "Theo, I love ghost stories and I'd love to experience the kind of spirits you're talking about." He shrugged. "Who knows? Maybe I will in Baudey House."

"It'll be fun," Amber said. "Cold spots, bloodstains, crazy laughter. But Dad'll nail them all."

Her father chuckled. "I'm sure we will."

"Just remember," Pelinore said darkly as she waggled a finger at them, "sometimes the spirits need help, not derision. Now, if you'd like to see your new home, you can follow me. It's easy to get lost here after dark."

"Dad can get lost—"

He squeezed her shoulder, inducing immediate silence.

A few moments later, they waited in the idling truck while Theo Pelinore locked up. "You're getting off too easy, Amber," her father said sternly. "Your behavior was miserable."

"No, it wasn't. You always tell me to stand up for myself. So I did."

"You toyed with her and that wasn't nice. She obviously knows very little about supernormal phenomena and it was rude to lead her on."

"I'm sorry but, Dad, she's a crystal-packer. You heard her. She probably *ohm's* herself to sleep at night and goes to a crystal-packing shrink slash channeler for past life regressions every week. She probably thinks she was Cleopatra in her last life."

"That wouldn't surprise me," he said begrudgingly, "but that doesn't mean you can be rude. She's just ignorant."

"And she wants to convert you. Dad, if she thinks she was Cleo, then you were her Antony."

"Come on, kiddo, don't exaggerate."

"Dad, you never see it coming!" Amber blurted in frustration. "She was practically drooling on you."

"You really think so?" He sounded pleased.

"It was disgusting."

"Daughter, dear, you think all attractive women are disgusting."

"No, I don't." She hesitated, not daring to bring up Melanie—her dad would have a spaz. "What about Jackie? I liked her." Jackie was his hair stylist back home and she wasn't a predator. They'd gone out three or four times after Melanie left.

"She was very nice. But that's all. There wasn't any fire."

"You only like women who abuse you."

"Amber." His voice filled the car with godlike wrath. "That is enough."

“Sorry.” She had a hard time not overstepping the bounds when he behaved so blindly. Fortunately, Theo Pelinore’s car pulled out right then, saving her from a sermon.

Three

Byron's Finger: 8:07 P.M..

Following Theo Pelinore's Volvo out of the hills and into town took only fifteen minutes, but Amber refrained from mentioning this to her father, who was intent on the tail lights glaring through his dusty windshield. A few moments of observed silence constituted a truce as far as he was concerned.

She watched the lights, too. God, the woman drove a *beige* Volvo. How yuppie and boring could you get? It wasn't really beige, of course. It was probably called "Pueblo Sand" or "Club Med Tan" or something equally snotty, just like Pelinore herself.

Amber stared out the windshield. Wisps of fog floated like ghosts in the Bronco's headlights. She'd been more happy than sad when her dad had announced they were moving out here. He'd always wanted to live on the west coast, and now he could afford the house of his dreams. Besides, his doctor kept telling him he was going to keel over from a heart attack if he didn't get away from the stresses of big city life. Amber figured that meant Melanie, the fans, and all those business lunches in Manhattan. When they'd discussed the move, he'd admitted to her that he'd been too caught up in the business and glamour and that now he just wanted to go off somewhere remote and write books. She liked that he confided in her and she liked the idea of making new friends who didn't know beforehand that her father was *the* David Masters. Unfortunately, from the looks of things, there would be plenty of fans to contend with in Red Cay, too, and that didn't make her happy, for her father or for herself.

As they passed through town and continued along on the coast road, the fog thickened. After about a half mile, Pelinore put on her right signal and turned off at a peeling old sign that said Byron's Finger.

"I live on Byron's Finger," her dad said, breaking the silence at long last.

She snickered. "But do you know where it's been?"

He grinned, but was too busy trying to navigate in the dark to reply. During their drive across country, they'd passed many miles telling stupid jokes.

The road was gravel. She could hear it crunch under the Bronco's wheels and wondered if Pelinore's Volvo was getting pitted. She hoped so. "Dad?"

"Hmm?" He was sitting forward, squinting over the wheel, trying to see where he was going.

"Will the electricity be on?"

"It's supposed to be."

"Gas?"

"Everything's electric. You'll get a hot shower, don't worry."

"And the moving van's arriving tomorrow, right?"

"Right." He glanced at her. "Anything else?"

The big question. "Are we going to get a good night's sleep tonight?"

"Yes." He pointed. "Haunted houses never act up on the first night. It's tradition."

"Dad?"

"What?"

"It's one thing to go check these places out, but do you really think it's smart to buy one? I mean, maybe we should just rent it first?"

"Are you worried, kiddo?"

The concern in his voice was genuine. "No," she said, then added, "Maybe a little. I mean, this place really has a reputation. I mean *mondo*."

"Yes . . . it does. If too much is going on—which I doubt,

judging by everything else we've ever encountered—we can take steps to neutralize it or, hell, I'm rich now, right?" He smiled at her. "We can move out. We don't have to live there forever, Amber . . ."

She groaned on cue.

"You will notice, my dear, that I didn't buy a murder mansion before I could afford a second home, just in case. Your old man's not stupid."

"Just crazy." She squinted into the fog. "This is taking forever. Are we almost there?"

"We're almost there. If Theo'd go over five miles an hour, we'd get there a lot quicker. The whole finger is only an eighth of a mile long, so it can't take much more time."

"The house must be at the very end."

"Not quite. The lighthouse is at the very end. We hit the house about five hundred feet before that."

"The fog's getting so thick, we probably *will* hit the house." The sifting white mist and the muted roar of the ocean on either side of them made her feel lost and vulnerable. A wisp of fog threaded in front of her face like a beckoning finger. Shivering, she closed the side window.

"There," said her dad. "There it is. Baudey House."

It rose out of the fog, the steep, gabled roof speaking of severity and discipline. The house, a Richardsonian Romanesque mansion, seemed to glower at them from beneath its two sharp-browed gables above the third floor windows. The heavy crossbeam supporting the front portico looked like a grim mouth.

"Well, it sure *looks* haunted," she said as her father pulled up next to the Volvo.

"Yes, it does." He turned off the engine. "Home, sweet home?" he asked lightly.

He *is* nervous, she thought. She was, too. Usually, a house that looked haunted, wasn't, and she knew the mansion's imposing appearance should be a relief. But it wasn't.

As she climbed from the truck, ocean air kissed her face, chill and moist. The house watched and waited, silent and still as death.

She heard a sound like distant laughter, cruel and feminine.

Startled, she glanced at her father. He just shrugged, and looked at Pelinore, who stood beside her Volvo. Again, the laughter, more distant, just as cruel.

"Birds," the woman said, her voice not quite steady. "It's only the birds. You'll hear them all over Red Cay at night."

You're lying, Amber thought.

"According to my research," her dad said, "one of the hallmarks of the Baudey House haunting is disembodied feminine laughter."

Pelinore cocked her head and gave him a brown-nosed smile. "Pish posh," she said.

Pish posh? Amber rolled her eyes for her father's benefit.

"Just a silly old wives' tale." the realtor added.

"Boy," Amber said innocently. "You really want to unload this place, don't you?"

"Amber, please. Theo, you don't have to be coy about the house's reputation. Remember, I bought it *for* its phenomena, not in spite of it."

"Well, I hope you won't be disappointed then, David, because I think you'll find this house will be a wonderfully peaceful and quiet place to live."

"Gee, I hope not." He grinned boyishly. "I'd be very disappointed." With that, he turned and walked across the dirt road then turned, arms folded, and stared up at the old house, a thoughtful smile on his face.

Four

Body House: 8:19 P.M.

Monolithic, stone cold, the Mephisto Palace seemed to grow out of the ground, its towers stretching up, like tortured fingers grasping at the moon.

"Is your father all right, dear?"

Pelinore's concern amused Amber. Her dad had been standing back there, staring at the house and wearing his goofy smile, for about five minutes now. She'd seen him space out like that about a gazillion times, but people who didn't know him sometimes thought he was having a fit or something. "He's fine," she said. "He's just writing in his head, he does it all the time."

Their words made David's cheeks warm with embarrassment, and he gave the two women a sheepish smile. "It's very impressive," he said, his eyes already drawn back to the huge old house.

Tonight, in the muted moonlight, it appeared to be breathing, sucking the oxygen from the air to make him lightheaded, then wrapping him in its foggy exhalations. Built of squared rough-cut stone and trimmed in dark brick, the pale gray mansion—the Mephisto Palace of his upcoming novel—was the archetypical haunted house, with its tall tower, cross-gabled roof, and dark, fathomless windows. Softening the severe lines of the house was a graceful wrought-iron railing that edged the second-story balcony situated on top of the heavy stone arches of the shadowy front veranda.

"Well," said Theo Pelinore as she tucked her hand into the crook of his arm, "I'll have to speak to Mrs. Willard first thing tomorrow morning."

"Mrs. Willard?" David asked.

"She's the housekeeper I hired for you. I specifically instructed her to leave the lights on when she finished up for the day." Theo smiled apologetically. "I'm afraid there isn't much to choose from around here . . . Mrs. Willard is usually quite reliable, though she has a little bit of a, you know, small-town attitude. And she does gossip a bit much for my taste."

"Don't worry about it," David said. "I'm sure she just forgot. This place could rattle anybody."

"Or maybe she's still in there," Amber added darkly, "splattered all over the walls."

"Knock it off, kiddo," he said mildly. Chances were, she was talking like that more to bolster her own courage than to get under Theo's skin.

David brandished the keys. "Shall we go in?" He took one step toward the house and halted as the soft sound of laughter filtered through the air. "What kind of bird did you say that was, Theo?"

Her grip tightened on his elbow and her laugh was artificial. "You know, I'm not sure what they're called. Nightbirds of some sort. I think they're a sort of whippoorwill. Sounds like laughter, doesn't it?" she added nervously.

Amber took his other elbow and he could practically hear her eyes rolling. "I studied orthinology in my natural science class last quarter, Mrs. Pelinore," she said sweetly. "Whippoorwills are not common to the western states. I think it's a blue-throated pacific night warbler. It belongs to the condor family."

Theo paused a long moment. "You know, I think you're right. Please, call me Theo, dear." To David, she said, "I'm not married."

"Come on," David said, pulling the women attached to his arms along with him. "Let's go in."

As they mounted the sweeping stone stairs and stepped onto the shadowy porch, the air chilled perceptibly. Theo's fingers dug painfully into his forearm. "I have to find the lock," he said as he gently reclaimed his arm and felt for the keyhole.

"I've got a flashlight." Theo rummaged in her purse and brought out a penlight. She aimed its weak beam at the door.

"Take a look at this, Amber," David said, inserting the key in the lock, which was the eye of an ornate brass peacock. The latchplate was a foot long and the tail plumage flowed halfway across the front door.

"Beautiful." Amber reached out and trailed her fingers over the molded brass.

"Utterly charming, don't you think?" Theo asked.

Instantly, Amber withdrew her hand, acknowledging the woman with a bare grunt. David resolved to talk to her about her hostility toward Theo later as he slipped his hand around the pull hidden in the peacock's breast and pressed the thumb latch. The door creaked and opened inward on perfect blackness. Chill, antiseptic air assaulted his nose.

"The switches are just inside," Theo said.

The little kid he kept buried deep inside him screamed *Don't put your hand in there—it'll get chopped off!,* and he hesitated for just an instant before he reached in and flipped a switch. Dim yellow light illuminated the porch, revealing the dull tarnish on the peacock, and several pieces of plywood—a two-foot square in the center of the door, and long strips at either side of the entryway.

"Is the door broken?" Amber asked.

"No," Theo said. "We kept the panels up to keep the stained glass safe." She turned to David. "Wait til you see what's under there."

"It's in good shape, then?" When he'd seen the house, all of the stained glass art had been hidden under layers of paint, the first no doubt dating back to 1917, when Baudey House was converted into a home for retired seamen. Though it cost him dearly to have the paint removed, David was glad it had been there: otherwise the erotic art beneath it would never have survived.

"Virtually all of it is intact," Theo said, "And it's beautiful. Utterly beautiful."

"I can't wait to see it." David flipped the upper switch and light blossomed within the house. "After you." He stood back and gestured to Theo to enter. She barely hesitated before stepping inside. Winking slyly at his daughter, he extended his arm. She took it, grinning approval, and they stepped inside.

"Wow!" Amber let go of David's arm and stepped forward. She slowly turned, taking in her surroundings.

The foyer opened into a spacious parlor. That room and what he could see beyond looked very different from the way it had the first time he'd viewed it. David smiled to himself. The damp, musty scent of mildew that had permeated the house had surrendered to fresh paint, wax, and Pine-Sol. Not a speck of dust or string of cobweb remained. Instead, the walls and woodwork were pristinely coated with eggshell-white paint and the Arenberg parquet floor gleamed, richly golden, under a fresh coating of wax.

"All the outside repairs have been completed, except for some touchups where the plywood panels are protecting the first story windows." Theo gestured toward the protected stained glass. "They'll take care of all that tomorrow."

Nodding absently, David examined the careful job the painters had done on the wood trim in the foyer. "My compliments to the workmen," he said. "And to Mrs. Williams."

"Willard, Dad," Amber called over her shoulder. "You know, like the rat."

"Thank you, dear," he said dryly.

"Here's something we found in the storage room off the kitchen, of all places." Theo led them to a cove across the room which contained a huge upright piano. "We cleaned it up, but didn't have any repairs done. It used to have a player action, but I'm sure it doesn't work."

The oak body badly needed refinishing, but the eight-inch tall stained glass mirror that depicted nude fairies cavorting the entire length of the instrument was in fine shape. Delighted, David lifted the key cover, revealing yellowed ivory keys stained here and there with dull dark-red spots. "Looks like somebody shot the piano player," he said, running his fingers over the keys. It needed tuning in the worst way, along with a few new strings, but the richness of the off-key tones told him the soundboard was intact. He resolved to get it refurbished immediately. "It's wonderful."

Theo had moved to the center of the room and was examining everything with a critical eye. "Hiring the painters was difficult," Theo said. "The locals are *so* superstitious, but we finally hired Mr. Willard and a young man from town, Eric Swenson." Theo paused to push a stray strand of glossy dark hair from her face. "Eric also helped Mrs. Willard with the heavy cleaning. He'll be here tomorrow to finish the work around the windows and to help you in any other way you desire. I think he'd be happy to do the gardening and odd jobs for you. He does excellent work."

"He sounds perfect," David told her.

"Well, not perfect, but close to it."

"Not perfect?" he asked doubtfully.

Theo smiled disarmingly. "Who is? Intellectually, Eric is a bit slow," Theo said. "You might need to explain unusual jobs more thoroughly to him. But he's well worth the trouble." She paused. "He also has a very vivid imagination."

"And he's willing to work *here?*"

"You know, it's funny. Sometimes, he talks about ghosts as if he can see them, but he's so matter-of-fact that I don't think he believes in them at all. He certainly isn't frightened of them. He's a sweet boy. I think you'll like him."

David glanced at Amber, who was examining the ribald stained glass doors fronting a series of cabinets and lawyer's cases built in to the far parlor wall, near the central stairwell. He turned back to Theo. "How old is Swenson?"

"Twenty-one or-two. You do still want the agency to find you extra help, don't you?"

"A housekeeper and a handyman, yes."

"As I told you before, it's difficult to find anyone willing to work in this house," Theo explained. "Mrs. Willard and Eric are both amenable, and they come with my recommendations." She frowned slightly, the corners of her full lips pulling down in an alluring pout, and shook her head. "This is a small town, David, and, well, people here are superstitious. Frankly, I was surprised that Mrs. Willard was agreeable."

"What about Mr. Willard?" David asked, thinking that if he could get a married couple, they might be willing to live in the house.

She shook her head. "No, we just talked him into helping with the painting. He owns the hardware store in town. They have a lovely little cottage on Gull Road."

"Oh."

"Eric refinished the dining table for you." Theo turned and walked through the parlor into the dining room, glancing back to make sure he was following.

The Tiffany chandelier in the center of the rectangular room blazed to life, illuminating one of the pieces of original furniture, a narrow, fourteen-foot-long walnut table with matching ladderback chairs. "Beautiful, isn't it?"

"Yes, it is." David cleared his throat. "Theo, may I ask you a question?"

She turned, looking at him with eyes like liquid chocolate. The light cast red and purple highlights into her gleaming black hair and her tongue poked out to wet her lips. "Yes, David?"

Suddenly, he became dizzyingly aware of her perfume and, for an instant, he lost his question in a testosterone haze. The fragrance, familiar and erotic, stirred an embarrassing physical reaction. *Down boy!* he ordered.

"Ah, I wanted to ask you a little more about this young man, Eric." He tilted his head toward the parlor, where Amber continued to explore. "In private."

"Certainly," she said, all business.

"Is there any chance he might . . . bother . . . my daughter?"

Her eyebrows lifted in brief surprise, then she smiled thinly and patted his arm. "What a good father you are! But you have nothing to worry about. Eric seems to have the mental capacity of a ten-or twelve-year-old."

And the gonads of a twenty-year-old—what a combination! He almost blurted out the thought. A dozen more comments occurred to him, all centering around Theo's ignorance concerning twelve-year-old boys. But he said nothing, remembering all the times Melanie accused him of being too protective of his daughter. He suspected she might be right. Besides, he reassured himself, Amber usually brought home intellectual or artistic types, boys who read books instead of Cliff Notes, or took art classes instead of drooling over comic books. And if a young man was tall and thin with dark hair and glasses, she seemed to like him even more. A slow-witted handyman with a blond name like Swenson wasn't likely to fit the bill in any way . . .

What the hell am I thinking? He was fixating on a man he hadn't even met yet. On top of that, he trusted Amber and she knew how to take care of herself. *Theo's perfume is making me crazy.* Finally, he said, "Theo, at twelve, all I could think about was the opposite sex." *Just like now.*

"You must have been a very precocious little boy." Theo slowly rewet her lips.

"Perhaps. At any rate, I'll trust your judgment and give Eric a try. After all," he couldn't help adding, "it's not like I won't be here to keep an eye on things."

"You won't be sorry, I promise," Theo said warmly.

Her renewed friendliness unnerved him and her perfume seemed to envelop him. He couldn't understand why he couldn't keep his mind out of his pants. "These insets are amazing," he said, forcing himself to cross to the short back wall and examine the built-in china cabinets. If you looked closely, you saw that the tile-like squares of stained glass which bordered the clear glass doors did not contain pink, red, and blue flowers, but human bodies, erotically entwined in subtle but endless daisy chains around each cabinet door. *Here I am worrying about my daughter, and I bring her into the porno palace of all time.*

"You're an overprotective daddy," Theo said, as if she could read his mind. She came up behind him and touched a finger to one of the glass squares.

Embarrassed, he turned away from the stained glass. "Melanie always told me that, too," he said.

"Melanie?" She sounded slightly taken aback.

"My ex."

"Wife?"

"Almost."

"Your decree isn't final yet?"

"No, she's my ex-girl—I mean ex-significant other," he corrected. "We were going to get married, but . . ." *Why am I telling you this? Because I'm as nervous as a cat, that's why.* "What kind of perfume are you wearing?" he asked suddenly. As soon as the words left his mouth, he prayed she wouldn't take them as a come-on.

"Obsession."

Obsession in a haunted house, he thought, amused. *How appropriate.*

"I'm surprised you noticed," she was saying. "I only put on a little dab, early this morning." She cocked her head at him. "Is something wrong, David?"

"No, no. Maybe it's not your perfume I'm noticing. It smells more like flowers. I can't quite place it, but it's something familiar."

"Probably flowers . . ." She sniffed. "I don't smell anything."

"It's faded away." It occurred to him suddenly that the scent might be part of the haunting and, despite his standing as a good skeptic, the hairs on the back of his neck stood on end.

"Dad?" Amber entered the room, her smile disintegrating when she saw how close Theo stood to him. "What are you doing in here?"

"Just looking around," David replied, happy that she had joined them. A pressure valve seemed to have been released the moment she walked into the room. "This is the original dining table, hon. Theo had it refinished for us."

"The table they found all those bodies on?" Amber asked, watching Theo. The right corner of her mouth curled up with restrained amusement.

"Yep." David noticed that the flowery scent had dissipated completely.

"You're joking," Theo said. "Aren't you?"

"Not at all." David pointed, warming to the subject. "Just there, in the middle, under the lamp, you can see some deep gouges."

"A maniac with a meat cleaver did it," Amber supplied.
"Amber, please."
"Sorry, Dad." She crossed to the china cabinets and frankly studied the glass insets. "Boy, these are dirtier than the ones in the living room."
"That's called the parlor, dear," Theo said.
"Whatever." Amber shrugged indifferently.
"If they bother you, kiddo, we can cover them or something."
"Nah. You really have to look to see what they are anyway." She grinned. "When you first said this house had really dirty windows, Dad, I thought you meant we had to wash them." Fixing Theo with a frank stare, she said, "So, let's see the rest of the house, Mrs. Pelinore."
"Certainly, dear. By the way, it's Ms., not Mrs., but in Red Cay, we're all good friends, so *please* call me Theo."
Amber looked supremely unimpressed.
"Let me show you the rest of the first floor," Theo said, leading them into a long tunnel of a kitchen. At the far end was a walk-in pantry, and a screened-in breakfast room that gave an illusion of width to the L-shaped kitchen. Stepping out onto the porch, David was pleased to see that the workmanship on the painting and screen replacement equalled that in the other rooms. A row of Monterey pines obscured the view of what lay beyond, their limbs scrabbling like fingers against the screen as fog sifted, wraithlike, through the branches. The muted crashing of waves and tang of seawater in the air reminded him how close the house was built to the southern cliffs.
Amber plucked at his sleeve and he followed the women back into the house. Bookshelves and cabinets, many with their lewd stained glass insets completely intact, were abundant. In the wide hall approaching the stairs, a floor-to-ceiling linen closet opened to a depth of five feet. Its doors were masterpieces of glass inlay, featuring lifesize nudes, their fleshy bodies entwined with vines of red hibiscus and blue morning glories. Amber studied the art with interest, then noticed Theo smiling at her and immediately rolled her eyes and muttered, "Gross."

Next to that was a large laundry room and then an even larger bathroom. Here the corridor ended, but another hall led to the left and right. Toward the front of the house were two more rooms. The front one, David intended to make into his office. About twenty feet square, it had three windows gathered at the far end of the room. The west one faced the front veranda, giving him a view of callers and the lighthouse at Widow's Peak. The northern window faced the cliffs and Red Cay, and the eastern provided a view of the road that led out the finger to the house. He would put his desk under the one facing the northern cliffs and have an instant three-way view—at least after the protective plywood was removed tomorrow.

"Look behind you," Theo said.

David turned to see a portrait of a woman hung above the fireplace at the other end of the room.

"The portrait was hidden away in one of the dormer rooms," Theo said. "She's beautiful, isn't she?"

"Yes, she is." David crossed to the portrait. A number of pieces of the original furniture remained, the stained glass was miraculously intact, and now he had a portrait, too. *I'm a lucky man.* He peered at the signature in the bottom left-hand corner and realized he was even luckier than he thought. It was a Jeremy Winslow, dated 1914.

"I wonder who she is," Amber said softly.

"It's Lizzie Baudey," David said with certainty. The elegant woman's coppery hair was swept up into a loose bun ornamented with a forest green plume. A few long, flaming tendrils had escaped to frame her heart-shaped face and lay, like fire, on her bare white shoulders. The green of her empire-waisted gown matched the plume, making her hair seem even redder than it was. The gown was typical of the nouveau era—the muttonchop sleeves began below the shoulder and the straight bodice was cut so low that it came dangerously close to revealing the nipples of her stylishly small breasts. Luxuriantly long ropes of pearls hung nearly to her knees and the straight skirt fell to the ankles, except in front, where the soft multi-layers of satin and chiffon were drawn up in a graceful fall of folds to reveal a curved flash of ankle and calf.

"She doesn't look very happy," Amber said.

"You're right, she doesn't." Everything about the woman in the portrait seemed soft and sensual until you looked closely enough to see the determined set of her full lips and the sadness in her large green eyes.

"From what I've read about Lizzie Baudey, she didn't always look that way," David said. "She was a great businesswoman, but she was also one of the original party girls, at least until she fell and injured her legs. She was never able to walk again without canes. That was in 1915, and some believe her own daughter pushed her." As he spoke, he became uncomfortably aware of Theo's eyes on him. "Whether that's true or not, by the time this portrait was painted in 1914, her daughter was giving her a lot of trouble," he added.

"What kind of trouble?" Theo asked, glancing at Amber, who sullenly stared back.

The glance annoyed David, too, but he didn't say so. "You don't know the story of Christabel?" he asked.

"No, not really," Theo replied.

"It's famous," Amber said dryly. "You can find it in almost any book on hauntings."

"I don't read things like that," Theo said, then hesitated, perhaps realizing she might be insulting David. "I know the house is supposed to be haunted, of course, and that Christabel was a poor, misguided girl influenced by her evil mother. I hope that her soul has gone into the light by now."

At those words, Amber poked David with her elbow, a little too hard. He cleared his throat to cover up his reaction, both to the poke and to Theo's words. He realized that Amber was right about the realtor being a crystal-packer. "Since Lizzie and Christabel are the subjects of my next novel, I've done quite a bit of research," he began, "and I hope to uncover a good deal more information now that we're here. But I can tell you that though Lizzie might not have been a model mother—"

"She was a prostitute, David!" Theo blurted.

The poisonous tone of her voice took David aback, but he

continued on as if she hadn't interrupted, "—she was, by all accounts, a warm, loving woman."

"I'll say." Amber snickered softly.

"Christabel's father was a sort of voodoo priest in the West Indies. Actually, it was voodoo mixed liberally with black magic. Anyway, Lizzie visited there with her father when she was just out of college. She met the hungan and, shortly after, her father died. Later, she claimed the priest cast a love spell on her, and blamed him for her father's death. At any rate, Christabel was born and Lizzie, a vital, well-educated young woman, languished on the island, a virtual prisoner. When her daughter was twelve, word came that her brother, Byron Baudey, had died, leaving her this house. She and Christabel managed to escape with the help of the captain of the boat that brought the news." He paused dramatically. "It's his headless ghost that's rumored to walk the lighthouse. As the legend goes, he was the first victim of Christabel's black magic. But she wasn't too good at it yet—the neck wasn't cleanly cut. Rather, it appeared that some huge beast had torn it off with its bare hands."

Lizzie's emerald eyes seemed to watch him from the portrait and, suddenly nervous, he cleared his throat. "Lizzie had wanted her freedom, but even more, she wanted to get Christabel away from her father. By the time they were rescued, the father had taught the girl the black arts—he'd been instructing her since she was barely a toddler—and Lizzie knew her daughter's mind was being poisoned. By giving Christabel a fresh start, enrolling her in a good eastern boarding school, Lizzie hoped to undo the damage."

"So she came here and opened a cathouse," Theo said sarcastically. "That makes a lot of sense.

"Boarding schools are expensive. So is maintaining a house like this. And Lizzie had no desire to be poor, so she carefully organized and opened a business, a very classy business, I might add, that would pay those bills. She took excellent care of the women who worked for her and she carefully screened the clients before accepting them.

"She never had any intention of having her daughter in the midst of the business and she sent her off to the school she herself went to as a girl. But she was soon sent home. For nearly two more years, she enrolled Christabel in school after school, and the girl continued to be expelled."

"Geez, Dad, what'd she do?" Amber asked. "Blow up toilets?"

He chuckled, despite himself. He'd told Amber a good deal of the story on their way out west, so she already knew. She was just adding to the drama to torture Theo, who still wore a look on her face like she was smelling a fresh pile of manure. His earlier attraction to her began to fade and he continued his tale with gusto. "Blowing up toilets would have been preferable to Christabel's proclivities. She liked to kill things. No chicken coop was safe, and if a school happened to have dogs or goats in residence, she took care of them also. But chickens were her favorite. She sacrificed them to Erzuli, the goddess her father had taught her to worship.

"So she ended up back here. Her mother interested her in art—dollmaking—and, for a time, she seemed to reform. But it didn't last. Against her mother's wishes, she became involved in the business. The information is sparse about how she accomplished that." David cleared his throat. "Then, eventually, she destroyed it. So," he finished, crossing his arms, "that's why Lizzie Baudey wears the expression she does in the portrait."

"Still, a cathouse," Theo said doubtfully. "It's no wonder she was so troubled."

"Lizzie had inherited the house and grounds but no money to speak of." He stared at the portrait. "Look at her. Does she look like the sort of woman who would take in laundry or sewing?" He shook his head. "Of course not. She used her business sense and opened a house of prostitution that was world famous at the time. Lizzie had a hedonistic nature to go along with her artistic talents, and her business sense allowed her to indulge in both." He saw the sour look on Theo's face and added, "You have to admire a woman of that era who knew how to get what she wanted, even if it wasn't approved of by other people."

Theo *hrmmphed* then said, "Shall we see the rest of the house?"

They moved to the other end of the hallway to explore a large bedroom with a wall of built-in wardrobes whose glass art was just short of scandalous. As he inspected the room, David began to suspect that this had been Lizzie Baudey's private sitting room. She would have wanted to stay near the front door, where she could keep an eye on the comings and goings of her customers. If, as the story often went, she broke her legs and couldn't walk without pain, she might well have slept down here, as well.

"God, Daddy," Amber cried, "do you know what these are?" She squinted at the glass on one wardrobe door. "They're . . . they're . . ." she paused, at a loss for the word, then sputtered, "Trouser mice!"

"They're what?" Theo asked. The dark mood that had hung over her like a pall in the other room had lifted.

David peered closely at the glasswork. "Penises," he said, catching a whiff of the sweet perfume.

"Dad!"

"That's what they are, kiddo." He glanced at Theo. "Amber's always felt that the correct terms for reproductive organs are more improper than almost any euphemism."

"They're gross-sounding words," Amber said huffily.

Theo joined them at the wall of wardrobes and put her fingers to the arched glass over the rosewood doors. Amber backed away, looking disgusted.

"When Lizzie Baudey inherited this house, she poured her artistic talents into it," David told them. "She replaced a lot of the original wood panels with glass. And since she was running a house of prostitution, I assume she thought that pornographic art was good for the mood. It probably appealed to her sense of whimsy, too, so that's what she designed and commissioned."

"They're not really pornographic," Theo said, her voice throatier than usual. "They're too beautiful to be obscene."

"Well, I don't want any of *those* things in *my* room," Amber stated with disgust. She walked out of the room.

"They *are* well done," David remarked to Theo, even more aware of the sweet scent. "I especially like the way Lizzie's sense of humor shows in some of the designs." The two-inch pink, rose, and purple penises in the glass arches were entwined with fig leaves and many of the elegant little organs seemed to be hiding, rather coyly, behind the foliage. He opened his mouth to say so then snapped his jaw shut, shocked that he'd been about to say this to a woman he barely knew. *Exhausted,* he thought, *I must be too exhausted to think straight.* "It's getting late. Shall we finish the tour?"

Theo smiled and gestured at the door. "After you."

He stepped toward the threshold, aware of Theo right behind him. A second later, he jumped as a hand caressed his left buttock. Shocked, he whirled to stare at Theo.

"What's wrong, David?" The surprise on her face appeared genuine.

"Uh, nothing. Nothing." He stood back and gestured for her to take the lead. *The woman copped a feel,* he thought, following her dumbly out the door. He couldn't believe it, but he knew what he had felt. Or maybe she'd just brushed him with her purse? That could be, he supposed. *Maybe . . .*

"I see you've found the billiards room, Amber," Theo said, entering the already-lit room. David followed her in, wondering how *she'd* react to a subtle goose.

Amber, standing on the far side of the huge billiard table, just shrugged. "This lamp's not bad," she said, looking at David.

"It's magnificent." The billiards lamp was five feet long and eighteen inches wide, and its leaded shade was comprised of hundreds of multi-colored circles representing billiard balls. "They cleaned up the wood," Theo said, pointing at the table's massive carved legs. "But we've had a hard time locating someone who knows how to re-cover the table top." She laid her hand on the stained threadbare felt. "My secretary finally located a man down in Santa Barbara who'll do the work, though. I'm really sorry it's not done already."

"No problem." The ancient material, once green, was almost colorless except for the huge blackish stains in the center of the table. David looked up and noticed that Amber had a slight smile on her face. Her eyes were on Theo's hands, one of which was actually resting on a big black spatter. Her gaze rose to the woman's face and she cleared her throat, obviously relishing the moment when she'd inform Theo that she was touching a seventy-year-old bloodstain.

"Are you ready to see the second floor, kiddo?" David asked, giving her the eye.

"Sure," she said, giving him a shrug that meant *I'll get her later.*

"We didn't see quite everything down here," Theo said as they headed back to the sweeping central staircase, "but there will be plenty of time tomorrow, won't there?" She put one hand on the ornate banister and the other over David's elbow, unaware of Amber's glare.

Or ignoring it. Troubled, David watched his daughter walk ahead of him up the staircase. Beside him, Theo was going on about the new roof, but he barely heard her because he was thinking about how possessive Amber had become. He supposed it resulted from all the time they spent as a family of two, though for the time that Melanie had lived with them, Amber never exhibited much jealousy. He wondered what it was about Theo that set it off so strongly and hoped that, whatever it was, he could nip it in the bud because he was thinking that he might like to see more of her.

As Theo snuggled her hand more securely about his elbow, he realized that one of the reasons Amber disliked the woman had to be her habit of touching people. His daughter wasn't used to that kind of familiarity. Neither was he, for that matter. *Some sort of West Coast thing,* he told himself. Amber even had a snide name for it that he couldn't recall. The sweet flower scent suddenly rose again, stronger, more familiar and exciting than ever.

"You smell that, Dad?" Amber asked as they reached the landing.

"Yeah." Relieved that she had picked up the fragrance too, he gently extricated himself from Theo's grasp. The air here felt cool and thick. "What's it smell like to you, kiddo?"

"Flowers. Jungle flowers."

"Do you smell it, Theo?"

"Yes, David, I do now," she said slowly. "That's what you were smelling when you asked about my perfume downstairs, isn't it?"

He nodded.

"It reminds me of night-blooming jasmine."

"You never noticed it before?" he persisted.

"No . . . but I haven't been here at night before, either. That's the only time the flowers have fragrance." She smiled at him as if he were a small child. "That's why they call it *night-blooming* jasmine, David. It's delicious, isn't it?"

Sweet and citrusy at the same time, the scent cloyed in his nostrils, so heavy now that the air seemed weighted by it. And suddenly he remembered where he'd smelled it before. Two summers ago, during his first book tour, he'd stayed in a ground floor suite at the Rolling Sands Resort in Palm Springs. Melanie had flown in, surprising him with a chilled bottle of Mumms and a scandalous lack of underwear. They'd spent the evening in his jacuzzi, soaking and drinking champagne. After a while, a sweet fragrance began to rise from the yellow flowers coating the bushes that edged the private patio. Back inside, they left the sliding door open, despite the desert heat, and made love, slept, made love again. It was a night of hedonism and excess and the exotic flowers' perfume had been part of it. The scent of the jasmine had faded with the dawn, and he'd forgotten it until now. No wonder Melanie was on his mind.

"David?"

"Hmm? What did you say?"

Theo stared at him quizzically. "Are you all right?"

"Maybe somebody left the windows open to air out the paint smell," Amber suggested.

"Are any windows open, Theo?" he asked.

"I don't think so. You can only smell night jasmine on very warm summer nights. It's summer, but it's certainly not warm." She glanced around apprehensively. "Perhaps Mrs. Willard used some air freshener . . ."

"Maybe it's just ghosts," Amber said.

The fragrance dissipated as quickly as it had materialized, and David turned to his daughter. "You might be right." In fact, he was virtually certain now that it was a manifestation of some sort and, if that were true, Baudey House was breaking with haunted house tradition.

"I thought you said nothing ever happens the first night, Dad," Amber said, reading his mind.

"So sue me."

"Do you really think it's a spirit, David?" Theo asked softly.

He studied the woman, thinking that she might be the reason behind the phenomena: certain people seemed to set things like this in motion and Theo appeared to fit the bill. It wasn't something he could define as much as sense: he thought of some people as "grounded," and others as the opposite. An ungrounded person seemed to feed their own energy into a manifestation and make it stronger. With Theo's sensuality and her thinly veiled volatility, chances were excellent she was feeding it an eight-course meal.

"It's not a spirit, Theo," he said finally. "It's a memory."

"I don't understand."

"When I was a little kid, I loved to go to my grandmother's house," David explained. "There was a scent—I realized later that it was my grandmother's sachet—that I always associated with the house. With her. When I was ten, she died and my parents brought some of her things to our house. Years later, when I was home from college, I went up into our attic hunting for a pair of skis—and I saw my grandmother's old steamer trunk. I knelt down in front of it and opened it," he said softly. "And was overcome by emotion because I felt like my grandmother was with me, like she was everywhere around me. I cried like a baby, remembering her—when I was ten I pretended her death didn't bother me—but the trunk held linens and little satin sachet bags which still held that sweet smell after all those years." Tears sprang to his eyes and, abruptly, he cleared his throat. "That's more the sort of ghost that we're experiencing here."

"What a lovely story," Theo said, her eyes glistening. "But how do you know it wasn't your grandmother's spirit?"

Give me a break. "That notion would make a nice story, but I'm afraid it simply doesn't work that way in real life."

"Unless your grandma happens to be a genie in a bottle," Amber threw in.

"Amber," he cautioned. The spiritualist viewpoint Theo held frustrated David, not only because he found it simplistic and superstitious, but because it caused many scientists to shun paranormal research. He decided that Theo, obviously an intelligent woman, was merely parroting what she had heard: she was another victim of pop parapsychology. "Perhaps I can explain a little better over dinner some time," he heard himself say.

"Why, that would be lovely, David."

Carefully, he avoided looking at his daughter. She'd probably rolled her eyes so far back in her head that only the whites showed. "Shall we?" Realizing he was exhausted, not to mention starving, he wanted to wrap up the tour as quickly as possible.

"This way," Theo said, leading them past the stairs to the other side of the house. At the cross corridor, she gestured to the right. "Several of the rooms have the original bedframes and we've replaced their boxsprings and mattresses, as you requested." Theo stopped at a door on the left side. "I asked Mrs. Willard to make up the beds in the two biggest rooms—this one and that one, two doors down." Smiling, Theo put her hand on the door latch then pulled her hand back, embarrassed. "These latches are still a shock."

"Gross!" Amber cried, catching sight of the tumescent brass entry latch. "If you think I'm going to—"

"No problem, Amber," David told her. Downstairs, the doors had traditional cut glass knobs, but up here, in the "business portions" of the house, most of the rooms, once used by Lizzie's ladies to conduct their business, had penile handles. "We'll change the latch on your room tomorrow."

"Why isn't it changed already?" she demanded, staring at Theo.

"It's my fault," David admitted, slightly embarrassed. "I told the agency to keep everything just the way it was. I'm sorry, kiddo, I should have had those changed. We'll take care of them right away." He'd go to the hardware store himself, he decided, and get enough knobs to change them all. Though they were valuable and fascinating pieces of history, he couldn't see himself grabbing one of these things every time he went in or out of a second floor room.

Opening the door and turning on the light, Theo stood back

so he could see the room. "This room, as well as Amber's, still contained some of the original furniture. We found a few more items to completely furnish them."

"Looks great," David said as he entered. Like the rest of the house, it was painted eggshell white—perhaps he would restore a few of the rooms to their original colors later, but the house was typical of the Victorian era and, therefore, dark and shadowy. It needed all the white paint it could get.

A dark cherry four-poster bed dominated the room, a navy spread covering it. A large chest rested at its foot. Across the rectangular room, a freestanding wardrobe waited, with an arch of stained glass that sported a daisy chain of subtly human forms resembling those in the dining room. Built-in bookshelves lined the short wall across from the bed, and a chiffonier and secretary were on the north wall. David crossed to the tall, narrow window near the bed. The top arch was stained glass, but refreshingly ordinary, containing conch shells and sea horses. The view was wonderful. From here, he could see the lighthouse and the cliffs. The beacon embedded in the cliffs beyond the conical structure cast intermittent light against the foggy mist, eerily illuminating the derelict structure at ten-second intervals. "I love it," he said. He'd put a small desk under the window so that he could work on his laptop at night with the most inspirational view he'd ever seen. "I absolutely love it."

"Let's see my room." Amber stood in the doorway, tapping her foot impatiently.

A moment later they stood in an identical room with similar furnishings, though there was a blessed lack of stained glass insets on the furniture. Central to the room was a sleigh bed with a sunny yellow spread. The window was identical also. Amber sat on the bed, bouncing to test the springs, a small smile of approval on her face.

"There's a large bathroom just across the hall from these rooms," Theo said. "Altogether, there are eight rooms plus the bath in this wing. The other wing is identical except there are almost twice as many rooms. Except for one big bedroom like these two, they've all been divided into very small rooms. Except for the bath, of course."

"Lizzie must have added the walls as her business grew," David said.

"You might want to remove some of the divisions later on."

"We'll see," David said. "I certainly don't need the space."

"Dad, could I move over to the big room in the other wing so I can have a bathroom to myself?" Amber asked from the bed.

Theo raised her eyebrows and David grinned. "I told you she's not afraid of ghosts!" He turned to Amber. "Sure, in a few days. Let's get a feel for what we've got here first."

"Okay." Rising, Amber crossed to the wardrobe, opened it, and began examining the drawers and closet space.

"Do you want to see the rest of this floor?" Theo asked.

"No, that's okay. We'll find our way around in the morning. Let's just take a quick peek at the tower and the third floor."

"Okay."

"I'm going to stay here, Dad," Amber said.

"I'll be back," David told her, and followed Theo from the room.

"This way," she said, leading him on past Amber's room to the end of the hall. Left of a window that aimed toward town, the wall rounded outward, destroying the squareness of the hall. A heavy arched door was set into the center of the round. Unlike nearly everything else in the house, the door to the tower was unornamented. Theo thumbed the simple brass latch and the door glided open, revealing utter darkness. "The switch is here," she said, reaching inside. She flicked it once, twice, then looked at him. "I'm sorry, they must have forgotten to put lights in here. I'll make a note to tell them to take care of it tomorrow." She pulled the door closed. "Heavens, it's cold in there."

"May I?' Curious, David stepped in front of Theo and re-opened the door, just sticking his head inside to get the feel of the air within. Theo was right, it was cold, but he knew that the tower walls were unplastered stone, so that was to be expected. Reputedly, the third floor tower room was the place where the daughter of the original builder, Byron Baudey, had strangled her baby then hanged herself, having gone mad from the rape that produced the child. It was supposed to be one of the most haunted places in the house, and David found it particularly interesting because it was a precursor to the scandals that changed Baudey House into the infamous Body House. It was a precedent that he hoped to research eventually.

Taking one step into the darkness, David did not hear the cries of a phantom infant, see the doomed mother climbing the steps or even sense any of the slimy-feeling psychic cold that usually accompanied major phenomena. *Another night.* Slightly disappointed, he reminded himself that the third floor, not the second, would be the heart of the manifestation. Besides, what he'd told Amber was true: first nights in haunted houses usually gave you nothing but a good night's sleep. He stepped out and pulled the door shut. The latchplate had not one but two skeleton-style keyholes in it and he could see old scratch marks on the newly polished brass.

"Someone wanted to keep this door locked," he said to Theo.

She nodded. "The doors on all three floors are just like that. As a matter of fact," she added, digging in her purse, "I have the keys for you." A second later, she pulled forth a pair of big old-fashioned keys, ringed and tagged. "Want to try them?"

"Sure." He inserted a key in the lock and found that it turned easily. "Works great." After an instant's hesitation, he withdrew the key without unlocking the door. His own caution amused him as he turned to Theo. "Shall we go upstairs?"

"Right this way." They turned right, pausing to admire the stained glass art on the french doors that opened on either side of the hall. The six right-hand doors opened onto a tall-ceilinged ballroom, its parquet floor gleaming warm gold. On the left, a half-dozen doors opened onto the wide veranda above the front porch. Small brass swing bolts kept them shut.

David unlocked one door and they walked outside. Three sides of the fifteen-foot-wide veranda were snug against the walls of the house. David would have liked to examine the stone walls and exteriors of the windows, but it was too dark. Instead, he walked to the railing, turned and leaned against it to peer up at the dark third floor. He thought the ribbon of windows on the tower above resembled blind eyes.

"It's cool out tonight, isn't it?" Theo said, joining him at the railing.

"Yes. And not a hint of jasmine out here—" Something pale flickered behind a dormer window just above them. "Did you see that?" he asked, his heart racing.

"See what?" She moved closer to him.

He pointed at a window to their left. "I thought I saw something move up there." He chuckled softly, still watching, but already calm. "It was probably a wisp of fog. I guess I just have ghostbuster's fever." He stepped away from the railing, but Theo stayed behind, still watching the dormer.

"Do you see something?" he asked.

"I—I thought I did." Suddenly, there was a creaking sound and Theo stumbled backward. "David!"

He jumped forward, grabbing her hands and pulling her toward him as the iron railing gave way. Instantly, her arms were around him and she clung to him, her breathing rapid. He held her, first looking at the crazy angle of the loose railing, then glancing briefly back at the dormer. As he held her, he noticed that he couldn't smell any jasmine on her skin or hair.

"Are you all right now?" he asked.

She nodded, letting go of him. "Just a little shaky. Let's go in."

"Of course."

Inside, as she threw the bolt, she stared back at the railing, brow furrowed. "The workmen removed the rust and repainted that railing. I can't believe they'd forget to tighten everything down. I'll have a word with Mr. Willard tomorrow."

"These things happen," David said as they continued down the hall and entered the other wing. "It's an old house. More than likely, it's no one's fault, just a weak spot that they missed."

"I'll ask him to check the entire terrace, no matter whose

fault it is." Theo flicked on the lights and they mounted the stairs to the top floor.

At the top of the steps, David was glad to see that the third floor wood and glasswork had been as carefully restored as the rest of the house, but, despite the light walls and ceilings, he still felt as claustrophobic up here as he had the first time he'd seen it. The ceilings were lower and the sloped dormer rooms had seemed cramped and tiny.

"The ballroom ceiling extends into this floor through the center of the house, but there's an unfinished attic to the rear that may contain more furniture. We didn't explore it," Theo said. "There's no electricity."

"I'll check it out soon, but right now, I want to go in here a moment," he said as they approached the room that overlooked the terrace, where he thought he'd seen something move.

Theo gave him a tiny, close-lipped smile and nodded. Obviously she was still shaken, and the high color in her cheeks and sparkle in her eyes made her very beautiful.

"You're sure you're all right?" he asked, his hand on a phallic door latch.

"Fine." More of her thick dark hair had escaped its bindings and she pushed it away unconsciously. "Ghost hunters first," she told him.

The door creaked open and, as he fished for the light switch just inside, he felt an unnatural coldness kiss the back of his hand. He paused, his hand on the switch, fascinated by the sensation as the cold areas wavered around his fingers. Like other cold spots he'd experienced, it reminded him of a kid's toy, a cool, oozing gel called Slime, with a weak electric current added to it. He almost told Theo, but decided to see if she sensed it for herself. He flicked the switch and walked in. She followed and the door closed softly behind them.

Mr. Willard, or Eric, or whoever had worked on this room, hadn't done their usual faultless job. Tarps still lay on the floor and, though the walls had been washed, only the ceiling and one wall had been painted. A stepladder lay on its side and, near it, a can of paint had spilled all over one of the tarps. David bent and righted the can. The paint inside was dry.

"Oh, my," Theo said. "I thought they were all done. I'm so sorry."

He picked up the paint-saturated tarp that the can had laid on and Theo groaned as they saw that some of the paint had spilled onto the wood floor. "I'm so sorry," she said again.

"The floor's already sealed, so there's no permanent damage done. With a little caution, the paint can be removed without harming the finish," David observed.

"Well, the agency will make sure you're not charged for any repairs—" Suddenly, her eyes widened and she yanked her hand back up and crossed her arms.

"What's wrong?"

"I thought something touched me. Something cold." She paused, then offered him a tiny smile. "It must have been a breeze."

David tried to hide his delight as he stepped closer to her and reached into the area where her hand had been. He found the cold spot immediately. An instant later, it dissipated. He walked back to the light switch, but felt nothing. "It's a free-floater," he said, smiling.

"A what?"

"I felt it when we first came in. It's a cold spot. You've heard of them?"

"Yes," she said hesitantly. "Of course."

"Some of them are stationery, some move around within a given space."

Theo yelped and swatted at the back of her neck. "I felt it again," she whispered, moving closer to David.

"We'll have to find out if that's what scared off the painters," David said, more to himself than to her. He felt it again, like a breath of frigid air on his face. At the same time, Theo started and touched her cheek.

"Sometimes these change size," he said, raising his hands to try to discern the shape of the spot. It hovered in front of their faces and seemed to be the size of a couple of beach balls.

"It keeps touching me." Theo's voice shook with fear now.

It wasn't touching him much at all, which told him he was right about Theo being particularly open to manifestations. "Don't be afraid," he said. "The more fear you give off, the more you'll feed it."

Theo made a disgusted noise and swatted at the air, then took three quick steps to the door and put her hand on the latch. "Christ!" she cried, letting go of it. "It's freezing! David, what's going on?" She grabbed his arm and clung to him.

"It's okay," he said, touching the knob. It felt very cool, but not freezing. "Touch it again," he said softly. "Is it still freezing?"

Gingerly, she put one finger on it and drew back quickly. "Yes!" she hissed. "Let's get out of this awful room!"

"Theo, listen to me. There's nothing to be afraid of. The latch feels colder to you than it does to me because you're frightened."

"That's ridiculous."

She looked ready to bolt, so he grabbed both her upper arms in his hands and made her face him. "No, it's not ridiculous. Your fear is feeding the phenomenon. The reason it's bothering you more than me is because I've seen these things before so I'm not afraid. It can't draw energy from me like it can from you because I won't feed it. Don't be afraid. You'll only increase its strength."

"David," she said slowly and sarcastically, "How can I *not* be afraid?" She flinched as something invisible floated between them. David could feel the coolness feather over his cheeks. It made the hairs on the back of his neck prickle up and he told himself it was cruel to make her stay there any longer.

Still, it was so utterly fascinating . . .

"All a cold spot is, is an energy drain. It doesn't think, it doesn't feel. It's mindless. It's drawn to humans because we have energy it can feed on. It's also drawn to electrical devices. Wherever you find cold spots, you're going to find problems with lightbulbs going out, clocks stopping, and things turning on and off mysteriously. Batteries don't last long in haunted houses. Now, does that sound very spooky to you? To me, it sounds merely annoying and—"

The cloying scent of jasmine suddenly dropped over them. A suffocating cloak, sweet and rich, it swirled within the growing coldness that touched his face and neck, his arms, and body. He could feel spectral fingers through his clothing, patting him, prying and familiar, touching his lips, hardening his nipples, caressing his buttocks and penis with horrifying intimacy. Adrenalin surged through him, eating away at his courage, filling him with utter panic.

Imprisoned in his hands, Theo stood utterly still, her eyes glazed, the chocolatey irises nearly eaten by her pupils. She moaned.

"Come on," he said raggedly. "Let's get out of here." He let go of her to open the door, but she had turned to stone.

He could hardly breathe. "Theo! Let's go!"

Slowly, her eyes met his, still glazed and slightly unfocused. Her tongue poked out and wet her lips. Her nostrils flared. She tilted her chin up toward him, her mouth slightly open.

He became aware of a putrid odor underlying the jasmine, a foul, rotting-meat smell, sweet and nauseating.

"Theo!" he said harshly. "Snap out of it!" He started to raise his hand to slap her cheek to get her out of her daze, but she caught his wrist in a cold iron grip.

"David," she whispered, her voice throaty with emotion. She pulled him closer, raising her lips to meet his.

The kiss was cold fire and David drew back, not believing she had kissed him, or that he'd responded. She put two fingers under his chin and drew him toward her again. Her other hand snaked around his waist and pushed against the small of his back, pressing his body into hers as they kissed again, her tongue forcing his lips apart, darting and exploring.

He responded, sucking her lush lower lip into his mouth, tasting her, smelling her beneath the scent of jasmine and decay. The erection he ground against her body was so hard that it hurt.

Roughly, she pulled her mouth from his, moving down over his chin, to his neck, licking and biting and sucking, raking her hands over his body, pinching, caressing, finally finding his belt buckle.

What's happening? Dumbly, he stared down at her as she fell to her knees and fumbled the buckle open and unzipped his pants. As her fingers slipped into the waistband of his shorts, she looked up at him and laughed.

And the room filled with the echo of that laughter, a separate laugh, but the same, the same laugh he'd heard just before they had entered Body House.

Theo fell silent, but all around them, the phantom laughter continued as she pulled his erection free, licked her lips, and gave him a vulpine smile. Her teeth glistened sharp and white.

"No!" he cried and slapped her, hard, across the cheek.

Stunned, she fell back, landing on her ass, her legs sprawling out from under her. The laughter faded, but not the scent. Theo watched without comprehension as he hurriedly zipped up.

"Come on!" he gasped. Grabbing her wrist, he pulled her to her feet as, around them, the cold air turned even colder, swirling like an invisible tornado within the room. The atmosphere seemed to charge and air pressure built in his ears, making him dizzy and nauseated, filling his head with a sound like a jet taking off. He dragged Theo to the door and yanked the obscene latch up and down. It felt like ice in his hands.

The door wouldn't open. "Come on, God damn it! Open!" As he yelled, the pressure in his ears faded and the door flew open so suddenly that it crashed against his forehead.

He barely felt it as he pulled Theo from the room and firmly shut the door.

"What?" she asked breathlessly. "What was—"

"Not now," he ordered. "Come on."

He guided her down the stairs and across the second floor to Amber's room. He knocked and she opened the door, her smile transforming into a circle of surprise when she saw his face.

"Is everything okay here, Amber?"

"Sure, yeah. Dad, what happened?"

Gingerly, he touched the bump growing on his forehead. "A run-in with a door."

"No, you've got lipstick all over your face." She glared at Theo, who was gripping his arm.

Damn, He hadn't even thought about that. "It's not what you think, kiddo. Listen, I'm going to see Theo out to her car, then I'll come back up and we'll talk. Don't wander around. Wait for me."

Doubtfully, she nodded and shut the door.

"I'm sorry," Theo said as they descended to the first floor. "I don't know what got into me."

"Do you remember what happened?"

"I'll tell you outside."

He understood her hesitation to speak within the house, and a moment later, they stood leaning against her car. "So tell me what you remember, Theo. From the time we entered the room."

"The paint can was tipped over. You were explaining that those cold spots couldn't hurt us and then that smell started. It was so strong, it made me feel ill."

"What did it smell like to you?"

"Jasmine, only stronger. And something else. It reminded me of a mausoleum I went in once, not too long after the '89 quake. I could smell flowers, and something else, too. It turned out to be a cracked vault. Something was leaking out of it and there were flies . . ." The memory made her wrinkle her nose.

Okay, we both smelled the same thing. "Then what happened?"

"I heard a woman laughing. It was like she was inside my head. I kissed you and—" She dropped her gaze and studied the ground "—and then I—David, I'm so embarrassed. I couldn't control myself."

"You remember everything then?"

She nodded. "I felt like I was watching while someone else borrowed my body. Can you forgive me?"

"There's nothing to forgive. You were merely responding to influences. So was I."

She smiled thinly.

Watching her, he wondered what, if anything, would have happened in that room had he been alone. Very little, he suspected, without Theo present to stir things up. "How do you feel now?"

"Absolutely exhausted," she admitted. "Why?"

"Do you remember what I said about the cold spots feeding on your fear?"

"Yes," she said without enthusiasm.

"Your energy was tapped to help fuel the manifestation. I can show you how to ground yourself so that you won't be so affected, but until then, I don't think it would be a good idea for you to go anywhere near that room."

"The entire third floor has a . . . a *heavy* feel to it," Theo said slowly. "Do you know what I mean?"

"Yes," he said, hoping she would elaborate. He was beginning to think that Theo had the makings of a psychic and—*and, oh boy, are there a lot of ifs*—if everything else worked out, her abilities could be very helpful in his research.

"I've only been on the third floor a couple of times," she was saying. "I hated it."

"As I recall, you waited downstairs the first time I looked at the house."

She nodded. "It wasn't very professional of me, I know." She hesitated. "David?"

"Yes?"

"I *have* smelled that odor up there before. Another agent and I came to check the house before you arrived and, when we went up, we both smelled it. I didn't recognize the scent earlier—without the rotting odor."

"What happened that day?"

"We left. For some reason, the smell frightened us. Nothing happened except, as I closed the door . . ." Her voice trailed off, her eyes fixed on the house.

"Except?" David prompted.

"I thought I heard the laughter." She studied her hands, then turned her gaze on him. "I'm sorry. I guess I should have told you about that earlier."

"That's all right," he reassured her. "Did your associate hear it too?"

"No, I don't think so." She paused, studying him. "I don't know what it is about that house. I don't understand why you want it. But I really believe that if there are spirits there, it's our duty to help them go into the light." She looked pained. "But I don't know if I'm strong enough. Perhaps if some of my friends from Beings of Light helped—"

"Have you ever noticed the jasmine scent downstairs before?" David, interrupted quickly.

"No. But one day, there was a horrible dead animal smell. I thought something had crawled inside and died, but Eric didn't find anything. The odor faded as suddenly as it rose."

The smell of decomposition was a well-known facet of the haunting and, though there were several theories concerning its source, David favored one that maintained that the dozen or so people missing after the massacre had been trapped below. But there was no proof since the entrance to the room—assuming it had ever even existed—had never been found.

"Theo, how do Eric and the Willards feel about the house?"

"Well, I wouldn't push it with them."

"I understand."

"David?"

"Yes?"

"I was possessed, wasn't I?"

He'd wondered how long it would take her to ask that. "No. You weren't possessed. Influenced, perhaps, but not possessed."

"What's the difference?" she asked skeptically.

"Possession implies that an actual spirit or demon, something that thinks and has a will of its own, takes control of your body for its own uses." He smiled. "That just doesn't happen, except in novels."

"You can't *know* that," Theo countered.

He cleared his throat patiently. "Possession is a concept that allows people to anthropomorphize an influence, to give it a personality, and human desires and motivations that really belong to the person bestowing them. Usually, the force will merely exhaust the person who feeds it. Sometimes, though, especially if a person has strong psychic gifts, as I think you may have, it can actually influence the person."

Theo appeared interested, so he continued.

"A poltergeist appears to have direction, to interact with the living. Sometimes it might speak to people or cause accidents. At that point, it becomes a revenant, which is, basically, a very powerful, very directed, poltergeist." As he spoke, he studied her with the sinking feeling that his definition of poltergeist and hers were miles apart. Her expression was one of sympathetic indulgence; she thought he was as full of shit as he thought she was.

Abruptly, she took a Kleenex from her purse and pressed it into his hand. "Your daughter must think I'm as wicked as that Baudey woman. I'm so sorry." She extracted a compact, opened it, and gave that to him, too. A tiny light illuminated the mirror and he began wiping the red smudges from his face.

"Don't worry, I'll explain it to her." He gave back her compact and helped her into her car.

She started the engine, then smiled. "I almost forgot. Our church is co-sponsoring a costume party at the Moose Lodge in town. I hope you'll come. As my guest, perhaps? It'll give you a chance to meet at least half the town."

"Costume party?" David asked quizzically.

"It's called the Come As You Were Dance. Everyone dresses as someone they think they were in a previous life."

That sounded bizarre but interesting. "When is it?"

"August twenty-second. About six weeks from now."

"Thank you for inviting me. If you can give me a few days to see how things are shaping up, I'll give you a definite answer. Amber may not want to stay alone in the house," he added.

"Oh, Amber can come too, of course." Theo put the Volvo in reverse. "She might like to go with some kids her own age."

"I'm sure she would," David said, mildly annoyed, "if she knew any."

Again, the winning smile. "I can help with that. Myra Cox—that's Ferd's daughter—is a good friend of mine and her daughter, Kelly, is exactly Amber's age. She's a nice girl and I'm sure she'd love to meet Amber and introduce her to the other kids. I can give her a call tomorrow."

"That would be very nice, Theo. Thanks. And thanks again for the invitation. I'll let you know."

"Great." She reached out and touched the back of his hand lightly. "I hope you'll say yes. See you later."

"Good night."

After her taillights faded into the night mist, he turned back toward the house and stared up at it, the dance forgotten. *What have I gotten us into?* It was a thought both thrilling and horrifying.

Except for the tower, the entire house blazed with light. The upper story pediments were brilliant with rich color, and the french doors leading to the terrace were absolutely exquisite. Achingly so. His gaze drifted to the third floor dormer room he and Theo had fled, but nothing looked out of place.

Then the light went out.

Shit! He felt paralyzed for what seemed like hours, then suddenly he was running toward the house. "Amber!" he yelled. "Amber!" If she'd gone up there by herself—

As he ran up the front steps, the door opened and his daughter stepped out, her jacket on, her purse slung over her shoulder. He slid to a stop just short of slamming into her.

"What's the matter, Dad?" she asked dryly. "See a ghost?"

"You weren't on the third floor just now, were you?" he asked, even as he realized it was a physical impossibility.

"No—"

"And just what do you think you're doing down *here*?" he demanded, his terror instantly and blessedly transforming itself into paternal anger. "I told you to stay in your room until I came for you!'

"Don't have a cow, Dad." She shook her head slightly, as if she couldn't believe what she was hearing. "I saw the wicked witch drive away and I'm *starving* to death, so I grabbed my stuff and came down to meet you." She fished in the pocket of her jacket and pulled out his car keys. "Let's find food."

His anger dissolved as quickly as it had arrived. "Just let

me go wash up." He handed the keys back to her. "Here, you warm up the Bronco. I'll be right out."

As he neared the stairs, he considered going up to the third floor to check the room again, but decided against it. He was reasonably sure no humans were hiding in the house, and that the light going out was merely another facet of the manifestation in the room, just as he'd told Theo. After all, that kind of garden-variety electrical phenomenon was about as mundane as it could get.

He entered the enormous bathroom for the first time since it had been cleaned. It was a delight. New grouting made the tiling, malachite green swirls with lush rose accents, seem new, and the huge clawfoot tub gleamed white in its niche. He walked over, wondering if it had been reenameled, a job he hadn't requested.

It hadn't. No one could scrub the bloodstains out of the old, porous enamel. These stains were newer, dating back to 1968, when a small band of hippies had died here—one had died in this very tub. "Definitely," he said aloud, "this needs new enamel."

He turned to the pedestal sink that rose gracefully out of the tile, widening into a large, shell-shaped basin, which matched the mirror and frame above it. The fixtures, nude fairies, were classic art nouveau. He turned on the hot water and scrubbed away the last vestiges of Theo's lipstick, using a sliver of Lava the workmen had left behind.

Looking at himself wasn't much fun tonight, he realized as he inspected his face. A purple-red welt was growing in a vertical slash in the center of his forehead, thanks to the smack on his head when the door flew open. Worse, it looked like Theo had left a hickey on his neck. He repositioned his collar so that it was almost hidden, then pulled his comb out and ran it through his thick caramel-colored hair. He needed a shave and there were bags under his eyes, but he'd do for now.

As he exited the bathroom, Amber leaned on the horn. Briefly, he felt guilty for taking so long, but as he grabbed his coat from the wall rack in the foyer, he reminded himself how often he had to wait for her.

He stepped out into the cool night air and locked the door behind him. As he walked toward the Bronco, he wondered if Amber would try to punish him for his seeming indiscretion with Theo. At least she was too hungry to sulk for now.

Five

Red Cay Public Pier: 10:10 P.M.

"There's no such thing as a blue-throated pacific night warbler," Amber said as soon as her father settled into the passenger seat. She wondered if he'd told her she could drive so that she couldn't be as mad at him for his behavior with that witch Pelinore, but she knew better than to ask.

"What?" Her dad had been staring back at the house.

"I made it up. There's no such thing as a blue-throated pacific—"

"Oh, yeah, I figured that. So what are you hungry for, kiddo?"

She glanced at the clock on the dash. "It's past ten. You think there's anything open around here? I mean, we haven't seen a McDonald's since Pismo Beach."

"You're right." Groaning, he rubbed his chin. "There was a truck stop five miles down on the main highway."

"Oh, joy."

"Yeah, I know, Amber. Wait, I have an idea. Turn left at the next intersection and head downtown. If there's night fishing, a diner around the pier might be open."

He was right. They found a place not just near the pier, but on the very end of it. A fishing boat was pulling out and a few night fisherman stood on either side of Doug's Diner, smoking and casting their lines. The foggy mist had cleared as soon as they left Byron's Finger and a three-quarter moon cast shadows of the fishermen against the wooden deck.

"At least it's got atmosphere," her dad said as they took red plastic baskets of fish and chips to a small picnic bench and sat down.

"Yeah, I wish it had a little less atmosphere." The stink of fish guts was ruining her appetite.

She wanted to talk to him about Pelinore—no, she wanted to scream at him that the woman was a piranha getting ready to eat him alive. But she couldn't, because her dad looked so tired and because she was feeling guilty about not noticing the ugly bruise on his forehead earlier. All she'd seen was the lipstick.

They sat and ate in peaceful silence until her dad went to squirt more catsup on his fries and the lid came off and drowned them. They looked at each other and laughed.

"How're you holding up?" Her dad shoved a sodden french fry in his mouth. "Tired?"

"I'm fine. Do you have a headache?"

"A little." Gingerly, he touched the bump. "It looks worse than it is."

She nodded. "Good. So, what do you think, Dad? Are you going to do talk shows and stuff now that you're here and they're making a movie and all?"

"If someone asks me, sure. But I wouldn't count on it, kiddo."

"They'll ask," she assured him. "You're not just any old writer, after all."

His smile was tired. "You're a wonderful daughter. You know just what to say."

"I know." She swiped one of his catsup-coated fries. "But you're different. Face it, Daddy, you're hot stuff. You're a male Jackie Collins."

He snorted.

"Well, you are. You look pretty good and you can talk, too." She pointed a fry at him. "Haven't you ever noticed the difference between you and most of your friends?"

"Nope."

She grinned evilly. "What about that guy who picks his nose at conventions?'

"Oh, please, Amber!" He laughed in spite of himself. "He's not my friend. That S.O.B. tried to put a move on Melanie, right in front of me." He paused, looking like he was startled to hear himself say her name. "Besides, he writes science fiction." He added the last like it was a curse.

Amber snickered. "He flirts with everybody and Melanie was just trying to get him as a client."

"She did it, too."

"Everybody but you, Dad."

"Everybody but me," he said sadly.

Amber was sorry she'd brought it up. She was pretty sure his refusal to throw over Georgina Gordon—the agent who'd been with him since the beginning—in favor of Melanie was what really broke them up. Plus, Melanie was a horrible flirt. "Dad?"

"What?"

"Most writers don't look so hot. Especially guys. That's why they aren't on TV much." She was determined to cheer him up if it killed her.

"Oh."

He still sounded depressed, so she pressed on. "A lot of your friends don't have much hair left and they practically all have big butts. But you still look pretty good, considering how ancient you are."

"Thank you, I think." He smiled, and the skin around his eyes crinkled up the way she wanted. "I seem to recall you pestering Rick half to death a couple of years ago at the horror writers' convention. You thought he was hot stuff."

She felt herself blush. "Well, I guess he looks pretty good, but I don't go for blondes anymore." For some reason that made her dad grin broadly.

"Is that why you decided you liked Tim?" he needled.

Lord! Once you start him you can't stop him! She almost wished he hadn't perked up. "Tim's got a great bod. Everybody knows that."

Like most of her friends, she'd started getting crushes on guys when she was around eleven. While most of her friends wanted rock stars, she'd been turned into a book nut by her dad and, until she was around fourteen, she'd get a crush on one writer or another, which was great, because they were always hanging around with her father.

She had started weaning herself about two years ago, when her father started getting famous and her friends wouldn't leave him alone. She hoped she hadn't acted as weird as they did. It was mortifying to witness. Thank God she hadn't been like Heather Ferguson and written stupid love letters—as it was, she could hardly look several of her dad's friends in the eye, and all she'd done was hang around and look moony. Heather, on the other hand, had written to her dad, and sent some Polaroids, too, but he wouldn't show them to her—he'd wadded them up and tossed them in the fire.

"Earth to Amber," her dad was saying. "Earth to Amber."

"Okay, Daddy, I know I had crushes on some of your friends, but I was just a little kid, so stop teasing me. I was trying to make you feel better."

He reached across the table and patted her hand. "I know. I'm sorry. I didn't mean to tease you."

She squeezed his fingers and looked him in the eye. "You know, if you worked out more, you could have a body like Tim's . . ."

"I guess I deserved that for teasing you."

"Yeah." She smiled. "You know, I'm a lot older now. I date."

"I know," he said glumly.

"So, maybe you should let me go out with your editor's assistant next time we go to New York. He's more my type."

He stared at her, obviously unsure whether she was serious or not. "He's too old for you, kiddo."

At last year's Christmas party, Amber and Joanna's assistant, Rex, had gotten pretty friendly, and he had asked her out on a date. Then her dad got wind of it and told the young man that he was her father and that she was a mere sixteen. He'd used that tone of voice he had that could make suitors wet their pants. Rex hadn't asked a second time, to Amber's sorrow.

Truthfully, she *was* a little serious. "I'm almost seventeen."

"He's too old for you," he said sternly.

"Okay, okay." She'd pushed one of her father's buttons

again and she didn't even know it. Wanting him to stay in a good mood, she backed off a little. "But you've gotta admit, Rex sure smells good."

"I hadn't noticed," Dad said impassively. "Are you finished eating?"

Nodding, she rose and helped him dump the trash, then they walked outside, pausing on the south side of the pier to gaze at the high cliffs of Byron's Finger. The house, visible because of the lights left on, was almost directly across from where they stood. The beacon at Widow's Peak was considerably farther out to sea.

A pair of fishermen, carrying their gear, came around the end of the pier from the other side. "Look at that. That fool writer really did move into Body House."

It was an elderly woman's voice and the male voice that responded, "I'll be damned," sounded just as old. Amber didn't turn to look and she prayed her father wouldn't do anything embarrassing, like introduce himself.

"Ferd, over to the store, told me the fool'd shown up," the man continued. "But you know Ferd."

"Half of what he says is *ferdilizer,*" the woman replied, and they both cackled.

Her father cleared his throat and started to turn, but Amber grabbed his arm as hard as she could. He got the message.

"You know what else Ferd said?" the fisherman asked his companion.

"What?"

"He's got a little girl with him. He's takin' a little girl into that hellhole."

"God help her, then."

The couple shuffled slowly down the pier and Amber sighed. "Little girl! I'm not a little girl. Thanks for not talking to them, Dad. I'd just *die.*"

"You're welcome. Besides, there's something I want to talk to you about before we go back."

She leaned against the wooden railing. "Okay. What?"

"About what happened with Theo."

"The woman's a slut!" The words, bitten back all evening, slid out before she could stop them. "I don't want you to explain anything to me, Dad. Instead, just listen to me this once, okay? Pelinore's a slut. I told you that about Lorna, but you wouldn't listen then, either. Theo's no good. She'll use you. And she's a New Age nut, to boot."

"I'm not going to argue about Theo's personality with you, Amber. But I need to tell you something."

"But—"

"Hush. Listen to me now."

He told her about the third floor, about the perfume and the cold spots and how Theo had kissed him. Looking at the hickey on his neck, Amber figured he was leaving a lot out of the story, but she didn't say so. He told her how the door had stuck, then flown open, hitting his head. Finally, he told her about the light turning off by itself.

"Wow!" she said. "I guess Body House wanted to prove your first-night theory was wrong." She paused, studying him, seeing the pallor in his face. "Dad? Are you worried?"

"No, not really." His chuckle sounded hollow and false. "But this manifestation is beyond anything I've ever seen before. It's incredibly strong. It even had an effect on me."

That surprised Amber. Nothing ever got its hooks into her skeptical father. Into her, either. "What kind of effect, Dad?"

He hesitated. "It definitely drew off a little of my energy. And I had . . . certain feelings . . . that weren't my own. The point is, hon, I think there's a good chance that Theo is probably psychically unstable and that she's the main reason the manifestation was so strong. But until we know what we're dealing with, the third floor's off limits."

"Even to me? Nothing bothers me, Dad."

"I didn't think anything bothered *me* either, kiddo. Look, the painter didn't finish painting the room this happened in. He left paint spilled all over the floor, and the ladder was tipped over. Something scared the bejesus out of him. So, don't go up there, not by yourself."

"Okay." She shivered, crossing her arms against the cold. "You ready to go home?"

He stared at her for a long moment, then smiled. "Let's go home." He put his arm around her shoulders and they began their walk back down the pier.

July 11

Six

Body House: 7:50 A.M.

In the dream, he did not refuse her, as he had last night, but pushed his fingers into her thick black hair and hung on for dear life. As she worked, she held him riveted with eyes that could see down to the very bottom of his soul.

Slowly, she reached up and took his hands, tugging him down to the floor. Her hypnotic stare kept him imprisoned as she straddled him and began to move with a ferociousness that made him lose control.

"Dad!" Fists hammered on the door. "Dad! Are you up?"

Dimly aware of the voice calling him, he shouted out as an orgasm washed over him. It was so powerful he thought it might kill him, but he didn't care.

"Dad!"

He came awake, eyes flying open, heart thudding in his chest.

"DAD!" Amber pounded on the door. "Are you okay?"

He glanced down, saw that he'd kicked off nearly all the covers. "Fine," he called, grimacing at the wet stain spreading on the sheet over his crotch. *Oh, God.* He hadn't had a wet dream since he was fourteen years old.

"Dad!" The phallic doorlatch started to depress.

"I'll be out in a minute," he rasped. "I'm getting dressed."

The handle returned to its original position. "Why'd you scream?" she called.

Oh God, I yelled out loud. No wonder his throat hurt. "Had a nightmare, kiddo. I'm fine."

"The rat lady's here."

"Who?"

"Mrs. Willard. Wait'll you see her. What a fox."

"Amber, be nice. She'll hear you."

"She's downstairs. She can't hear me. Sound doesn't carry for spit around here. I'm supposed to tell you breakfast'll be ready in a half-hour."

"Great. Are you done with the bathroom?" He hadn't showered since they left Barstow yesterday morning and he was beginning to feel pretty ripe. He caught sight of the sheets again. *Make that ready for harvest,* he thought wryly.

"Yeah, I'm done. The shower's funky."

"Are there towels?"

"When we got back from the pier last night, we brought in the knapsack with all the bathroom stuff, remember?"

He's going senile was the unspoken codicil. "Oh, right. Listen kiddo, why don't you go downstairs and get acquainted with Mrs. Willard while your old man tries to wake up."

"Give me a break, Dad. I'm going to explore."

He swung his legs over the edge of the bed. "Not the third floor." The words came out sounding more urgent than he wanted.

"No, not the third floor," she said in a put-upon voice. "I'm just going to check out the lighthouse."

"It's not safe. The stairs—"

"I'm not going *in* it, Dad," she said in her best long-suffering tone. "I'm just going to walk out to it and back."

"Okay." Against his will, he added, "Be careful."

"Oh, Daddy, you know I will."

After waiting a moment and not hearing her leave, he called her name. There was no reply. Amber was right, Body House ate sound. *Body House,* he mused, realizing he'd already forsaken his determination to restore its proper name. *Oh well, I'll fit in better with the locals.*

Quickly, he made the bed, so that Mrs. Willard wouldn't discover his embarrassing secret. After the washer and dryer arrived, he'd launder the sheets himself. Gathering together his day's clothing, he wondered if the bedding was on loan from Theo or her agency or if she'd purchased it for him. He'd have to find out.

He padded across the hall to the bathroom. He'd been so exhausted last night that he'd barely noticed the room, but now he looked around, exhaling air through his teeth as its garishness sank in. The room was a virtual twin to the green and rose one downstairs, but here the primary tiles were a disturbing shade of crimson—sort of a bloody cherry—with pearlescent pink trim. The other way around would have been much easier to take. Examining the shower fixture, which was ornate brass that matched the nouveau faucets and spindles quite well, he thought that it had probably been added in the late thirties, when Drake Roberts, a popular matinee idol, acquired the place as a weekend retreat. Though it wasn't apparent in his films, the actor was only five-foot-two, and the shower head was mounted just high enough to hit six-foot-two David in the chest. Amber, at five-seven, probably got it square in the face. Another eighteen inches of pipe, plus a massage head, would remedy the situation. As for the rabid red tile, perhaps a ceiling full of fluorescents would cheer the place up for now.

He showered and shaved, happy to see that the bruise on his forehead was barely noticeable, then, uncomfortable in the room, tucked a towel around his waist and carried his clothes back across the hall. He pulled on a pair of khaki Dockers, a T-shirt, and an Irish wool sweater. July or not, the weather was evidently always cool here, so far out on the headland. Sitting down to pull on his shoes and socks, he wondered why he disliked the bathroom and concluded it was purely an effect of the color. It depressed him.

Too, Drake Roberts had probably died in that particular bathroom, if David recalled correctly. The actor had had a heart attack in a bathroom not long after he'd moved in. *All that red,* David thought, *probably set it off.*

He smoothed the bed, then went to the window and released the latch on the casement windows and pushed the upper pane down. Inhaling deeply, he savored the freshness of the damp salt air. Stratus clouds etched the blue sky and gulls cried over the muted roar of the ocean. Pleased, he thought these sounds would be the perfect background music to write by.

The lighthouse, ominous and imposing last night, now looked as scenic as a photo on a travel brochure. As he watched, Amber appeared from behind the structure and started back toward the house. He remembered that she'd said something about breakfast and his suddenly growling stomach ordered him to go downstairs immediately.

But when he reached the stairwell, he decided to first take a peek in the third floor room that had hosted the spectacular phenomena the previous night. He only hesitated an instant before trotting quickly up the stairs.

A little thrill of excitement wormed through his belly as he opened the door on the dormer room. Everything looked the same as it had last night, though the heavy atmosphere had dissipated. The light switch, he noted, had been switched off, which was a much more interesting phenomenon than the lightbulb merely burning out. He flicked the switch and found that the bulb was fine.

He walked into the center of the small room, then, hands out, walked in a spiral, feeling for cold spots. "Gotcha," he whispered, when he finally found a small slimy-feeling area near the west-facing window. Calmly, he pushed the fingers of his right hand into the orb and, as he expected, it slowly oozed further onto his hand, like a cold glove. These spots, he theorized, were akin to miniature black holes, and he always wondered what would happen if a bolt of lightning struck one. That, in fact, had been the subject of *Dead Ernest,* his first bestseller. He smiled as the cold crawled onto his wrist. He had a soft spot for cold spots.

The sensation of cold increased suddenly and he pulled his tingling hand back, shaking it, realizing he shouldn't let it consume any more of his energy. The very fact that it had grown in strength surprised him because it meant it had actually managed to draw from him, and that was something that had only happened once before.

While researching *Dead Ernest,* he'd spent the night in a notoriously haunted house in Boston. He'd been fighting off a miserable case of the flu, was working under a deadline from hell, and had recently broken off with Lorna Dyke, the woman before Melanie, and she'd spent the last several weeks screaming at him by phone, sending him suicidal letters, and driving by his house at all hours of the day and night. He should have listened to Amber, he realized later. She'd told him that Lorna—an unpublished (and unpublishable) poet who worked in a gas station—was a psychopath, and she'd been right. The night he broke it off, she'd even threatened to kill him.

So, when he decided to sleep in the most haunted room in the most haunted house in Boston, he'd been a little stressed out—a little under the weather, as it were. He hadn't been physically or mentally up for the experience, but he refused to put it off.

He awoke at three in the morning, trembling because of a nightmare about swimming in a room filled with blood, and shivering from the cold. The whole room was frigid even though the little space heater nearby glowed red. The manifestation simply ate the heat. When he stood, he found that his legs would barely hold him up and, as he staggered toward the door, an apparition appeared. Fascinated he watched it—it was his first visual ghost—and it floated toward him, nothing but a pale amorphous ovoid. Just before it touched him, he panicked and tried to run for the door, which seemed to take forever because he hardly had any strength left and because a telescoping phenomenon—an effect that made the door look like it was a million miles away—impeded him. But he had made it out before the apparition touched him. To this day, he wondered what would have happened if he hadn't woken when he did, even though, intellectually, he thought he was being a superstitious idiot. Not only did the experience frighten him badly, but he ended up in the hospital with pneumonia. The fever dreams became an integral part of *Dead Ernest,* his fifth book, and his first bestseller.

Now he caught a faint whiff of jasmine, and he smiled. After *Dead Ernest,* he arranged to secretly witness a black magic ritual that was to be held in an abandoned warehouse in Chicago. The building had been the scene of a horrendous gangland slaying in the thirties and, naturally, it was supposed to be haunted. From everything he'd read, he'd believed it probably was—but that was nothing compared to the ritual. It so horrified him that he was glad he was hidden too far away to see everything in detail, but it taught him that reading or writing about such a thing and actually witnessing it were very different experiences. The energy the cult members expended was eaten by the haunting and soon he began to feel the unnatural cold, even up on the catwalk where he hid. Below, he saw vapor issuing from the mouths of the cultists as they chanted. Then something happened that scared him as badly as the Boston haunting had: first he heard—felt, really—the rush as the air pressure changed, hurting his ears just as it had in this room last night. Then suddenly the catwalk started swaying and his microcassette slid off the narrow metal walkway. The cultists heard it and looked up.

Fortunately, he'd come prepared with colored smoke bombs and, as he rose, he began dropping them to hide his escape. The catwalk swayed harder, slowing him down, and the air pressure played havoc with his inner ears, almost causing him to fall several times. By the time he got to the ladder, the cult members were almost upon him. He slid down the ladder and threw the last smoke bomb in front of them, then ran like hell, only a few steps ahead of them. If his new lady friend, Melanie Lord, who was parked across the street, hadn't seen him coming and careened her T-Bird around in the best Hollywood rescue style, they would have caught him. Caught them both.

He went home and wrote *Bloody Little Secrets* in a frenzy and it went to the top of the *Times'* Bestseller List and stayed there. The next book, *Remains to be Seen,* currently on the stands, was also a bestseller—there was already a miniseries deal in the making. It had been inspired by a close brush with a suspected serial killer, one that would have resulted in his becoming a victim if Melanie hadn't alerted a friend of hers on the police force. Her friend got the glory of the arrest and David got invited to be present at the exhumation of bodies buried under the monster's house. He still had nightmares about that.

Quite unexpectedly, the scent of jasmine grew strong

enough for him to catch the scent of decay underlying it. Fear trickled coldly down his spine as the odor continued to strengthen. The coldness moved onto his hand and, forcibly, he shook it off. *Don't panic!* he ordered himself. *Don't panic! Just leave!* He knew his fear was allowing the manifestation to feed on him. "See you later," he said as calmly as he could, then walked out and pulled the door firmly shut behind him. He thought he heard the laughing woman as he headed for the stairs, but wasn't sure.

He descended, nervous but happy because he knew that *Mephisto Palace* would be another bestseller. He sensed that Body House had the potential to scare him worse than anything ever had and he knew the fear was the secret of his success. Once his fears overrode his intellect, he could trip on his endorphins, ride a roller coaster of emotions, and love every minute of it. He was, he thought as he reached the main floor, nothing but a perverted thrill seeker. *At least,* he told himself, *no one can say I don't sacrifice for my art.*

Seven

Body House: 8:44 A.M.

"What are you smiling about?" Amber asked her father as he walked into the parlor.

"I have a feeling *Mephisto Palace* is going to be the best book I've ever written, kiddo."

She laughed. "You always say that at first, then when you finish it, no matter how good it is, you decide it stinks until your editor tells you it doesn't."

"Of course," he said lightly. "That's how it works."

Amber rolled her eyes.

"I smell food, my dear. Let's find it."

Though she didn't want to run into Mrs. Willard again, Amber was too hungry to disagree. As they entered the dining room, the woman bustled in from the kitchen carrying a carafe of orange juice and glasses.

Despite her ratty name, she looked like a fat little forest creature right out of *Bambi,* a grandmotherly rabbit with glasses. The silvery-white hair with its beauty-shop wave and the pale blue print dress and ruffly white apron screamed cookies and milk. She didn't match her name at all until she opened her mouth, and that was the horror of the rat lady: she could talk you to death. Amber cringed as Willard cleared her throat.

"Why, hello there, you must be Mr. Masters," she bubbled. "I recognize you from your bookjacket photo, oh my, you're so handsome if you don't mind my saying so." She barely paused for a breath. "I've read all your books and I've *so* been looking forward to meeting you, why, I don't think wild horses could have made me work here in this nasty, nasty house, if Miss Pelinore hadn't told me it was *you* who were going to be here." She set the juice and glasses down and whisked forward, snaking her arm around Amber's waist before she could get away.

Oh God, Amber prayed, *oh God, strike her with terminal laryngitis.*

"You have such a lovely little girl, I mean young woman, here Mr. Masters. We had such a nice talk, didn't we, honey?"

Mrs. Willard smiled, staring at her with bright robin's-egg eyes that were magnified through her rimless glasses, until Amber felt compelled to say something. "Yeah, I guess."

"You must be so happy to have such a famous daddy," she went on as she set Amber free and continued toward Dad, both hands extended. "I'm just pleased as punch to meet you, Mr. Masters! Just so pleased! May I ask you a question?"

He smiled benevolently. "What is it, Mrs. Willard?"

"Well, I read all your books and everything, and I've always wondered how you come up with all those awful ideas? I could never think of such things." She barely paused for a breath. "Mr. Masters, something horrible must have happened to you as a child. Am I right?"

"Nothing out of the ordinary," he replied calmly. "Everybody has an interest of some sort. In grade school, the kids would get to order little paperback books. Arrow Books," he added fondly. "I'd take my list home and check off all the books about ghosts and witches and haunted houses, and Mom would check to make sure I had my math right, then give me the money to buy them."

"She didn't try to get you to read something else? That seems so morbid for a child—"

"Of course not. Mom had bookshelves full of books on the Civil War. Dad was a nut for experimental gardening. The man had twenty-three books on grafting fruit trees." He smiled to himself. "I counted them once. They understood that everyone's different. That's what makes the world an interesting place."

But she just beamed at him and took his hands again. "My, you're such a handsome young man, and talented too. And your daughter, so lovely. It's a shame . . ." She trailed off, a dreamy expression on her face, then her bright little chipmunk eyes shot back to his face. "Mr. Masters, did your wife divorce you because of all those scary stories you write?"

Amber stifled a gasp, and turned to see her father's reaction. The first question had been bad enough, but this one was the worst. He hated how people always assumed that his wife must have divorced him, usually for any one of several reasons, number one being that he turned into an egomaniac when he became famous. Number two was that he couldn't keep his hands off his fans. Number three was that, like all writers, when David Masters wasn't drinking, he was shooting up heroin, and number four, Minnie's choice, was that anyone who wrote what he did had to be a psychopathic fiend who sacrificed children and small furry animals to Satan himself.

The nervous tic in Dad's jaw barely twitched as he said softly, "Carol died in a car accident not long after Amber was born, Mrs. Willard, but I'd like to think that if she were here, she'd be proud of my work."

The tiny woman's cheeks colored instantly and she let go of his hands and began fussing with her ruffles. "I'm so sorry, I—"

"That's all right." He smiled gently.

"My Mickey, that's Mr. Willard, he always tells me, 'Why don't you learn to stop and think before you start talking. That foot of yours is always in your mouth."

"No harm done, Mrs. Willard."

"Please call me Minnie. You, too, dear," she added, dimpling up at Amber.

"Are you sure?" Amber asked before the old lady's mouth could go back into overdrive. "I mean, Miss Pelinore calls you Mrs. Willard and she's a lot older than me." She ignored the look her father was sending and smiled a major shiteater at Minnie.

"Oh yes, you can call me Minnie, dear. Miss Pelinore has to call me Mrs. Willard."

"Why?" Amber asked, continuing to ignore her dad.

Minnie patted Amber's hand. "Well, I'm not one to talk out of turn . . ."

Oh, yes, you are. Amber smiled sweetly. "You can tell *us.*" She glanced at her father and saw that his warning look had turned to bemusement. "Can't she, Dad?" She added that, knowing he couldn't resist: he always said his two favorite things were Italian food and people who talked too much.

"Our lips are sealed," he said, right on cue.

That was true. He could keep secrets as well as she could. If you told him anything, though, if it was good enough, you'd eventually find it twisted and deformed in one of his books. "Sealed," Amber repeated.

Minnie Willard glanced around, as if she were afraid of eavesdroppers. "Miss Pelinore," she began conspiratorially, "is a hussy!" She blushed again. "Excuse my French. I shouldn't talk that way around a nice young lady like you, dear. I'm so sorry, I—"

"I read my dad's books," Amber said, suddenly warming to the woman. "Nothing shocks me." Anyone who didn't like Pelinore couldn't be all bad.

"Theo seems nice enough," Dad said, obviously feeling he should come to her defense.

"Oh, Mr. Masters, all men think Miss Pelinore's sweet as peach pie." She lowered her voice. "But she's a rotten apple."

"Why?" he persisted.

"She's loose."

Amber giggled.

"She takes what isn't hers. Miss Greedyguts, that's who she is. Any woman can tell just by looking at her." She gave Amber a knowing nod. "Aren't I right dear?"

"I couldn't agree with you more, Minnie."

Minnie lifted her eyebrows above her glasses. "See? Now, you two sit down and I'll bring the rest of your meal out."

"I told you," Amber hissed as soon as Minnie left. "I told you."

"She didn't say anything important," her dad whispered back. "Theo warned me that Minnie's a gossip."

"Oh, Daddy, Pelinore was ready to lick the eyebrows right off your face last night."

To her surprise, Dad turned as red as punch, but before he could say anything, Minnie was back with plates of scrambled eggs and bacon. She set them down, then snitched a piece of bacon. "Mmm. Just right. That old stove works just as good as new. Well, I'll just go back to work."

"Minnie?" Dad paused as the woman stole another piece of bacon. "All Miss Pelinore told me was that you agreed to keep house. She didn't mention cooking."

Minnie snorted. "She didn't, did she? Well, that's just like her." She shook her head. "Once you're settled in and don't need as much help, I thought I'd come in Mondays, Wednesdays, and Fridays around ten in the morning and stay for two or three hours, or longer if there's something special that needs doing. I'll make your lunch on those days and, as often as you want, put together casseroles or whatever for your suppers." She dimpled up again. "You just have to tell me what you like. I grocery shop on Wednesdays and I'll do yours, too, if you give me a list."

"That's very nice of you. Where do you shop?"

"We couldn't find the supermarket last night," Amber chimed in.

Minnie scratched her chin thoughtfully. "Well, you'd have to go all the way back down to Pismo for a real supermarket. There's a pricey gourmet market up in the hills, it's called Greenaway's, but only people like Theodora Pelinore shop there. The real folks shop at Ferd's market on Main Street, right near my Mickey's hardware store."

"I know the place. Amber and I met Mr. Cox last night."

"Well, if you want the town to accept you, shop at Cox's." She lowered her voice. "Then go up the hill to Greenaway's and get your caviar. Just don't let the locals see you. And don't tell Ferd Cox. He about has a conniption fit every time Greenaway's is mentioned."

"He told us we're going to die in here," Amber chirped.

"Oh, don't pay any attention to that line of talk. Ferd's

okay, he just pretends to be a grouch. In fact, Mr. Masters, Ferd could probably tell you a lot of stories about this place. His granddaddy had his own ship back then and Ferd said he met Miss Lizzie herself."

"Ferd did?" Amber asked. He looked as old as God, but . . .

"No, sweetie, his daddy did. Ferd wasn't born until the twenties, nor his brother, so he never knew Lizzie."

Gee, there are two of them? Amber wondered with distaste.

"There've always been whole herds of Coxes in these parts," Minnie rattled on, "so there were plenty of relatives to pass the stories along. The Coxes are a fine old family. Fishermen and politicians," she added, "and they do love their tales, tall or not."

Amber was shaking with barely contained laughter, but Minnie and her father seemed oblivious.

"Ferd didn't seem to care for me," Dad said.

"Honey, he doesn't *seem* to like anybody. If Ferd ever cracked a smile, it would break his face. He goes to Barnacle Bob's just about every night. Buy him a beer. He'll talk, him and Andy both, though Andy's less lively than Ferd. They're twins, you know. If you want them to open up, just don't wear anything with designer labels showing." She barely paused for a breath. "If I might ask, Mr. Masters, do you have a lady friend?"

David looked slightly taken aback. "No."

"Well, I didn't mean to pry, but I had to know because I know someone you simply *must* meet. She's sweet as honey and cute as a bug in a rug, isn't that a silly expression, but she is. That cute," she added breathlessly. "And she's a writer, too. Just like you."

"There's another novelist in town?" he asked, intrigued.

"Oh my, yes. She's written fifteen books!"

"That's very impressive. Perhaps I've read one," he said.

"Oh, no, I don't think so. Calla is a lit'ry novelist. She's my daughter, too," she added proudly.

He smiled thinly. "I read all sorts of books, Minnie, not just horror novels."

"Oh, no, I didn't mean to imply you weren't well read. You couldn't have read one because Calla hasn't sold any yet, though Lord knows she's tried. She's tried for fifteen years. I know she'd be honored if you'd read them for her, they're very good, so very lit'ry, you know. Maybe you could put in a good word with your publisher." She paused, eyes sparkling. "Or with your agent. She hasn't found the right agent yet. The book she's working on now is wonderful. It's called *A Woman's Purple Onion.*"

Amber watched her father try to control the muscle that had begun twitching in his left cheek. She felt sorry for him as he worked to stay composed while Minnie blithely pushed almost every one of his hidden buttons.

"I'm sorry," he said uncomfortably, "but my, ah, agent has advised me not to read unsold manuscripts."

"What?" She obviously didn't believe him.

"It's a legal thing. If an unsold manuscript happens to have something in it similar to something I've written that isn't published yet, an unscrupulous would-be writer might claim I stole his or her idea."

"Calla would never do such a thing! Not my Calla!"

He raised his hands. "Of course she wouldn't, but I can't break the rules. Sorry."

"Well, that's terrible, having your reading censored like that."

"Yes," he said with false helplessness, "but it's a price I have to pay."

"Calla gets published all the time, though, in the *Guardian.* She's their star reporter. She did a story on your moving here that came out yesterday morning. She's going to review your books and she wants to interview you, won't that be nice? Well, I have work to do. Just leave the dishes when you're done. I'll clear them out."

As soon as Minnie exited, Amber patted her father's hand. He still looked rattled. "How come you didn't ask Minnie Mouth if she'd had any haunting experiences here?"

He laughed. "I never got the chance."

"Yeah."

"Hey, kiddo, do you think we really need a housekeeper? We used to get along just fine without one."

"We lived in a two-bedroom house, Daddy, and it was a sty, except for when Melanie was there."

"Yeah." He grimaced humorously. "Melanie and her list of Saturday morning chores that we all had to do."

"No fun. Anyway, this place is huge and I can't cook any better than you can."

"It would be nice to get some home cooking, wouldn't it?" He leaned back and stretched.

"You said it, Dad."

"Okay." He lowered his voice to a soft whisper. "We'll just have to work together to keep our problems at a minimum."

"I'll tell her what a monster you are if someone bugs you while you're working," she whispered back.

"Thanks. Lay it on thick, will you, sweetheart? I'm going to buy new latches for upstairs and locks for your room, my room, and my office today. I'll give you an office key, but you have to keep it hidden." He leaned over and whispered in her ear, "I think Minnie's a snoop."

"Sure, Daddy, but she's probably not that bad," Amber said, even though she was picturing Minnie on the other side of the door straining to hear their conversation. "You're always a little paranoid about your books."

"I can't take a chance on her getting into my manuscripts—"

"She won't," Amber replied, though she wasn't so sure. "I mean, she's nosey and all, but she's nice."

"You like her?"

"I didn't at first."

He smiled slightly. "I saw you when she badmouthed Theo. That's when your attitude changed."

"And you say you're not psychic." She grinned, then asked in a normal tone, "When are you going into town?"

"Now, I guess. I want to get back to interview our potential gardener and to oversee the movers while they break all our stuff." He stretched. "Why? Want to come along?"

Amber smiled sweetly. "I think I'll stay here and look around—"

"Not the third floor—"

"If you say that enough times, I'll get so curious that I'll *have* to go up there, just like the people in your books."

"Point taken."

"Daddy?"

"What?"

"When you get back, can I take the Bronco and go exploring?"

"As long as you stay in the general vicinity and get back by four or five in case I need to go out again."

"It's a deal." She paused. "Did you hear anything last night? After we went to bed?"

He cleared his throat and asked in a funny voice, "Noises?"

"Um hum. I thought I heard music."

"Singing?" he inquired cautiously.

"No. Piano music." She shook her head. "I'm not even sure I heard it. I might have dreamed it. Is something wrong, Daddy?"

He visibly relaxed. "Nothing's wrong, kiddo. What kind of music did you hear?"

"Old. Kind of like the music from *The Sting*."

"Ragtime?"

"Kind of." She hummed a few notes. "I can't think of the title."

"Hello, my baby, hello my honey, hello my ragtime doll," he sang.

"That's it. Maybe that old piano's got a ghost, huh Dad?"

He grinned. "We can hope."

Eight

Byron's Finger; 12:24 P.M.

When David returned to the house, his Bronco laden with groceries, doorknobs, and shower fittings, the first thing he noticed was his daughter sitting on the tailgate of a beat-up blue pick-up truck with the handsomest man he'd ever laid eyes on.

Anxious to get back, he'd resisted the urge to stop in at the library, or to try to drag Ferd Cox or the young clerk at the hardware store into conversations and, seeing his daughter swinging her jeans-clad legs and laughing with this stranger, he was suddenly very glad he'd returned so soon.

Amber saw him and pointed. The man looked at him briefly, then waved. An instant later, the two of them trotted over, the young man only getting better looking as he neared.

"Daddy, this is Eric Swenson. He's helping Mr. Willard with the house."

No he's not, he's helping himself to my daughter. David tried to smile. "I've been looking forward to meeting you," he said, giving the boy's hand a strong shake. Eric met his grip firmly, thereby passing the handshake test.

"Yes, sir. You too, sir." He smiled shyly. Eric Swenson's face possessed the bone structure of a Nordic god and he had the body to go with it. As tall as David, his hair was a wavy thatch of blondness, his smile winning, and his cornflower blue eyes as open and trusting as a child's.

"Is that your truck?" David asked him, nodding at the pick-up.

"Oh, no sir. That's Mr. Willard's. I came with him. I just ride a bike."

"Where's Mr. Willard?"

"Inside." Eric looked apprehensively toward the house. "He's working on the downstairs plumbing. The tub was clogged."

David nodded, deciding he wanted to ask the boy a few questions as soon as possible. "How about you two helping me carry the groceries inside, then you can take off, Amber."

"Yes, sir." Grinning, Eric immediately scooped up three heavy bags and started for the front door.

Amber started to pick up a bag, but David stopped her. "Kiddo, I need to tell you something about Eric."

"He's supposed to be slow. Minnie already told me."

"I don't think you should be alone with him until we know him a little better, okay?"

"Yeah, I knew you'd say that. You're such a worrier. He's very nice, though." She shook her head, watching the boy mount the porch steps. "What a waste of a great bod."

"Amber, please. You make me nervous when you talk like that."

She stood on her toes and kissed his cheek, then grabbed a sack labeled Willard Hardware. "You're so silly, Daddy. Eric reminds me of the golden retriever Aunt Barbara had, you know, big and gorgeous, but kind of goofy." She peered into the bag. "What's this stuff?"

"It's the stuff to fix the doors. And," he added triumphantly, "a shower massage with twelve settings. You can take that bag upstairs and leave it in your room for now."

"You're a good father," she said with fake somberness, before heading for the house.

With Eric's help the groceries were in Minnie's care before Amber even drove away. The housekeeper put the perishables in the cooler she'd brought the breakfast food in, fretting that someone would have to go for ice if the movers didn't show up soon. But as soon as the words were out of her mouth, the van pulled up and, to David's relief, the supervisor promised to have his men unload the fridge, pronto.

After giving him written directions for placement of the furniture and cartons, he left Minnie in charge, and led Eric back outdoors where they would be out of earshot.

"Let's walk down to the lighthouse and back," David suggested. "I haven't seen it yet."

Eric halted. "I don't want to go in there."

"We won't go in," David promised. "We'll just go out to Widow's Peak and look at the town." The youth's reticence intrigued him.

Eric brightened. "You can see the pole beacon if you lean over the railing a little. It's on all the time. It's fun to watch."

Grinning, David said, "That sounds good. Let's go." Eric began to move again.

They walked in silence a moment, David wondering how to get Swenson to talk about his experiences in the house. He was sure he'd had one by the way he'd looked at the place when he'd informed him that the still-unseen Mr. Willard was in there. David also guessed that Eric was the one who had spilled the paint and that he was worried about the wrath of Mickey Willard when the damage was discovered. If that were true, David would take care of things.

"There're ghosts out here, you know."

Eric's words stopped David in his tracks. Ghost stories were the last thing he expected to hear out of a young man like Eric. But then again, he realized, the boy couldn't be too frightened or he wouldn't have been willing to work here at all.

"Ghosts?" he asked vaguely.

"There's one in the lighthouse, he's real scary, but he doesn't mean to be. And there're a couple that hang around outside a lot. They're nice, but kind of sad. You know who they are?"

David realized that his mouth was hanging open and promptly shut it. "Who?" *What the hell is going on here.*

"They're Mr. and Mrs. Byron Baudey, Byron and Margaret Cross Baudey, that's who they are." He stopped walking and stared at the sky before continuing to speak in a tone that suggested he'd committed someone else's words to memory. "In 1887, Byron Baudey built the house, that's why it was called Baudey House, and when his sister, Miss Lizzie, inherited it, she called it that too because that was her name and also because she thought it was a good joke to have a bawdy house named Baudey House. Then all the bad things happened and now the joke is Baudey House is Body House."

"That's fascinating, Eric," David said enthusiastically. "Tell me more!" Through long experience, he had learned to never let on he knew anything about a subject because it caused the informer to censor himself, and some priceless bit of information might be lost.

The grin that spread across Eric's face was one of pure pleasure. If he was considered slow, then being taken seriously was probably a rare treat. "Well, Byron Baudey, he got rich in the spice trade. He had his own boat and everything, and he decided to retire young because he was in love with Margaret Cross, who said anyone who married a sailor was a widow whether the sailor was dead or not and she wouldn't be a sailor's widow.

"Well, he already owned this land and he'd built the lighthouse with his own money because so many boats had sunk here. The town really liked him for that." He paused to watch as a flock of pelicans flew overhead.

"So then Byron Baudey hired a bunch of men to help him build the house. It was hard to build because the land is mostly rocks and he wanted to have a big cellar for potatoes and stuff and for his wine collection—"

"Cellar?" David asked quickly. "Do you know more about it?" The cellar was the focal point of various theories about the house and he hadn't been able to find out much about it in his research so far. According to legend, Lizzie used it as a sort of soft-core bondage and discipline playground, though her daughter, Christabel, later converted it into a torture chamber worthy of the Spanish Inquisition. After the night of the massacre in 1915, a dozen bodies, Lizzie's and Christabel's included, were never found and, because of the stench that emanated for sometime thereafter, which was said to still manifest occasionally, it was theorized that if anyone could find the secret entrance, they'd find the bodies, too. It was a mystery that David hoped to solve.

"Well, I think it's there. Byron Baudey took a bunch of dynamite and blasted the cellar out of the rock. Then he evened it out with a pickax, or that's what Uncle Craig guesses."

"Is that who told you about the Baudeys?" David asked as they resumed walking.

"Mostly, but everybody knows about them. Uncle Craig, he got real interested because he almost got killed there once."

"He did?" David could hardly contain his excitement at having found this treasure trove.

"Uh huh. He just missed getting killed. He was—" Eric hesitated, "a new policeman—"

"A rookie?"

Eric's eyes sparkled. "Yes sir, that's right. A rookie. The chief sent him and his partner over to check the house because there were all these hippies having a . . . a commune in it."

1968. That's when it happened. David envisioned the headline from the copy of the old *New York Times* article he had in his file: "TWENTY DIE IN DRUG/SEX ORGY IN HAUNTED HOUSE." The bodies were nude, horribly mutilated, and bizarrely arranged. David had never been able to find out the exact positions of the corpses but he suspected they bore a resemblance to the positioning of the victims in the 1915 massacre. Maybe now he could see the police photos. "Is your uncle still a policeman, Eric?"

Eric nodded proudly. "He's the chief. Sometimes he takes me for a ride in his cruiser."

"What does he think of your working here?" David asked as they came to the end of the promontory.

"He thinks it's just fine." Eric leaned over the railing and pointed down at the rocks. "See the beacon? It's right there."

David looked and got a faceful of brilliant white light. He pulled back quickly. "That about blinded me."

Eric straightened. "It makes me see spots. That's kind of neat. Red Cay's right there."

They turned north and looked out at the town. Tiny cars traveled the compact downtown area and the pier he and Amber had been on last night jutted out into the halfmoon bay. Gulls and pelicans flew around it and boats were docked in a small harbor adjacent to the pier. The sleepy little fishing village was almost painfully picturesque. It was no wonder it had attracted so many artists.

"Eric, what does your uncle think about all the ghosts here?"

"He doesn't believe in them."

"But you do?"

"Sure. I see them sometimes," he added matter-of-factly. "You know that where we're standing right now is really called Widow's Peak?"

"Yes, I'd heard that."

"It's just this part that's kind of uphill, from the lighthouse back."

David smiled. "How did it get the name?"

"Margaret Cross Baudey threw herself from this very spot after her family died. She was too sad to live," he added pensively. "That's why she walks around out here sometimes." He paused. "I think other widows came here too, before her. Uncle Craig would know."

"And you've seen Margaret?"

Eric nodded, as if David's question was completely ordinary. "Uh huh. I've been here a lot with Mr. Willard since you bought the house and I've seen her three times. Once in the daytime, twice when it was getting dark. I saw Byron Baudey too, once." He smiled. "I hope they get to see each other sometimes. That'd be nice, don't you think?"

"Very." Eric hadn't told him anything he didn't already know. The first deaths in the house were those of Byron and Margaret's young daughter, Charity, and her infant son. In 1905, Charity was raped, the baby being the product of that assault. Charity never recovered from the violence of that night and the murder-suicide in the tower was the result. Then, in 1909, Byron was found dead near the lighthouse, most likely the victim of a simple heart attack. The following year, Margaret threw herself from the cliff. David had read vague accounts of their ghosts walking the grounds, but hadn't paid them much attention: he assumed these stories to be garden-variety ghost stories. He found the later murders far more interesting.

He glanced at Eric Swenson, who was avidly pointing out landmarks in the town, and David guiltily realized he hadn't heard a word the boy was saying. He resolved to concentrate.

"See that boat pulling away from the pier? That's the *Painted Lady.* It belongs to Andy Cox. So does that one, and that one." He pointed at two fishing boats tied to the dock.

"I see. Who does that one belong to?" David pointed at a large ketch just heading out to sea.

"That's Bo's tour boat. He rents to sport fishermen."

"Eric, how come you don't like to go in the lighthouse?" David asked bluntly. Seeing the boy's look of surprise, he added, "I mean, if Byron Baudey isn't a mean ghost or anything—"

Understanding dawned on Eric's handsome face. "Oh no, Byron Baudey walks around *out here.* The one in the lighthouse is just really scary. He can't help it. He's really sad and angry all the time and he's kind of hard to take."

Either Eric Swenson was mentally ill, or David had found himself a genuine psychic. If Swenson wasn't making it up or imagining it, then he was actually sensing things, and unlike Theo Pelinore, he seemed to be very down-to-earth about the whole thing. Theo, David had decided in retrospect, probably possessed just enough sixth sense to feel a haunting—much as many other people did. After all, she hadn't claimed to have experienced anything unexplainable except for last night's events. He'd have to quiz her more carefully, though he expected to find that she was merely a battery for the manifestations to draw on. He studied Eric. "Do you know who the ghost is?"

Eric made a face. "It's Captain Wilder, but I don't like thinking about him because he's so sad and awful to look at. He's got no head."

"No head?"

"No, sir. It got chopped off by Christabel."

"Lizzie's daughter."

Eric nodded. "Captain Wilder was the first one she killed." He unbuttoned the cuffs on his denim shirt and started rolling up his sleeves. "It's getting warm."

"It sure is." David thought it would be nice to get back to the house and lose the sweater. "And the captain's killed a few people too, hasn't he? Since he became a ghost, I mean?"

"No," Eric replied somberly. "He just scares people because he can't help it. He wouldn't mean to kill them."

"They're scared because he's headless?"

Eric thought about it. "No, sir, I don't think so. I'm the only one I know who sees him like that." He hesitated. "Of course, there could be others, but I don't think they'd say so. I don't talk about it, usually, because it just makes people think I'm crazy."

"I don't think you're crazy," David assured him.

"I figured you wouldn't, since everybody in town says *you're* crazy."

"What?" David asked, taken aback.

Eric cleared his throat and took his voice up an octave. "That crazy writer is gonna die in that house."

"Ferd Cox!" David laughed.

"That's him!" The boy beamed.

"That was a great imitation."

"Thanks!"

David couldn't contain his curosity. "Who else says I'm crazy?"

"Oh, most everybody."

"Do you think I'm crazy, Eric?"

He scratched his head. "No more than me."

Wondering what that meant, David prompted, "Tell me more about the captain. What does he look like to most people?"

Eric shrugged. "I don't know. Different. Most people don't see him at all."

"Do you know anyone else who's seen him?"

"Yes, sir. Billy Galiano saw him."

Pay dirt! Galiano was the boy who survived the lighthouse accident last May, just before David bought the house.

"Billy's friend, Matty Farmer, he saw the ghost too. That's why he died—he got scared stupid and he fell."

"The ghost didn't kill him?" David nudged.

"No, sir. Uncle Craig told me that Billy said they were up at the top of the lighthouse and they heard footsteps coming up the stairs. There wasn't anywhere to hide, so they came down. They just thought they were going to see a drunk or maybe even get in trouble, if one of the police saw them go up there. But they saw a black cloud—that was the captain. Billy said he was really scary. He told Matty Farmer that they were going to run right through it. And that's what Billy did. But Matty chickened and ran back up the stairs and he fell."

"Why is the captain so scary if they don't see him like you do?"

"I guess you could say he feels scary." Eric considered, scratching his chin. "I think the captain's still mad that he got killed. I think maybe he loved Miss Lizzie and didn't want to die."

A star-crossed love affair between the madam and the mariner. Images crowded into David's brain, making him itch to get to the keyboard. "The captain loved Lizzie? Did your uncle tell you that?"

"Oh, no, I just think he did. I kind of feel it, you know?"

"I understand." Even if it hadn't actually happened, that romantic thread was just the sort of thing he needed now to flesh out *Mephisto Palace*—David liked to draw from reality whenever he could. "Did Billy say exactly what the captain looked like to him?"

"Black stuff," Eric said simply. "Sort of like a big old ball of black fog. Calla Willard said she thinks she saw him once, but he just looked like a ripple in the air or something."

Both the darkness and the ripples were common forms of manifestation and that lent credence to Eric's tales and David began to think the boy was truly gifted. For that matter, though there was a simplicity about the young man, David wasn't so sure it was a simplicity of intellect. It might be, he thought, that Eric Swenson possessed an unerring bullshit detector and a willingness to accept the unexplainable. Those traits would logically go with more overt psychic abilities and someone whose thinking processes were so different from your average person, especially in a small town, David suspected, might not feel the need to conform. As this occurred to him, Eric extended his arms and began turning circles, swooping and twirling and obviously enjoying the hell out of himself. David watched, thinking he'd been turning Eric into a character in his book rather than seeing him for what he probably was: a mildly handicapped young man who might possess some psychic abilities.

"Eric!" he called. "What're you doing?"

Eric stopped twirling. "You were busy thinking, so I took a ride on a Tilt-a-Whirl." He grinned broadly, showing straight white teeth. "It's fun. Not as good as the one that comes with the carnival, but it still gets me dizzy." He studied David. "Are you done thinking?"

David couldn't help smiling. "Yes. Eric, you couldn't tell me what I was thinking about, could you?"

He stared at David curiously. "You mean you don't remember?"

"No, no." He almost laughed, then seeing the look in Eric's eyes, began to wonder if the boy might be pulling his leg. "Actually, you seem to have some psychic abilities and I was wondering if you're telepathic at all."

"Well, I guess you were thinking mostly about me and if I'm crazy or not. And you're all excited about those ghosts."

"You're right. On both counts."

"But I didn't read your mind, sir. First, you wouldn't be here if you weren't all excited about ghosts. And that's what we were talking about. Second, everybody in Red Cay wonders if I'm crazy." A slow smile spread across his face. "Just like they do you, sir."

"Touché." Quite suddenly, Swenson made him nervous. *You're reading things into his words,* he cautioned himself. Still, he resolved to get Minnie Willard's view on Eric as soon as possible. "Call me David, please, Eric."

"Yes sir. I mean David."

David smiled. "Let's get back to the ghosts."

"Okay."

"Have you ever seen ghosts in the house? Maybe in the tower?"

"Oh, I won't go in the tower. I can hear that baby cry sometimes and I hate that. I sure don't ever want to see those ghosts in there." He looked at his shoes. "Mr. Willard told me to put new bulbs on every floor in the tower and I said I did it. But I was chicken," he confessed. "I didn't do it. I just opened the door and stuck my hand in and left them. I was afraid he'd fire me if I said I was afraid. I'm sorry."

"That's all right, Eric. I'll take care of it."

David took a step in the direction of the house and the boy fell in beside him.

"Eric, have you ever seen *any* ghosts in Body House?"

"Well, there's lots of *stuff* in there . . ."

"Stuff?"

"Yes, sir," he said patiently. "There's lots of stuff everywhere people have been, not just in that house. The stuff in there feels bad mostly, but there's some really nice-feeling stuff too. It feels sort of like a party."

"Eric, slow down a minute, you're losing me."

Eric appeared to be pleased. "I am?"

"Yes. Tell me what you mean when you say 'stuff.' "

"Stuff is . . ." Eric stopped walking and stared at the sea. Finally, he spoke. "It's like leftovers." Suddenly, he chuckled to himself. "Do you go to a gym to work out?"

Last year, David had bought a year's membership at a health spa. He only went once. All those perfectly sculpted bodies encased in Spandex intimidated him so much that all he could think was that he had walked into the middle of a horror movie called *The Stepford Bodies*. Looking at Eric, he realized the muscular young man would fit right in. Finally, he said, "Yes, I've been to a gym."

"Well, you know when you walk into the locker room and all you can smell is B.O. like crazy, but nobody's in there? That's leftovers. That's stuff. Body House has a lot of that stuff."

It's not a spirit he'd told Theo last night when they had smelled the jasmine, *It's a memory.* He'd likened it to smelling his grandmother's sachet. David thought for a moment and decided that Eric had very nearly the same take on hauntings as he himself had.

"Did you smell the flowers?" Eric asked.

"Yes. And something bad, too," David told him.

"Something like the dead opossum I found rotting under our house last fall."

"That would be the smell. So you haven't actually *seen* any ghosts in the house?" David wanted a straight answer.

"Well . . . I don't want to ruin your dinner or anything, but . . ."

"But what?"

"There's a real ugly one in the dining room. He's been sliced down his middle, but usually you don't see that. He looks alive, but he's still really ugly. He has kind of long hair and a beard and he looks really, really dirty, fat and dirty. But he's funny. He does that President Nixon thing a lot."

"What's that?"

"You know, with his hand." Eric made a peace sign. "He mostly crawls around on the table. He gets on it and crawls from one end to the other. When he does that, his pants go too low." Eric snickered. "I call him Buttcrack."

So much for dignity in the afterlife. "Fortunately, Amber and I usually eat in front of the television."

Eric nodded approvingly. "I saw another one floating in the bathtub downstairs."

"Another one?"

"Another hippie. She's naked—" Eric blushed "—and real white because the water's completely red. Her guts are out of her. I saw her once when I was washing my hands. Her eyes were open. I washed in the kitchen after that. That's why I told Mr. Willard I needed to take a break. I didn't want to help him in there."

"I don't blame you."

"There's a man and a woman on the floor in the ballroom." He paused, blushing harder. "They're making love. And there's a little man in that red bathroom. He just likes to stand there and look at himself in the mirror."

Drake Roberts. David was relieved to know that it wasn't just the torrid color of the room that made him uneasy. Curious to hear how Eric would reply, he said, "A lot more people died in the house. Aren't their ghosts there, too?"

"No. Most of them don't hang around. There's a real nice one in the front room, though, that makes pretty music."

"My daughter thought she heard piano music last night."

"Yes, sir. I've heard it lots of times. It's usually really hard to hear, but sometimes it's pretty strong." He grinned. "I like it. It makes it easier to work."

"Do you see a ghost playing it, Eric?"

"I never have. I think the piano is its own ghost."

David decided to figure that one out later. "Eric, have you ever seen a red-haired lady in an old-fashioned green dress, like in the portrait on the first floor?"

"No, sir. It *feels* like Miss Lizzie's around, though, in a way. It *feels* like lots of people are around, but I think they're just leftovers." He grinned, probably thinking about Buttcrack again.

"Is the flower perfume hers?"

"No, sir."

"Please call me David," he said again. "Is it Christabel's?"

"I don't know . . . Mr. Willard's probably wondering where I am," he said nervously.

They began walking again and David decided to push just a little further. "Have you seen Christabel, Eric?"

Swenson stared straight ahead as he answered. "I saw something, but I can't think about it now. I'm sorry."

"Just tell me this: was it on the third floor?"

"Yes sir, David. Don't go up there, that's where it lives."

Eric was saying "it," where he'd referred to gender with the other ghosts. David asked him why, but he just shrugged. "It's not exactly a ghost."

"Is it leftovers?"

"No. Leftovers are nothing. Ghosts are fancy leftovers that are kind of caught up in their own world and they don't pay much attention to things we do. They usually hang around one place, like Captain Wilder, but that thing up there . . . it's interested. It's a bad thing and it's . . ." He searched for a word for a long time. "It's hungry. I think it can make ghosts and leftovers *do* stuff, too. And David?"

Goosebumps trailed deliciously down his spine. "What?"

"I think maybe it can go wherever it wants. You need to be careful not to get it excited. Billy said he saw it at a couple of windows that day when Matty got killed."

"What did it look like?"

"Like curtains blowing, I guess."

"Only there were no curtains." David cleared his throat. "Eric, have you seen it?"

The boy didn't answer.

"Did you see it in the room where the paint's spilled?"

Eric stopped walking and whirled to face David. "You went in that room?" he demanded.

"Yes, but don't worry about the paint—"

"Don't go in that room! Don't *ever* go in that room!"

"Theo Pelinore and I were up there last night."

The blood drained from Eric Swenson's face.

"Don't go up there. Don't let your daughter go up there either."

"I've asked her not to already. Why, Eric? Do you think it can hurt her?"

Somberly, Swenson nodded. "Amber's like you, so she's pretty much safe, except up there. It can hurt anybody that goes in there."

"Did it hurt you?"

Eric started walking. "We need to get back."

David walked silently. He longed to ask more questions, but knew he'd gone far enough. As they neared the house, he groaned, seeing a silver and blue telephone truck parked out front. He hoped they hadn't been there long, since he'd left no instructions.

A moment later, they passed the truck and, to David's relief, the engine was still clicking.

Nine

Body House: 1:57 P.M.

A short, stocky man in olive coveralls stood on a stepping stool on the front porch, carefully prying boards from the fanlight above the door. He had already removed those covering the sidelights and David was rather relieved to see that these, like the fanlight pediments over the windows, were traditional art nouveau, rather than pornographic. The sidelights were a riot of brilliant colors, primarily blues and greens, and when he moved two steps nearer, David realized that the designs in the glass were an eclectic but graceful display of peacocks and scallop shells.

"Mr. Willard?" David asked as the man pulled the last nail from the fanlight and climbed down.

"He's a little hard of hearing," Eric said quietly.

As David opened his mouth to speak more loudly, the man turned around and, startled, dropped the plywood on his toes. He uttered a single heartfelt "Damn!" then placed the board in a stack with the others before looking at David. "You Masters?" he grunted.

"Yes."

"Willard," he said, extending his hand.

"It's a pleasure to meet you, Mr. Willard."

"Phone man's waiting on you." Willard stood back from the door so that he could enter.

"Thanks." David moved past him, Eric on his heels.

"Swenson," rumbled Willard. "Take those boards to the truck and get the wood putty."

"Yes, sir."

A swarthy moving man with a pack of Lucky Strikes rolled into his T-shirt sleeve came from the direction of the stairwell, glanced at David doubtfully, then picked up one of the huge cartons that were stacked around the parlor, and headed back the way he'd come. David continued through the maze and into the kitchen, tracking the faint, unceasing sound of Minnie Willard's voice.

"Well, that's how Bea Broadside is, always sticking her bosoms into other people's marriages—not that I'd say anything bad about her, she's my dearest friend. Oh, Mr. Masters, there you are!"

The phone man, a callow youth with a sprinkling of freckles, a neat red ponytail, and an embroidered nametag that read, "Conan," toppled a coffee mug in his hurry to escape the captivity of Minnie's rampaging tongue. Coffee sloshed all over his pants and the table. "Whoa, sorry," he said helplessly.

"That's all right, dear." Brandishing a paper towel, she passed by the puddle on the table and headed for his crotch.

He sidestepped with the alacrity of a bullfighter and snatched the towel from her. "Thanks, ma'am. Mr. Masters? Where do you want your phones?"

David led Conan out of the room. "I'd like a wall outlet in the kitchen, but that can wait until she's done in there."

The phone guy nodded gratefully.

"Let's start with my office. I need two separate lines in there."

"Cool."

Fortunately, there were old-fashioned phone outlets all over the house, the surface wiring skillfully hidden amongst the trim. With David helping, the modernization went quickly and they were soon working on the second floor.

"So, like, is that your mother down there?" Conan asked as he tested the new outlet in the hall by the stairwell.

"My mother?" David asked, puzzled. "Oh, you mean Minnie." He chuckled. "No. She's my housekeeper."

"Better you than me, man," the phone man said, shaking his head.

"You're not from around here?" David asked.

"No. I just moved up here from Phoenix."

"Have you heard anything about this house?"

"Huh? Like what?"

"Oh, anything. Anything at all."

Conan thought a moment. "No. So tell me about the house, man. What should I have heard?"

I'm not going to get another chance like this. David smiled broadly at the only person he was likely to run into who had never heard of Body House. *Thank you, God, for sending me this man!* "You haven't noticed the stained glass, then? The house is famous for it."

"Sure, it's real pretty." Conan glanced briefly at the cabinetry above, then finished screwing in the new phone outlet. He rose. "Where else?" he asked, looking a little more closely at the glass arch at the top of the shelves.

"My room. It's this way."

Conan squinted at the cabinets once more—from looking at the glasswork in the hall here he couldn't decide if it was Georgia O'Keefe-style orchids or dew-dropped vaginas. David smiled, watching him. The art was too subtle for the man to say anything, even though he obviously suspected something.

A moment later, in David's bedroom, Conan stared at the unobscene fanlight topping the window and shrugged. "It's nice, but you can see stained glass anywhere."

"True. Look at the glass on that wardrobe over there."

"Okay." Glancing over his shoulder at David, he crossed the room and stared closely at the glass for about thirty seconds. Suddenly, he whistled appreciatively between his teeth. "Whoa! Nice tits on your furniture, Mr. Masters!"

David stifled a laugh. "That's why the glass is famous." He paused. "You *really* haven't heard of Body House before? You haven't read about it or seen it on television?"

"Huh uh, no! Body House, that's what it's called? I can see why!" He studied the twist of feminine bodies on the wardrobe. "Body House. Is there more like this?"

"Yes. And many different patterns, too."

"Those flowers out in the hall, man . . ."

"I don't think they're flowers," David said, smiling beneficently. *He doesn't know, he really doesn't know!* This was a dream come true.

"Body House," Conan said again as he bent to install the outlet. "Body House."

"I'm really surprised you've never heard of it." David wanted to give him every chance to remember.

"I don't watch much TV. I like tunes." He made a face. "And I *hate* to read. It's such a big waste of time. I just put my earphones on and my CDs and listen to my tunes." He stood up, put his screwdriver in his belt, and grinned. "Any more lines to go in?"

"One more. It's this way."

David led Conan down the hall and into the corridor between the terrace and ballroom. In the daylight, the orgiastic stained glass was impressive. David could see the gleaming wood of the ballroom floor and wondered where the coupling ghosts were located. Finally, Conan let himself be led to the stairwell and they mounted the steps to the third floor.

"The room's still messy," David explained. "A can of paint was spilled and we haven't cleaned it up yet. Forgive the mess."

"No problem."

David held the door and the phone man entered and looked around the room. "We have a problem," he said, scratching his carroty hair.

"We do?"

"There's no wiring in here. I'd have to run it in from . . ."

A whiff of jasmine permeated the room. "Is something wrong?" David asked innocently.

Conan turned to face him, his flushed face split by a sheepish grin. "No, nothing's wrong. I feel really good. I guess I just had a stained glass flashback. Wow."

"Did you see something?"

"No. I just got this rush." His eyes strayed downward and David noticed the erection straining against Conan's pants before the young man dropped his hands to hide it.

The jasmine scent strengthened, became edged with decay.

"Man, get another air freshener. Whatever you're using up here is foul." He stopped talking and, momentarily, a blank expression came over his face. "Whoa. I gotta get out of here." With that, Conan left the room.

David followed, pulling the door securely closed behind him. "What's wrong?" he asked the phone man as ingenuously as he could.

"Man, I don't know. I got cold and, you know, hot." He shook his head, but didn't stop walking. "It felt like somebody was stroking me off." They were on the stairs now. "I'm sorry—you won't tell my supervisor I said that?"

"Don't worry. You thought somebody was touching you?"

"Yeah. For a second there, I thought I was gonna spew, man." They reached the second-floor landing. "God, I'm rattled, Mr. Masters, I wouldn't talk like that if I wasn't. Please don't—"

"I won't tell." He smiled, leading Conan down to the first floor. "I'd noticed something like that myself, but not so strongly."

"Well, you're kind of an old dude," Conan said sympathetically. "It's harder to get it up when you're so old."

"I'm forty-one," David said defensively.

"Yeah, an old dude."

"Let's get that kitchen connection in," David told him.

Fifteen minutes later, it was done. Conan had tested the line by phoning his girlfriend and making a date for "the sooner the better."

As David saw him out the front door, Amber pulled up behind the moving van. She got out and David watched the book-hating phone dude as he took in her dark blond hair, glistening in the afternoon sun, her long legs encased in stretch jeans, and her well-proportioned torso, covered by a white shirt tied just above the waist so that when she moved, a flash of skin showed.

"Wow," said the phone dude.

"That's my daughter," David growled in his ear.

Conan went rigid. "Gotta go." He strode purposefully toward his truck, turning his head away as he passed Amber, who stared curiously after him.

"What's the matter with him?" she asked, coming through the door. She fixed David with a look, her hand on her hip. "Daddy, did you tell him I'm your daughter?"

"Well, you are." He grinned at her. "Aren't you?"

"Daddy, I'm going to be forty years old and still living with you because of the way you tell guys you're my father."

"Did you pack a phone in the Bronco like you were going to, kiddo?" David didn't feel like being chewed out right this minute.

She nodded.

"Well, go get it and you can call your friends and tell them you're still alive." *Bad choice of words, Masters.* But she didn't seem to notice, just turned and ran for the truck.

Leaving the movers to Minnie and the repairs to the taciturn Mr. Willard and Eric Swenson, David went to his room and turned on his laptop computer. By the time he finished entering everything pertinent that had happened since their arrival at Ferd Cox's store twenty-four hours ago, two hours had gone by and Amber had given the phone the workout of its life.

Ten

New York City: 7:46 P.M.

Melanie Lord was trying her damndest to get Harry Rosenberg drunk, but the Dorner Books editor seemed to be a bottomless pit. He'd had three scotch-rocks and showed no signs of melting down. As the waiter passed, she signaled him. "Two more, please." Then she cocked her head coquettishly, so that her short auburn pageboy shimmered around her face. Batting her lashes, she said, "Harry, I hope you don't mind my ordering more drinks—"

"No, no. Not at all." He drained his glass and sat forward. "So, let's talk about someone besides Meat Blaisdell. He's just not what I'm looking for."

Melanie studied Rosenberg. This guy was very high up in the publishing feeding chain and she'd been pleased as hell when he'd accepted her invitation for drinks after she'd sent over Ray's latest proposal. She thought that maybe she was going to get over that last hurdle and hit the big time if Rosenberg went for Ray.

Ray "Meat" Blaisdell was a science fiction writer trying to go straight, or as he put it, he wanted to "pull a Masters." More than half the genre writers she represented, no matter what their specialty, talked like that. "Masters writes horror," one would say. "No, he writes science fiction," another would argue, and a third would insist he wrote thrillers. They argued on and on about why he was so lucky and how they themselves could get that way.

Melanie thought that Ray had a chance because he actually understood that genre trappings had little to do with that bastard Masters' success: it was the scope and humanity of said bastard's work that had taken him, along with a handful of other authors, over the top. Melanie wanted to help Ray get there, first because he was the best writer she represented; second, because he was her current lover. He didn't quite have that prick Masters' natural talent for either activity, but he was young and had stamina. With luck, he'd learn.

". . . just not quite our kind of writer," Harry was saying.

"When you accepted my invitation, I assumed you wanted to talk about Ray's proposal," she said as the drinks arrived. She sipped her wine spritzer, then ran her finger around the rim of the glass and waited expectantly.

"Melanie, Meat's a good writer, but it's too generic for Dorner. Too much science fiction razzle dazzle." His lip curled up as if he smelled something bad. "Too techy. But, if you could get him to write something set here, on earth, and in the present, I'd very much like to see it. I'd especially like to see a UFO proposal." He smiled thinly. "Lots of sex and humiliation. That's very hot now, you know."

"I know." Melanie sipped her drink slowly. That was all the editors were talking about this year. Last year it was serial killers, next year they'd probably have hard-ons for medical thrillers. The disgusting truth was that having a feel for coming editorial hard-ons—"trends" was just too nice a word—was what could make your name as an agent if you didn't already have a best-selling author to help you fly. And since that best-selling S.O.B. David Masters would fall into her bed but not her agency, she'd decided she'd have to make it the hard way.

Besides, she had to admit, Harry had a good idea with the UFO thing. "Ray might go for it," she told him truthfully. "I'll call him first thing tomorrow." She lifted one eyebrow. "So, Harry, who else can I sell you?"

"You can sell me David Masters."

"I wish I could," she said sourly. "You'll have to talk to Georgie Gordon about him."

"So steal him. I thought you and Masters were . . ." His voice trailed off suggestively.

"We were." Tempted to spew invective about that she-snob Gordon, she decided to take the high road instead. "You have to understand how David thinks. Georgie discovered him and stuck with him while he was slogging around in mid-list. He's very devoted to her. Very loyal." She heard the sneer in her voice and tried to force it away. "I suppose that if I had discovered him and he left me for an agent he had a personal relationship with, I'd feel very used." Whenever she said that, usually silently and to herself, she understood David better, which made it harder to feel hurt and angry, which was how she preferred to feel.

"My dear Melanie," Harry purred. "You're a charming woman. Seduce him away from Georgie and Randall House, bring him to me, and you'll have million dollar clients dripping from the diamonds you'll wear on your fingers. I guarantee it."

Christ, she thought, *when the booze finally hits him, it really hits.* She reached across the small round table and patted his hand. "Darling," she said, falling into perfect Manhattan Bitch, "I'd *love* to hand him to you, but David has these annoying *scruples.* He doesn't like to mix business and pleasure."

"Scruples? Who needs them?" Harry rose, a little unsteadily. "Please excuse me. I'll be back in a moment." He walked carefully in the direction of the restrooms and Melanie took the opportunity to pour her spritzer into a potted plant she'd sat by for that very purpose. She should have poured out more of the first two drinks, but Rosenberg had proven himself to have the bladder of a large, ocean-going mammal and she never had a chance. She waved at the waiter, who was taking another order and as soon as he approached, ordered another round.

A moment later, watching Harry lumber back, she regretted not telling the waiter to leave the booze out of her spritzer.

The bearlike Rosenberg still walked with the confidence of a nearly sober man. This could be a long, long night.

"So, how can you get me David Masters?" he said as he slid into his seat.

"If Georgie falls off a cliff, I might have a shot at him." She hesitated, then asked the question she really wanted an answer to. "Why aren't you talking to Georgie?"

"Simple. Masters won't move, and Georgie's in too tight with Randall House to want to pressure him. Besides Masters, she's got Hall and Cory over there."

"That's only three biggies," Melanie said doubtfully. Normally, she'd recall exactly who Georgie had at Randall, high and low, but the wine had clouded her mind.

"Three constant bestsellers. Three who bring down more than a million a book," Harry said. "Then she's got a raft of occasional bestsellers, the six-figure crowd."

Melanie nodded. "If I could get him, what can you offer that Randall House can't?"

"More money. A guaranteed promotion and publicity budget. Higher royalties—"

"Unfortunately, David's world doesn't revolve around money. Don't get me wrong, he likes it, but he's perfectly content with two or three mil a book." She took a sip of wine. "He'd be content with less than that, to be honest. And, as for the other things, well, I'm afraid he's probably quite content with what they do for him at Randall House."

"Well, what *does* he want?"

She snorted. "David already has exactly what he wants. He has Joanna." That was his editor. "He's as loyal to her as he is to Georgie." Melanie made a face. "He always points out that she bought his first book and stood by him through the thin times."

"God, spare me the loyalty shtick." Harry looked at the ceiling. "The agent's loyal to Randall for her own ambitiously greedy reasons—" he smiled smarmily "—not that I don't have the greatest respect for that sort of thing, mind you. And the writer is blindly loyal to his editor." He finished his drink. "Masters should give me a chance. I'll wager I can outdo Joanna Scanlon's best author-coddling any day of the week."

"He likes the way she edits, too, Harry," Melanie said dryly.

He nodded. "Because he doesn't know any better."

"She's good, Harry." Melanie had writers with Scanlon, too, and her own loyalties to keep.

"I know. I trained her." He sat back. "That sounded terribly arrogant. Forgive me."

"I know you're a hell of an editor, Harry, you don't have to sell me. I saw the unedited Tarnmeyer manuscript. I know you practically rewrote the thing. It was brilliant."

"Thank you." Harry's smile slid across his face like a slow-moving snake. "However did you get a copy of that, my dear?"

"Tarn sent it to David for a quote."

"He did?" Genuine surprise showed in Harry's eyes. "Why would he do that before the galleys? He knows we'd send it to Masters at that point."

She chuckled, low in her throat. "Exactly. His cover letter said that he wanted David to see it in its original form before, and I quote, his 'editor gets hold of it and tries to rewrite it because all he is is a frustrated writer.' " *What the hell do you think you're doing, telling him this?* Mortified at her own lack of discretion, she felt her face heat up. "My turn to apologize, Harry. That was a bitchy thing for me to say." She let out a throaty little laugh. "I've had a little too much to drink."

This time, Harry reached for her hand. He didn't pat it, he took it and held it. "Don't apologize. I can outdrink most any agent. And, believe me, I already know Tarn's a prima donna. So, let's get back to David Masters. I want him. You need him. I think we should work together to meet the challenge."

She stared at his hand on hers. Half the male editors in town were gay and here she was, stuck dealing with a drunken hetero who could do wonders for her career. His finger moved lightly over one knuckle, then he became aware of her gaze and withdrew his hand.

"Sorry, I'm a little smashed myself."

Melanie felt one of those proverbial lightbulbs go off over her head. "Harry, let's talk about Joanna Scanlon."

"Shoot."

"Joanna started at Dorner as a junior editor. David was one of her very first buys."

The right side of Harry's mouth crooked up expectantly.

"David left Dorner for Randall House because he wanted to stick with Scanlon." She sat back and looked him in the eye. "Your house didn't know what they had. You let him get away."

"I believe I heard something to that effect," Harry said, his smile growing.

"So if Dorner were to hire Scanlon away from Randall, your house would have a much better chance at acquiring David."

"What about Georgie?"

"Ultimately, she'll do what her author wants." She smiled coyly. "If she won't go for it, David would have to make a choice—his beloved editor or his beloved agent." *Melanie, you're a drunken bitch!* Still, she liked the idea of making him choose, although she knew that wouldn't mean he'd bring his business to her. "Harry," she continued, "you wouldn't be his editor, but you could get the glory by bringing David here."

"Well, that's almost as good, isn't it?" Harry beamed at her. "Melanie, I like the way your mind works. How long have you been in business now?"

"Just four years."

"That's not long." He paused, studying her. "You've built up quite a list. You're going places. I might be able to throw a new author your way, a guy who sent a manuscript over the transom. I bought it. It's a political thriller and it's going to be big stuff. We're ready to buy another book, and he's looking for an agent. You interested?"

"You bet."

They discussed a little more business, then argued politely over the bill. Melanie was relieved when Harry finally snatched it away. Emerging from the Oyster Bar, they were suddenly drowned in the humid evening heat. Melanie's beige silk dress immediately started to stick to her skin and, as she tried to adjust it, she nearly collided with a group of luggage-wielding Frenchmen heading into Grand Central Station.

"I'm going to Gramercy Park." Harry said as he steered her away from the tourists. He began hailing. "Care to share a cab?"

"No, thanks. I live the other way, near Sixth and Fifty-Second. I'll walk."

"You're sure?" he asked. A taxi pulled up and he opened the door. "We can go by your place first."

"Thanks, but no. I really want to walk."

"You're the boss." He kissed her lightly on the cheek, then slid into the cab. "I'll be in touch."

Still slightly thick-headed, she walked slowly through the oven-like heat to Sixth, then took the train to 48th. She walked from there, stopping at a little market at Fifty-First for a bottle of orange juice, mainly so she'd have an excuse to pet the big black and white store cat, Pretzel. She needed a cat of her own, she decided as she turned west on the next block. A moment later, she was in her building and riding the elevator up to the twelfth floor. She needed company; if not a cat, then a parrot or something. She hated living alone.

Unlocking her door, she was immediately assailed by stale hot air. If she had a pet, she told herself, she'd have an excuse to leave the air conditioner on while she was at work.

She closed the drapes, turned on the air and stripped down to her slip, then took the bottle of orange juice and sat in her old easy chair directly in front of the refrigerated air.

She held the chilled juice bottle between her breasts, rolling it back and forth, then moved it higher, over her shoulders and neck, across each cheek. Finally, she unscrewed the cap and drank greedily from the bottle. The wine had dehydrated her and she felt thick and a little drunk, and she had the beginnings of a headache.

"You behaved abominably tonight," she said aloud. "In fact, you were a complete ass." She looked around the dimly lit little room and wondered again what it would be like to have a cat come and greet her when she got home. Nice, she thought. The apartment was just too lonely.

She'd moved here when she'd left David last January, and the place still made her think about him. *That bastard!* A single, stupid, tear escaped and rolled down her cheek. Maybe she should move.

No. That was foolish. But so was she.

When they'd met, just before he hit the big time, neither knew what the other did for a living. David claimed to be a school teacher, which was true, though he didn't bother telling her he'd been able to quit his full-time job, and only subbed now and then to make ends meet. When she asked him what he liked to do for fun, he said he got a kick out of writing, never mentioning he'd published several books. When he asked Melanie what *she* did for a living, she lied, afraid that he'd inunadate her with horrid manuscripts if she said she was a literary agent. She told him she was a hair stylist. She smiled, remembering the night he'd suggested they play "naked barber." He never said a word about the bald patch she left on the back of his scalp, probably because of her lack of attire. He must have suspected something wasn't quite kosher, though.

A few months later, when the truth came out, David wasn't offended. In fact, he found it very nearly hysterical, and loved to tell the tale. He told Georgie, whom she had no right to dislike, and the overworked agent soon sent several promising writers her way. He told Joanna, who recommended Melanie to a few new writers, and soon her business had grown to where she could pick and choose.

Shortly after *Dead Ernest* made the bestseller list, she tried to pressure him into dropping Georgie Gordon in favor of her agency and was hurt when he refused, even though, on some level, she admired him for it. "I don't mix business and pleasure," he'd told her gently. She wished she'd listened and tried harder to understand, wished she hadn't been so oversensitive and arrogant. Most of all, she wished she hadn't told him that if he wouldn't switch, that meant he didn't love her enough to trust her. She knew now that it had been a stupid, juvenile thing to say.

But she had made the threat and she felt obligated to follow through on it. He softly said he was sorry she felt that way and that remark made her so furious that she'd responded by telling him to fuck off, in just those words. Then she'd called him names. She'd regretted it ever since and that was why she hated him: he'd had the audacity to remain reasonable in the face of her irrationality. It was humiliating.

Amber had told her he'd forgive her if she apologized. The girl had begged her to do so. But she couldn't. She didn't think she could ever even look him in the eye again.

It's amazing how much I've matured in six months. In that time, the self-protecting anger had receded—it still flared, as it had tonight, but not like before. Intellectually, she had understood his reasons all along, but emotionally, she was just beginning to get it. "David," she whispered. "Oh David, oh David, you fucker, I miss you."

Tears flowed freely and orange juice dribbled down her chin. *What a sight I am.* She had the career, the contacts, she would get her bestselling writers sooner or later, she knew that, but she didn't have David. When they were together, they'd called themselves Lord and Masters, and they thought they were the perfect couple.

"God," she sighed, and turned her thoughts back to this evening.

She'd done something not quite respectable in plotting with another editor to get Joanna Scanlon to move to Dorner.

Or had she? Scanlon was a big girl. Maybe she'd done her a favor. Maybe she wanted to leave Randall, or maybe she'd use it to get a counteroffer and a nice raise from her current employer. That certainly wasn't bad.

It *seemed* bad though, at least in motive. She had no business manipulating David—it certainly wouldn't make her feel better about herself. *What should I do?*

Her first thought was to call David, but if he even had a phone yet, she didn't know his new number. Maybe she'd ask Joanna to lunch and fill her in . . . Maybe she wouldn't. "God, never mix business with pleasure," she moaned. "Masters, you were absolutely right about that." She rose and padded into the bathroom to brush her teeth and down some aspirin, then went back to the living-room and dragged the futon off its frame, unfolding it between the air conditioner and the chair. She stripped to the buff, snagged an afghan for later, and lay down, letting the chill air dry the sweat beneath her breasts, enjoying the feel of the breeze shrinking her nipples into hard buttons as she thought about David and how he knew exactly how to twist them between his thumb and forefinger to drive her absolutely . . .

The jangling phone brought her bolt upright, her heart beating too fast, her stomach in her throat. She turned on the lamp and squinted at her watch. It was nearly midnight.

She sat up and grabbed the phone. "Yeah." Her voice cracked with sleep.

Ray Blaisdell's voice oozed into her ear. "Melanie, baby, you didn't call."

"Sorry. It was a long night, Ray."

"What did Rosenberg say?"

Not now, please, not now. "He had an idea. I'll call you tomorrow and tell you about it."

"Tell me now. Does he like my proposal?"

Oh, God. Never mix business with pleasure. You're a slow learner, Melanie. "He says it's not right for Dorner, but he had another idea and I'll tell you about it tomorrow."

"That asshole. Tell me now, babe. I can't wait, it'll drive me crazy."

"No, Ray." Anger started to rise. "Tomorrow. I'm exhausted. I have a headache."

"How about if I come over and massage it away for you?"

"Not tonight." She felt lonely, but not for him. "Not tonight. I'll call you in the morning. I'll have to check my schedule. Maybe we can do lunch."

"I'd just like to do you. Meat misses you."

Ray, only twenty-six, had long dark blond curls, arrogant features, long fingers and an amazing penis. *In fact,* she thought dryly, *he likes talking about his penis almost as much as he likes using it.* And he adored its nickname, but what he lacked in savoir faire, he made up for in enthusiasm and in a pleasant obsession with giving her multiple orgasms whether she wanted them or not. All in all, except for the arrogance, which was actually not that bad, he was a great guy, she told herself. A catch.

But he's not David. "Tomorrow night I'm all yours," she said with little enthusiasm. Why couldn't she get over that damned Masters?

"Okay, Mel. I'll be waiting to hear from you in the morning. Are you sure you won't tell me now?"

"No, Ray, not now. Goodnight. "She heard him start cajoling again as she dropped the phone in the cradle. Soon, she began to drowse, visions of David Masters cavorting in her head. The dreams to follow would put her in an excellent mood by morning.

Eleven

Body House: 7:49 P.M.

"That wasn't too bad," Amber said as David handed her the last dish to dry. "For a casserole."

David had been thinking just the opposite and he suspected his daughter was just trying to look on the bright side. Minnie had left them something she'd brought from home that morning, "taco fiesta casserole," she called it, and it featured soggy tortilla chips, canned chili peppers, and ground beef that must have had a fifty percent fat content. It felt like a sack of cement in his stomach and he suspected that only a teenager could digest it.

"If she keeps cooking like that, I'll have to double my hypertensives within a month."

"Oh, yeah, cholesterol and all that junk. What are you going to do?" Amber asked mildly. "Fire her?"

"No, don't worry." He laughed. "I'll try to retrain her, instead. Everything I bought is low fat. I even got a low fat cookbook. She'll get the message."

"I hope so." She paused. "Dad?"

"Hmm?"

"Do you really think Eric Swenson is retarded?"

"Why do you ask?"

"Well, he seemed kind of weird to me, but . . ."

"How do you mean?" Eric had been on his mind ever since

they'd met, and he was eager to get his daughter's take on the odd young man.

"He doesn't seem stupid," she began, then shrugged helplessly.

"Theo said he has the mind of a ten-to-twelve year old," David told her. "And there are plenty of twelve-year-olds who can out-think adults. They may not have the life experience . . ." It was David's turn to shrug.

"That's it, Dad. He seems like he's spent his whole life locked away by himself and they just let him out."

"Unsophisticated," David said as the phone began to shrill in the parlor.

"I'll get it," cried Amber, tossing the dish towel at David and running from the room. Closing the cupboard and hanging up the towel, he hoped they'd find the box containing the rest of the phones tomorrow.

"It's for you!" Amber called, her tone mildly disgusted.

As he entered the parlor, he became painfully aware of the inadequacy of his few pieces of furniture. After *Dead Ernest* hit the bestseller list and stayed there, he had moved Amber and Melanie from the rental and bought a modern condo that was made mostly of glass and chrome. Melanie had helped him with the furniture and, except for the rather timeless overstuffed gray suede couch and chairs, it was all too modern for the house, even he could see that. He wanted the parlor, at least, to be perfect by September, when it was likely that independent human interest programs like Eye on LA might contact him about filming ghost spots for Halloween programming. Gaylord Price, his Hollywood agent, had promised to give it his best shot, especially since *Remains to be Seen* was still on the charts and his recently completed novel, *Star Light, Star Bright,* would hit the stands in early October. *Maybe Theo can give me some guidance with new furniture.*

Then he focused on Amber as she tapped her foot impatiently and held the receiver out to him and decided to ask her to come up with some ideas first. For one thing, it would keep the peace; for another, it would give her a project to fill the summer, if she was interested. All he knew for sure was that he didn't want to get involved in anything creative except his new book. Though he'd begun *Mephisto Palace* before they'd moved, he was already behind schedule on the damned thing.

Who is it? he mouthed at Amber as he took the phone.

Gaylord she mouthed back. *Speak of the devil!* Maybe he had something lined up already.

"Gaylord," he said, returning Amber's wave as she headed toward the stairs. "How'd you get my number so fast?"

"Called that real estate agent of yours." Gaylord's British accent gave him an air of dignity you didn't normally find in the film business. He was as cutthroat as the rest of the agents, he just didn't sound like it, and that was why David liked him.

"And she just *gave* you my number?"

"No, no, dear boy, no need to worry. She put me through the third degree first. So tell me, lad, is that woman as sultry to look at as she is to listen to?"

"At least."

As usual, Gaylord insisted on going through the pleasantries before he got down to business. "There is a reason for this call," he said ten minutes later.

"Good news or bad news?" David asked with trepidation.

"You tell me. They cast the part of Max."

"Uh huh." Max was the hero of *Dead Ernest* and the last part to be cast before filming could begin. "Did they get Evan Winters?" he asked hopefully. That would make it good news. Winters was a newcomer David had spotted in a bit part in a Costner movie and he had the same diamond-in-the-rough style that the hero in the book did—dark, young but craggy, with a voice that rumbled pleasantly. *Ernest* would be a big break for Winters and Gaylord had guessed that he could be acquired for a song.

"I'm sorry, David, they didn't get Winters."

"Why the hell not?"

"Because they got someone bigger."

"Who?"

"Gere."

"Gere as *Max?* That's ludicrous! That's stupid! He's too soft and smooth and handsome. You can't have a man with a baby face playing a rugged bad-ass like Max! That'll ruin it!"

"There, there, my boy," Gaylord said when David finally ran out of steam. "Remember what I told you about the movie business? Unless you follow Friedkin's path and write *and* direct, you're going to have zip to say about creative control. You sell them the rights, and they do what they want. Your book sales will go through the roof." He chuckled. "As if they haven't already."

"Yeah, yeah, I know." Gaylord had explained to him how it worked and, at the time, it sounded fine. Now, it sounded horrible, but there was nothing he could do about it. Gere as Max. *What a travesty.*

"Gere could play Scoleri," he said hopefully. Scoleri was Max's ladykilling best friend.

"David, it's done. Let it go."

"My input counts for nothing?" he asked resignedly.

That cultured chuckle again. "You know the joke about the starlet who came to Hollywood and 'slept with a writer, David."

"Yeah, I know the joke." David cleared his throat. "And Gere's a draw. I'm sorry, Gaylord, I didn't mean to blow up."

"No apologies necessary, dear boy, you barely let off steam. You haven't seen "blow up" until you've seen—" Another chuckle. "I suppose I should be discreet. She's a client."

"Well, at least we got Turner to play Sargeant Pimental," David said. The air in the parlor suddenly seemed very chill to him and he picked up a faint whiff of jasmine.

"And that's exactly who you wanted."

"Um hmm." With his free hand, David began feeling the air for pockets of cold.

"David, here's some good news for you. The studio asked about *Mephisto Palace* today."

Slimy cold crawled over David's fingertips, up to his knuckles.

"David?"

"Oh, sorry? I missed that."

"I said the studio inquired about *Mephisto Palace.* Any idea when the manuscript will be ready to show? They're *very* interested. I think we'll get into a bidding war. You'll be a rich man."

"I already am." The cold was up to his wrist now, and climbing, and the jasmine cloyed in his nostrils.

"Peanuts, my boy, peanuts. Now, when can I have a look at it?"

His arm had chilled to the elbow and the sensation began to move more quickly. "It'll be a while. I'm just beginning the real research."

"Oh? Taking your time, are you?"

"Gaylord, I moved in *today!*" His whole arm felt numb with cold. Chilled fingers edged across his shoulder toward his neck.

"There is that, isn't there? Well, I'll string them along a bit, then, you know, do the old mysterious bit."

"Sounds great, Gaylord." Cold oozed into his chest as he spoke. "Any bites for the talk show circuit?"

"Maybe. Let me do a little more work before I say more. But I'll be in touch soon." He paused. "Have you seen any ghosts yet?"

"There's onc here now."

That elicited an appreciative chuckle. "Well, if you see Drake Roberts's ghost, you can offer him a cameo."

"I'll do that. Good night, Gaylord."

"Good night, David. Sleep well."

He dropped the receiver in its cradle and moved to the center of the room. The cold, in and around him, moved with him. His body seemed filled with it now and he realized he was shivering. A sudden thrill of fear ran through him and, instantly, the strength of the manifestation increased. "Okay, that's enough," he said aloud. He hadn't meant to feed the thing. He willed it to leave him but, instead, it seemed to grow, filling his abdomen, shriveling his genitals, and stiffening his legs.

"Amber," he called. "Amber! Come down here!"

She didn't reply and he remembered her telling him this morning that the house ate sound.

"Get! Off! Me!" he said, focusing his will. He could see the vapor from his words hanging in the air. His lungs began to feel brittle with the cold. *It's your imagination, Masters. That's how people like Theo get into trouble with this stuff. Now, concentrate!*

But it wasn't working. A suffocating sensation made him gulp for air. "Amber!"

He took one unsure step, then another, toward the front door. The chill numbness was in his knees, almost to his ankles, and he could barely feel them. Despite his intent, his fear grew. *Get a grip, Masters! Get a grip!* He staggered into the foyer, the litany, *Get off me, Get off me, Get off me,* running through his mind. The sound of his own blood pumping rushed into his ears.

Grabbing the door handle with unfeeling fingers, he depressed the thumb latch, but nothing happened. He tried again, this time with both hands, and as he struggled, he heard the laughter.

It surrounded him, deafening him in its proximity. It seemed to emanate from within the cold itself. Feminine and musical, the tones carried undeniable cruelness.

Gasping for air, he depressed the latch with both hands, and started to pull as the laughter continued.

"Dad?" Faintly, he heard Amber's voice. "Dad?"

Black spots danced in his vision. *You're doing this to yourself, Masters! You're panicking!* "NO!" he cried. "GET OFF ME!"

"Dad! What's wrong?"

Just like that, it left him, the cold, the suffocation, the laughter. Dizzy, queasy, knees trying to buckle, he gulped at the air, almost tasting the decayed jasmine scent that lingered.

Something touched him, just behind the elbow. "No!" he yelled, and whirled.

Amber stepped back, her eyes wide.

"Amber, honey, I thought—I'm sorry. I didn't know it was you."

"Are you okay?"

"Yeah." He walked slowly to the couch and dropped heavily onto it, wondering if he was going to vomit. "I'm okay now."

She sat down next to him and touched his hand. "God, Daddy, you're frozen."

"Yeah." Purposefully, he forced himself to breathe slowly and deeply. Amber waited, watching him, and in a few minutes, he felt calm enough to talk. "Why did you come downstairs when you did, kiddo?"

"I heard that laughing again." She made a face. "You know, Pelinore's night warbler."

"Was it loud or soft?"

"Pretty loud. I was writing letters and it started all of a sudden. I about jumped out of my skin."

"Did it sound like it was in the room with you?"

"Not exactly. It just seemed to be all through the house, especially when I opened my bedroom door. It was a lot louder down here."

"Well, kiddo, you know how we've played with cold spots in the past?"

"Uh huh?"

"Don't do it in this house. It's like playing with fire." He grimaced. "Make that ice."

"What happened?"

Briefly he explained, then shook his head. "It took control, Amber. That's never happened to me before. And I couldn't get rid of it. I was trying to open the door and walk outside when I finally got control and it dissipated. Maybe I could have taken control back faster if I had been better rested, but it shouldn't have been able to take it from me in the first place." He gave her a meaningful look. "Just like it shouldn't draw on you. So, if you run into any cold spots, steer clear. Don't play with them."

"Oh, Daddy, that's *your* thing. I don't like playing with them like you do. Don't worry." She peered closely at him. "Are you totally wasted?"

"I've been better."

"Well, it's only nine. When I went out, I joined the video club in town. I brought back a movie." She glanced at the big set temporarily sitting across the room. "Want to watch it with me?"

"Sure. What is it?"

"Blazing Saddles."

He gave her a genuine smile. "Just what the doctor ordered. Especially after the grease casserole."

"Oh, Daddy, it wasn't that bad. But speaking of ordering, when are we going to get cable? I mean, we can't even get regular stations out here."

"We're too far out for cable," he said as she fetched the movie from an empty bookshelf.

She turned. "What?"

"I'll call the satellite dish company tomorrow."

She stopped looking like her world was about to end.

"Hey, kiddo," he said just before she slipped the movie into the VCR. "I bought microwave popcorn this morning. Shall we do this right?" He started to rise.

"Sounds good. But you stay there, Daddy. I'll make it."

He waited about two seconds, then trailed her into the kitchen, ostensibly to ask if she wanted root beer floats instead. In truth, he just didn't want to be alone.

Twelve

Beings of Light Church 8:00 P.M.

Promptly at eight P.M., fifteen members of the Beings of Light inner circle had assembled for their weekly meeting and channeling session. Old business included a report on their recent sale of crystals and essential oils at the annual Artists' Conclave up in Cambria and new business included finalizing plans for the upcoming Come As You Were fund-raiser, cosponsored with the Seaside Preservation Society. They had made arrangements to rent the Red Cay Moose Lodge and they expected a good-sized turnout of non-members. There would be no mention of metaphysics or anything else that might scare off locals: it would merely be a costume dance where people would be invited to dress as they might have been in another life.

They finished the party plans with a few jokes about the number of Cleopatras and King Arthurs that would probably be in attendance, then Reverend Alice Birch announced that Theo Pelinore had a special request.

"As you know, David Masters and his daughter have moved into Body House," Theo told the others. "I think it would be a good idea to send them a cone of light to make sure they remain safe. I'd like to make a motion to that effect."

Kevin West, who worked at Greenaway's Market, raised his hand.

"Yes, Kevin?"

"Theo, do you think it was smart to sell them the house?"

"I don't know, Kevin. The house was for sale and the man wanted to buy it. I couldn't stop him."

Kevin nodded, evidently satisfied. "Then I second the motion."

Everyone was in favor and, a moment later, the group stood in a circle, hands joined. In the center of the circle, Theo, their best channeler, raised her hands and closed her eyes.

"Envision white light, see it pour from your souls and into me that I may send it to David and Amber Masters." Theo slowly turned in place, repeating the command over and over.

Five minutes elapsed, and then Rodger Stern, a graphic artist who specialized in psychic painting—he made his living selling past life portraits—began to shake. "I give you my white light," he intoned. Theo crossed to him as the group raised their clasped hands like points on a crown. Her own arms still raised, she positioned herself against the man, slipping her feet between his, so that they had full body contact from toes to finger tips. Rodger moaned and trembled, Theo did the same and soft sounds came from the rest of the group.

Next, Lydia Mandrake, poet and heiress, called out and Theo went to her. This continued until the energy had been collected from everyone, then Theo returned to the center and, with several more incantations, sent the cone of light over to the new residents of Body House.

Finally, the Beings of Light members sat down cross-legged on the carpeted floor of the meeting room, Theo joining the circle between Lydia and Rodger. Theo spoke again.

"Thank you all for sharing your energy tonight. I've now been in the house several times and I can tell you that there are spirits trapped there, spirits in need of our help." She paused significantly. "I'd like to make a motion that, next week, we begin discussing ways that we can try to send the spirits there into the light."

"Will Masters allow that?" Art Candell, a marriage counselor, asked the question.

Theo smiled. "Mr. Masters and his poor misled daughter claim they don't believe in ghosts. So I don't think they'll mind."

"A horror writer who doesn't believe in ghosts," commented Kate Grabski, owner of a gourmet coffee store up in Morro Bay. "That doesn't sound natural."

"Nobody who believes in ghosts would go near that place after dark," Art said.

"I wouldn't go there by myself in the daytime," Kevin added.

"I'd like to do some paintings in there," Rodger said, pushing his long curly hair out of his eyes.

Reverend Alice clapped her hands. "Well, now, everyone, shall we begin tonight's channeling session? Theo, dear, are you ready?"

Theo freed her hair from its pins and shook it out until it fell in glossy waves nearly to her elbows. She took a deep breath, exhaled, repeated the process. "Ready," she told Alice.

Alice lit a stick of incense and turned on the stereo. Soft New Age music filled the room as she joined the circle.

Theo let her head fall forward and, after a moment, she moaned and raised it again and looked around, eyes bright and inquisitive, her whole posture changing from her usual feline grace to something quicksilver and alert, birdlike.

"Who seeks to speak to us tonight?" she asked in a voice that sounded like a basso profundo chipmunk with a slight Mideast accent.

"The Beings of Light request your presence, Spiros," Alice said.

"Ask your questions, then. I am ready."

"May I?" asked Rodger.

"Go ahead, my friend," said Spiros/Thco.

"I'd like to know more about the life I led in first century Rome."

Spiros/Theo giggled maniacally. "Ah, you who are now Rodger, in that life you were an orator. You spoke eloquently and well, for your wit was strong and, I might add, a bit ribald. You were popular with some, but made many enemies. Eventually, you were stoned to death upon your podium for speaking ill of the Emperor's penis size." Again, the giggle, joined now by others in the group.

"Who's next?" Spiros/Theo asked.

Thirteen

Body House: 11:31 P.M.

Sitting at her vanity, Amber brushed her hair. She was glad she'd rented *Blazing Saddles* because, no matter how distinguished and proper her father sometimes tried to act, the poor man couldn't resist fart jokes. Give famous novelist David Masters a whoopee cushion and he became a ten-year-old, hiding it under his jacket until you forgot about it, then squeezing it and saying "Excuse me." It was totally embarrassing. Give him Mel Brooks and all the tension left him in fits of helpless laughter. He'd been so uptight, she wasn't sure whether it would work tonight, but it had.

She began braiding her hair to keep it from tangling. When she'd heard that awful laughter earlier tonight, she'd felt pretty uptight herself. The minute she'd opened her door, the sound had increased tremendously, and it was everything she could do to force herself to walk the long hallway and go down the stairs to see if her father was okay, instead of locking herself back up in the safety of her room.

She couldn't remember Dad ever acting so nervous. Recalling his stories about the house in Boston, the satanic cult, and the research for his newest book that brought him face to face with a serial killer who claimed to be possessed by a demon, she knew he'd been scared every time and that he believed that the fright was responsible for his hitting the bestseller list. For a self-avowed skeptic, her dad was awfully superstitious about his books.

Still, she'd never seen him like this. Since she was old enough to remember, he'd taken her into haunted houses and other strange places, and she never quite understood what turned him on so much about such things. Maybe because she'd seen so much of it, always with him whispering scientific explanations in her ear, and maybe because she'd seen him bust several fake ghosts and phony psychics, the stuff just didn't scare her. Knife-wielding maniacs made of flesh and blood were another matter altogether. When she'd heard the laughter again tonight, she thought perhaps someone was hiding in the house and that had scared her half to death. When she got downstairs and felt the weird cold in the room, she'd actually been very relieved, thinking, *Big deal, it's only a ghost.* Even so, some of Dad's nervousness had rubbed off on her and she'd spent half the movie furtively glancing over her shoulder.

She finished with her hair and stood up, stretching her arms high above her head. She was exhausted. After the movie, her dad mentioned that witchy old Pelinore wanted to fix her up with some girl who lived in town. For a moment, she'd been righteously pissed, but after she thought about it briefly, she decided it was better than nothing. She hoped the girl, Kelly Cox, wasn't a major nerd. Being associated with geekdom at a new school was all she needed.

Walking slowly across the room to the window, Amber paused to admire the beautiful fanlight above the window, before staring out toward the lighthouse. It was swathed in shifting wisps of fog, and she thought she might like to try painting a watercolor of the derelict building, with a huge full moon reflecting on the mist. Touching the window glass with her fingertips, she was surprised at its chillness and wondered how miserable it would be here in the winter if it was this cold in the middle of July.

Tomorrow, Dad was going to let her take the Bronco all the way down to San Luis Obispo to go shopping at the mall and he was even letting her take his Visa card. She was going to pick out curtains for their bedrooms and for the kitchen, plus a couple more phones, including one for her room. She'd been completely shocked when he'd asked her if she wanted to do this, but she'd eagerly agreed. Then when he'd suggested that she bring back some furniture catalogs to study and said he'd like her help in furnishing the place, complimenting her on her eye for such things, she'd totally flipped. He wanted to do most of the downstairs in the same style as Lizzie Baudey had and he hoped she'd research it for him and show him her ideas. He even offered to pay her for her time.

In a way, she wished Melanie would be there to go shopping with her. Melanie had taught her all sorts of things about clothing and when her dad bought the condominium back east, she'd found out that Mel knew all about furniture too. But Amber had already learned a lot and it all sort of fit with her career plans in different ways. So, she decided, as much fun as it would be to have Melanie here, it was better not to, because she figured Melanie would have taken over the job without her dad ever even thinking about asking his own daughter.

Amber crossed to the huge wardrobe on the other wall and opened it, looking through her clothes, pondering what to wear tomorrow. She chose a pair of white jeans and a blue scoop-necked T-shirt, then reached for the hanger that held her belts.

"Damn!" she said as the hanger unlatched, spilling the belts all over the wardrobe floor. She got down on her knees and started pulling them out, when she felt a funny little depression in the wood. After fiddling with it a moment, something clicked and the wood slid smoothly out from under her fingers. Startled, she drew her hand back before gingerly touching the edges of the opening. It was a foot long and six inches wide. Carefully, she reached inside and touched something that felt like cloth.

Knowing she should get a flashlight, but too impatient to do so, she plunged her hand in and wrapped her fingers around the slender object within. Slowly she brought it out into the light.

It was a doll, a beautiful antique doll with a handpainted

porcelain face and red hair. "You're Lizzie," she whispered, recognizing the features and the green dress from the portrait in her dad's office.

Briefly, she thought she detected the faint, light fragrance of lavender, but it was gone in an instant and she returned her attention to the doll. Everything was perfect, from the rosy blush of the glazed cheeks to the minute stitches on the dress. The china hands were delicate and flawless, even down to the tiny fingernails.

She lifted the skirt, seeing first the little green slippers covering delicate feet then, miserably, the white porcelain calves, both of which were badly cracked above the ankles. She wondered how it had happened, then thought, *Oh well.* Despite the damage, the doll was beautiful.

Curiously, she undid the tiny buttons on the back of the dress and removed it, revealing a lavender and black laced corset and matching bloomers. She removed these carefully, gasping as she saw the doll's body.

The breasts had perfect pink-tipped nipples and the pubic mound had a thatch of short auburn hair that matched the hair on the head. Turning the doll over, she saw that the buttocks were unusually realistic. The legs fell forward at the hips, revealing the doll's crotch. "My God," Amber whispered. The porcelain genitals were painted pink and were anatomically correct. "My God."

Slowly, she rose and shut the wardrobe, then took the doll to the dresser and replaced the clothing. Tomorrow, she'd have to ask her dad more about the dolls. He'd said that Lizzie had taught her daughter how to make them—today, she'd noticed the old kiln outside the sun porch, where the dolls must have been glazed. He'd also told her that none of them had ever been found, that they were only rumored to exist.

Now she knew they existed, and wondered at her fortune at finding this one. But the genitals bothered her. Christabel wouldn't have made a doll of her own mother like that, would she? Maybe Lizzie created this one, though instinctively Amber doubted it. Before she left for San Luis Obispo, she'd leave it with her father and tell him to undress it after she was gone. "Lizzie," she said softly, turning the doll in her hands before setting it on the dresser and walking over to the bed.

As she turned on her bedside lamp and picked up *Gone With the Wind,* the novel she was reading, she glanced at the doll. "Goodnight, Lizzie," she said softly. Though the window was closed, a soft breeze fragrant with subtle, soothing lavender permeated the room.

Amber had thought her room wasn't haunted. In fact, she'd sensed that it was one of the most neutral places in the house, a pleasant sanctuary. But now she realized that there was something leftover in the walls, something nice, that made her think of her father's story about his grandmother's sachet. She smiled, glad that it was here, realizing that it probably kept the laughing ghost that reeked of jasmine and decay out of this room, and decided she'd stay here and share the ugly red bathroom, instead of moving to the other wing.

She fell into pleasant dreams, lulled by the melodic almost imperceptible, ragtime music that drifted up through the floorboards.

Fourteen

Body House: 11:46 P.M.

David sat at his small writing desk in front of his bedroom window and finished entering the evening's events in the computer, then added another line. "All in all, I had the crap scared out of me tonight. This bodes very well for *Mephisto Palace.*" Yawning, he turned off the laptop and tossed his robe on the chair, then climbed naked into the luxurious poster bed, slipping between clean pale blue sheets that he'd unpacked earlier.

As soon as Minnie had left for the day, he'd taken the soiled sheets downstairs and washed and dried them. It made him recall a day when he was twelve. He was trying to wash away the embarrassment before his mom caught him. She'd walked into the garage and seen him loading the washer and started to shoo him away, saying she'd do the laundry. He must have looked horrified, because she suddenly focused on the sheets, and apparently realized what they were. Then she colored slightly and backed off, saying maybe it was good for him to learn to do laundry. Of all the things she could have done, that was the best, but he still remembered the mortification of realizing that she *knew.*

He wasn't worried about Amber—she was used to seeing him do his own laundry, but Minnie catching him at it would have been worse than Mom. Minnie'd gone on at some length today about men with bad aims missing the toilet, citing the case of poor Mrs. Candell, whose husband Sal must have some sort of vision problem because she was "always cleaning up after that man." David could just imagine what that foretold for him if she found out about his sheets. "David Masters has wet dreams," she'd tell the town. Probably that daughter of hers, Calla, would plaster it across the front page of the weekly paper.

Cool it, Masters, you're getting bitchy. He sighed and lay back. Today had been stressful, no doubt about it. If Amber hadn't shown up with that goofy movie, between dealing with the Willards, and the rest of the locals, not to mention the movers, most of whom had IQ's as big as their dicks, he would have been ready to climb the walls. And of course there was the little matter of the manifestation he could barely control. *I hope buying this place wasn't a mistake.* At least Amber seemed to be unaffected by it.

Still, there was no way he would leave her alone in Body House, at least for now. He wasn't sure *he* wanted to be alone here, for that matter. *You're just tired,* he told himself. *Tomorrow will be better.*

As he picked up a book to read himself to sleep, he thought he heard a strain of melody, soft and sweet, Scott Joplin's slow, moody rag, *Solace,* but he was too tired and too unsure if his ears were playing tricks on him to get up and check. Too, he had no desire to go downstairs again tonight. The music faded, if it was ever there at all, and he turned back to his book. He barely finished a page before his eyes grew heavy and the words became a blur. Gratefully, he set the book aside and turned off his reading lamp.

Eyes closed, he drifted toward sleep over and over again, but each time his mind began to fill with the shifting hypnogogic images that signaled the dreams to come, he would panic and wrench himself back to consciousness, then lie in the dark, staring at the ceiling, while his heart pounded and the sea air from the open window dried the sweat on his skin.

You've gotta knock it off, Masters, he told himself after the fourth or fifth episode. The house was quiet, the atmosphere in the room spoke of the ocean, not ghosts, and there was absolutely no reason why last night's dream visitor, whether she was a product of the house or of his imagination, should return. *And if she does, enjoy it, Masters. What's there to be afraid of? Minnie Willard telling the town you stain your sheets?* Finally, his fear moved into the proper perspective, and he closed his eyes once more. This time, he gave himself to the hynogogia, relishing it as he normally did, and was soon rewarded with a pleasant dream about a romantic weekend he and Melanie had spent in a ski lodge in the White Mountains.

Toward the end of the dream, which had consisted of warm, pleasant emotions experienced while they sat in front of a huge stone fireplace, hands and feet entwined, and watched the blizzard rage outside, Melanie did something out of character.

Despite all the other people in the lodge's common room, she began undressing. He protested, suggesting they go to their room, but she only smiled, and the smile changed her into someone else.

She held herself above him and her breasts were small but perfect as he kneaded them with his fingers while she fed first one, then the other, between his lips, into his mouth. He tasted the smooth saltiness of her skin as he sucked the nipple, licking and gently chewing it. Her cool flesh smelled of jasmine, a scent he thought he might die for.

She lifted herself up, taking away her breasts, making him moan his desire for them. He tried to reach for them, but she stopped him, grabbing his wrists in her incredibly strong hands and holding them to his sides as she slid her body down over his.

Her tongue flicked over his lips, lightly at first, then probing more and more forcefully until he parted them. As she explored his mouth, she continued to pin his arms at his sides and began rubbing her body over his. He could feel her rubbery-hard nipples against his chest and then, the tickle of her pubic hair against his erection as she moved downward, trailing her tongue over his lower lip and down until she reached his neck.

Suddenly, she slipped her sex over his and he felt himself surrounded, imprisoned within her cold fire. She bit his neck, painfully, then sat up and began to ride him like a horse. She let go of his hands, but he didn't move them.

"My God," he moaned. "My God, Melanie." He opened his eyes to look at her, his head swimming with desire, his body on the verge of release, but it was too dark to see her.

"Melanie." He felt her weight, felt the tight sheath of her muscles entrapping him, using him, felt her cold hands pinching his skin, yanking his chest hairs as she moved over him. A nail scratched his nipple, but he was so excited, it only added to his passion. He heard her laugh, smelled her perfume, the heavy erotic scent of jasmine.

Still half asleep, he reached out to caress her ass as it pressed rhythmically against his groin, and she laughed again as his hands floundered in the chill, chill air.

Melanie's not here he realized, and at that moment, the woman dug the nails of one hand into his chest. An instant later, he felt her other hand reaching down between his legs, felt a finger probing between his buttocks, and he shivered in erotic agony as it entered him like an icicle. At the same time, she squeezed her muscles around his erection, up and down, milking him until everything in the world disappeared in a climatic delirium that went on forever and ever.

Dimly, he heard himself screaming with release, heard *her* laughing, laughing, laughing.

Breathing heavily, shaking, dizzy, he lay there beneath her cold weight for one second, then two. At three, he yelled and grabbed for the light, almost knocking it over as he pushed the switch.

The weak, golden light illuminated the room and the bed, and he forced himself to look down.

"My God," he whispered, still feeling the cold weight upon him, but seeing nothing except his spent penis standing at an unnatural angle, still inside the invisible thing that had used him.

His body wouldn't respond, wouldn't move. He felt paralyzed. "Get off me!" he whispered.

Laughter was the only response, that and a renewal of the cloying perfume, now tinged with decay. The entity squeezed his penis again as he watched and he saw a ripple move up and down the shaft as invisible muscles moved. The cold finger began to probe once more and, against his will, his body started to respond.

"Get off me!" he growled.

But the succubus continued to use him, to start its horrible rape all over again.

Rape, he thought. *Dear God, I'm being raped!* Anger welled inside him, gave him strength, killed his fear. "Get off!" he screamed at the top of his lungs. Refusing the paralysis, he propelled himself upward and, where physical strength had failed, the sheer force of his will succeeded. He threw the thing from him. "Get the fuck out of here!" he hissed. "Get the fuck out!" He shoved at the chillness, recognizing it now as the same sort of clammy cold as he'd experienced downstairs. This time, it had taken a form. "Get out!" Hatred filled his heart and mind.

There was a brief surge of the odor of flowers and rot, and then it faded. Trembling uncontrollably, he padded naked around the room, feeling for cool spots, wondering how he was going to keep the entity out of the room. There were many methods and he hoped that one might work.

He found it hovering near the door, small and icy cold, slushy-thick. Quickly, he withdrew his hand from the manifestation. "Get the fuck out of here," he ordered, still fueled by anger.

He heard the laughter, right in his ear, and then he heard the feminine voice say, *David, David, David.* And then it was gone.

My God. It knows my name.

Hurriedly, he slipped on his robe and trotted to Amber's room. The door was locked. "Amber!" He pounded on the door. "Amber! Wake up!"

A moment later, he heard her fumbling with the lock, and then she stood there looking at him with sleepy-heavy eyes. To him, she looked ten years old again, with her braided hair and Garfield sleep shirt. She looked so vulnerable. *What have I done? What was I thinking, bringing her to this house?*

"What, Dad?" she asked.

"Is everything okay in here?"

"Sure. I was asleep." She seemed to wake a little bit. "What happened to you?"

"Why?" He glanced down, relieved to see his robe was closed.

"You look like you just ran a marathon."

"I had a visitor." He paused. "Frankly, I'm not sure it's safe for us to have that empty room between us. If it visits you—"

"It won't," she said simply.

"How do you know that?" he asked, exasperated.

"Because," she said patiently, "this room's already got a ghost."

"It *what?"* He couldn't believe his ears.

"It has a ghost, a good one. That other thing won't come in here."

"How do you know?"

"I know."

He believed her.

She studied him. "You want to sleep in here?"

He considered it, then thought that if she was wrong, if the jasmine manifestation could enter the room, what might happen would, at the least, humiliate him forever, and at the most, destroy both their lives. "That's okay, kiddo. It won't bother me again tonight."

She nodded. " 'Night, Daddy."

He gave her a gentle kiss on the forehead before heading back to his bedroom.

"Goodnight."

July 12

Fifteen

Body House: 12:35 P.M.

By noon, David had his office set up exactly the way he wanted it, from the Navajo rugs on the floor to the Felix the Cat clock, and the Edward Hopper prints, movie posters and blowups of his own book posters on the walls. His favorite Hopper, *Gas,* hung to one side of the front window, so that he could see it anytime he looked up. He stared at it now, marveling at the way it never failed to inspire him. It depicted a 1930s Mobil gas station beside a wooded highway at dusk. A lanky man in vest and tie stood near a pump and, beyond him, the forest and road disappeared into a curve of unending blackness. David always wondered what was lurking just beyond the turn in the road, what was waiting to emerge, what was watching the oblivious man as he straightened cans of oil, and if other things observed him from the blackness beneath the nearest trees. The wondering always brought him different answers and different questions and, ultimately, different ideas for his books.

He and Eric had moved the portrait of Lizzie Baudey to the parlor, hanging it in a place of honor above the fireplace built into the wall separating the parlor from the dining room. After the job was completed, he'd briefly wondered if Theo would be irritated, then decided not to worry about it.

Settling in had gone far more smoothly than he'd expected. His oversized L-shaped oak desk hugged the north and west facing walls, affording him views of both Red Cay's half-moon bay and the old lighthouse. To his dismay, he'd managed to hook up the big computer correctly on his first try and it only took a couple of tries to get the fax and the answering machines for both his phone lines working.

Now, having finished copying the files from his laptop onto the main machine, he sat in his chair, feet comfortably propped on the desk and the door optimistically shut against Minnie's unending verbiage. In his hands, he held the doll Amber had given him this morning. It was unfortunate that the legs were marred but, in spite of this, it was still an exquisite piece of work.

Before bringing it downstairs, he had removed its clothing, as Amber suggested. He'd been shocked by the anatomical detailing, though he didn't know why, considering the history of the house. Now, he repeated the process, setting the clothes aside, and holding the effigy of Lizzie Baudey under the bright desk lamp, he scrutinized it more thoroughly. Finally, on the inside of the right thigh, he found what he was looking for: the artist's initial. The tiny, curling "C" was so subtle that it was nearly invisible, but it was there, all right.

"C" for Christabel, it had to be. So, Christabel Baudey had made a doll of her own mother . . . complete with genitalia. That struck David as one of the most unnatural things he had ever encountered.

As far as he knew, no one had ever found one of Christabel's dolls before. There were all sorts of theories on the whereabouts of the collection, the most popular being that they were secreted in hidden compartments throughout the house or in the infamously unfindable cellar below. It seemed to him now that the secret compartments theory might at least be partially correct.

This morning, Amber had showed him where the wardrobe's hidden compartment was located, but neither of them could get it to open again. Finally, she'd grinned wickedly and told him, "Maybe I was supposed to find it!"

Maybe she *was* supposed to, he thought now.

He began dressing the doll. Amber had said nothing more about the haunting in her room and he'd decided not to bring it up until later since she was in such a hurry to get going on her shopping trip.

Not very much was known about the dolls. Several of Elizabeth Baudey's beautiful creations had been in a private collection back east, but that entire collection had been destroyed by fire in the nineteen forties. Still, there were photographs and enough documentation for him to know with certainty that Lizzie's dolls were not anatomically correct, as this one was. He wondered what had happened to the rest of them, suspecting that Lizzie had probably given many of them away as gifts to the people they represented—which meant there were probably a few still in town. As for the rest, he had an intuitive feeling that Christabel might have destroyed them. From all accounts, she had a jealous, vindictive nature, and as talented as she was, she wouldn't want to have to compete with her mother.

The stories concerning Christabel's dolls were rather sparse, as if people had been afraid to talk about them, or her. This, combined with her alleged black magic powers, made David suspect that the dolls might have been used for magical purposes, or at least were believed to be by the superstitious sailors and townspeople of the era.

Looking at this doll, beautiful as it was, made him think he'd been right about that. There was something about it—probably the unnatural detailing—that chilled him.

Just as he started trying to fasten the frustratingly tiny buttons on the back of the dress, he hoard three raps on the door. Quickly, he placed the doll in a desk drawer.

"Mr. Masters?" Minnie called.

Without waiting for a reply, she opened the door and beamed at him. "Oh my, this is just the loveliest room. Is this how writers like to work, in a great big office like this? My Lord, just look at that big computer, I don't know how you manage such a complicated thing. I'd just fall apart if I had to figure out how to work it, but then, I'd fall apart if I had to figure out how to write a book. You're just so astounding, Mr. Masters, just amazing, and that TV screen or computer screen, whatever you call it, it's such a pretty blue, don't you think? Do they come in different colors? Computers, that is? Yellow is my favorite color, so I'd want a yellow screen. Do they sell those?"

I'll install the lock on the office door before the afternoon is out, he promised himself as she blathered on about God-knew-what. If such a thing were possible, she was more verbose today than yesterday.

". . . and I was telling Calla just last night what a fine, handsome man you are and how you offered to read all her books and give her some advice—"

He winced. *I not only didn't offer to read that stuff, I told her no!* "Minnie, when I'm in my office, I'm working and I prefer not to be interrupted unless it's *very* important."

"Oh, I'm sorry." To her credit, she appeared to mean it. "I didn't realize—"

"It's okay, Minnie. What's up?"

"Eric's finished planting the flower beds in front and wants to know if you have another job for him."

I'll have to leave her lists if I want peace and quiet. "Yes, I have something for him to do," he said, thinking about the door lock again. "But may I ask you a question first?"

"Anything you want—"

"I was told that Eric is a little slow," he said carefully. "Could you tell me exactly what that means?"

She eyed him. "Miss Pelinore told you that?"

Nodding, he said, "Yes, she did. I thought perhaps you could tell me a little more about him."

Folding her hands over her apron, she smiled. "What would you like to know?"

"Is he? Slow?"

She thought about that for a moment. "I suppose." One hand went up to rub her chin. "Or maybe he's just busy thinking about other things."

"What kind of things?"

"I have no idea, but I can assure you he's a good boy, honest as the day is long."

"Theo mentioned that he sometimes tells tall tales. Do you think that's true?"

"No," she said simply. "No, I don't. And you shouldn't listen to anything Theo Pelinore says," she added. "She's the one who tells the tales." Minnie's eyes narrowed and she darted a look behind her before whispering, "You know about Miss Pelinore, don't you?"

"Know what?" David wondered whether or not she was defending Eric just to be contrary to Theo.

"She sleeps around," Minnie confided.

"You mentioned that yesterday."

"You should have seen her following poor Eric around, telling him to take off his shirt so he wouldn't get paint on it, and just eyeballing him like he was so much beef roast on a platter. Why, she's old enough to be his mother."

"I doubt that," David said lightly.

"She's older than she looks," Minnie said vehemently, "and she wants to soil that poor young man!"

Barely stopping a chuckle from escaping his lips, David decided to take a different tack. "When Eric's in the house, does he ever seem frightened to you?"

"Only of Theo Pelinore," Minnie replied stoutly.

On the verge of anger or laughter—he wasn't sure which—David raised his hands. "Okay. Okay. Minnie, I know you don't like Theo, and that's just fine. I want to talk about Eric. Only Eric." He forced a smile. "Has he mentioned seeing any ghosts or anything else along those lines?"

"Well, sometimes he laughs when he's in the dining room. Last week, I walked in and caught him just standing there staring at the dining room table and laughing to beat the band. I asked him what was so funny, you know, I wanted something to laugh about too, but he wouldn't tell me. I got to thinking maybe he thought those dirty glass pictures were funny, but they're all over the house and that's the only place he laughs. It probably doesn't mean a thing, though."

David suppressed a smile, remembering the boy's story about Buttcrack the Ghost who crawled down the table. He decided to show as much restraint as Eric had and not tell her about it. "He's never told you any stories about the house or the lighthouse?"

"I told you, Mr. Masters, Eric's a good boy. He doesn't tell stories. Only Theo Pelinore tells stories. Why, that woman, she thinks she's God's gift to men, and she doesn't care a whit about who she hurts as long as she gets what she wants and—"

"Minnie?" he interrupted as patiently as he could. "Can I ask you a personal question?"

Her mouth still open and ready to fire, she nodded.

"Did Theo do something to you? To you personally?"

Minnie *hrummphed.* "I'm not one to talk, mind you, but, well, you met my Mickey yesterday."

"Yes." Technically, he'd met the man, though the grizzled little fellow barely grunted two words his way. He probably gave up talking long ago, David realized. He had too much competition.

"Well, then, you know how handsome he is. Any woman would want my Mickey." She crossed her arms and *hrummphed* again. "But that's no excuse for trying to seduce a married man."

"Wait a minute. You're saying that Theo—"

"That hussy!" Minnie blushed. "Excuse my French."

"How did you find out?"

"Mickey told me."

"I see." He nodded sagely. The only teller of tall tales revealed thus far, David decided, was Mickey Willard. "Would you ask Eric to come in now?"

"Certainly." She bustled out, forgetting to shut the door behind her.

"Oh well," he sighed, and picked up his copy of *Great American Hauntings.* It held the same sketchy Body House lore as a dozen other books, but what made it special was that somehow the author had managed to lay her hands on several blurry photographs of the dolls. He opened the book to the black and white—or brown and tan, to be exact—photos. There were three dolls, two fancily-dressed females and one male in fisherman's garb, including a pea coat and watch cap. The captions identified them only as representations of two of the working ladies and of one of their customers. *That's a big help.* Holding a magnifying glass over the page, he studied the two female dolls. Both were dark-haired and their clothing was similar enough to Lizzie Baudey's evening gown—both on the doll and in the portrait—but closer scrutiny revealed a number of subtle differences. He wished he knew the colors of the clothing. Raven-haired Christabel was known for always wearing black.

"Mr. Masters?"

David swiveled his chair to face Eric Swenson, whose tall, broad-shouldered body nearly filled the doorway. He smiled. "Come on in, Eric. Close the door behind you."

He was amused to hear Minnie *hrummph* in the hall just before the door latched. "Have a seat." He gestured at a channel-back chair beside the desk. "I want to show you something."

Eric sat down and waited patiently.

David took the doll from the drawer. "Amber found this last night."

"That's Miss Lizzie, isn't it?"

"Yes, I believe so." He extended the doll to Eric. "What do you make of it?"

Gingerly, Eric took the creation in his big square-fingered hands. He turned it over and back, a slow smile dimpling his face. He touched the fiery hair, ran one finger down the skirt of the bottle-green satin gown. "It's nice," he said simply.

David, who had been hoping for more signs of psychic ability, hid his disappointment.

"It feels good," Eric continued a long moment later. "She's a nice lady."

Aha! "Does the doll make you think that?"

"Yes, sir." He paused, a look of concentration on his face. "But her legs hurt."

He didn't look under the dress, he couldn't possibly know the legs are cracked! "What do you mean by that?"

Eric looked up. "They hurt, David. They just hurt. Did Amber find this in her room?"

"Yes, she did."

"In the wardrobe?"

Barely controlling his excitement, David nodded. "In a hidden compartment. Did you know it was there?"

"No, David."

"Did you find any other dolls when you were working on the house?"

"No, but . . ."
"But what, Eric?"
"Well, I guess this is why that wardrobe felt nice. Miss Lizzie was in it."
David asked him if he meant the doll was haunted by Lizzie's spirit.
"Kind of. I mean, she's around it sometimes."
"Do you see her?"
"Oh, no. Usually I just see those leftovers—"
"Like the ghost of the fat man crawling on the dining table?"
"Yes. He's not here, he's just leftovers." Eric grinned. "Or more like a gym sock."
"Are you saying you believe Lizzie is actually here?" He'd mentioned something to that effect yesterday.
"Yes, she is." Eric sounded positive.
"And she's not just a movie? A leftover?"
"No, I don't think so."
"Yesterday, you said something exists on the third floor that can travel around. Is that Lizzie?"
"No, Miss Lizzie's nice." He looked at his knees. "I don't want to talk about that other one."
"Eric, listen to me. If I tell you something, can you keep it secret?"
"Oh, yes."
David believed him. "It's important that I know what or who it is. You were right when you told me it can move around. It came downstairs last night and it came into my bedroom. It was very cold and powerful. It was scary."
Eric only nodded.
"Can it go anywhere in this house?"
"Mostly."
"Where can't it go?"
"I don't think it can go in your daughter's room." He gazed at the doll. "But I think you should maybe put the doll back in there, just to be sure."
"Why?"
"To make her stronger, I think."
"Amber?"

"No." Solemnly, he shook his head. "Miss Lizzie. That was her room."

"I thought the room with all the closets at the other end of this hall was probably Lizzie's."

"Yes, I think it was her office, like this is your office, but she slept there, too. When her legs hurt."

"How do you know this?"

"I don't know." Eric shrugged. "I really don't. It sort of popped into my head just now. It's just feelings I get when I touch things or see things. That's why I stopped talking about ghosts to people. They think I'm crazy."

"I think you're psychically gifted, particularly with psychometry." Eric smiled uncertainly, prompting David to explain, "That means you can sense things by touching inanimate objects."

"Wow. Are you psychic too?"

"No, not at all," David admitted. "I don't have a bit of intuition about ghosts, but when I saw that downstairs room, I thought it was Lizzie's room, just because it looked like something she'd like and because it was very luxurious with all the closets and cabinets. It was . . . logical."

"Yes."

"But ask yourself why you know so many other things, Eric. Have you read about the house?"

Eric blushed. "I'm not much of a reader."

"Well, you've lived in Red Cay all your life. Maybe you've heard stories."

"Well, sure, Uncle Craig told me about finding the dead hippies."

"What about older stories? Ones about Lizzie and Christabel?"

"Well . . ." Eric rubbed his chin. "I guess I mostly heard stories from Andy Cox."

"Ferd Cox's brother?"

"Yes, he's the town expert. The historian. He told me a little about Captain Wilder. The ghost in the lighthouse."

"He must have told you about Wilder being in love with Lizzie."

"No, sir."

"You just knew that?"

"Yes."

That would be easy enough to check out, David thought. He'd have to try to get over to Barnacle Bob's in the not too distant future. "Did you know that Lizzie was crippled not too long before she disappeared?"

Eric nodded. "Andy said Christabel did it because Miss Lizzie wouldn't let her do what she wanted."

"It makes sense, then, that she'd sleep downstairs after that." David felt relieved and disappointed. Maybe Eric wasn't as psychic as he appeared. "It does make sense."

"I guess it does. I just know for sure because my legs hurt when I go in that room and I know it's Miss Lizzie I'm feeling." He looked dreamy. "Her leftovers in there feel nice, but really, really sad. And hurt."

"I thought you said she's not leftovers—" David began.

"*She* isn't." Eric looked at David and explained as if to a two-year-old. "There are leftover feelings in the room. There are in most rooms."

Eric Swenson's tendency was to refer to "leftovers," ghosts and certain spirits as if they were all different things. David was sure now that "leftovers" were inanimate objects and feelings, while "ghosts" were the boy's term for human apparitions. But that didn't matter at the moment. Right now, he had a hunch about the doll, Lizzie's accident and Christabel's involvement. "Eric," he began, "What part of your legs hurt when you're in that room?"

"Here." Eric touched one of his legs halfway between the knee and the ankle, then the other closer to the ankle. "And here."

Goosebumps prickled on David's neck. "Lift the doll's skirt," he said softly. *Voodoo.*

Another blush. "But—"

"Go ahead. Look at her legs."

Eric glanced at David once more, then did as he asked, pushing the dress only to the knees. He looked at the cracked legs a moment, and nodded. "That's right. Those are the places it hurts."

Everything he'd read said that Lizzie had fallen and that

Christabel *might* have been behind the accident. There were no other details to judge by. Occasionally, the daughter's twisted voodoo practices were mentioned, though usually in conjunction with her sexual proclivities. Judging by what Eric had told him, it appeared that she had tried to kill her mother with magic, too.

"Eric, would you mind coming upstairs with me?"

"I don't want to go to the third floor."

"The second floor."

"Okay."

David took the doll and locked it in his desk drawer. Eric started to protest, but he assured the young man he would return it to Amber's room before she returned.

As they exited the office, David wasn't particularly surprised to see Minnie dusting the already dustless framed Edward Gorey print he'd hung in the hall. He gave her a knowing look, which she refused to read.

"Mr. Masters, would you like me to tidy up your office?" she twittered.

"No, thanks." He pulled the door firmly closed behind him. "No matter how messy it gets, *never* touch my office. I'll take care of it myself." He sounded too gruff, so he smiled and added, "Writers are superstitious about things like that."

"Surely you don't mean that you don't want me to vacuum." She said it in a tone that suggested not vacuuming and never changing your shorts were one and the same.

"Surely, I do." He glanced at his watch. "It's after one. Why don't you knock off for the day?"

"I haven't made your casserole yet."

"Don't bother, we'll fend for ourselves tonight."

"I can't have you doing that."

I'm going to kill her. He smiled through gritted teeth. "Amber and I are going out tonight. Go on home, Minnie."

"If you insist. Eric, if you want to put your bike in the back of my car, I'll give you a lift."

"No, Minnie," David interjected. "Eric still has some work to do."

"Well, then, I'll wait."

"No." He looked at Eric. "I'll be right back." He took

Minnie's arm and guided her up the hall and toward the door. In the foyer, he held her coat for her, then handed her her purse. "Thank you, Minnie, for all your hard work. Now you go home and relax." He could feel the muscle in his jaw twitching as he spoke. He wondered how much more of her he could take as he opened the front door. "Goodbye, Minnie."

She looked at him sideways. "Goodbye." Inside, the phone began to ring. "Do you want me to get that?" she asked hopefully.

You nosey old bag. "No, thanks." He practically pushed her out the door. "I'll get it," he said, shutting it just as she cleared the threshold.

He walked back in and found Eric had picked it up for him. Smiling, the boy held out the receiver. "It's Amber."

Oh, no, the truck broke down. "Hey, kiddo," he said.

But the truck was fine, she only wanted to consult about curtain colors, and a moment later, David and Eric were headed upstairs.

"Who picked the bedrooms?" David asked.

"Well. I gucss Miss Pelinore did," Eric replied slowly. "Kind of. She picked yours."

"What about Amber's room? Did she pick that one too?"

"No." At the landing, Eric paused, leaning against the balustrade. "She was going to put her in that one big bedroom on this side of the stairs."

"Why didn't she?"

Eric turned beet red. "Mr. Masters, I put Amber in Miss Lizzie's room." He stared at his finger tips. "I pretended I made a mistake. She almost fired me."

"Amber likes the room, Eric," David said warmly. "She says she feels safe in it."

Eric smiled slowly. "I'm glad."

"Tell me, why did you do it?"

"Well, I guess because most of the bedrooms have leftovers that aren't very nice. That big room, down there," he pointed toward the other wing again, "had a whole lot of leftovers. A bunch of people got killed in there."

"In Lizzie's time?"

He shook his head. "No, just a while ago. A family. With kids. There's stuff in there from Miss Lizzie's time too," he added thoughtfully.

In 1952, an entire family was found butchered in an upstairs bedroom, David remembered. The police chalked it up to a group of degenerates. They caught one who, before he killed himself, said he'd been possessed. *Oldest excuse in the book.*

"So you were trying to protect Amber in case she was sensitive to the ghosts?" David asked, the last of his worries about Eric Swenson dissolving into positively syrupy appreciation.

"Yes. Most people don't seem to notice leftovers. I mostly did it because Miss Lizzie's room feels good. And the other *thing* never goes in there." His voice sounded terribly somber.

"The thing from the third floor?"

Eric nodded.

"Let's go in Amber's room and see if it still feels good to you without the doll present."

"Okay."

A moment later, they were inside and Eric walked to the center of the room then turned in a slow circle. "Miss Lizzie?" he whispered.

A faint breeze stirred in the room.

"Do you smell that?"

Eric's words produced a sudden rush of adrenalin and David sniffed, expecting jasmine, smelling instead nothing but a faint, clean scent. Lavender, he realized. "Yes."

"She's here."

"Who's here?"

"Miss Lizzie," Eric said matter-of-factly. "I think she'd feel better if the doll was here."

"Does that increase her strength?"

"I think so. I'm not sure."

Suddenly, the boy looked at the closed door. David followed his gaze. The handle jiggled, as if someone had their hand on the hallside doorlatch.

"What is it?" David whispered.

"It's the *other.*"

"Christabel?"

"Don't say her name," Eric whispered urgently. "Don't *ever* say her name." As they watched, the handle began to depress.

"Why not?" David realized his body had begun backing toward the other side of the room without mentioning it to his brain. Eric stood his ground and he forced himself to rejoin him.

"Just don't say it." The handle, moving in slow motion, had almost reached the point where the latch would release. Abruptly, Eric ran at the door and grabbed the handle, tried to force it upward.

Too late. The door exploded open. Eric yelled as the force of it hurled him across the room like a rag doll.

Vaguely, David heard Eric scrambling to his feet somewhere behind him, but he couldn't turn to help him. His eyes were on the transparent dark mass hovering in the doorway, and his stomach churned from the overwhelming stench of jasmine and putrescence that filled the room.

Vertigo set in, worsening David's nausea. Gagging, he staggered backward until invisible hands roughly grabbed his upper arms. He yelled, struggling to get away.

"It's me!" Eric hissed in his ear.

Quickly, David moved aside, and leaned against the tall, curved end of the sleigh bed. The chill air seemed poisoned with the decaying odors and he couldn't seem to get any air into his lungs. *Don't panic, Masters.* He forced himself to breathe deeply and slowly. Though his gorge rose with each inhalation, the dizziness began slowly to pass.

Then the undulating darkness crossed the threshold, its odor nearly overwhelming him. In front of him, Eric stood statuelike, his feet planted far apart, his muscular arms at his sides, but tensed, the hands curled almost into fists.

The door slammed shut behind it.

"I thought you said it couldn't come in here," he said softly.

Eric didn't answer.

Freezing cold emanated from the mass. Its stench was so strong now that David could taste it, sickeningly sweet, cloying foulness that made bitter saltwater rise under his tongue, made his stomach spasm. *No!* Again, he fought down the urge to vomit.

As he watched, the hovering darkness seemed to stretch and elongate, changing from a vague chest-high globe into an ovoid, then into a long, rounded rectangle that reached nearly to the floor.

A phantom zephyr pattered around David's face. Though it was cool, it was far warmer than the bone-chilling cold emanating from the dark manifestation. He caught the faint clean scent of lavender in the breeze.

The light fragrance suddenly drowned out the rancid rotten stink of the other. It flowed into his nose, invaded his mouth and ears. He peered through a grayish haze and now the breeze felt more like finger tips patting his face and neck and hands. *It's trying to get inside me!* "Eric!" he called, panicked.

Swenson half turned and stared at him, wide-eyed. "It's Miss Lizzie!" he gasped.

"What—what does she want?" David asked helplessly. Behind Eric, the dark manifestation grew taller.

Eric's eyes darted back and forth. He shook his head, then blurted, "Let her in!"

"What?" David cried in confusion.

The cold dark form moved closer. Eric glanced at it, then screamed, "Let her in!"

"I don't understand!" The air behind Eric roiled as the phantom moved toward him. David saw the boy's blond hair rising in response to the static electricity filling the room. He could feel his doing the same and his whole body felt like it had been asleep and was now being prickled by pins and needles. The air pressure changed suddenly, hurting his ears.

David felt caught in a vacuum.

"Let her in!" Eric commanded.

A piece of darkness detached itself from the long ovoid rectangle and rose, like an arm reaching for Eric's shoulder.

"Watch out!" David cried.

Eric screamed as the darkness touched him. His eyes pleaded with David.

Suddenly, he understood that Eric wanted him to open up

to Lizzie. The thought scared him nearly to death, but he had to do it. *Lizzie! Lizzie Baudey!* His thoughts were answered by more insistent pressure from the lavender-scented spirit.

Eric continued to scream. A second arm had detached itself from the main body of darkness and sunk its phantom hand into his other shoulder.

Okay, Masters, let her in. It's a paranormal experiment. Still, he hesitated, unwilling to let down his defenses. Eric's scream became a pain-filled moan as he gasped for breath.

David inhaled deeply, held and exhaled, then took another breath, trying to relax, to stop resisting. "Lizzie, come into me." The roar of his own voice startled him.

She entered him like a cool summer breeze, flowing through ears and eyes and mouth to fill his chest, his heart, his mind, with her essence. In a brief instant, he knew her emotions, knew her sorrow and rage, knew her love—and her hatred—for her daughter. He knew the torture she had endured.

She began to leave him, too soon, too soon, and he knew that he would fall down because she had fed on his strength, had taken it for herself. A blank instant passed, then the haze left his eyes and he lay gasping on the floor, unable to move. In front of him, a pale haze glimmered and thickened in the air, then began to take on a vaguely human shape.

Eric was still fighting off the darkness—fighting off Christabel, trying to keep her from getting inside him. She jerked him about like a puppet. Christabel was winning.

Christabel! No! David heard Lizzie's words in his mind. As he tried to pull himself into a sitting position, he watched the spirit metamorphose into human form. A few wispy trails of fog became long white fingers, others transformed into red hair that escaped in long tendrils from its pinnings, and into green satin and sheer chiffon, like the gown from the portrait. A curve of her pale ankle flashed above Lizzie's green-slippered foot and, as she stepped toward Eric, David thought he heard the soft rustle of satin and lace.

Christabel. The name entered David's mind again as Lizzie glided away from him.

Suddenly, the dark entity tossed Eric roughly aside. Immediately, he scrambled to his feet and edged a wide circle around the phantoms to join David near the bed. "Come on," he grunted, pulling David to his feet.

His legs were jelly, nearly useless, and he let himself be pulled along. Swenson dragged him back around the edges of the room until they were nearly at the door. "Wait!" he groaned. A coughing fit doubled him over as he tried to catch his breath in the asphyxiated atmosphere.

"Come on!" Eric dragged him to the door. "We have to get the doll!" His hand on the latch, he paused, his eyes on the apparitions.

Uncomprehending, disbelieving, in awe, David gazed at them. Lizzie appeared much as she did in the portrait, though her face was drawn and her emerald eyes sparked with anger. *I could reach out and touch her.* David wondered if she felt like flesh and blood.

Christabel began to take form now, much as Lizzie had. Glossy raven hair waved halfway down her back and, below that, her dress was translucent black chiffon, revealing the pale skin of her back. At the very top of her rounded buttocks, the chiffon joined with more layers of material, forming a straight skirt in the style of the nouveau era. The layers of chiffon hung like scarves, revealing glimpses of her legs as she moved toward her mother.

Christabel's horrible laugh sounded then, and David was glad he couldn't see her face.

Eric began pulling him out the doorway. He started to resist, wanting to watch the specters, but, vaguely, he realized how dangerous it might be to remain there. He staggered out of the room.

"We have to get the doll," Eric whispered urgently. "Miss Lizzie needs it."

"But she's strong. Stronger than Christabel."

Eric shook his head. "No, the other's stronger. The strongest. She's like a witch. But Miss Lizzie, she's just a spirit, she's just trapped here."

Christabel's laughter rang out again, making Eric grimace. Quickly, he led David to the side of the hall. "Wait here. I have to get the doll."

"No! Wait!"

"There's no time!"

David fished in his pants pocket, withdrew his keys. "It's locked. Use the little key, there."

Eric snatched the ring and ran down the hall. After he turned down the hallway that led to the stairs, David couldn't hear his footsteps anymore, not even on the stairs.

The laughter sounded again, and another voice, pleading, soothing. He couldn't understand the words. He sank to the floor, let his spinning head rest between his bent knees. He couldn't understand anything anymore. He was confused by his feelings, how the sensation of letting the spirit—*rerun, energy drain,* his skeptical brain insisted—into his body had been pleasant and had made him feel that he knew Lizzie Baudey intimately. Was that how Eric and other psychics he'd worked with in the past sensed things? They felt them with a sort of magnified intuition? Christabel laughed again, louder, sending chills through him, sickening him.

Dimly, he heard footsteps and lifted his head to see Eric pounding toward him, the doll clutched in his hands. David struggled to his feet, fighting his rubbery legs, but by the time he stood, Eric had disappeared back into Amber's room.

Then, before he could take a step, a storm of swirling darkness filled her doorway. He heard the laughter, much fainter, and the dark mass, once again a globe floating several feet off the ground, moved into the hallway, and hovered, becoming fainter and fainter until it had disappeared entirely. A moment later, Eric reappeared, his hair disheveled, his cheeks red.

"What happened in there?"

"Miss Lizzie got rid of—you know." He walked to where David stood. "We have to keep the doll safe."

"What are you talking about?"

"Come on, I'll show you." Eric tried to put his arm around him, but David stepped back.

"I'm fine."

Dubiously, Eric nodded. "Let's go."

They reentered Amber's room. No trace of foul odor remained, though David thought he detected a light scent of lavender. It could have been his imagination. He watched as Eric crossed the room and removed the doll from beneath the bed pillows. "The *other* will break this if she can. We can't let her."

David knew he meant Christabel. "How do you know that?"

"I don't know. I guess Lizzie told me."

"What happens if it breaks?"

Concentration pinched his features. "If the doll breaks, Lizzie won't have a place to go where *she* can't get her."

"Lizzie lives in the doll?"

"Mostly. I think it's why she can fight her at all. It's a safe place. She goes there to rest." Eric pushed his hair off his forehead. "I don't know if I'm right. That's just what I feel."

Mine is not to reason why . . . With that thought, David directed Eric to get some towels from the bathroom. Eric wrapped the doll safely and put it in a shoebox in the bottom of the wardrobe as David rested against the dresser and watched. Finally, he asked, "Is it safe for Amber to stay in here?"

"Yes," Eric sounded certain. "As long as Miss Lizzie is safe, she'll keep the other one away from her." He studied David. "But you know that."

"How could I know that?" David asked impatiently, though it was true, he did know it. Even if he didn't want to give it credence, he had felt Lizzie's fierce protectiveness during that brief moment when she'd passed through him. She reminded him of a lioness protecting her young and he had also known that, for some reason, this aspect of her personality had concentrated on Amber. Perhaps it was because she had failed to save her own daughter. *Okay, Masters, reality check. You know you don't believe in sentient spirits hanging around.*

Eric was staring at him, a look somewhere between frustration and disgust on his face. "Don't play games, David. Miss Lizzie was on you. You *know.*"

David had always prided himself on his open-mindedness, on his willingness to consider possibilities. And on his skepticism. To him, they went hand in hand. He made fun of the

New Age movement, calling its followers crystal-packers and worse, because they often believed everything, unconditionally. And he made equal fun of their opposites, the people who debunked everything they couldn't prove materially and absolutely. They called themselves skeptics, but they weren't—they were disbelievers, every bit as fanatical as the believers. As Eric waited for an answer, David knew he didn't want to fall into either category, but here he was automatically disbelieving that sentient spirits could exist just because he'd never seen any reasonable proof before. *Reasonable proof just zapped you for all you're worth, Masters, old boy. Consider that.*

"I guess you're right, Eric." His mind was reeling and he was having a hard time accepting any of it. A very hard time. "But, I'm curious. How do *you* know? Was Lizzie on you too?"

"No. I just sort of picked it up."

"Did you feel her emotions as if they were your own?"

He shook his head. "No. I guess I would if I did what you did, and let her into me." He looked down at the floor, then back up at David. "But I—I felt some of the . . . *other's* emotions when it touched me . . ."

"Christabel's?"

He nodded. "Don't say the name out loud, don't even think it. It felt like she was trying to drain away my life. She's not nice."

"I gathered that." Suddenly, David's adrenalin deserted him and he had to stifle a yawn.

"She hates," Eric told him. "She's practically made out of hate."

"I think I need to take a nap," David said as they left Amber's room. "I've been having trouble sleeping. I think it's because of Chr—her. What do you do to protect yourself here?" *I'm asking this kid for advice, my God, I don't believe it.*

"I wouldn't sleep here," Eric replied, as they arrived at David's doorway. "But if I were you, and I had to, I'd sleep in Amber's room. I don't think the other will go back in there."

Unable to bring himself to tell Swenson about his somnambulant sexual activities, he said, "Amber wouldn't want her old man bunking in with her. What about my room, though? How would you make it safe?"

In reply, Eric walked into the bedroom and looked around. "*She* used this room a lot," he said at last. "*She* slept here."

"Was it her bedroom?"

"For a while." He stared hard at David. "She liked the room by the terrace on the third floor best."

"The one with the spilled paint?"

"Yes."

He'd check into that later, David decided. He gestured at the room. "Can you tell what happened in here, Eric? Were there murders?"

Eric shut his eyes a moment. "Some, but not too bad. *She* did *things* in here."

"Things?"

"She had—" Eric blushed uncontrollably.

"What did she have, Eric?" David prompted.

"She had lovers. In that bed. Lots of them."

"The mattress and box springs are brand new."

"The frame isn't." Eric walked over and touched one tall poster, again closing his eyes. "She used rope. She liked to tie them up." His eyes glazed. "The men. Women sometimes. They couldn't say no." He snatched his hand from the frame and gazed squarely at David. "They did whatever she wanted. She used magic on them. They let her hurt them."

David tried to keep his expression blank. "What if I get rid of the bed?"

"That might help. When you're asleep it's really easy to pick up on leftovers." He rubbed his hand. "And these are extra strong. Almost like upstairs." He cleared his throat and added, "Getting rid of the bed will make the leftovers weaker, but *she* could still decide to come in here, especially if you think about her."

"I think she already has," David admitted. "While I was asleep."

At this admission, Eric blushed again, and that told David

that the boy had also been approached sexually by the succubus.

"Well," he said quickly, hoping to lessen the boy's embarrassment, "Let's change the bed and see what happens. I have another bed." He'd had the movers put the components of his huge, beloved waterbed and matching bedroom furniture in the room between his and Amber's. He'd originally intended to have them set it up, but the beauty of the antique poster bed had delayed that order. Already, he missed the waterbed's temperature controls, its gentle movement, its welcoming warmth when he slipped between the sheets.

"Eric, I have two more jobs for you today. First, we need to put a lock on my office door, and then we need to take the poster bed out and set up the one I brought with me." He forced back a yawn. "Guess I'll have to skip the nap."

"I can do those things by myself."

"Putting my bed together is a two-man job. Easy with two, impossible with one."

"I'm really strong."

"I know." Eric could do it, he knew that, but there was no way he was going to nap while Eric was there—the possibility of humiliation was too great. "Actually, I'm starting to feel quite lively. I want to help."

"If you say so, David." Eric nodded at the old bed. "What do you want to do with that?"

"I guess I should have a guest room. Maybe the large room in the other wing? We'll put the rest of this furniture in there too, except for my writing desk and chair."

The thought of his familiar oak bedroom set, utterly sleek, completely modern, the wood stained a rich warm gold, really did revive him a bit. Standing up, he found that his knees barely buckled. "Let's do it."

August 5

Sixteen

Body House: 11:45 A.M.

"Jerry Romero?" David repeated into the phone. "Really?"

Gaylord Price responded with his cultured chuckle. "Yes, Jerry Romero. A whole hour, and not the daytime show, my boy. He wants to use you and Body House in a prime time special."

"When will it air?"

"Currently, it's scheduled for the week before Halloween." Gaylord cleared his throat. "Your new novel will be on the stands."

"I know," David said happily. "I know. Tell me the details."

"He'd like to film sometime around the end of August. He would also like to set up a band in the ballroom to play music from the cra and have appropriately dressed actors do a bit of turn-of-the-century cavorting. Color, you know."

"Great."

"He also wants to bring in a psychic and film a seance."

David's stomach did a quick square knot. "I don't know about having a seance here."

"Whyever not? It's all in fun, after all."

"I understand that," David said carefully. He wished he knew how to explain his reasons to Gaylord without coming off like a superstitious idiot. "When we first moved in, we had a lot of trouble with the house. I'm afraid a seance might start it up again."

"Trouble? What sort of trouble?"

Well, Gaylord, a succubus was screwing my brains out and her mother is protecting my daughter. "Electrical phenomena," he said instead. "Strong poltergeist activity. It, ah, was very frightening. To Amber." He thought that would satisfy his Hollywood agent.

"I thought your daughter was quite the trooper where these things are concerned."

Damn my bragging mouth! "Yes, she is. But Body House doesn't harbor your garden-variety bumps in the night." He forced a light chuckle. "Body House does it up brown."

"I see. But David, Romero's shows are built around sensationalism. A haunted house special without a seance? Why not send Amber to spend a night at a friend's?"

He almost argued, then decided not to. *Star Light, Star Bright* would be out in hardcover and the paperback edition of *Remains to be Seen* would be hitting the stands when the program aired, and that kind of prime time exposure was a dream come true. Also, he'd get an early plug in for *Dead Ernest.*

Unfortunately, Gaylord was right about haunted houses and seances: one was ice cream, the other hot fudge, each incomplete without the other. A TV journalist/sensationalist like Romero would probably want to use one of his usual very theatrical but very fake mediums—and that, in itself, would help keep anything supernatural from happening. Between that and the fact that true hauntings had a habit of refusing to perform for cameras, everything would probably be fine. "Okay, Gaylord, I'll work something out."

"There's a good fellow."

"Is Romero intending to focus the entire hour here or will there be other segments?"

"That depends."

"On what?"

"He wants to uncover the secret of, as he puts it, "The Lost Chamber of Sexual Tortures." He'd like to build the entire show around it."

David groaned. "No one has ever found it, Gaylord, including me." In the last few weeks, he'd spent hours in the

Red Cay library, though he'd perversely avoided the newspaper office. But he'd found nothing new so far and, if he wanted a shot at locating the thing, he had a feeling he'd have to go to the *Guardian* and brave Calla Willard.

"Well, if you do find the chamber," Gaylord was saying, "and I have every confidence that you will, dear boy, Romero would like you to keep it mum so that he can focus the show around it. He's willing to send an escape artist out to help you find the entrance. At his expense, of course."

"I see. I don't think I want to try that at this point."

"It's your choice, of course, David, but if you can find that dungeon, he'll give you the entire hour. If not, you still get the majority of air time."

"Sounds good either way," David replied, still mildly worried about the problems a seance might cause.

They discussed a few more details before hanging up, then David tilted back in his desk chair, putting his feet up and twining his fingers behind his head. "The Jerry Romero Show," he thought. *Not bad, Gaylord, not bad.* On second thought, it was better than that—it was fantastic. Over the last few weeks, he and Amber had acquired a number of antique and neo-nouveau pieces with which they were slowly restoring the parlor, dining room, billiard room, and downstairs bath to their early twentieth century glory. By the end of the month, the final pieces should have arrived and the house would truly be a showcase.

Sitting back up, he stared out the window at the lighthouse rising stark and scenically severe against the blue sky. Since the atmosphere of the house had calmed down, something which Eric attributed to Christabel's withdrawal into the still paint-stained third-floor room to recuperate from the energy-draining fight in Amber's room, David had spent too much time trying to find the entrance to the cellar, in an attempt to satisfy his curiosity. *The Lost Chamber of Sexual Tortures,* he corrected, smiling to himself. He was behind on the book now and knew he should got down to serious work, but the mystery continued to haunt him.

He first began to feel guilty when he'd found himself knocking on walls and pressing on odd-looking spots inside cabinets during writing hours. The frustration ate at him and he'd remind himself that Houdini had once attempted to locate the elusive entryway and had failed, and that he himself was a fiction writer and could very well rely on his imagination, which was probably far more gruesome than reality. He'd go back and try to write, but he couldn't stop thinking about it.

Now, Jerry Romero would be phoning next week and that gave David the excuse he needed to redouble his efforts. He had several more leads that might yield clues. One was poking around in the unfinished attic at the back of the third floor. He thought he might do that today, especially if he could talk the radar-like Eric into helping. Theo had told him that as far as she knew, it had been locked up since shortly after the 1915 investigation ended: no one had ever stuck around long enough or had the desire to poke around in its lightless depths.

He also intended to talk to the townsfolk, including the dreaded Calla, who'd taken to leaving messages on his machine at all hours. Until now he'd avoided her calls requesting an interview, a torture he decided he'd have to endure soon, not only to keep the locals from thinking he was a snob, but mainly because the lit'ry Miss Willard with her newspaper connections might prove invaluable as a source of information on Body House's history. More likely, though, she'd probably prove to be as fun as a boil on his ass.

He expected that a chat with history buff Andy Cox would be far more useful, but he needed to spend an evening in Barnacle Bob's for that and he couldn't bring himself to leave Amber alone in the house.

He might get his opportunity soon, though. Theo had made good on her offer to introduce Amber to Kelly Cox, Ferd's granddaughter, and the two were not only spending a lot of time together, but as a consequence, Amber had met most of the kids who'd be in her senior class next fall. She was also practicing to try out for the cheerleading squad—Kelly, the head cheerleader, had assured her she was a shoe-in. Though Amber normally abstained from such activities, she seemed to be getting a real kick out of it.

In fact, this very morning Amber had asked him if she

could spend the night at Kelly's, and he'd readily agreed. She'd teased him then, asking if he'd be okay alone in the house, and he'd said of course, with total honesty. Since that day when he and Eric had encountered the two apparitions, nothing more had happened other than catching an occasional whiff of jasmine. To be honest, the third floor room was as horrible as ever, but the horror was staying put, putting credence in Eric's theories. David had also experienced half a dozen more wet dreams, though they were more fun than disturbing because they seemed like dreams, not reality. Still, he'd become very clandestine about washing his sheets

Before she left for the beach today with a batch of her new friends, Amber had also told him she'd been invited to the Come As You Were Dance, coming up in a little over two weeks, by one Rick Feldspar, a boy she described as tall, thin, and dark-haired. He wanted to be a graphic artist, she explained, and when David had asked her if Rick wore glasses, she'd looked at him oddly and said, "How'd you know?" David just smiled and told her it was fine by him, especially since they were double-dating with Kelly and her date.

The minute Amber took off, he'd realized he could leave the house tonight, so he immediately called Theo Pelinore and asked her out to dinner, something he'd wanted to do since he'd met her. Tonight, in the Rusty Anchor, a pricey seafood restaurant overlooking nearby Morro Bay, he'd accept her invitation to the dance. She'd issued it several times since he'd moved in, the last time just two days ago. He was glad he could finally stop putting her off.

His thoughts drifted back to the missing dungeon and he turned to his computer, wondering what clues might be staring him in the face. He called up a file he'd compiled on the house's history and began to review it, searching for anything he might have previously overlooked.

According to his notes, Byron Baudey built the house for his wife Margaret Cross Baudey. Their child, Charity, was raped in 1905, when she was only fifteen. *Even younger than Amber.* After the child was born, she took it to the third floor of the tower, where she strangled it then took her own life, accounting for the first two hauntings.

In 1908 and 1909, Byron and Margaret died, the former of a heart attack near the lighthouse, the latter by throwing herself from the aptly named Widow's Peak at the seaward tip of the finger. That made four hauntings altogether.

Lizzie and Christabel Baudey moved in in 1912 and in 1914, the decapitated body of Ezra Wilder, spice merchant and captain of the clipper ship *Golden Horde*, was found. Soon, his ghost was sighted. The captain was in love with Lizzie, according to Eric, and that was something David wanted to verify.

The captain fascinated David. On the surface, the tale was such a traditional ghost story that he had always assumed that, though Wilder had been murdered in the lighthouse, the haunting aspects were probably born of repeated telling of the tale.

Wilder's was the first mysterious death to take place on Byron's Finger after Lizzie and Christabel moved in. He had, according to history, been the son of a naval officer who had been a close friend of Lizzie's father, and it was he who detoured his ship to the island where Lizzie was thought to be living.

Wilder had brought Lizzie and her daughter back to America, spiriting them away in the night and, though Lizzie was extremely happy to be rescued, the daughter was horrified. She wanted to stay with her father, who was also her teacher, but according to the legend, Lizzie hoped she would turn into a normal child once she was away from the voodoo priest's influence. *She should have left her there.*

Christabel would have despised Wilder, whom she considered her kidnapper. And, if Eric was right, and Lizzie and Wilder had fallen in love, this would have served to further anger the girl. She had to hate the man. Given the circumstances and her nature, how could she not?

Early in the morning, the lighthouse keeper had descended the stairs and discovered Ezra Wilder's headless body just inside the lighthouse. The head, never found, was assumed by police to have been thrown into the ocean, but the condition of the neck had confounded police: the severing had not been done with a blade, but gave the appearance of being torn off by a huge wild animal. The police finally closed the case, saying that a bear had probably wandered down from the mountains fifty miles to the east, and done the damage.

This was accepted for lack of a better explanation, even though the lighthouse keeper had insisted that sound carried very well up the tower and he would have heard the struggle. In response, it was suggested that the bear killed the captain elsewhere and deposited his body in the lighthouse. *Pretty neat, for a bear.*

The fact that Christabel had begun making dolls before the captain's death fascinated David. Was there a doll of Ezra Wilder and did she try to use it to murder him? David didn't believe sticking a pin in—or pulling the head off—a voodoo doll would work on anyone unless they believed in voodoo and knew it was being done. Wilder was well educated, which made it unlikely that he would buy into such things, but he was also a sailor, and they were often superstitious.

Masters, you're reaching. If he believed Christabel stuck a pin in a doll's heart, he maybe, maybe, could have a heart attack, but there's no way, no matter how devout a believer he was, that this knowledge would tear his head from his body! Christabel, David thought, might have been behind his death, just as the rumors said, but a couple big brawny guys who were well paid to take their time and make it messy, most likely had more to do with Wilder's appearance than anything Christabel did with an actual doll. Still, it made for fascinating fiction, and was all going gleefully into *Mephisto Palace.*

After Wilder's death, several more people died mysteriously in 1914 and 1915, though he could find no more reports of hauntings until late in 1915, after the mass murder occurred. About nine months before the massacre, Lizzie's legs were broken, and rumor had it that it was Christabel's doing. Then, after the tragedy, rumors of Christabel's ghost began to supersede all the others. He also found a few possible references to Lizzie's ghost, but, surprisingly, the expected raft of ghosts of dead customers and prostitutes didn't manifest. Also the doll collection disappeared, and many bodies, including the Baudeys', were never found. *Find the dungeon,* David thought and you'll find the bodies *and* the dolls.

He moved his cursor down the screen. The house remained empty until 1917, when Maxwell Patton moved in. A retired naval commodore and Lizzie's doting godfather, he had been named as beneficiary in her will. Patton opened the home to other retired seamen in 1918, but things never went smoothly. There were a few humorous anecdotes about a lascivious ghost—rumored to be Christabel—who used the men for its carnal pleasures. Several of the elderly gents died of heart attacks in bed. The lighthouse ghost was seen repeatedly. In 1921, Patton closed the failing home and moved away.

In 1924, a silent film was made in the empty house. The leading lady died there—a fall down the stairs—and a stand-in was used to complete it. The film was quickly and poorly made and David hadn't been able to find more than this reference to it, let alone a copy. He wondered if the movie company had ended up more interested in getting out alive than in making a picture.

The house began to fall into disrepair, then, in 1931, the commodore's heirs decided to have it restored and sold—but the project stalled after several workmen died under mysterious circumstances. It began again in 1934 and was successfully completed in 1936. The house was sold to swashbuckling actor Drake Roberts, he of the red bathroom, who wanted it for a weekend retreat. Roberts made great use of the ballroom to entertain his famous friends. A couple was found murdered, in a very compromising position, in the middle of the room after one party, and the double murder was never solved. Another guest fell from the lighthouse and Roberts died shortly thereafter, of a heart attack.

Still nothing about that damned dungeon! Scrolling further, David saw that Roberts's estate attempted to rent the property out in 1939. The only tenant who lasted longer than a few weeks died after two months. There were no details on that death, but there were repeated reports in Drake Roberts's time concerning the lascivious female ghost and odd smells, including an odor of rotting bodies that sometimes rose through the floorboards of the house. The sounds of a baby crying in the tower were also reported by various visitors.

The house remained empty and forgotten from 1942 until 1946, when a group of spiritualists came in and tried to contact the spirits. Very little happened and the reputation of the place began to fade, though no one wanted to buy the house.

Then, in 1952, the house was sold to the Buckners, who by all accounts were a typical all-American family. A "Leave It To Beaver" family, though David wondered about the truth of that considering the phallic latches had evidently remained in place. The Buckners were violently murdered six months later. Again unsolved, these murders were attributed by local police to sexually deviant drifters. David made a note to go down to the police station and introduce himself to the chief, Eric's uncle Craig Swenson, and ask about these murders. He returned to scanning his notes.

In 1953, the house went up for sale, but again there were no takers. Two years later, in 1955, then-famous ghost hunter Henry Gunn wrote a book about the place, playing up the notion that the house was cursed because it was built on a lost Chumash burial ground—an out-and-out fabrication, David knew. Gunn also claimed to have exorcised a few demons and a succubus or two. The book was a bestseller, but Gunn was full of shit.

The windows were boarded up for good and the house closed, then, sometime in early 1968, a hippie commune clandestinely moved in. They were largely ignored since no one went near the old place, but later that year, they were found viciously murdered in the house. The police reports stated that they believed the atrocious murders were committed by one of the commune members during a mass orgy. There were, according to Eric, at least two ghosts from that time, the fat guy on the table and the girl in the tub.

He paused, considering. Now he was getting into modern history. Eric had said that his uncle had been a rookie on the scene, so that was another thing to talk to him about. Wondering if anyone knew any of the commune members, he wrote another note to himself.

In 1971 and 1984 the first real scientific investigations

were conducted. Many anomalies occurred, but there were no conclusive results. David made one more note, to try to locate the head of either or both investigations and make sure nothing had been held back.

Nothing more had happened here, according to reports, until last May, when ten-year-old Matty Farmer had fallen to his death from the lighthouse. His companion, also ten, was a boy named Billy Galiano and David wondered if it would be possible to talk to the child.

What first? He pondered a course of action until there was a light rap on the door. "Yes?" he called.

"I'm leaving now, Mr. David," Minnie twittered from behind the door. "That is, unless you need anything else. There's a macaroni and cheese casserole in the fridge."

He rose, stretching, and walked across the room. Turning the lock, he pulled the door open and smiled at Minnie. She looked rather sullen in a fat-cheeked chipmunky way; she had ever since the lock had gone on the door. He didn't care. "That's all for today, Minnie. I'll have the casserole for lunch tomorrow—I have an engagement tonight. So does Amber."

She waited for him to tell her his plans, but he waited longer.

"I'll be going home now," she said at last.

He walked her to the front door. She was nice enough in her way, he supposed, but she was the sort of woman who belonged in a book, what with her nosiness and non-stop chatter. He'd been controlling the urge to put her into *Mephisto Palace* as the 1915 bawdy house's maid: it was just possible she'd recognize herself and that would give him trouble of some sort. He didn't need that.

She drove off in her dented white Civic and David breathed a sigh of relief because he could now roam his own house without having to hear another story about the Marvelously Literary Calla, Bea Broadside's hormone shots, or why every pickle you eat takes seven minutes off your life span. He wanted to fire Minnie, but he needed the help, and until he found someone else—a difficult proposition—he didn't dare do so. He also had the sinking feeling that if he let her go before making friends with enough of the townsfolk, she'd make sure he was considered a pariah one way or another. Between the lock on his office and his continued avoidance of Calla, he was already treading on unsafe ground.

He walked out onto the front porch and set on a step, enjoying the summer saltwater breeze that ruffled his hair. *So beautiful,* he thought, staring out at the cliffs. *Melanie would love it here.*

He had tried not to think about her since he'd moved here, but it was hard. Hopefully, tonight's date with the sultry Theo Pelinore would help cure him of his longings for ambitious, childish Melanie Lord.

Lord and Masters. The thought made him smile but, swiftly, he wiped the expression off his face. Someone like Theo, despite her bizarre New Age notions, would be much easier to get along with. Every time he spoke with her, in person or on the phone, no matter what she said, the sound of her voice implied that she lived to please him and only him, that she'd do anything he wanted sexually.

A sudden memory of Lorna Dyke and her similar behavior, along with Amber's similar dislike of her, gave him momentary pause, but he dismissed it quickly: Amber was, quite naturally, jealous.

Except of Melanie. But Melanie bore similarities to the others. She liked to control things, in business and pleasure. Unlike Lorna and Theo, she never exhibited any of their sex-slave behavior, but she knew exactly how to drive him wild—not always in ways he expected, either, not always what he hoped for. He smiled despite himself. *No, Masters, she was always better than you hoped for.* Another pang of desire washed over him. Melanie was smart, strong-willed, sensual, and a royal pain in the ass. *We were two peas in a pod, that's what we always said. Lord and Masters.* He shook his head, watching an arrow-shaped flock of cormorants pass overhead.

Melanie always made sure he knew what she wanted, too, and he liked that a lot. He didn't have to play guessing games with her—she was too blunt for such nonsense. And they talked, too. They talked for hours and hours, sometimes all night, and both would be surprised that it was already dawn and they didn't remember the time going by.

The one thorn in their relationship had been work. That was where her ambitions took control of her common sense, her vanity overcame her intellect. She had taken it personally because he wouldn't put his career in her hands and he wished she could have understood. She was young yet, only twenty-seven, he reminded himself for the millionth time, and she might begin to understand his notions about old loyalties in a few years. The romantic in him wanted to wait forever for this to occur, if necessary, but the other parts of him were uniformly angry with her. *It would never have worked out.*

Theo Pelinore. He would date her and other women, and get on with his life, and some day he'd find the right woman. He frowned, thinking that no matter what, the romantic seemed to win out. *You already found her,* that part of him asserted, *and you left her behind cutting book deals in Manhattan.*

He told the romantic to shut up, but it wouldn't. Perhaps, it suggested, he should have let Mel represent him. After all, he was only one of a number of Georgie's big sellers—she didn't need him . . . But Melanie asking him to drop her was too much like crazy Lorna constantly wanting him to assure her he'd give up writing before giving her up.

He couldn't say it, though, not even to get laid. He couldn't even comprehend why Lorna felt she was in competition with his work—he couldn't not write, not for anyone or anything. It was too much an integral part of his makeup, and Lorna ended up infuriating him as no one else ever had.

Melanie was different. Even though she pissed him off, he understood her motives to some degree.

"Mr. Masters!"

David looked up as Eric Swenson glided up on his bicycle. "Hi, Eric!" He was glad of the company. "Listen, we've already discussed this. Would you please call me David? Mr. Masters is my father."

"What do you want me to do today?" Eric asked as he got off his bike and flipped down the kickstand. "David?" he added awkwardly.

"Well, I thought we'd work together. Amber's been invited

to the dance and she needs a costume. Frankly, so do I. Do you?"

"No, sir, David, I've got mine already. I'm going as a cowboy. If I ever lived before, that's what I would've liked to be."

"Good idea." David stood up and they walked to the front door. "I've been putting off exploring that old attic for weeks, but I need to see if there are any papers in there and if there are any old clothes Amber and I can wear to the dance. Are you up for it?"

Eric stalled, just inside the door, his eyes staring upward, as if he could see through the ceilings, right through to the third floor. "Well, I guess. As long as we don't go near that front bedroom."

David held up his hand, his palm facing outward. "You have my word."

Seventeen

Body House: 12:37 P.M.

David almost wished he could cancel this evening's date with Theo as he looked at the booty he and Eric had found in the attic.

Despite their trepidation when they first broke the lock on the door, they found that the cramped, dusty room that ran most of the length of the back of the third floor was utterly without ghostly laughter, cold spots or anything else more unnerving than a few spiders.

At first, the room appeared to be empty except for a few beat-up pieces of upholstered furniture draped in sheets that crumbled when touched. They uncovered a bergeré chair and an elegantly sloping méridienne lounge, both with cabriole legs of rich dark walnut and acanthus leaf and cockleshell extensions. They hauled both downstairs to send out later for reupholstering. David didn't notice the jagged rips and massive, ancient bloodstains until the pieces were in the parlor, but they only made the pieces more interesting to him, even though he planned to replace their decaying red velvet and tassels quickly and identically, so that they'd be ready for Jerry Romero's cameras.

But the furniture was only the icing. Back in the attic, as he was almost ready to give up the ghost, so to speak, they discovered the wooden crates. There were six of them, four feet tall and eighteen inches wide, filling the spaces between the beams and joists so perfectly that they were virtually invisible. If David hadn't tripped and put his hand against one to steady himself and, consequently, felt it move, they might never have noticed them.

Eric had gone downstairs and brought an aluminum handcart back up then, carefully, they'd moved the boxes down to David's huge office, where they lined them up against the wall near the desk. They spent the next hour prying them open. David felt like a kid on Christmas morning, and wished Amber had been home to participate. The first four were full of fancy clothing that could only have belonged to Lizzie's ladies. Nearly out of time, he only peeked in the upper layers. The feather boas had gone to dust, but many of the dresses were perfectly preserved, and he knew Amber would be delighted. He thought he'd take them all to get cleaned, then hang them on old-fashioned hangers in the wall-to-wall wardrobe in the downstairs room that he and Amber had dubbed "Lizzie's Salon." They'd serve as decor and Amber could take her pick of costumes for the dance.

In the top of the third crate, he found two sets of men's clothing. One was a mariner's uniform, complete with captain's bars and hat, though it wasn't precisely military. *Captain Wilder?* he wondered. The man captained a spice ship, after all. Holding up the clothing, he was pleased to see that the uniform might fit him after the cuffs and trousers were taken up. That would solve his costume problem.

The other set had probably belonged to a fisherman. The clothes were considerably smaller, and the pants, watch cap, coat and sweater were all unadorned black. There was even a pair of crumbling black leather gloves. *These belonged to a kinky fisherman,* he told himself with amusement. Eric, briefly touching the gloves, pulled away, saying they had belonged to "a bad man." He refused to touch the clothing and David decided not to push.

But he did, eventually, get Eric's impression of the captain's uniform and, to his delight, the boy proclaimed it had belonged to Captain Wilder. The shallowly-hidden romantic in David was ecstatic. As silly as he knew it was, he just couldn't stop thinking that like the long ago captain, he didn't have his true love either . . . Melanie would make a great Lizzie, with her similar bone structure, coloring, and frank green-eyed gaze. *You're going with Theo Pelinore, Masters. Try to appreciate that instead of pining away for that selfish excuse for a woman!*

They were running out of time. David needed to take a bath before going to pick up Theo, and though he would have liked Eric's impressions of some of the other items of clothing, it would have to wait. They opened the fourth and fifth boxes, saw clothing and opened the sixth.

The last box, by far the heaviest, which they opened hurriedly, was the true treasure. At first he thought it was full of hats, then, lifting them out, had found the books. He removed a few, finding journals and papers beneath them. "Let's take this down to my office and lock it up," he told Eric.

Once that was done, he sent the young man home, and resisted the urge to call Theo and cancel. Instead, he forced himself to refrain from looking through the crate's contents, reminding himself that there would be plenty of time for that tomorrow. He went upstairs and showered and shaved, and was soon on his way to Theo's house.

Eighteen

Rusty Anchor Restaurant: 9:15 P.M.

Without the interference of moving vans, paranormal manifestations, or a resentful teenager, Theo and David relaxed and got to know each other, starting with the twenty-minute drive to Morro Bay. It had been delightful, with the sun setting a romantic mood by dropping, jewel-like, into an ocean that reflected clouds colored salmon and lavender.

Once they reached the Rusty Anchor, things had gone from good to better. They shared a secluded candlelit table on the restaurant's glassed-in patio that rested on stilts above the bay. To the north loomed Morro Rock, a dark sentinel, and due west, the full moon cast silvery ribbons across the choppy water. Theo couldn't have asked for anything better.

As they dined on scallops, the Rusty Anchor's specialty, and split an excellent '87 Reisling, vintaged locally, their conversation had been light and low-key and without any awkward moments. Theo had carefully refrained from saying much about her involvement with the Beings of Light, sensing that David, like many other uninformed individuals thought the New Age movement was just a fad. When he'd asked about it, she'd even played it way down, making it sound more like a social club for local artists than anything else. She would have to introduce him to her beliefs very slowly and carefully and, though it would be difficult, she fully intended to do so. Enlightening a famous novelist would allow him to write better, more meaningful, books, and that would help spread the message of the Beings of Light Church.

Now, over brandy and coffee, she realized that the alcohol had made her slightly tipsy: a warm spot burned low in her belly. "I'm so glad you're going to come to the dance with me, David." She slowly pushed her hand across the table and laid it down so that her fingers were a bare inch from his.

He smiled and let his fingers brush against hers. "Amber has been invited to go with friends. I just couldn't commit until I knew she wouldn't be home alone." He withdrew his hand to drain his brandy snifter. "I can't thank you enough for introducing her to Kelly Cox. In fact, she's at her house tonight."

"That explains the sudden invitation." Theo gazed into his eyes and lowered her voice a notch. "I was beginning to think you'd never ask."

"How many of these fund-raisers have you held?"

"This will be the twelfth annual Come As You Were Dance."

David lifted his eyebrows questioningly. "And they're successful?"

"Yes, very. The whole town will turn out and we'll have people from Pismo, Morro Bay, and Cambria as well. Even a few from Los Angeles." She smiled. "You seem surprised."

"I'm surprised that you say the whole town will turn out. By whole town, you mean people who make their living running the gas stations and hardware stores?" He paused. "Will Ferd Cox be there?"

She laughed. "Oh yes. All of them, even Ferd."

"Ferd mentioned your church and sounded, ah, unimpressed."

"He called it the 'High Hooey Center,' I'll bet."

David blushed. "Well, yes."

"Most of the townies do. But it doesn't matter, they still enjoy the dance." She gave him a knowing look. "Our cosponsors help, too—no one's put off by the Seaside Preservation Society, and they take seventy-five percent of the proceeds."

"Why is your group involved?"

"We're very involved with ecology as a cause," she said sincerely. Then she smiled. "And, frankly, we enjoy the subject matter. Everyone loves a costume party, and the reincarnational aspect is our specialty. The Beings of Light Church offers past life counseling at a special price this time of year and you'd be surprised who comes—"

"Past life counseling?" David interrupted, smirking.

She was treading on thin ground, thanks to the brandy. "Yes," she said, holding his gaze. "It's rather . . . romantic. Don't you think? Knowing that you were, say, a court jester in a Renaissance court, or a soldier in the Civil War, and getting to dress up that way for the dance?"

"I suppose it is romantic, at that." He smiled slowly. "But how do you find out things like that?" The skeptical look returned.

"David, you wouldn't believe it if I told you."

"Try me."

"We channel it." She waited for the retort, and it wasn't long in coming.

"You're kidding. You believe in channeling?"

"Don't knock it until you've tried it." Her words were purposefully light, even though his skeptism irritated her. If he knew she was the channeler, he'd write her off as a hopeless loony. "I would think that as a novelist, you would be fascinated by such things—and more open-minded than most."

He stared at her a long time before answering. "You're right, I should be. Instead, I'm being a complete turd. Forgive me."

"You're forgiven," she said warmly.

"Well," he said, sitting back, "I don't know for sure, but I'd guess I was a monk doing illuminated manuscripts."

She'd been hoping he'd say something like that. "David, I asked for information on you already."

"Oh?"

He looked surprised instead of offended. "Yes. First Spiros said—"

"Who's Spiros?"

"Our guide."

"Is that the spirit you people channel?"

"Yes, Spiros is his name. He lived his last life on earth ten thousand years ago in the great Atlantean society. He's a spiritual teacher." She'd gotten carried away again and now watched him warily.

"I'm not going to tease you," he assured her. "So what did your Spiros tell you about me?"

"Most recently, you were a German housewife renowned for strudel."

David laughed heartily. "You know, I can almost believe that. I detest, absolutely *detest,* strudel."

"You probably got sick of it." She smiled broadly. "And I didn't think that you would want to dress as a *Hausfrau,* so I asked for a past life where we knew each other, just in case you accepted my invitation. I thought it would be fun to dress as we were when we last knew one another."

David said nothing, just raised his eyebrows expectantly.

"You were a composer in the court of Napoleon in the early eigthteen hundreds. I was a courtesan." She paused, waiting for him to respond, but he remained silent. "We knew each other very well," she added finally.

"Oh?"

"In every way. In fact, the emperor, who was a very jealous man, sent a spy to observe me. We were caught in the act and eventually beheaded."

"Ouch," David said, wetting his lips. "It's a good story. A very good story." His eyes roved over her face, searching.

"David, you'd look marvelous in a powdered wig and leggings. I've already rented my costume and they still have one that would be just right for you." She decided not to mention she'd put down a deposit to hold it for him.

"Thanks, but I already have a costume."

"You do?" She hid her frustration. "I wish you would have told me. I wouldn't have gone on so long."

"Oh, but I wanted to hear it. It's fascinating." He cleared his throat. "I just found the costume today. Eric and I took some old trunks from the attic and they were full of clothes. From Lizzie's time," he added proudly.

"You're *not* going in drag, are you?" she asked, shocked.

He laughed again. "No, no, no. There was a sea captain's uniform in one carton. It fits perfectly."

"But you're supposed to dress as you were in another life." Theo tried to hide her disappointment under gentle chiding.

"Who's to say I wasn't a sea captain?" he asked, his tone mild.

"Well, maybe you were. But since you know who you were—might have been—don't you think you should represent that life?"

"I don't see why. I doubt if many of the attendees will be so appropriately dressed." He leaned closer. "Or if most of them even believe in reincarnation."

"You have a point." She made herself smile at him again. "I guess I'm just disappointed that your costume won't match mine."

"Change yours. Be a captain's lady."

"Thanks, but I'm obligated to dress correctly. The other members of Beings of Light would disapprove if I didn't. Are you sure you won't reconsider?"

"I'm sorry. I wouldn't be comfortable dressed so theatrically. You know, we writers aren't too outgoing. We prefer to put our characters in colorful clothes, not ourselves. That's probably why we write instead of act; we don't generally want to call attention to our physical selves."

She laughed throatily. "But you have a wonderful physical self, David. You shouldn't be so shy."

He blushed again. "Thanks. But I'll stick with the conservative costume. Otherwise, I might die of embarrassment." He drained his coffee cup. "Also, Eric Swenson said something that really made sense."

"Eric?" she asked, surprised.

"Yes. I don't know who told you he's slow, Theo, but it's not true. He's been misjudged. He's different, yes—I think he lacks a certain ambitiousness present in most people and its absence scares them and makes them think something more serious is missing." David shrugged. "He doesn't care about impressing anyone, but he's not slow or retarded or handicapped, or whatever you want to call it."

Theo carefully hid her annoyance. "So, what did our Eric say?"

"That he's going to dress as a cowboy because that's what he'd *like* to have been if he'd lived before." He paused. "Inventing a past sounds more satisfying to me than following the advice of some dead guy from Atlantis. No offense."

Silently, she counted to ten, keeping her expression as serene as she knew how. "And you'd like to think that you were a ship's captain?"

He nodded. "Sure. And the costume won't embarass me. Uh, Theo, I'm sorry if I offended you. I didn't mean—"

Smiling sweetly, she said, "Don't worry about it. I'm a member of a very unusual group and I've heard much worse. So, do you know what Amber is going to wear?"

"I thought I'd let her pick out something from the trunks, if she wants. She's been gone all day, so I haven't told her yet."

"David, you don't mean you're going to let your own daughter dress as a prostitute?"

He chuckled. "She can call herself an elegant woman from 1914. There is nothing cheap about the clothing." He paused. "Well, most of it."

Theo wet her lips. "Most?"

"Um hmm." The waitress brought the check and David grabbed it before Theo could see the damage. "Just a moment," he told the girl. Pulling a gold card from his wallet, he laid it on the little tray, then waited for the waitress to move out of earshot. "There were some very naughty underthings in one crate. Corsets. Garters. You know."

"I'd love to see them," Theo whispered.

"I'd love to see them on you," David retorted. Abruptly, he sat up straight, obviously startled by his own words. "I'm sorry. I guess I'm a little too relaxed."

"No need to apologize. I'd *like* you to see them on me." Excitement squiggled from her crotch into her belly. "Would you like me to try them on tonight?"

"You're blunt, Theo," he said as the waitress brought him the receipt.

"Sorry."

He signed the check with a flourish, then looked Theo in the eye. “Don’t be. I like blunt women.”

“Good,” she purred.

August 6

Nineteen

Theo Pelinore's House: 8:30 A.M.

He awoke slowly, luxuriously, stretching his nude body between the cool sheets, keeping his eyes closed, acutely aware that for the first time in weeks, he'd slept the whole night through. Ever since his second night in Body House, when he'd awakened to find the ghost—or succubus, or whatever it was—using his body, he hadn't slept well, even though he'd half convinced himself that the whole thing was a dream. The sleeplessness was due in part, he suspected, to his concern for Amber's safety after the manifestations of Lizzie and Christabel in her room, though primarily it was due to his nervousness concerning the succubus. He'd continued to have orgasmic dreams—sometimes two or three in one night—and would wake at the moment of release, then remain awake, always wondering if it was really only a dream or if he would again find the invisible woman straddling him again. Fortunately, it hadn't happened again. Turning over, he let himself drift back toward sleep . . .

And a moment later, he awoke, aware of the sudden coolness enveloping his penis, stroking it, using it—

"NO!" he screamed, sitting bolt upright. Dazed, he stared around the room . . . The unfamiliar room.

"David! I'm so sorry! Did I hurt you?"

Theo. He'd spent the night with her in *her* house, in *her* bedroom. On the way back from the restaurant, they'd decided to come here instead of going to Body House, because of the possibility of Minnie or Amber catching them together.

He gazed at Theo now, at her face, pale yet beautiful, even without make-up, at her long dark hair falling in waves over her full breasts so that it artistically hid one nipple and exposed the other.

"I had a nightmare," he told her. "It had nothing to do with you."

She moved closer and sucked the lobe of his ear into her mouth for just an instant. "I thought I'd stabbed you with a fingernail," she whispered, then started nibbling again.

"No, no. It was just a dream," he murmured as she trailed her tongue halfway down his neck before resuming nibbling. He groaned, desire returning with memories of the night before.

They'd sipped champagne while curled up on the sofa in front of her fireplace, watching the yellow flames consume a large piece of hickory. After that, she'd led him into her huge bedroom with its inch-thick white carpet, central air, and enormous bed with black satin sheets. Everything in the room was black or white except for a vase of blood-red roses.

She took the initiative, playing with him, making him wait, extending the foreplay for nearly two hours.

Theo was an animal, every man's dream, but, he thought, even as he ran his fingers over the lush curve of her ass, but something had been missing. Something, he didn't know what.

The smell of her now nearly drove him mad. She pulled him over on top of her, wrapping her legs around his waist as he entered her, using them to force him deeper inside her with every thrust. Her nails dug into his back, and tears came to his eyes as her teeth sank into his earlobe. He pulled his ear free and raised himself as far as she would allow, looking down at her flushed features, trembling lips, and brilliant dark eyes glassy with desire. Her nostrils flared with each rapid breath she took.

"Fuck me!" she ordered. He cringed as her long red nails broke through the skin of his back.

Last night, when he was intoxicated, he knew she had done

the same, but he'd been imprisoned in an erotic cloud that made him nearly unaware of the pain. Now, it was too much and his erection began to fail. With all his strength, he pulled away from her, trying to ignore the fingernails as they raked over his back and across his ribs. He took hold of her hips and pushed. Immediately, she understood what he wanted, and turning herself, she rested her head on the satin-sheathed pillow and thrust the globes of her perfect ass up toward him.

Roughly, he plunged into her, giving her the depth and roughness she craved, excited by her expert muscle control and her breathless demands for him to fuck her.

Safely out of reach of her teeth and nails, he gave her exactly what she wanted, and when they were done and he rolled off her, she took his limp penis in her hand and squeezed it. Looking him in the eye, she told him he was an incredible fuck, the best she'd ever had.

He didn't answer, only gave her a small, tired smile. His body was satisfied, but he felt used, very much like he had after the succubus episode. *Guys don't care if they're used, Masters, so what's wrong with you?*

Abruptly, a vision of Melanie swam across his mind, smiling and bright, giggling over the silliness of some position they'd tried, he chuckling with her as they tried it again. Now he knew what was missing: laughter. Theo Pelinore was deadly serious in her lovemaking; she never laughed.

Theo, long and tall, unfolded herself and rose from the bed. She padded into the bathroom and he heard the shower come on a moment later. As he lay there listening to the water, he wondered briefly if perhaps he should compromise his morals and give his career to Melanie to agent. Then he would have her to talk to and to love. To laugh with.

"Care to join me?" Theo's voice carried above the sounds of the shower.

He glanced at his watch. *Holy shit, it's nine in the morning!* Rapidly, he searched for his socks and underwear but found only one sock and no shorts. "Oh hell," he muttered and pulled on his pants and shirt, then slipped his bare feet into his shoes. He glanced around once more, but saw no sign of his underclothing. He'd have to pick them up later. Haphazardly dressed, he stepped into the steamy bathroom, unmoved by the dappled silhouette of Theo behind the shower glass. "Theo, I have to go. It's late!"

"Are you sure you don't want to shower first?" she asked. "I've got a shower massage."

Watching her, he realized that she held the instrument in question between her legs. Maybe she was just washing . . . maybe she was ready for more. "Sorry, but I'll have to take a raincheck. I've got to get home before Amber catches on."

"If you say so." She finished her sentence with a little moaning sound. Five seconds later, David was out the door, trotting toward the Bronco.

Twenty

Body House: 9:00 A.M.

Where is he? Amber had left Kelly's house early because she'd been worried about her father being all alone in the house, but when she got back, she was dismayed to find he wasn't home.

An hour had passed and she was a little worried and a lot annoyed as she carried a basket of laundry downstairs. Though he'd acted pretty normal for the last week or two, judging by the circles under his eyes she suspected he was probably just getting better at hiding his nervousness.

Carefully balancing the overfilled basket, she opened the laundry room door and went inside. She'd thought she'd never have to wash her own clothes again, thanks to Minnie. "Fat chance," she muttered, putting the basket on the table and turning on the light. Sighing, she opened the washer and started tossing in underclothes. "Minnie, I could kill you," she muttered under her breath.

Yesterday, she and Kelly Cox had gone to cheerleading practice, then met up with a bunch of other kids, including her date for the Come As You Were Dance, luscious Rick Feldspar. They'd spent the day at Pismo Beach, with Rick valiantly trying to teach her how to ride his surf board, while Kelly and her boyfriend, Jason Swenson, showed off on their boards. Amber had declared herself a klutz, partly because she felt that way, but mostly because it made Rick renew his efforts to teach her, and she liked that very much. At the end of the day, they'd built a big bonfire and roasted hot dogs.

Jason Swenson dropped the girls off at Kelly's house and the pair had a pleasant evening. She'd expected Mr. and Mrs. Cox to be weird like Ferd Cox at the store, but they were nice and normal. They'd all sat together in the family room and watched *E.T.* Amber had seen it maybe a million times, but it was still lots of fun.

Mrs. Cox asked her a few questions about Body House and about her dad, but Amber handled them just the way she had when her new friends questioned her: she made everything sound boringly normal, saying her dad was a terrible nag about chores and that the stories about the house being haunted were complete baloney. Mrs. Cox had looked disappointed, but Amber figured that if she said anything at all about the rotten-flower stinkfest that arose without warning almost every day and lasted seconds to minutes, or told her about the creepazoid cold spots, or even the ghostly piano music, she'd probably decide Amber was weird and wouldn't let Kelly hang out with her. She didn't tell her friends, except for Kelly, whom she'd sworn to secrecy, for the same reason.

Amber leaned down and opened a cabinet next to the washing machine, withdrew a box of Ivory Snow, and poured a cup of it on top of the clothes. "I could kill you, Minnie," she repeated.

The reason she was so ticked at the housekeeper was her big fat mouth. At first, she'd liked Minnie because of all the interesting stories she told, many of them nasty ones about that witch, Theo Pelinore. But last night, she found out from Kelly that Minnie had been gossiping about her to Mrs. Cox. "You bitch," she whispered, closing the lid and starting the water. She had set it on the delicate cycle, so there was no point in leaving the room: she'd have to add softener in ten minutes, tops. She backed up to the built-in folding table, put her hands on it and easily hoisted herself up so she could sit.

Swinging her legs back and forth, she thought about what Kelly had told her Minnie said, and started doing another slow burn. *How dare she!*

"I gotta tell you something, Amber," Kelly had said, once they were sprawled out on the twin beds in her room. "You better watch out for Minnie Willard, she's been talking about you to my mom."

"What?"

"And my mom's way down on her list of people to visit. Like, twentieth or something. By the time she gets to Mom, she's already told half the town." Kelly started brushing out her thick chestnut-colored hair.

"Christ, Kel, what did she say to her?"

Kelly leaned forward. "She was talking about your underwear."

"My *what?"*

"Shhhh. She told Mom you had really sexy underwear and that she didn't think it was proper for your dad to buy you things like that."

Amber couldn't believe her ears and it took a major effort to keep her voice lowered. "What the hell is she talking about? Who the hell does she think she is?"

"She probably thinks you're supposed to wear white cotton fat lady pants like she does, and shit like that." Kelly stopped brushing a moment. "Don't get too excited, Amber. Everybody knows what a prude she is."

"How dare she! That bitch! What my underwear looks like isn't any of her business!"

"That's right, so you better start washing it yourself. Do all your laundry yourself or she'll talk about how low-cut your shirts are and what size you wear and the length of your skirts." Kelly made a face. "I guess she'll do that whether she washes your clothes or not. But at least don't let her wash your bras and panties."

"God."

"Can you lock your bedroom door? She'll read your diary and everything and then tell the whole town."

"My dad put locks on both our doors already. God, for once he was right."

"Right about what?"

"He said she's a snoop. He's usually really stupid about women, but he didn't like Willard from the moment he met her. I did." She smiled sheepishly. "I liked the nasty things she said about Theo Pelinore."

"Theo's kind of a twat."

"She's after my dad, big time."

Kelly cocked her head. "Come on, Amber, what'd you expect? Your dad's kind of a hunk for an old guy, and he's rich and famous."

"Yeah, I know. That's why she wants him. She's a predator, I just know it, but he thinks she's nice."

"She's got big boobs." Kelly covered her mouth to muffle the trail of giggles that followed.

Amber started giggling too, and soon they'd pretty much trashed Theo Pelinore. Then Kelly told her Theo didn't fuck *everybody* in town, just rich, good-looking guys, no matter what Minnie the Bitch claimed. "Willard says she tried to seduce that toad she's married to."

"Mickey Rat?"

"Yes! Can you believe that?" They giggled hysterically. "Can you even *imagine* it?"

Amber held her sides. "I don't *want* to imagine it! Gross plus!"

About then Mrs. Cox knocked on the door and told them it was after midnight and let's get some sleep, shall we?

They whispered in the dark, talking about Rick Feldspar and Jason Swenson, who turned out to be Eric's cousin and Chief Swenson's baby brother.

"My dad wants to meet the chief," Amber said.

"Why?" Kelly gasped in the dark and lowered her voice a notch. "He's not on probation or anything, is he?"

"God, no! Why would you think that?"

"Who wants to talk to a cop if they don't have to?"

That made sense. "My dad talks to all kinds of weird people. Once he went to a mortuary."

"Gross!"

"Tell me about it!"

"So why's he want to talk to Craig Swenson?"

"To talk about the history of Body House. Eric said Craig was a rookie cop when those hippies got killed, so my dad wants to ask him about it."

"Oh. Isn't Eric cute?"

"He's not my type," Amber said, "but I like him. He's sweet."

"I don't know him, but my dad says he's retarded."

Amber considered that a moment. "Minnie the Bitch says he's retarded, too. Maybe your dad heard it from her. Theo the Witch said it too. But I don't think so. My dad says he's just different and that he's really psychic."

"Theo the Witch and Minnie the Bitch. Are you gonna be a writer, too, Amber?"

She threw her pillow at Kelly. "God, no way!"

Kelly threw the pillow back. "Why's he say Eric's psychic? What's he mean by that?"

Amber told her a little, then asked her not to repeat it, for Eric's sake.

They fell silent for a few minutes, and Amber's eyes grew heavy. Then Kelly spoke again.

"You know that stuff I told you about the underwear?"

"Yeah?" Inwardly, Amber cringed.

"Can I ask you a question?"

"You can't try on my underwear."

"No, seriously, Amber. Can I ask you a question without you getting mad?"

Amber propped herself up on one elbow, instantly alert. "You can ask," she said, using her dad's standard reply.

"Well . . ."

"Spit it out."

"*Did* your dad buy your underwear?"

Amber couldn't answer for a long time, all she could do was feel her heartbeat reverberating in her head. "Kelly, you said nobody listens to Minnie, but you just asked about what she said. If *you* ask that, everybody's going to ask that. Shit." She felt like crying.

"I'm sorry, Amber. I mean, you guys live by yourselves and all and . . . Oh shit, I'm sorry."

"I buy my own clothes, okay? My dad had a girlfriend in New York who lived with him a long time and they were going to get married, but they broke up. Melanie was great. She was the only female my dad ever brought home that wasn't a golddigging bitch." The words came out venomously, but she didn't care. "Melanie is a literary agent and she's gorgeous. She taught me all about clothes and make-up and stuff and she and I used to go shopping at Bloomie's all the time. Melanie helped me pick out lots of things, like shoes and purses. And underwear."

Kelly quietly switched on the lamp between the beds. "I'm sorry, I didn't mean to offend you. I'm really sorry."

"It's okay. I'm glad you told me about Minnie Rat. I've gotta get my dad to fire her."

"If he doesn't like her, that should be easy."

"It would be if there was another housekeeper around he could hire. But he's not going to want to do it until there is."

"So tell him the underwear stuff. He'll fire her ass in a New York minute."

Amber grinned, feeling affection for her friend. "I guess I could, maybe. I'll have to think about it. But, I don't really want to, you know?"

"Yeah, it's weird to talk to your dad about underwear." Kelly paused. "So what about this Melanie? Does your dad still love her or was the argument too serious?"

"He never says anything, but he's got her picture in his wallet and he's got one on his desk. He hides it in his drawer when anyone comes in."

"So he's got it bad."

"Yeah."

"What about Melanie?"

Amber shrugged. "I don't know."

"Can you call her?"

"Why? So she can swear out an affidavit saying she helped me choose my underwear?"

Kelly shook her head. "Don't be a goof. If you could get them back together, nobody'd believe any of that stuff about your dad buying your underwear. You could get Minnie fired really easy."

"Melanie could hire someone new," Amber admitted. "She's really good at stuff like that."

Kelly nodded. "And she'd sure cramp old Pelinore's style."

* * *

The washing machine cycled and Amber put the softener into the water. Later, she might call Melanie, maybe, to ask her about some lamps she was trying to talk her father into, and just see how she acted, see if maybe Mel was missing him. Meanwhile, Amber could barely control her anger. The minute Minnie Willard walked in today, she wanted to fire her. *Who knows? Maybe I will!* Her dad might be a little ticked, but it would be worth it. She'd do a lot of the household stuff herself to make it easier. Then she realized that the rat lady wouldn't buy it unless her dad did the firing—and she'd have to tell him why she wanted Minnie out of the house. *Christ!*

She glanced at her wristwatch. It was nearly nine-thirty. Where was he?

She slid off the table and walked around the room, idly opening and closing the myriad of cabinets lining the walls. One lower door stuck and she thought it was the fresh paint, so she yanked harder. Suddenly it opened and she squatted down to look.

"Wow." This one was too deep to see into, just like the giant linen closet between the bathroom and this room. She squinted, thinking she saw a golden glint deep inside. Finally, getting down on her hands and knees, she ducked her head and torso inside and reached for the tiny object.

"Ouch!" She pricked herself on whatever it was and, gingerly, she put her fingers around the object and drew it out. She heard a vague clicking sound deep within the cabinet.

It was a small jeweled brooch, an art nouveau butterfly. A drop of blood oozed from her finger, but she ignored it. *How could this be here?* she wondered. With all the people moving in and out of the house, it seemed impossible, but she felt sure it dated from Lizzie's time.

She rose and set the brooch on the counter then went to wash her hands, squeezing the blood out of the pinprick to clean it. A faint whiff of lavender reached her nose and she turned and looked at the open cabinet. "Lizzie?"

No reply, but what did she expect? The lavender fragrance strengthened. "You want me to look in the cabinet again?"

The smell was all around her as she got on her knees and crawled partway inside once more. Where the pin had lain, the bottom of the cabinet had slid away to reveal an opening similar to the one in her wardrobe. *Another doll!* Excited, she reached inside and, sure enough, her hand touched cloth. One, no, two dolls! They were stacked on top of each other. As she pulled them out, the opening smoothly slid shut.

The lavender scent had faded away to nothing, but she barely noticed as she peered at the top doll. It was a bearded male, dressed all in black, and it's expression was so vicious that she quickly laid it on the counter. It held a tiny multi-tipped whip in one hand.

After placing it carefully on the table near the laundry basket, Amber studied the other doll. It wore some sort of navy uniform, was also male, but had no head. Cautiously, she touched the ancient dark stain that marred the doll's neck and the front of the uniform, and it flaked off in her hand. It looked like dark rust. Or dried blood.

The thought startled her, and she let the doll slip from her grasp. *Idiot!* she thought as it tumbled, as if in slow motion, toward the floor. She swooped to catch it, but too late. The shattering porcelain sounded like windchimes in the distance.

"Damn!" *God, I'm such a klutz!* She squatted and put her hand around it, hesitating as she felt something sticky and warm coat her fingers. Fighting back a rush of panic, she lifted the headless doll, revealing a small crimson puddle beneath it. "Oh, God." Paralyzed by shock, she watched hot, thick fluid drip off her fingertips.

As she stared at the broken doll, its uniform grew dark and damp. *Blood!* It looked like blood, but it couldn't be. *Maintain!* she ordered herself as her hands began to tremble. *Maintain!* No, it couldn't be blood. The twisted girl, Christabel, must have filled the doll with something resembling blood . . . She must have done it for the shock value. Real blood would be dried up after all these years, it would be nothing but a clump of dark redness.

Revulsion crawling up her throat, she forced herself to lift one of the china hands. Red fluid oozed sluggishly from a crack across the palm. As she gingerly examined it, half the hand suddenly snapped off. Blood spurted from the opening, spraying hotly across Amber's face, her cheeks, her nose, and into her mouth.

She heard someone screaming as she hurled the doll across the room. It splatted against the white wall, then slid slowly down to the floor, leaving a broad bloody streak behind it.

Suddenly, she realized she was the one screaming. She put her hands to her mouth, then saw the blood and pulled them back, staring at them in shock, still screaming, vaguely tasting the unmistakable metal tang of blood in her mouth.

"Amber! Amber, where are you?" Dimly, she heard her father calling her.

"DADDY!"

Twenty-one

Body House: 9:31 A.M.

"DADDY!"

Hearing his daughter's ragged scream, David left the keys in the open front door and ran toward her voice. She screamed for him again and again as he checked in the kitchen, then the sun porch, panicking in his inability to discern the origin of her voice.

"AMBER! WHERE ARE YOU?" he yelled as he pounded back through the dining room into the parlor.

He ran past the laundry room to the bathroom, thinking she was in there. Nothing.

"DADDY!"

He heard her voice to the right as he came back into the hall, and glanced at the closed laundry room door.

"DADDY!"

"AMBER!" He screamed her name as he grabbed the glass doorknob and tried to turn it. It wouldn't budge. "Amber! Open the door!"

Her screams turned into hysterical sobbing as she pulled on the knob from the other side. It barely jiggled. "Oh God, oh God, oh God," she moaned between huge, hitching sobs.

"Get away from the door!" he called. "I'm going to break it down!"

He backed up ten feet and ran, hitting the door with a strength born of panic. It creaked and groaned, but held. He shoved his shoulder into it as hard as he could, once, twice then, abruptly, the door opened and the force meant for the door sent him flying across the laundry room, bending him over the folding table and knocking the breath from him.

"Daddy!"

Panting, he whirled, and saw Amber standing before him, her eyes huge in her blood-soaked face. "My God. You're hurt!"

Her shoulders shaking with repressed sobs, she shook her head no.

"The blood."

"It's . . . not mine," she said, her voice shaking as badly as her body. "Oh God." She tucked her arms around her stomach and ran for the big sink next to the washer. She turned on the water and bent over, retching.

David held her while she was sick, pulling her hair back away from her face, then waiting while she rinsed her mouth for what seemed like hours. Finally, she bent over even further and let the water wash the blood from her hands and face. When she righted herself he let go of her hair and pulled paper towels from the roller so that she could dry herself.

At last, she looked up, her gaze traveling to the door, then back to him. "Don't let it close," she said quietly.

Nodding, he took the box of detergent and set it in the doorway, then turned to his daughter. "Amber, are you sure you're not hurt?"

"No, I'm okay. I came home and you weren't here and I decided to do my laundry and I was looking in the cabinets and found this—" She took a small piece of jewelry off the counter and handed it to him. It was exquisite. "Then I smelled Lizzie's perfume—"

"Lizzie's?" He thought she'd made a mistake.

"Yes, Lizzie's. The lavender."

David nodded.

"And I thought she wanted me to look again so I did and where the pin had been there was a secret latch like in my wardrobe, and it opened. There were two dolls in it. This one." She shoved the laundry basket over so he could see the effigy laying behind it.

As his fingers closed around it, she whispered, "Be careful!"

"I will," he said, turning the doll over in his hands.

"Don't drop it," she added.

"Don't worry." It was a vile-looking thing. Thrusting against its black pants, he could see the outline of a huge erection. "This has to be another of Christabel's creations," he murmured as he carefully set it down. "Amber? Where did the blood come from?"

"The other doll." She pointed behind him.

He turned and saw the bloody skidmark on the wall and the dark lump on the floor beneath it. Taking a pen from his pocket he squatted down and pushed at the thing. It reminded him of a dead bird.

"I dropped it and I when I picked it up, it was bleeding."

"The *doll* was bleeding?" David couldn't believe his ears.

"Then it sprayed all over. It got in my mouth and I threw it." She looked at the floor. "I'm sorry, Daddy."

"Sorry? What are you sorry for?" He rose and put his arms out to her.

Immediately, she was in them, burying her face against his chest like she had when he carried her in his arms when she was little. "I'm sorry I dropped the doll. I got scared and threw it."

"Don't be sorry, kiddo. I would've thrown it too."

A sick giggle escaped her. "Then I'm sorry Minnie didn't find the stupid dolls."

He chuckled. "Me too. Can you imagine?" He stroked her wheat-colored hair and waited patiently until she pulled away from him. "Amber? You know that can't really be blood."

"That's what I thought. That's why I picked it up again even though I saw the stuff. I thought old Christabel had filled it with something gross."

"You're a smart kid."

"It's blood, though, Dad."

"How do you know?"

"It was hot. And it tasted like blood."

August 8

Twenty-two

Body House: 1:15 P.M.

Amber, her dad, and Kelly Cox stood in the downstairs room they called "Lizzie's salon." One entire wall of wardrobes stood open to show off the two dozen antique evening gowns hanging within.

"Wow!" Kelly said. "There're so many! And they're gorgeous!"

"There were tons more," Amber told her, "but they fell apart."

"So, are you two sure you want to wear these to the dance?" her dad asked.

"Yeah!" Kelly breathed. "Jason's grandfather is letting him and Rick get old-fashioned sailor's uniforms out of his attic, so we'll all look great together."

"For sure," Amber seconded.

A look of concern crossed her dad's face. "Okay, but there's one condition you have to agree to before I let you use these dresses—"

"We're not little kids, Dad. We won't spill anything on them."

He smiled thinly. "That goes without saying."

"Anything, Mr. Masters," Kelly breathed. "Anything."

"All I ask is that you don't tell anyone where you got them or who their previous owners were. You can call yourselves opera enthusiasts, stage actresses, pre-flappers, or anything else you want—as long as it's not ladies of the evening."

"Sure, Dad."

"No problem."

His smile turned genuine. "Good. I wouldn't want the town gossiping about how I'm ruining the morals of teenagers by letting them dress up as hookers!"

"You told him about the—?"

"Shut up, Kelly," Amber hissed. She hadn't said a word to her dad about the stories Minnie had told about him picking out her underwear. It was just too mortifying. She hadn't called Melanie, either, because she knew her dad would be ultra-ticked if he found out she was messing around in his personal life.

"Told me what?" he asked, his brows raised questioningly.

"Forget it, Daddy," Amber said quickly. "It was just some stupid gossip. You know how you hate gossip."

He shrugged. "Okay. I'll be down the hall in my office if you need anything." He gestured at the hanging dresses. "You two go ahead and start trying them on."

"Can we model them for you when we're done?" Kelly asked.

He looked surprised. "Sure, if you want. Just give a knock." He turned and left, pulling the door to the salon closed behind him.

"You want to *model* the dress for my dad?" Amber asked as soon as he was gone.

Kelly blushed and shrugged.

Amber put her hands on her hips, disgusted. "You think he's cute, don't you?"

"Well . . ."

"Don't you?"

"Sort of."

"Yeah, well, listen Kel, you'd better not let him know it. A couple of my girlfriends back in Boston kept hanging around him and stuff and he caught on that they had the hots for him and you know what he did?"

"What?" Kelly asked breathlessly, her eyes wide and waiting. "Did he—"

Amber didn't want to hear it. "He wouldn't let them come over to see me anymore, that's what he did." She fixed her friend with a knowing look. "You wouldn't want that to happen, would you?"

Kelly shook her head.

"Then be cool. He's really, *really* sensitive about stuff like that, okay?"

"Okay. But how come you didn't tell him about the underwear stuff? If he's so sensitive, he'd fire that old busybody on the spot, wouldn't he?"

"Yeah, he would." Amber took a red dress from the wardrobe and held it up. "But it's just too embarrassing, you know?"

"Yeah, I guess," Kelly said as she examined a slinky violet dress. "I'm going to try this one on." So saying, she laid the dress over a chair and began undressing.

Even though it *was* mortifying, Amber had been ready to tell her dad two mornings ago, but then that weird stuff with that disgusting doll had happened and they decided to hurry and clean up the laundry room so Minnie wouldn't see it. Then everything got put on hold after that. He put the dolls in Ziploc bags and locked them in his office, then insisted on taking her out for brunch and a matinee. She knew he was really scared, mostly for her, even though she kept telling him she was fine.

And she was, pretty much. A little creeped-out, maybe, but that was all. She didn't care to be alone anywhere in the house except in her room, which she shared with the pleasant ghost identifiable only by the faint fragrance of lavender that she secretly believed belonged to Lizzie Baudey.

The smell of lavender preceding the laundry room attack didn't really worry her because she thought that Lizzie's spirit had wanted her to find the pin and the dolls. It had gone bad because she'd dropped the doll—she couldn't conceive of the gentle ghost meaning her any harm.

Amber put the red dress back and began looking over the four rich green ones, which she thought had belonged to Lizzie. She would have liked to wear any one of those beautiful gowns, but Lizzie must have been very tiny-boned, maybe a size three or five, at the most. Amber needed a nine. It was too bad Melanie wasn't here; she could wear one—and she even had red hair, just like Lizzie. *Oh well.* She picked a black dress next. It appeared to be the right size and she decided to try it on—after all, Kelly was getting into a third dress already, and was completely off in another world.

The other day, after the matinee, her dad had insisted on a walk on the beach. Finally, they sat, jeans rolled to the knee, bare toes dug into the warm sand.

"Do you want to leave the house, kiddo?" he'd asked her quietly.

"And go where?" she asked.

"Well, I think that after the Jerry Romero show, I might try to sell Body House," he admitted. "I don't sleep so well there, you know."

"It'll be hard to sell."

"Not too. Gaylord was telling me that George Frankenberg has been asking if I'm ready to sell it or lease it yet." He laughed. "He wants it now that it's restored."

Frankenberg was one of the hottest directors in Hollywood. "You'd take a big loss, wouldn't you?" she asked.

"No. Nothing's set in stone yet, but George wants to buy the rights to *Mephisto Palace.* And he wants to film it on location. I can make the house part of the deal." He paused. "Don't repeat any of that, okay."

"No problem," she had replied, realizing how serious he was about this—her dad's most major rule was that he never, ever said anything about any projects until everything was signed. "Are you thinking about renting another house in town for now?"

He didn't speak for a long time. "Frankly, I hadn't considered that. I don't really want to leave here until I'm done with the first draft."

"Atmosphere?"

"Yeah. I was thinking that you could go back to Boston and stay with your Aunt Barbara. That way you could go back to Revere High to finish your last year. I'd come back before the end of the year and we could find a new house."

She was silent. Her father's plan held a lot of appeal for her. On the other hand, she had new friends here and she really liked the California weather, the beach, and the slower pace. But most importantly, she'd go nuts wondering if Dad was okay all alone in Body House. "I'm not going anywhere until you do," she said at last.

"Are you sure?"

"Positive. Besides, you told me hauntings can't hurt you, remember? You can only get scared and hurt yourself."

"I can't argue with that." He studied her. "Okay, then, we stay, but I don't want you ever to be alone in that place again. If you happen to come home and no one's there, wait outside. Deal?"

"Sure. Or I can stay in my room."

"I'd prefer you stay outside. It'll probably never happen, but if I'm away, I'll be back fast."

"Dad, my room is completely safe."

"I'm not so sure."

"Why?"

"No reason," he said uncomfortably.

She could tell he was keeping something from her, but she decided not to bug him about it. "Okay. I'll wait outside." She had pushed her toes deeper into the sand. "Dad?"

"Hmmm?"

"Where were you this morning?"

"Oh, ah, I had an errand to run . . ."

If David Masters was lousy at skirting the truth, he was an absolute disaster when he tried to lie. "Dad," she said reprovingly. "Come on."

"An errand," he said slowly.

"Where?"

"I didn't expect the Spanish Inquisition," he said, but his attempt at humor failed dismally. "Theo Pelinore called. I had to go sign a paper. You know, a real estate thing."

"Oh." She'd forgotten Pelinore, who was reason enough in herself for Amber not to return to Boston. Her dad would be a sitting duck and she could end up with a bona fide wicked stepmother.

"So, you want to go back to the house and start checking out those crates of goodies you told me about at lunch?" she asked abruptly.

He'd put her in charge of the clothes while he slowly began

examining the contents of the trunk that contained the books. The rest of that day and night had passed uneventfully. Yesterday, things seemed really normal and he even asked her if she'd like to stay in the house permanently if they could dispose of the hauntings. She'd very honestly said yes, at least if she could get a car of her own to go into town with, and he'd said it wouldn't be a problem, then talked about getting in touch with a parapsychologist and physicist he knew from way back and seeing if he couldn't fly them out to run some scientific studies. He went on and on about electromagnetism, physics, and hauntings, saying he thought it might be possible to neutralize the house, though he didn't want to do it until he'd finished with Romero and the first draft.

Fastening the black dress, Amber thought her dad was the weirdest thrill-seeker in the world.

"Wow, you look incredible!" Kelly told her.

"You think so?" Amber studied her reflection in the mirror. She did look pretty good, she thought. The off-the-shoulder sleeves were made of thin chiffon that fit so that they began below her shoulders, even with the lacy sweetheart neckline. The layered satin and lace skirt trailed gracefully down from the empire waistline, stopping a few inches below the knee, where the luxurious folds of material were gathered to drape to the sides and extend to the ground, much as Lizzie's dress in the portrait. She took a step and showed a brief flash of calf.

"Sexy, sexy," Kelly told her. "Rick's tongue will be on the ground when he sees you."

"You really think so?" she asked, but it wasn't really a question because, suddenly, Amber felt confident and adult. "Dress for success, isn't that what they say?"

"For sure," Kelly breathed. "Can you hand me that red dress?"

"Sure." Amber examined her reflection while Kelly slipped into the crimson gown. The black dress made her look grown up. More than that it made her look *experienced,* she thought, but not slutty. Rather, it gave her an unapproachable air. "It says 'Look but don't touch.' "

"Huh?"

"This dress. That's what it says, I think."

Kelly grinned. "Yeah, like the Spider Woman or something. It'll keep all those dirty old men away."

"Oh, my dad'll do that." As she said it, she realized that he might have a cow if he saw this on her. It wasn't that it revealed much more than any of the other dresses. It was just so . . . sexy. She started to unfasten it. "I guess I'll keep looking."

Kelly turned. "You're kidding. That's just so perfect! You *have* to wear it!"

"Really?"

"Really! It's totally sophisticated. Now, what do you think of this dress?"

Amber studied it. "Your boobs are too big for it. You'd have to bind them."

"Oh, gross!" Kelly made a face.

"That's what they did back then. Strapped them down. Flat chested girls were the ones everybody wanted."

"Eoo-ooh!" Kelly whined. "No offense, but I like Candy and Sue just the way they are and I'm not going to tie 'em down for anybody."

Candy and Sue? Amber turned to the wardrobe, hiding her amusement among the gowns. "Here's another red one," she said, "And it looks like it's got mondo boob room."

"Cool." Kelly said breathlessly, "Hand it over."

Amber did, then changed into her street clothes and settled down on the floor. She'd been to Nordstorm's once with Kelly and, from that experience, she knew her friend would have to try on everything in the wardrobes before she could choose.

Twenty-three

Body House 2:35 P.M.

Out of the half dozen crates, only the sixth one contained anything other that clothing. Like the other boxes, though, this four-foot tall, eighteen-inch wide wooden carton was constructed so that it could only be easily opened at one end, and David had to dig down, deeper and deeper and layer by layer, through crumbling magazines and newspapers, as if he were an archeologist looking for prehistoric treasures.

Perversely, he enjoyed the job and had been taking his time, examining each item slowly and carefully before going on to the next. He had only inspected about a fourth of the contents thus far and he had every intention of extending the process for as long as possible.

Yesterday, Amber had watched him for a while and told him how annoying he was, pointing out that he was acting just like he did when he got a Christmas or birthday present: he routinely took fifteen minutes to unwrap a single gift. She was right of course, but he didn't apologize. Instead, he gave her a big stupid grin and drawled, "Anticipation, my dear girl, is the best part." With a groan, she'd gone back to sorting the dresses to take to the dry cleaners.

He'd watched her work for a moment, thinking that, despite his worries about letting her remain in the house after the laundry room incident, he was very glad she'd refused to leave. *Chip off the old block.* The thought made him proud—

the girl had been born with nerves of steel. After they'd returned to the house, he'd felt obligated to tell her about the encounter he and Eric had had with the two female ghosts in her room—though he didn't want to worry her, he couldn't, in good conscience, allow her to choose to remain without that knowledge. The story told, he waited an anxious moment before she told him that she still intended to stay, that she had faith that her room would remain utterly safe.

She'd been so level-headed about the whole thing that he wished now that he could discuss his nightmare problems, however circumspectly, with her. But he couldn't. Wishing he had someone to discuss them with made him think fleetingly of Melanie.

The phone rang, interrupting his reveries. Seeing it was the business line, he snagged it up. "Hello?"

"David." Georgie Gordon drawled his name in her sophisticated, smoky voice. "Darling, how are you?"

"Georgie," he said warmly. "I was just thinking about you."

She laughed, low and knowing. "Wondering where your royalties are, huh?"

"Not at all," David laughed. "Did Gaylord call you?"

"Yes, it's wonderful, isn't it, what a hard-on Frankenberg has for *Mephisto Palace*."

"It's terrific."

"He told me about the Jerry Romero Show too," Georgie continued. "He's just such a *turd,* don't you think?" She laughed. "Jerry, not Gaylord."

"Is he?" David asked. "I don't know too much about him."

"Oh, he's a charming turd, but he can be so obnoxious. You'll need to hire a guard to keep him from snooping through your whole house."

David chuckled. "There's a thought. We have a room on the third floor that seems to turn people into raving sex maniacs. Maybe I should take him up there."

"Really? Sex maniacs?"

"I swear it on a stack of contracts."

"That's *marvelous,* David. Are you writing about it?"

"I haven't worked it in yet. Who knows?"

"Why don't you tell Jerry he can spend the night in there if he promises to behave himself?" she suggested with a throaty laugh.

"He wants me to find the dungeon, Georgie. He's calling it the "Lost Chamber of Sexual Tortures.' "

"Sounds like a gas, darling. I wish I could get away. I'd love to come for a few days sometime around the filming."

"We'd love to have you!" he said, very honestly.

"You're a love, David, but that's not why I'm calling."

"Oh?"

"I had lunch with your editor today. She looks wonderful. She's such a dear, isn't she?"

"Yes, she is."

"And she *adores* you," Georgie added, mimicking a Joan Rivers gush perfectly. "She had drinks with Melanie last week."

David's good mood twisted into a leaden knot in his stomach. "Oh?"

"No, no, David, don't get upset."

"I'm not upset."

"Don't lie to your agent. You sound like you just sat down on a broomstick."

"Georgie, what's this about?"

"I thought you'd like to know that Harry Rosenberg at Dorner Books made Joanna a huge offer to get her and you to leave Randall House."

"Oh, God." He could feel the headache coming on already. He hated the business end of publishing. "What does Melanie have to do with this?" Suddenly, he couldn't understand why the hell he'd been missing her so much.

"It's not what you're thinking, David. It seems she told Joanna about the offer before it came down."

"*Melanie* did that?" He couldn't believe it: Melanie never did anything that wouldn't further her career, and though warning Joanna Scanlon might not hurt her, it couldn't possibly help in any way he could imagine. *"Why?"*

"Well, David, I don't know, but I'm guessing she had an attack of conscience."

"What do you mean?"

"Melanie told Joanna that it was her idea, that she suggested to Harry that he make the offer as a way for Dorner to acquire you, and that she'd felt like a shit about the whole thing ever since. She decided to confess."

"That doesn't sound like Melanie," David said slowly.

"No, it doesn't, does it?" Georgie cleared her throat. "Anyway, the offer was made—"

"What happened?"

"Joanna parlayed it into a nice raise and a corner office with two windows at Randall House."

"Good." David couldn't think of anything else to say; all he could think about was Melanie.

"I've got to go, darling. I'm late for a dinner engagement."

"Wait—"

"Yes, David?"

"What's Melanie up to these days?"

Georgie chuckled. "Well, she's frequently seen with Ray Blaisdell."

"She's seeing Meat? The cocksman of science fiction?"

"Be nice, David. She wouldn't have confessed to Joanna if she wasn't still pining away for you, Meat or no Meat." She cleared her throat suggestively. "How much do you want to bet he shrinks when you cook him? Now, darling, I've got to go."

"Thanks for telling me, Georgie."

"You're welcome, David. Goodbye."

He set the receiver back in the cradle, pleased and confused about Melanie's behavior, wanting to believe it was because of him, but wondering if she had an ulterior motive. She usually did. And the thought of Meat Blaisdell—the nickname said it all—absolutely infuriated him.

He had no right to worry about whom she slept with—after all, they'd broken up more than six months ago. But Meat Blaisdell . . ."God damn it, Melanie. You have better taste than that."

You crawled right into bed with Theo Pelinore, Masters, it goes both ways. And you don't have time to waste worrying about it. You have work to do.

With that, he glanced at the two dolls in their plastic bags on the other side of the desk, and his worries about Melanie retreated to the back of his mind.

The headless one—the one that had "bled"—lay in a powdery rust-colored dust. The red fluid had dried and powdered within one hour of the incident. He should, he reminded himself, take a sample of the powder to a lab for testing: he thought that the doll had been filled with something that resembled blood and he was very curious to know the chemical content of the stuff. If the voodoo-versed Christabel had used some sort of alleged "magic," he might discover a chemical compound as amazing as the one that true voodoo practitioners used to create the zombie effect.

Another thing that intrigued him was the fact that the doll was the effigy of the decapitated Captain Wilder, right down to the lack of a head. Before giving the real naval officer's uniform to Amber to take for cleaning, he had examined it again, but found no sign of blood, so either the captain hadn't been murdered in this particular clothing or it belonged to someone else.

Then there was the mysterious evil-faced doll in black seafarer's clothing. David assumed it represented one of the customers, one who owned a razor-tipped cat-o'-nine-tails. *Any woman willing to bed down with this guy for any price must have had a death wish.* It was endowed with an obscenely huge erection that sprouted from a crotch coated with bushy hair that extended in a thin line to the navel where it blossomed across the thing's torso. Its back, shoulders, and buttocks were nearly as hairy as its chest.

He turned his attention back to the open crate, thinking that perhaps he would find an answer within.

Thus far, he had only discovered impersonal, though fascinating items, which would serve as useful color in *Mephisto Palace.* On top, he'd found items from 1912, including a copy of *Collier's Weekly,* piano sheet music for the brand new hit, "Alexander's Ragtime Band," and, best of all, a copy of the *Red Cay Guardian,* dated April 17, detailing the sinking of the Titanic two days previously.

The next layer contained items dating back to 1913 and 1914. There was a copy of the *Guardian* containing the debut of the new comic, "Bringing Up Father." David read it, remembering the same comic from his childhood, but by then it was known as "Maggie and Jiggs." Next came a small pouch of Indian-head nickels, and another copy of the *Guardian,* this one reporting the opening of the brand new Ford Motors plant. There were advertisements, carefully cut from the paper, for *The Perils of Pauline,* starring Pearl White, and Cecil B. DeMille's epic western (or so said the ad), *The Squawman.*

Now he gently lifted out the next clipping, a story about the movie, *Birth of a Nation.* The article bore the title, "Movie Causes Race Riots in Atlanta: Is D.W. Griffith Member of KKK?" Lizzie, he decided, must have been fascinated by politics and music. These things, sterile as they were, helped the woman come alive in his mind. She had been a feminist of sorts.

He smiled, as he found a carefully folded poster for *The Tramp,* Charlie Chaplin's first major film. Beneath that, lay a copy of the *Guardian* dated May 8, 1915, its headlines detailing the sinking of the Lusitania the previous day. It was an extra edition.

If the items were roughly in chronological order, there would be little left, he realized, at least if Lizzie had stored these trunks away herself. Curious as to what he'd find next, he set the May 8 newspaper aside for later perusal and lifted out a handful of paperbacks, including a 1912 edition of Zane Grey's *Riders of the Purple Sage* and a 1914 *Tarzan of the Apes* by the relatively unknown Edgar Rice Burroughs. There were many more pulp books and magazines, several inches' worth, and David began to think they filled the rest of the crate, when he came to another newspaper, dated September 2, 1915.

I've struck gold! A little thrill ran through him as he stared at the date. Lizzie *hadn't* packed the trunk—she couldn't have. The massacre had occurred on the night of August 31, 1915. He wondered who had packed them and if the same person had constructed the crates to fit so invisibly among the wall studs?

The words "EXTRA EDITION," were emblazoned across

the top of the sheet. The headline, in huge type, took up nearly all the rest of the front page: "Bawdy House Becomes Body House In Bizarre Midnight Massacre." Below that, in slightly smaller typeface, were the words, "25 Bodies Found, Many Missing, Including The Notorious Madam And Her Daughter."

"Oh, boy!" David settled back in his chair and put his feet up, then began to read:

> Sometime during the night of Friday, August 31, a terrible massacre took place in the quiet seacoast village of Red Cay, on the central coast of California.
>
> At 11:00 A.M. on September 1, Miss Charlotte Manderley of Red Cay entered Baudey House, the residence of Misses Elizabeth and Christabel Baudey, where she was horrified to find the gruesomely murdered bodies of twelve women and fifteen men.
>
> Miss Manderley, a resident of the house, had gone to visit her sister in San Luis Obispo on Friday night. "If I hadn't spent the night with Rebecca, I would have died too," Miss Manderley told this reporter.
>
> Upon entering the mansion, which has long been known as a house of ill repute, Miss Manderley saw a sight that will visit her nightmares for the rest of her life. A red velvet méridienne lounge held the body of Miss Lucy Latour, a resident of the house and Miss Manderley's close friend. The body had been eviscerated, and the gut had been draped around the lounge and body in a garland-like manner reminiscent of the murders committed by Jack the Ripper of Whitechapel, England, two decades ago.
>
> Upon seeing this dreadful sight, as well as dimly noticing other bodies and huge splashes of blood, Miss Manderley fought her desire to faint and ran outside, where she soon recovered herself enough to drive into town, and notify Police Chief Robert Lee of the murders.
>
> Chief Lee promptly summoned all five of his officers as well as Doctor Louis Shayrock, and they set off for Baudey House. Officer Thomas Lockhart was stationed

outdoors to keep curious parties, as well as the press, away from the murder scene. He was instructed by Chief Lee to answer no questions.

Another officer, Mr. Jonah Willard, who has only been on the Red Cay force for six months, was seen to exit the house and subsequently became violently ill.

"Horrible, beyond belief," said the officer, who exchanged posts with Officer Cox. "It's the devil's work, no mistake." The officer refused to elaborate further.

After two hours, Chief Lee appeared and made the following statement:

"A mass murder, taking twenty-seven lives, possibly more, occurred sometime last night. At this point we have no suspects in custody. The Red Cay Police Department will conduct a thorough investigation which will not end until the perpetrator of these heinous crimes is captured and justice is done."

When asked if Elizabeth Baudey and her daughter were among the victims, Chief Lee replied that they did not appear to be on the premises. He answered no further questions, but announced that a list of victims would soon be released.

Baudey House has been officially known as The Baudey Home for Young Women since Miss Elizabeth Baudey inherited the property, though local residents have always continued to call it Baudey House. Due to gossip about the alleged "home," some locals in Barnacle Bob's Tavern, as well as many transient salesmen and sailors, have taken to referring to the morally questionable establishment as "Bawdy House."

Now, the house has acquired a new and yet more terrible epithet: Body House.

David perused the article again, then glanced through the paper for any other pertinent information, but found only a brief article detailing Byron Baudey's building of the lighthouse and mansion, and several editorials blasting the town government for looking the other way in the face of prostitution.

The next paper, a regular edition, was dated September 5, 1915, and contained several articles and editorials. David read through them quickly, then slowed, when he came across new information:

Red Cay Chief of Police Robert Lee has issued an official list of murder victims found September 1 in Baudey House. Details of the murders were withheld, although locations of the bodies were revealed.

All the female victims listed were residents of Baudey House. Found on the first floor were the bodies of the following persons:

Parlor: Harrison Cox, 48, Mayor of Red Cay; Chelsea Latour, 23.

Bathroom: Roberto Misella, 40, locksmith; Laurel Drake, 22.

Drawing Room: Unknown Male Transient, 30-35; Kitty Clausen, 31.

Billiards Room: Douglas Cleghorne, 45, Merchant Marine; Nancy Jones, 24; Ginger Buckminister, 19.

Kitchen: Max Nicolatti, 35, Grocer, Red Cay; Jane Vander Putten, 29.

Dining Room: Turner Cox, 26, Officer, Red Cay Police; Tucker Cox, 26, Lawyer, Red Cay; Daisy Johnson, 19.

Found on the second floor:

Front Bedroom, East Wing: Jesse Sampson, 33, Fisherman, Pismo Beach; Shirley Webster, 21.

Third Bedroom, East Wing: Samuel Willard, 54, Selectman, Red Cay; Claudia O'Toole, 26.

Fourth Bedroom, East Wing: Reverend James Worthy, 41, of Red Cay; Timothy Waters, 19, Merchant Marine; Sarah Seville, 18.

Ballroom: Aaron Swenson, 17, of Red Cay; Lawson Cox, 67, State Senator, Red Cay; Unknown Male Transient, 40-45; Emily Pelinski, 31.

Terrace: Noah Fester, 47, Captain, *Sailing Queen,* out of Portland, Oregon.

Found on the third floor in the front dormer bedroom was Mariette Cantori, 17.

No suspects are yet in custody, but Chief Lee expects developments soon. The chief again refused to comment on the method or methods used by the murderer.

Three drawings accompanied the article, depicting the layout of each floor and the locations of the bodies. David studied them, not surprised to see that the body of the young woman murdered on the third floor had been found in the room overlooking the terrace. David made a note to try to find out more about Mariette Cantori who, at seventeen, had been the youngest victim.

The second floor schematic showed that no bodies were found in the west wing, where he and Amber slept, and that pleased him and further convinced him that these larger rooms had been the private quarters of Lizzie and Christabel.

He was surprised to see, however, that the diagram of the first floor revealed that the drawing room, in which two bodies had been found, was the office in which he now sat. *At least it doesn't feel haunted,* he thought, glancing around. According to the drawing, the man and the woman would have been lying right about where he was sitting now.

He perused the names, amused at the number of highly placed citizens, Coxes in particular, that had met their fate in the bawdy house. The town fathers must have worked very hard to bury the well-connected names.

A third paper, dated September 9, 1915, contained an interesting article concerning people who had been missing since the night of the massacre. The article first stated that the police chief considered the disappearances of Elizabeth and Christabel Baudey highly significant, but offered no explanation—undoubtedly the tight-lipped Lee hadn't given one. It then listed the other missing persons: Flossie Sullivan, Colette Seville, and Lucy McGuire, all residents of the house, were unaccounted for, as well as Thomas Wright and Adam Fletcher, both of the *Sailing Queen,* Peter Castle, a Morro Bay fisherman, Luke Peters, a local carpenter, and Luis Sandoval, who owned the Double Bar Ranch near Red Cay.

Near the end of the piece, David saw the first mention of the cellar:

> . . . One avenue Chief Lee is investigating is the possibility that a secret chamber exists below the house, one that is accessible only by an unknown passage. An anonymous source told Chief Lee that it was Miss Baudey's practice to blindfold any men who wished the services available in the chamber before she escorted them to this nefarious den.
>
> Chief Lee is attempting to locate the chamber as the uncharacteristically warm weather has produced unmistakable odors associated with unburied corpses. Word has been sent to the great escape artist, Harry Houdini, who is currently touring Europe, that the Red Cay Police Department would appreciate any advice he can dispense.

David had known that Houdini had been contacted, but nothing ever came of it. Chief Lee never found his murderer or murderers, either.

Following that article was a colorful feature playing up the lurid aspects of the history of Byron's Finger, and David lingered over a section of it:

> Baudey House is located a mile from town on a small peninsula known as Byron's Finger. Except for the Widow's Peak Lighthouse, it is the sole structure upon this land, which the Chumash Indians have always considered cursed.
>
> . . . Perhaps the Chumash were correct . . . Many sailors have lost their lives on the treacherous rocks of the headland, even after Byron Baudey built the lighthouse.
>
> . . . The tip of the peninsula acquired the name "Widow's Peak" in the eighteenth century. Widows of seamen gathered on the anniversaries of their husbands' deaths to throw flowers into the unforgiving waters below *in memoriam*. More than one heartbroken woman threw herself onto the sharp rocks below.
>
> Even in modern times, the land seems cursed, just as the Chumash have said. The mansion and the lighthouse

have continually been plagued by unexplained deaths and tragedies. Byron Baudey, his wife, daughter, and grandchild, all died in dire ways, as have those who came after them.

In the last two years there have been several unsolved murders and disappearances. All involved unidentified transient merchant marines and sailors, with the sole exception of Captain Ezra Wilder, whose hideously decapitated body was found within the lighthouse early in 1914.

Wilder, whose spice trade is now operated by his son Ajax was coincidentally the man who rescued Elizabeth Baudey and her daughter from her imprisonment on a Caribbean Island by a voodoo priest. It is believed that Wilder and the elder Miss Baudey were intending to marry at the time of his death.

Now, that's something new. Eagerly, David read on:

Some of our citizens suspect that the beautiful young Christabel, who was only sixteen at the time of her disappearance, is responsible for the captain's death, as well as the deaths of the others. It is said that her voodoo priest father taught her everything he knew and that she was an extremely powerful priestess.

A local citizen who wishes to retain anonymity told this reporter that Christabel Baudey used magic to obtain any man she desired and that she used other perverse magic upon them once she had them in her thrall. He also said that after Elizabeth Baudey's unfortunate accident in November of 1914, in which she broke both her legs, Christabel altered the secret chamber from merely a "fanciful den of pleasure" into a "torture chamber where no man was safe."

Laying the paper aside, David put his hands behind his head and leaned back, staring at the ceiling. It was definitely time to contact Craig Swenson, the current chief of police, and see if he could learn anything more about the murders. He hoped that Swenson could be talked into letting him take a look at any photographs that might be on file, as well as Chief Lee's original reports.

His thoughts drifted back to Melanie and, for a long time, he stared at the phone. Twice, he nearly picked it up. Nearly.

Twenty-four

Body House: 3:31 P.M.

"See you later!" Amber called as Kelly Cox waved from her yellow VW Bug and pulled away. It had been a great afternoon, with the two of them trying on every dress that remotely fit before they were through. Amber was pleased that her friend had taken the hint about not showing off their costumes for her dad, mostly because she didn't really want him to know which one she had chosen. She wasn't sure he'd let her wear the black dress to the dance: it was rather revealing and very sexy, and what he didn't know wouldn't hurt him.

She walked down the steps and took a deep breath of ocean air. The weather was perfect; the sky was blue with a sprinkling of puffy clouds, and the lawn Eric Swenson had planted a few weeks ago had come up greener than green amid the flower beds full of pink and white impatiens and yellow marigolds.

Deciding to stroll out to the lighthouse and back, she began walking toward Widow's Peak. She had plenty of time: her father would probably stay holed up in his office for a couple more hours, then after that they were going out to eat. Minnie had left some kind of godawful casserole in the refrigerator yesterday, to "tide them over" while she took the day off. Amber had taken one look at it, decided something with sliced cocktail weenies, bell peppers, and macaroni swimming in pink-colored sauce wasn't something she'd be eating any time soon, and scraped it into the trash, with her father's crinkle-nosed blessing.

She sighed. Minnie would be back tomorrow and that made her wish she could bring herself to call Melanie, but she just couldn't: the more she thought about it, the more she felt that telling Mel about the underwear rumor would be a whiny, babyish thing to do. She had to get rid of the old busybody herself. But how? Maybe Kelly could help her cook up a plan.

As she neared the lighthouse, she saw that its old wooden door was ajar. Shaking her head, she approached the tower, intending to close the entry again. She wondered how it came to be open because her dad had asked Eric to put a new hasp and padlock on the door to make sure no one entered the dangerous structure.

The hairs rose on the back of her neck as she got near enough to see that the hasp had been torn from the door. It hung crookedly from its fastenings in the stone wall, the padlock still secured. *Who did this?* She thought it had to be the work of transients or kids.

Nervously, she peered inside, wondering if she should call out before she shoved the door shut. If there were still kids in there, she should, but what if it was some old bum? She sure didn't want to attract his attention. Staring at the geometric spiral of sun and shadow within, she decided it would be best to do nothing except go back to the house and tell her father.

The black metal stairs clanked slightly as a cool easterly breeze washed in through the windows and out the entryway and, simultaneously, something scuttled behind the half-open door. Staring at the floor, she told herself it was nothing but a rat, though she instinctively stepped backward, fighting down the mindless urge to turn and run.

Suddenly she noticed a black boot tip sticking out from behind the threshold. Stunned into immobility, she knew it hadn't been there a second before—she would have seen it.

She heard a scraping noise and a second boot appeared.

Frozen, she let her gaze travel upward, seeing dark blue trousers, a long-fingered hand, then—

He stepped out from behind the entryway and in one unending second, she saw the navy jacket with its gold piping, saw the blood, shiny and fresh, that stained the uniform shirt and jacket lapels. It had spattered the little ribbons and medals affixed to the jacket. Incredulously, she saw the ragged bloody flesh and a flash of bone at the neck as the headless thing stepped closer, its pale, well-manicured hand rising, as if it wanted to touch her.

Paralysis broke and she stumbled backward, then turned and ran as fast as she could, heading for the house.

As she neared the front steps, heart walloping against her ribcage and sides aching, she saw the beige automobile pulling to a stop just ahead of her. Theo Pelinore's stupid car.

She stopped running and crossed her arms against her stomach trying to catch her breath as Pelinore stepped out of the Volvo and quickly walked toward her.

Amber glanced back at the lighthouse and saw nothing. The monster hadn't followed her.

"Amber, dear," Theo gushed, trying unsuccessfully to put her arm around Amber's waist. "What's wrong? You look like you've seen a ghost!"

She's smarter than she looks. Amber took in Pelinore's form-fitting royal blue dress and the amethyst and quartz-crystal amulet that hung between her prominent breasts.

"Nothing's wrong," she said, making a major effort not to sound too out of breath. "I was jogging." She tried to smile innocently. "It's pretty out there by the lighthouse. You'd like it." The thought of the headless thing grabbing Pelinore's pair of pride-and-joy's nibbled away at Amber's lingering fear.

"What a nice thought," the woman said with a patronizing smile. "I came by to talk to David and there's no reason we can't talk and walk at the same time. Thank you, dear, for the lovely idea."

Anger, black and unbidden, rose in Amber. *Barracuda!* She glanced at her Swatch. "He's working right now."

Pelinore put one foot on the bottom step. "I know he'll want to see me."

"He doesn't see anyone while he's working. He doesn't even answer his phone unless it's New York." She paused, considering. "Or unless it's Melanie."

One of Pelinore's elegantly plucked eyebrows shot up like an exclamation point. "Melanie?" she asked sweetly.

"His fiancée."

"Dear, he doesn't see her anymore. Didn't you know that?" she asked in a voice that dripped with condescension.

"I think they might get back together."

"And *I* think *I* might know a little more about that than *you,* dear." Pelinore's smile barely masked controlled anger. "Now, would you please tell him I'm here?"

You goddamned bitch! "He works until six o'clock. Then he returns phone calls. He probably won't come out of his office before six-thirty or seven. Then we're going out to dinner," Amber retorted smugly.

"Dear, he'll want to see me. Please tell him I'm here." Pelinore's eyebrow came up again, this time in a calculating way. "I have something for him."

"You can either wait or leave it with me."

The eyebrow stayed in arched mode. "Very well." Pelinore smiled like Cruella de Ville and pulled a small white paper bag out of her purse. "Would you give this to him, dear?"

Don't call me dear. Amber took the bag. "No problem."

"Tell him I'll call later."

"Sure." Without saying goodbye, Amber turned and walked up the steps and let herself in the house, closing the door firmly behind her. She watched through the sidelight until Pelinore drove away. "Good riddance," she muttered, glancing around to make sure that her dad wasn't out and about before unfolding the top of the small bag.

She saw a pair of navy blue socks, neatly rolled, and, beneath them, a pair of pale blue men's briefs. "Oh, no," she whispered, her stomach knotting. "Oh, no." That bitch had already gotten to him. Pelinore's words *I think I know more about that than you, dear,* took on new meaning. *Shit!*

A door opened nearby, then her father's voice called, "Amber? Is that you?"

She finished refolding the top of the bag just before he

entered the room. "Hi, Dad," she said without enthusiasm. "Are you done working already?"

He nodded. "I'm having a tough time concentrating today." He saw the bag. "What's that?"

"That real estate agent dropped it off. She said to give it to you."

"Theo? When was she here?" he asked, extending his hand.

"A while ago."

He took the bag. "What is it?"

She gave it to him. "I don't know."

He looked inside and the color drained from his face. He closed it quickly.

"What is it, Dad?" she asked dryly.

"Nothing important." He tried vainly to stuff the packet in his jeans pocket. "Did you and Kelly find your costumes?"

"Yes."

He stared hard at her. "What's wrong, kiddo?"

"Nothing." She wasn't mad at him, she was mad at that bitch vampire. Her dad was Pelinore's victim, she knew that and she wasn't mad at him, not exactly, but she just couldn't force herself to act normally.

"When did Kelly leave?"

"An hour ago."

"Amber, what's—" He paused and glanced at the bag in his hand, perhaps worried that she really had looked inside. "What have you been up to for the last hour?"

"I took a walk . . ." *God, I'm losing my mind!* She'd been so pissed at Pelinore that she'd forgotten the thing in the lighthouse.

"Come on," he said, taking her elbow and guiding her to the couch. "Talk to me."

"The lighthouse. The door was open."

"It wasn't locked? You didn't go in there, did you, kiddo? I told you it's very dangerous—"

She jumped to her feet, "No, Daddy!" she exploded. "I didn't go in the stupid lighthouse!"

"Amber—"

"The hasp was pulled off the door," she continued. "And

as soon as I saw it I was going to come back here and tell you, then I saw the shoes."

Her father rose too. "There was someone in there?" he asked, putting his hands on her shoulders. "Amber, are you all right?"

She nodded. Her lower lip had started trembling and she tried vainly to stop it. "It wasn't a someone. It was a *something.*"

He waited.

"I saw it, Daddy."

"Saw what, honey?"

"The sea captain. Like . . . like the doll." Suddenly, all the earlier terror hit her like a dead weight. "It wa-walked out from behind the d-d-door and it reached for me." She felt tears streaming down her face. "It was all bloody and it didn't have a head. It's neck was . . . was all torn up and—and there was th-this b-b-bone sticking out."

He pulled her against him and she allowed herself to sob against his shoulder. Finally, when she was cried out, he led her into his office and sat her down in his big desk chair, then picked up the phone. "Eric has seen it, too, kiddo," he told her as he punched in a number. "I think he might be helpful."

She doubted that. But, already, she felt a little better. *I'm Amber Masters and I'm not afraid of anything.* She'd been telling herself that since she was five years old and saw a candlestick float across a room in one of her dad's investigations. And it was true, a ghost couldn't hurt her, she knew that, but this one was just so . . . so *gross!* She attempted to smile at her dad as he waited for someone to answer at Eric's mother's house. She couldn't let him worry about her or he might insist on sending her away. And then he'd *really* be lost to Theo Pelinore. "It just startled me, Daddy. It was like something from a horror movie, you know?" Her voice sounded stronger. "I'm fine. I don't need any help."

"Well, at least let's get Eric to describe how he sees the ghost. And I want to know if he thinks a manifestation like that could break the hasp. I have a feeling that a human did that."

"Are you going to call the cops?"

"I wanted to talk to Chief Swenson anyway. This might be the right time." He paused. "Hi, Mrs. Swenson? This is David Masters. Is Eric around?" He listened, then jotted down a number, said thanks, and broke the connection. "Eric's at his uncle's," he told Amber as he dialed again. "Yes, hello. Chief Swenson? Hi, this is David Masters. May I speak to Eric?"

"Hi, Eric," he said a moment later, then proceeded to tell the young man about her experience at the lighthouse. It didn't sound like Eric was saying much and Amber figured that he didn't want to talk in front of Uncle Policeman. Finally, her dad hung up.

"So?" she asked.

"Eric says he's seen the same thing as you and he sounded really surprised that you saw it. Anyway, he and his uncle were just going out, so they're going to stop by here first. Eric told him about the broken lock and he wants to take a look."

"Does his uncle believe in ghosts?"

"Nope." He gave her a sly smile. "Judging by your story, though, he may soon."

The phone rang, the personal line, and they waited for the machine to screen the call.

"David? This is Theo. I know you're working now, but—"

Amber cringed as David picked up the receiver and said hello.

"Yes," he continued a moment later. "Sure, um hmm. That sounds great, but let me check with Amber first. No, she's sitting right here. No, she *hates* surprises!"

The bitch is up to something!

"Theo would like to take us out to dinner tonight, down to McClinton's in Shell Beach. She says they have the best ribs anywhere."

"She wants to take *us,* huh?" Amber asked dryly.

Her dad put his hand over the mouthpiece. "Yes, us."

"That's only because she knows you won't leave me here alone."

"Amber—"

The doorbell chimed, stopping her from saying something she would have regretted.

"Theo? Can I call you back about dinner?" He chuckled. "Well, you know how it is. I'll call within the hour. 'Bye." He looked at Amber. "Why don't you like Theo?"

"We need to answer the door, Dad."

He rose. "I know. But be honest—why don't you like her?"

"You wouldn't believe me if I told you."

"Give me a try," he said as the bell rang again.

She walked into the hall, then turned and looked at him. "She's a hunter, Dad. And you're a trophy."

To her surprise, he didn't argue, just nodded slightly, as if considering the idea. "Let's get that door."

Twenty-five

Body House: 4:45 P.M.

"Amber," Eric Swenson said as he seated himself on the front steps. "Have you ever seen any of the other ghosts?" He watched Uncle Craig and David as they walked slowly toward the lighthouse. They were gesturing a little while they talked and he could tell they'd hit it off, despite their wariness of one another. He wasn't too surprised. David was a likable man, and so was his uncle.

"How do you mean, 'seen'?" Amber handed him a Pepsi, then sat down next to him and pulled the tab on her own soda. "I know there's a nice ghost in my room."

Eric nodded. "Do you see her?"

"No. Sometimes I smell lavender. And the room feels friendly . . . if that makes any sense."

"It makes lots of sense."

"I've heard the piano play, smelled the flowers, and felt the cold spots," Amber added. "But if you mean have I seen anything else with my eyes, then, no."

"I wonder why you'd see the captain, then." He didn't understand why the echo of the murdered man was suddenly strong enough for her to see: no one else ever saw anything more than a sort of black fog, if they saw anything at all, and he didn't feel that Amber Masters was particularly psychic in any way. On the contrary, she was very similar to her father, in that she also possessed a groundedness that wouldn't let them pick up on certain things.

"Is he dangerous?" she asked.

"He never has been," Eric replied slowly. "But I guess I need to take a look at him before I say no, just to be safe. He's just a leftover ghost. He's not really there."

Amber nodded. "My dad calls them 'reruns,' but it's the same thing. It was really creepy, though. He reached for me. Right *for* me."

"A person is like a flame and a leftover is like a moth. They're attracted to your energy, so sometimes it *seems* like they know you're there."

"Yeah. If it had touched me, would it have been cold?"

"Probably. Or sometimes they can feel exactly like real people, if they're really strong."

"There was a haunting my dad checked out once where this woman kept getting slapped and pinched, all over her body. She was covered with bruises and bite marks. Dad said it was a poltergeist and revenant combination thing," she added.

"Mostly, all that's in Body House are leftovers. I don't know what your dad would call them."

"Mostly?" Amber probed. "What about the ghost in my room? And the other nasty one that got in there with Daddy and you? Are they leftovers?"

"He told you about that?" Eric asked in surprise.

"Yesterday."

"Well, I *think* maybe they're not leftovers, at least not like the others. They might be, but with more direction."

"That makes them revenants."

"Can you explain that to me?"

"Revenants are reruns—leftovers," she amended, "that are directed by a human being, sometimes subconsciously, sometimes on purpose."

"Then they're not revenants. I felt Miss Lizzie when I walked into that room the first time and nobody was here to direct her. Same with the *other*."

"Christabel."

"I don't feel good about saying her name, not even out here. The moth to the flame thing goes double with things like that: if you think about them, you feed them and they get stronger. I think it's good to think about Miss Lizzie, but never about the other one."

They sat in silence for a long moment, watching David and Craig standing near the lighthouse door. A moment later, the two men disappeared inside.

"I wonder why you saw the captain . . ." That question kept eating away at him.

"The doll, maybe?" Amber suggested.

"The doll of Lizzie?" he asked, confused.

"No. The captain doll . . ." Her eyes opened wider. "Oh, you weren't here. You don't know what happened." And with that, she launched into a story about dolls and blood in the laundry room that shocked him and made him wish he understood the implications of her tale.

"Eric?" she asked when he didn't make any comment.

"Amber," he forced himself to say, "Can I see the doll?"

"It's locked up in my dad's desk. When they come back you can." She gave him an apologetic smile. "But if Dad doesn't bring it up in front of your uncle, don't say anything. He gets really paranoid about stuff. I'll make sure you see it tomorrow if that happens."

In addition to seeing ghosts, Eric had always been able to sense things with his hands, so he wanted to touch the dolls. When he was little, he liked to close his eyes and feel colors with his finger tips. It was almost like a guessing game. He nearly always knew what they were and it wasn't because he saw them in his mind or anything. His fingers could *feel* the colors; red felt like hot liquid mercury, orange like a friendly sun. He could detect other things with his hands too, good things and bad, and touching the dolls might be very important.

"Look!" Amber pointed at the lighthouse.

David Masters was already back outside and as Eric watched, his uncle raced out, gun drawn. Both men turned to stare at the structure. Something moved into the doorway, blocking the beams of light that had shone through, and for

Amber's sake, Eric was glad they were too distant to see any details.

Craig yelled something, then fired his gun once, twice. The darkness in the doorway dissipated all at once. After a moment, the two men straightened and slowly began walking back, casting glances over their shoulders every few seconds.

"Come on," Amber said, rising. "Let's go find out what happened."

"They're coming. Let's wait."

"Why?" she asked impatiently.

"Well, Uncle Craig just tried to shoot a headless ghost. He's probably really mixed up about that right now. Let them talk so they can calm down a little."

"I guess that's the smart thing to do."

Her words made Eric feel good.

Twenty-six

Body House: 5:10 P.M.

"I don't believe it," Craig Swenson said as he planted his broad-shouldered body on the couch. "I just don't believe that I saw it."

David slid into the cushiony chair across the coffee table from him. "Neither do I." He shook his head.

"Did you think *I* made it up, Daddy?" Amber asked, her indignation obvious. "Did you think *Eric* made it up?"

David shook his head. "No, kiddo. I believed you both. It's just that seeing it for yourself is . . . Well, it's shocking."

"Tell me about it," Amber said dryly.

Craig Swenson nodded and looked at his nephew. "Eric, I owe you an apology.

"That's okay," Eric said, sitting down on the piano bench.

Swenson looked at David. "When Eric was younger, he told people about seeing things like that—that thing out there. Nobody believed him."

"They thought I was tetched in the head," Eric explained.

"I guess I'd rather think I'm tetched too, than believe my own eyes," Craig Swenson said. "When I felt that hand on my shoulder . . ."

David saw Amber and Eric exchange glances.

"What happened?" Amber asked.

The chief looked at his massive hands, then back at Amber. "Your dad was waiting below while I went up the stairs. It took a while to get up there because they're so rickety, but I finally did, and didn't find a thing. So I came back down, just as slowly, and after I made the last turn and could see your dad waiting below, that's when it happened. David yelled something just as I felt a big old hand dig into my shoulder." He looked at David. "What was it you yelled, anyway?"

"Run."

He nodded. "Good advice. But I turned and came face-to-face—make that face to neck," he amended sickly, "with that *thing.* I just hauled off and socked it, but my hand went right into it like it wasn't there. It was like sticking my paw in a bucket of ice." Uneasily, he ran his fingers through his thick gray-sprinkled blond hair.

"What did the captain's hand feel like on your shoulder?" Eric asked.

"The captain?" Swenson paused, then nodded. "The captain. Well, it felt just like a hand clamping down on my shoulder."

"It could touch him but he couldn't touch it," David explained.

Swenson rose and walked over to the bay window and, again, David was fascinated by the similarities between Eric and his uncle. Swenson was off duty and both were dressed in shorts and bright Hawaiian-type shirts. They were tall, broad-shouldered, muscular types—Amber would class them as California beach hunks—with brilliant blue eyes, and strong jawlines softened by friendly smiles. The chief had a hint of middle-age spread, a little gray peppering his thick blond hair—which appeared to be pulled back into a ponytail hidden under his shirt—and maps of crinkles around his eyes, the result of a lifetime of sun worshipping. David thought he might make an interesting character in some future book.

He ran after the murderer, his zorries flap-flap-flapping *against the boardwalk as he dodged a group of rollerskaters, six women whose tanned, sculpted bodies were framed by fluorescent G-string bikinis that seemed to defy gravity. But Craig had no time for that now. As he passed a sun-sleepy surfer, he flashed his badge and yanked the banana-yellow surfboard from the sand. He ran with it held high above his head until he was less than a dozen feet behind the killer, then, barely pausing to take aim, he hurled the board at his target. Like a torpedo, it found its mark.*

". . . can't report this," Swenson was saying. "I'd be out of a job quicker than you can whistle 'Dixie.' David, you'd be more of an expert on handling this sort of thing than I would anyway. I hope you understand."

"No, Chief—"

"Craig."

"Craig, I wouldn't want it reported. This place would be crawling with the curious." He paused. "What do you think pulled the hasp from the door?"

Craig shook his head. "Just looks like simple vandalism to me. I'll file a report about that. It might be useful if it happens again."

"Who's going to fix it?" Amber asked softly.

"I will." Eric stood up.

"It can wait until tomorrow," David told him. "Nobody will go in the lighthouse tonight—it seems to have its own security system anyway," he added with a sick chuckle.

"We should get going," Swenson said. He looked from Amber to David. "You two been clamming yet?"

"No!" Amber said enthusiastically.

"That's where we're headed. You guys want to come along, you're more then welcome."

"Can we, Daddy?"

"Theo's expecting—" David said, then hesitated. Amber certainly didn't want to see her and he wasn't at all sure any respectable part of his anatomy wanted to, either. A relaxing evening on the beach with the Swensons sounded far better. "Sure," he said. "Let's clam. I just have to make a quick call first." He could feel Amber's smile following him out of the room.

Twenty-seven

Pismo Beach: 8:35 P.M.

Craig poked the dying campfire with a long piece of driftwood. "You remember ever having that much energy?" he asked David.

Masters stared at Amber and Eric as they energetically tossed a Frisbee back and forth on the hard-packed sand near the water's edge. "It's a dim recollection, at best," he said, not without fondness.

Only a slight orange glow at the horizon remained to remind them of the sun, but a brilliant full moon cast enough light across the beach for the kids to see. *Kids,* thought Craig. *I never thought I'd call a twenty-year-old a kid.* He hadn't been much older than Eric was now when he'd joined the force. He glanced briefly at the writer, who seemed to have something on his mind. Craig figured he'd hear about it sooner or later. "Beer?"

"Sounds good."

Craig took two Buds out of the cooler and tossed one over to Masters. He was glad David and Amber had come along. Usually it was just himself and Eric, which was fine, but Eric didn't drink—said it didn't agree with him—and it was nice to share a brew once in a while. As he pulled the tab, he felt a fresh wave of guilt about his nephew. He'd always been close to Eric, like a father really, since the boy's father, Craig's own black sheep brother, had run off eighteen years ago, leaving Holly and her toddler to fend for themselves. But he hadn't believed Eric's wild stories any more than anyone else had. "I wish I'd seen one of those things a long time ago," he said. The fire crackled.

"I think Eric understands."

Eric sees ghosts and this guy reads minds. Craig considered for a moment, then understood that Masters' brain was simply working in the same channel as his: he was thinking like a parent, probably upset as hell he hadn't been there for his little girl when she'd run into that creature. *That hallucination.*

"My first month on the force, a few years before Eric was born, there was an accident on that road near where the High Hooey Center is now." Craig took a long swallow of beer. "It was bad. Really bad. I took one look and lost my dinner on the side of the road. Fisher Cox was a seventeen-year-old punk and, as usual, he was drunk off his ass and tearing around in the hills.

"That day, as far as we could tell, he took a blind curve on the wrong side of the road and plowed into a car, a little tin box of a car." The memory still made him wince. "Car had a family in it, folks from Denver. Parents, a couple of little kids. The wife was eight months pregnant." The beer suddenly tasted way too bitter. "That was back before people wore seatbelts much. The bodies were pretty torn up. Some were thrown clear—we found one in a tree that was growing a ways down the mountain from the road. Some were crushed right into the metal. Couldn't really get 'em out, you know?"

Masters nodded solemnly.

"The father was impaled on the steering column, neat as you like, but the pregnant mother had gone through the windshield, right through it and then through Fisher Cox's windshield, so she was face to face with him. Forehead to forehead." He shivered "Almost like they were kissing, but when you looked closer, you saw that her whole front was sheered off by the windshield glass. In effect, her belly was scalped. The hood of the car had gone off to one side and the skin hung off it like a red flag."

He shivered, then took a couple more beers from the cooler. "We found the fetus all kind of smushed down in the engine."

Purposefully, he opened a fresh beer and swallowed. "A few years later, when Eric was about two, whenever we'd drive that way, I'd notice that he'd cover up his eyes right there at that curve where the accident had been. When he was four, I asked him why he did that."

"What'd he say?"

"That he 'didn't like to look at the bloody, sad people, especially the mommy.' "

"Christ!"

"Yeah, Christ! When he was a little older, he described the people in detail. Fisher, the parents, the kids. At least he didn't seem to know about the fetus."

"So, what'd you think?"

"I did like everybody else in this backward little town and decided he was a little off." Disgusted with himself, he added, "He described what *I'd* seen. I *knew* it was real, but I still wrote the poor kid off."

"That's a normal human response to something we don't understand," David said, opening his second Bud.

"As he grew, he pointed out other things, things no one else saw. Between that and his personality, which is pretty non-aggressive, everybody just began to ignore him." He paused, listening to the kids' laughter rising over the crash of the waves. The tide was coming in. "I realized a long time ago that he wasn't slow, but I still thought he was a little abnormal." Craig tilted the can to his lips and took a long drink. "By the time he was eight or nine, he'd quit telling people about the things he saw, but I could tell that he was still seeing them, you know?"

David nodded. "I know."

"So," Craig continued. "Now *I* see something myself and, I swear, if you and your daughter hadn't seen it too, I'd think I was losing my mind, regardless of Eric. I'd probably run to a doctor to see if there was some sort of insane gene in the Swenson makeup. When I think of what that boy has been through . . ." He was glad it was hard to see around the fire because his eyes were watering like crazy.

"Don't feel too bad," David said softly. "You know now."

"I guess I do."

"Rather than accept that we've come across something we can't comprehend, the human race creates rational answers. And we accept those rationalizations, no matter how ridiculous they are, because they're the only things we can comprehend, at least until we learn something more." David cleared his throat. "It sounds like I'm a little drunk."

"Feels good, doesn't it?" Craig set the can down and stretched. "I get what you're saying and I appreciate it. It's a good excuse for not giving Eric the benefit of the doubt."

"You sound bitter."

Craig shrugged.

"Don't be," David cautioned. "You're only human and, even if being human *is* an excuse, it's a valid one." He set his own can aside. "I'm surprised the Beings of Light haven't pestered Eric, quite frankly."

"They tried, but Eric wouldn't have anything to do with them." Craig chuckled, remembering. "He suggested that someone had started a rumor about his talents and that none of it was true."

"Good for him. I know Theo Pelinore doesn't have a clue about his psychic gifts." He considered a long moment. "I guess he's extra cautious around Minnie Willard."

That struck Craig as particularly funny. "Who do you think he blamed for the rumor? Another beer?"

"I don't know—"

"We'll kill the sixer and that's it." Craig pulled the last cans out by the plastic rings.

"Sure, let's kill it." David opened his can, then sat back and stared at the stars a moment. "I have so many questions."

"Such as?"

"Why isn't Eric allowed to drive?"

"He's allowed. He doesn't like to. I think he sees things, things like that accident I told you about. I think it makes him nervous."

David nodded. "He told me that sometimes he can't tell a ghost from a living person until he gets good and close."

"*I* have a question." Craig belched. "Excuse me."

"Thank God you did that." David burped too, a refined

little city noise with his hand over his mouth. "I thought I was going to explode. So, what's your question?"

"When did he start telling you about the ghosts?"

"About five minutes after we shook hands."

"He doesn't hide it around you." Another belch escaped, but he barely noticed. "Why is that?"

David shrugged. "You know about his other talent?"

Craig tried to think, but it had been so long since Eric had mentioned anything that he drew a blank. "Give me a clue."

"Did you ever notice that your nephew is a good judge of character?"

Scratching his head, Craig thought about it. "Yes," he said finally. "I guess I did, at that. But what does that have to do with it? There are plenty of good people in this town and he's not confiding in any of them."

"Eric has a talent that commonly goes with his other ability. It's called psychometry. He senses a lot about things and people when he touches them. He's told me all sorts of things about the house that he couldn't possibly know—and that I've since verified."

"And he shook your hand and knew you'd believe him?"

"Yes, I think so. He may know that I've seen a number of things no one else would believe. Things I put in my fiction."

"Wait a minute. You're telling me you're like Eric? You've got ESP?"

David laughed heartily. "You're probably more psychic than I am. I work with psychics occasionally, but left to my own devices, I have about as much psychic ability as that Frisbee they're throwing."

"Then how?" Craig was halfway through his third beer and it was making him a little foggy. He hoped he didn't sound too stupid.

"Same way you saw the headless guy today. I just put myself in places where weird things happen."

"On purpose?" Craig was incredulous.

"Of course!"

"Why?"

"It's fun."

"Jesus Christ, you're weird, you know that?" Shaking his

head, Craig added, "Chief of Police, and I about wet myself out there today. And you enjoy it?"

David gave him a shit-eating grin. "Sick, isn't it?"

"Yeah." He turned the can in his hands, then rubbed it against his forehead. "But I'm glad you moved here. You're good for Eric."

"He's good for me. He's so accepting and unafraid." David laughed. "You know when we got back to the house earlier and I disappeared for a minute?"

"Uh huh."

"I *did* lose control out there at the lighthouse."

"No shit?" Craig grinned. He liked a man who had the courage to admit it when he was afraid.

"No shit." David laughed lightly. "Rule number one: always wear black jeans when you go ghostbusting."

Craig laughed. "I'll remember that. You know, I didn't know what to expect with you. I guess I thought you'd be a pretentious snob."

David forced a belch, as if to waylay suspicions. "Why?"

"Famous big time writer, moving into Body House. I thought that was kind of a show-off thing to do."

"I only write bestsellers if I scare myself shitless first. It's the secret of my success. That's why I bought the house."

"You're weird," Craig repeated, not unkindly. "You live in a house like that and you're superstitious?"

"Maybe a little." David paused. "You mentioned the Minnie Willard rumor mill . . ."

"Uh huh," Craig said slowly.

"Am I in it?"

"Sure." Minnie had been spreading some particularly vile stuff about Masters and his daughter and Craig figured he ought to tell him, but really didn't want to. "Minnie talks about everyone."

"What's she saying?"

"I don't pay any attention to her stories. No one with any sense does—we've all been embarrassed by her at one time or another, though some people never learn. She oughta be writing soap operas. A lot of people tune in to Millie, even though they're ashamed to admit it."

"Jesus, what has she been saying about me?" The alarm in Masters' voice was unmistakable.

"Oh, that you're a crazy writer, of course," Craig said lightly. "You won't let her in your office so she figures you've got some really interesting secrets in there. Says old Theo has her hooks in you."

David snorted. "Is that all?"

Craig knew he really should tell him the one about how Masters kept his daughter supplied with sexy underwear. But, he wondered, was it really necessary? Only the handful of old hens that were Minnie's buddies paid any real credence to the woman's stories. One of them, Bea Broadside, the second biggest gossip in town, had gone so far as to call him about it. He grunted something about looking into it, which almost made him laugh while still on the phone, then shamed her, just a little, since he didn't want her phoning anyone else and making trouble for an innocent man. As David had rightly pointed out, he really did rely a great deal on Eric's judgment and Eric had said nothing that made him worry about the man sitting across the fire from him.

"That's about it," he finally said. He hated himself for his lack of honesty. "But if I were you . . ."

"If you were me?" David prompted.

"If I were you, I'd let her go. She's the worst kind of gossip, Masters." He took a deep breath. "Minnie takes a fact, a little bitty fact, and twists and turns it until it's bad."

"Are you trying to tell me something?"

"Let's put it this way. I got married in '89 and Linda packed up and left me in '91. It took me months to find out exactly where she got the notion that I was cheating on her." Old anger boiled at the memory.

"Minnie."

"Give the man a cigar. First, she saw my cruiser parked at Pelinore Realty, then one of her cronies saw it again a week later. Those two times, I really was there—Theo was having some trouble with vandalism at the time and we had two or three calls a week from her for more than a month, until we caught the culprit. Anyway, other officers were there at other times . . . but it just was my turn to be talked about." He paused to take a deep breath. Exhaling noisily, he continued. "Right around that same time, I was sitting in Fran's Cafe having lunch, reading the paper, minding my own business. Minnie and Bea were in the booth across from me. Well, Theo comes in to see Fran about a house she was buying. When she's done, she walks over to talk a minute about the vandal problem. Masters, she never even sat down and it got turned into one of a string of rendezvous, just like the two stops at her office turned into dozens. Linda left me two weeks later. Left a note, but wouldn't even speak to me because her good friend Minnie had advised her that her husband wasn't trustworthy." He coughed. "And that's what Minnie's mouth can do."

"I wonder why Theo even hired her for me. Minnie despises Theo. She must be out to ruin her reputation. Theo must know that."

"She knows. But I have two theories. Maybe one or both are right, or maybe both are bullshit. Personally, I'm theorizing they're both right."

"Well, spit 'em out."

"You told her to hire you a housekeeper, so she took what she could get." He snorted derisively. "Nobody but Minnie would do it. Her curiosity outweighs her fear. That's one theory. The other is, she's blackmailing Theo, so Theo had to hire her."

"What could she blackmail Theo about and why does she hate her so much?"

"Who knows?" Craig asked, then grinned. "Of course, I've got theories on that, too. Minnie was a member of the Beings of Light Church some years back but they excommunicated her—or whatever it is the High Hooey Center does when it kicks you out. Well, that was right around the time that Spiros appeared—"

"Spiros is the 'high being' they claim to channel?"

"She's told you about him, then?"

"Briefly." David nodded. "Very briefly."

"I figure they were afraid she was going to tell who the channeler was, so they dumped her. And that pissed her off."

"Is she mad at all of them, then?"

"Sure she is, but Theo is a particular target. Seems she gets to all the eligible men before Calla can and 'spoils' them for Minnie's darling daughter."

"Minnie has implied, particularly to Amber, that Theo sleeps around, that she's a golddigger." David shook his head. "But Minnie or no Minnie, Amber hates Theo."

"Most women do. Holly, my sister-in-law, says Theo's predatory. Women sense those things. We don't."

"You've got that right. So, is Theo a maneater, like Minnie—and Amber—say?"

"Let's put it this way. If you get invited into her bed, make sure you've got rubbers. She's been around. I wouldn't take any chances."

"Rubbers." David chuckled. "Haven't heard that word for a while. All us aging big city baby boomers say condoms, so no one'll know how old we are. I say condom, but in my head, it's still rubber."

"Guess I'll have to say that too," Craig said. "You ever see the old-fashioned kind?"

"What do you mean?"

"My granddad had this rubber. This *one* rubber. He kept it in a wooden box by his bed and when I was ten, he decided to explain the facts of life to me. He took that thing out of the box and kinda waggled it in my face, you know? And then he explains to me how you had to be careful to wash it out every time you used it, and how you needed to dry it and talc it. I was horrified—my grandfather was having sex with my grandmother."

Masters guffawed. "What an awful thought!"

"It still is," Craig chuckled. "When he picked the thing up, talc flew out of it, and there were water stains—fresh ones—in the wooden box. A kid doesn't need to know his grandma and grandpa are still doing the wild thing. And you should've seen this thing. It was as thick as a plumber's glove. You wouldn't even know you were having sex." He laughed. "It warped me, Masters, it truly did."

"Can I ask you something?" David's tone was serious.

"Shoot."

"Why did Minnie try to break up your marriage?"

"Try? My friend, she did it up brown. My own theory is that Minnie wanted to get rid of Linda. She never liked her—" He grinned. "Like you, she was from the big city, which is a pretty exotic thing to Minnie, who claims never to go anywhere. Anyway, as far as she was concerned, Linda waltzed in here and stopped her plans to fix me up with her daughter. After Linda left, she went back to trying to matchmake me and Calla."

"I'm sorry."

"No. It was a lousy marriage anyway. If it hadn't been, Linda would have trusted me, at least enough to hear my side. So, in a way, the old bat did me a favor." He finished off his beer. "Has Minnie tried to fix you up with Calla yet?"

"I've been given the sales pitch a dozen times." David groaned. "And Calla keeps leaving phone messages about interviewing me for the paper. She's left notes on the door and she's come over when her mother's there. I guess I can't avoid her forever, but . . ."

"How the hell do you avoid her now?"

"I screen all my calls, and I lock myself in my office all day." He grinned sheepishly. "I got nasty with Minnie early on after she came into my office without knocking, then I followed up by making sure she knew about the lock I installed. Amber then explained to her that I'm a monster if anyone disturbs me during working hours. A regular Jack Torrance."

"Jack who?"

"Jack Nicholson in *The Shining*."

"The maniac writer." Craig nodded appreciatively. "That's nothing *I'd* want to mess with."

"Let's hope Minnie continues to feel the same way. But I think I'll just let her go. I knew I should—I just didn't want to do any housework."

"You might ask Eric about working more hours for you. He's got a part-time job at the bait shop that he would love to give up."

"I'll ask him. Thanks. So, tell me about Calla. You were going to marry her?"

"Lord, no. Minnie thought I should. I'd about rather turn gay."

"Bad news, huh?"

"She's not exactly ugly or anything, just homely. Real skinny, with a long horsy face. Wears granny glasses."

"How unfortunate," David said.

"And she fucks with her hair. It's always different and always looks like a cat threw up on her head. It's always short, but sometimes it's brown, and sometimes red. Once she frosted it so she looked a lot like the Bride of Frankenstein. She cuts it herself, too, and sometimes little chunks are gone out of it. Then, when that happens, she perms it so it looks like an Afro from the seventies. The boys at the station have a pool every week on Calla's hair." He grinned. "I won last week."

"She sounds horrible."

"Yep. She's sort of got this rebellious save-the-world attitude that you'd expect from a college kid. She handcuffed herself to a trash can once to protest rising refuse bills. Had a photog from the paper take pictures and wrote up a story trying to accuse my men of brutality. Since half the town witnessed the event, she just did herself a big disservice. She's the bee in your bonnet type, always looking for causes no one else cares about. Calls herself a liberal or a socialist or a humanitarian, depending on her mood. Always shows up in old jeans and Hawaiian shirts. Wrinkled ones. I mean, this is California, we don't much care, but she wears this stuff to weddings because it's 'her right,' as she says."

"Old hippie," David observed solemnly.

"You've got it. The worst thing about Calla, though, is her earrings. Now, understand, I've been here most of my life. Went to college in San Luis Obispo and I get out to LA or Frisco once in a while, but basically I'm a socially ignorant country boy. But even I know those earrings of hers must come from inside cereal boxes. They're big and they're cheap and she has a million of them. That's Calla."

"You haven't mentioned her qualities as a writer," David said dryly. "Her mother told me she's written fifteen books and volunteered me to read them so she can get published."

"Lord have mercy on our souls," Craig said with false fervency. "She once had an offer to sell one of those books. It was a long, long time ago. You know what she did? She wouldn't sell it because they said there'd be some editing."

"There's always some editing."

"She said it was perfect the way it was and if they were too stupid to see that not one word should be changed, then they couldn't have it. She wrote a scathing editorial about the publishing industry and selling out in the next issue of the *Guardian.*"

"She sounds utterly charming."

"To the core. And her mother never gives up trying to get her married off. Christ, Masters, I guess I'm just as bad a gossip as Minnie."

"It will go no further, I promise." David hesitated. "Can we change the subject?"

"Please."

"Okay. Do you know if there are any police records still around for the Body House Massacre of 1915?"

"You've been wanting to ask that all evening, haven't you?"

"Yeah, I have."

"There's nothing. Not a scrap. After I became chief, I had a really good look around, but it's all been destroyed. If it ever existed."

"What about doctor's records? Any idea where Louis Shayrock's files got to?"

"No, and not for lack of looking. I thought I'd find out plenty, since the same family's been doctoring around here since God knows when. Keith Shayrock, his grandson, is our doc these days, but all he told me was that his granddaddy died in a fire in 1918. The family feeling is that he was murdered."

"Don't tell me. The fire was in his office and all his records were destroyed."

"Exactly right. You ought to give Keith a call and talk him up a little—you seem to be pretty good at that. Because of my job, sometimes people clam up around me even when there's no reason to." Craig cracked his knuckles with great enjoyment. "Old Red Cay wasn't exactly the most upstanding place in the world, you know, and now and then, you hear talk about how many of Lizzie's customers were Red Cay's most upstanding citizens."

"The mayor and a senator were mentioned as victims," David told him.

"Mentioned where?"

"In the *Guardian*."

"From 1915?"

"Yes. There are several articles. I haven't even finished going through them yet, but—"

"The *Guardian* office burned down three weeks after the massacre, so all the morgue copies were destroyed." Craig lifted his eyebrows. "And all the copies of the papers mentioning the Body House massacre disappeared. Where the hell did you find the papers?"

"There were some boxes in the attic that Eric and I found. They were built to be invisible. The contents date back to 1911, the year Lizzie moved here, and they appear to go on for some time after her death. I'm guessing the retired navy man she left the place to packed the items away."

"Can I give you some advice?"

"Sure."

"Don't tell anyone else about the papers. Sure enough, they'll disappear on you. Copy them and send the originals somewhere safe out of town. Memories are long around here."

"I'll do that. You've done a lot of researching yourself."

"I have. I got interested in the original massacre in 1968, after the hippie slayings."

"Eric mentioned you were there. Was it bad?"

"It was very bad. Not as bad as that fetus stuck in the engine, I guess, nothing could be as bad as that. What got me curious about the old murders was that I'd heard stories about the methods of the murderer and they seemed very similar to the hippies'. Jack the Ripper type stuff. But I couldn't find anything factual to verify it. All we have are word-of-mouth stories and some write-ups in books and magazines to go on, but those mean nothing since they were based on hearsay. No witnesses survived." He looked up hopefully. "You probably know more about the massacre than anyone else. I'd be real interested in taking a look at those articles."

"I'll be happy to make you copies." David grinned. "You can expose the ancestors of half the people in town as part of the scandal. There were a whole bushel of Coxes dipping their surnames that night."

"Really!" Craig laughed, delighted. "Any Swensons?"

"There might have been one, I can't recall offhand, but I'll look."

"Exactly what have you got? I'd sure like to find out about the condition of the bodies."

"I have lists of the victims and the missing persons. I also have a schematic of the locations of the victims, but so far I haven't found any detailing on the murder methods, except for one mention of a Ripper-style disembowelment. I don't really expect to find anything else, either, not in newspaper clippings."

"Probably not." Craig lasped into silence. The murders weren't important anymore, but the fascination held.

"Amber has found several of the missing dolls," David suddenly announced.

Craig looked up in amazement.

"They're in hidden compartments in furniture and walls. You know . . ."

"What?"

"It's probably a coincidence, but . . ."

"Spit it out, man!"

"Yesterday, Amber found an effigy of a sea captain. He didn't have a head."

"Oh?"

"She dropped it and was upset because it broke. She saw a pool of something that looked like blood underneath it and figured it had been filled with a red-colored oil or something. Then she picked it up and it spurted the stuff in her face. She says it was warm and that it tasted like blood." David paused. "It wasn't, of course, it couldn't be, but phenomena can suggest such things. It dried to a powder very quickly. I think these dolls were Christabel's creations—they have very obscene genitals—and I think she used them in her voodoo rites."

"Um hmm," Craig said doubtfully. "So Amber's okay?"

"She was shaken and I offered to move her out of the house, but she refused. She's no newcomer to weird phenomena. It's just a little too personal when it gets in your mouth."

"That's an understatement."

"I wonder . . ." David said slowly.

"What?"

"It sounds far-fetched, but I wonder if finding, or even breaking the doll could have some correlation to the appearance of the lighthouse ghost."

That did sound far-fetched, but Craig didn't say so. "Maybe I'm being overly cautious," he began, "but I wouldn't tell anyone about those dolls, either. Things disappear around here—hi, guys!"

"You two looked like you were having so much fun, we decided to leave you alone," Amber said as she and Eric stared down at them.

"Thanks," Craig said. "We grunted and burped and told stories."

"Guy stuff," David added.

"Well, it's almost eleven."

"Holy sh—cow!" Craig said, in deference to the girl. "Last time I looked at my watch, it was eight-thirty."

"Time flies," David said. "Amber, you look frozen to the bone."

"I am. Can we go home now?"

"You've got it." David rose and started gathering their trash while Eric doused the fire.

"Did you have a good time, kiddo?" David asked his daughter as the four walked back to the car.

"Yeah, Dad, great." She grinned. "But you two look like you had a better time."

Masters shrugged, a mildly embarrassed expression on his face.

"You're right, Amber," Craig said, as they reached the car. "We had a good time." He tossed her the keys. "In fact, we had such a good time that you get to drive us home."

She stared at him a long moment, then bubbled, "Sure!" and Craig, bemused, thought she looked like she'd swallowed the proverbial canary.

August 13

Twenty-eight

The Lighthouse: 2:31 P.M.

Eric Swenson wanted to visit the lighthouse by himself, so he waited until Amber had left for cheerleading practice to go out and repair the lock; Minnie was polishing floors, and David was shut away in his office. He'd meant to do it earlier in the week, but there had been no time until now.

Now, as he reinstalled the hardware with thicker, heavier bolts, he felt uncharacteristically nervous and half-wished he'd called David to help him, as the writer had requested.

He finished screwing in the top bolt and started on the bottom. The eerie feel of the lighthouse—of Body House and the entire finger, for that matter—had changed, had grown somehow stronger, so that now there was so much electricity in the air that it practically thrummed around him, filling his ears with thickness, making the golden hairs on his arms stand at attention. *Creepy!* Quickly, he finished attaching the bolt, then hesitated, his hand resting on the latch, and wondered whether to go in or not. After all, he'd come out here by himself for that express purpose. He'd wanted to find out just what had changed. Now, his guts were insisting that he didn't want to know.

Abruptly, the latch turned ice cold under his fingers and with a cry of surprise he let go. "What the heck?" he whispered, staring at the heavy wood-plank door.

It began to shake, almost imperceptibly at first, then harder and harder. Eric stepped back as the new metal fittings began to rattle and the four-inch-thick wood started to creak and groan.

Then as suddenly as it began, the shaking stopped. The silence was huge as Eric stepped forward and laid his hand on the latch. The freezing cold metal now felt nearly normal.

Suddenly, something crashed against the door from inside, a huge, heavy weight. Despite the shock, Eric held his ground. Two seconds passed. Again the door was struck and, as he heard the sound of cracking timber, he leaped backward.

Again and again the force hit the door, until the new bolts were giving way and a crack appeared in one of the planks. One or two more strikes would open it.

"Captain?" Eric called tentatively.

Silence, then a sound like nails scrabbling against the door.

"Captain Wilder?"

More scrabbling, like rat's claws moving over slick pavement, a pause, then thunder as the door was struck again.

Eric sensed frustration. "You want me to open the door, Captain?"

A single rap was the reply.

"Okay, I'm going to open it now." Swallowing hard, Eric stepped forward and depressed the latch, then moved back as the door swung slowly open.

The captain nearly filled the doorway, even without his head. Eric stared, amazed at the changes in the apparition he'd seen so many times before.

Previously, Captain Wilder had appeared to be not quite solid, not quite opaque, allowing Eric to make out whatever was behind the figure. But now, as he stepped onto the threshold, he appeared as solid as any human. And he didn't feel like a leftover anymore.

"Y-you're real, aren't you?" Eric whispered.

Slowly, one pale hand rose and rapped once on the door frame. The blood on the front of the uniform appeared fresh and sticky and a vertebra glinted whitely where the sun hit the neck.

"Are you Captain Wilder?"

Another rap. Then the hand moved toward Eric and gestured for him to come closer. When he didn't move, the apparition repeated the gesture, more impatiently.

"Okay," Eric whispered. Despite the horrifying appearance of the thing, he didn't feel it meant him any harm. He inched toward the ghost, trying not to flinch as its cold hands took his upper arms and drew him to itself. The roaring in his ears increased and his mind was lost in the dark lake of a strange consciousness as he felt the tall, bloody body, cool and solid, against his own.

Twenty-nine

Body House: 2:33 P.M.

When the Masters's and the Swensons had returned to Body House a few nights ago, David had shown them the dolls and let Craig scan through the articles. Eric hadn't been interested in touching the dolls—in fact, he'd refused, apprehension plain in his eyes, even though he'd expressed interest before he actually saw them. David had intended to ask him about it, but the next morning, prompted by a phone call from his editor Joanna, David had left Eric, the dolls, and the crate full of papers alone in favor of getting a chunk of book done.

He'd been making excuses—research being the best excuse—not to get down to serious work on *Mephisto Palace.* No matter what he was working on, the first half of a book took him five times as long as the last half because, until he got over the middle hump, he could never quite shake the notion that he'd started a project that he was incapable of completing.

Intellectually, he knew it was bullshit: he had enough books behind him to know that, but the feeling never quite left him. Until he began writing novels, he'd never in his life attempted a project he couldn't do in one sitting, whether it was a term paper or a crossword puzzle, building a birdhouse or learning to swim. If he stopped before the task was complete, he invariably walked away and never took it up again. It had proven to be a hard habit to break.

He'd learned to control it to some extent by thinking in scenes and chapters, but what had helped most of all was Joanna, who knew his neuroses better than he did. She knew he'd fritter away time, becoming steadily more anxious and depressed with each passing day, and she knew that, around mid-point, he'd turn manically gleeful as the end became a possibility in his mind. During that stage, she'd call him up and remind him to relax, to go see a movie or get laid, or whatever else occurred to her, but more importantly, during the early stages she'd call every couple of weeks, just as she had the other day, and make herself into his confessor whether he liked it or not. She'd give him annoying little inspirational speeches until he broke under the need to confess his lack of production to this angel of a woman. Or maybe she was a devil. Either way, the Catholics had it right: confessing felt good. The one she'd extracted most recently would be good for a couple of weeks worth of good, hard work, and that would get him over the top and into the manic phase he loved in no time at all.

He smiled at the screenful of words, knowing that if he kept going at the current rate, he'd be on over the hump in less than a week. In fact, he realized as he tore back into the keyboard, the manic phase was perhaps already in its first stages. As hard as it might be on his body, it felt really, *really* good. By the time he finished the book a few weeks—or sometimes only a few days—later, he'd look about five years older, but in a month or so, about four of those years would disappear. He didn't begrudge the book the other year: the devil always demanded his due.

After this latest confession, Joanna had told him the same story about Melanie as Georgie had and every time he remembered it, he lost his train of thought. Just like now.

So call her! His fingers remained poised above the keys. *Thank her for her selflessness and get her out of your system! Stop wasting time, Masters!*

He didn't want to give in and call her, though, so he tried to concentrate on the book. But it didn't work. *Melanie did something nice and you should acknowledge that. It's the only polite thing to do. Call her, say thank you, and hang up.* Then: *No! You broke clean, keep it that way.*

Now he watched his hand pick up the phone, and sat helplessly by as his fingers pushed her number, evil fingers with minds of their own. He listened to the phone ring and smiled as her answering machine granted him a reprieve. The machine was the answer: he could thank her without having to actually speak with her.

The machine beeped at him. "Hi, Mel, this is David. I just called to say thanks. *Throw Meat Blaisdell out and come back to me!* Ignoring his thoughts, he said he hoped she was well, and that he and Amber were fine, then hung up.

Okay. Write! But it still wasn't working because he missed her and she'd done something that made him think they might have a chance together.

It wasn't sex—between the continuing wet dreams and Theo's constant attempts to seduce him, sex wasn't high on his list of priorities. He'd turned down several invitations from the real estate agent in the last ten days, though he had agreed to see her two nights from now, when Amber was again spending the night at Kelly's. But he wasn't at all sure he was looking forward to the liaison. Theo and her claws were, perhaps, more than he could handle.

But you have to give it a chance. You have to get Melanie out of your system.

Heaving a sigh, he decided he needed a Pepsi, then remembered that Minnie was out there and decided maybe he didn't. It was ridiculous, being a prisoner in his own office, but if he so much as stuck his head out, she'd grab his ear and twist it with a barrage of words.

He'd decided to fire her at the end of the week, but thought he'd give her a chance to earn some extra money first—*and let's be honest, save myself some trouble*—by asking her to wax the floors and generally get the house in shape before a regional magazine came to do a piece on him and the house. He didn't think it would be a smooth move to mention "The Jerry Romero Show." If he did, he'd never be rid of her.

Standing up, he stretched his arms in the air, then reached down to touch his toes. He did it again, then did a few waist twists before bending his neck backward and forward until his stiff muscles started to relax. The phone rang as he was about to sit down. *Melanie?* He turned the sound up on the machine and waited.

"This is Keith Shayrock returning your call. If you want to make an appointment, please call between—"

"Dr. Shayrock?" David said, snatching up the phone. "I wasn't calling about an appointment. Well, not a medical appointment . . ."

Shayrock cleared his throat. "You have me at a disadvantage. I'm afraid you left your number but not your name. Do I know you?"

Good thing he's not a shrink, he'd want to commit me. "I'm sorry, no, you don't know me—"

"I buy my supplies from American Med—"

"I'm not selling anything," David interrupted, afraid the man was getting ready to hang up on him. "Craig Swenson suggested I call you. My name's David Masters."

"Oh!" Shayrock's voice warmed. "I know *who* you are, at least, Mr. Masters. What can I do for you?"

"I'm researching a book and Craig thought you might have some information I haven't been able to locate."

They spoke briefly and, as David hung up, pleased that he would be visiting Shayrock the next day, someone pounded on his door.

Minnie, you insufferable monstress!

"Mr. Masters! Open up!"

"Eric?" he called, surprised.

"Let me in!"

Quickly, he crossed the room and unlocked the door. Eric was a mess, his hair and eyes equally wild. "Eric? What happened?"

Eric entered, Minnie on his heels. David stopped her with a gentle hand. "That will be all, Minnie."

"But—"

"Why don't you call it a day? Yes, call it a day and go on home." He gently but firmly shut the door in her face, turned the lock, and looked at Eric.

"He wants his head!" the boy cried loudly. "He needs it and it's in here!"

"What?" David asked in confusion.

"The captain. Captain Wilder, in the lighthouse. He wants his head. It's in here. He wants it *now!*"

"Shhhh!" David glanced at the door, certain that Minnie was eavesdropping, then grabbed Eric's arm and pulled him to the other end of the room. "Don't say another word," he ordered, as he directed him to the chair next to the desk.

"But—"

"One more second." David switched on the stereo and the room filled with the brilliant sounds of Verdi's *Requiem* Mass. Not even Minnie would be able to hear them over that.

"Okay. Now you can talk."

"He wants his head!" the boy repeated excitedly.

David shook his head. "I don't understand. Start at the beginning."

"I went to the lighthouse to fix the lock, and—"

"I thought we were going to do that together. It's not safe—"

"I needed to go alone so I could figure out what's going on. It's safe."

David held his tongue, knowing that what Eric said was true. Besides, he didn't really want to see that headless monstrosity again—he'd only said it out of prudence. "What happened?"

"The captain told me he wants his head."

He doesn't have a mouth, he can't tell you anything. David felt the beginnings of a hysterical giggle building. "He *told* you?"

"In my head," Eric explained, looking at David as if he were a total imbecile.

Embarrassment blessedly killed David's impending snicker. "You said that the captain's a leftover. How could he communicate with you?"

"He *was.* He isn't anymore."

"I don't understand."

"I don't either, not exactly, but I know that's why you can see him. Anybody could see him now, Mr. Mas—David." Eric gazed steadily at David. "He showed me a doll. In my mind," he added quickly. "It's head was gone. He needs it."

David opened the desk drawer and pulled out the bags containing the two effigies. He held up the broken one, though it was half-hidden in the reddish dust. "This doll?"

Eric nodded. "Most of him got out when it was broken."

"What do you mean?"

Eric shook his head, his frustration obvious. "Captain Wilder was a rerun until the doll was broken. He was in the doll. Most of him."

"Him? You mean his soul? His *spirit* was in the doll?"

"Yes. But not all of it. He needs me to break the head so he's all put together again."

They're coming to take me away, ha ha, he he, ho ho . . . The giggle grew and freed itself in a little hiccup. David swallowed. "And did he tell you where the head might be?"

"In there." Eric pointed at the trunk containing the papers.

"I've been nearly all the way through it, Eric. There's nothing in there but papers. I would have seen a doll's head."

"It's in there," Eric insisted. "Underneath."

David rose and crossed to the trunk. "Let's see." Carefully, he bent and lifted out the last few papers, a bare half-dozen. "That's it. There's nothing else in here."

Eric squatted down next to the tall box. "Tap the side, right where the bottom is."

David did, then looked at Eric.

"This is where you tapped," Eric said, pointing at a spot about a foot above the floor.

"It has a false bottom . . ." David said in amazement.

"I think the others do, too." Eric patted the box around the outside, then reached in and felt around.

The other five cartons lined the opposite wall and David glanced at them in wonder.

"There!" Eric whispered triumphantly. "It's open."

He lifted out several dolls, each wrapped in unbleached muslin, and handed them carefully to David, one at a time. Gently, David satisfied his curiosity by partially unwrapping them, and saw that two were feminine. One had a noose around its neck, though both appeared to be in perfect condition. The third was a detailed likeness of a portly balding gentleman with white sideburns and Ben Franklin glasses. David smiled as he placed the dolls one by one in his file cabinet.

"That's all," Eric said.

Hearing that, David locked the cabinet. He glanced at the two bagged dolls he'd been keeping in the drawer, and moved to put them in the cabinet too, but Eric crowed triumphantly and David turned to look. The boy held up a little china head, complete with whiskers and an old time sea captain's hat.

David held his hand out and, reluctantly, Eric handed it over. The masculine face was perfectly executed, with a hawk nose and deep-set eyes beneath bushy eyebrows. The expression looked hearty, perhaps even friendly. "This is beautiful."

"We have to smash it, just like the rest of the doll is smashed."

"We can't—"

"We have to!" Eric's words rang out forcefully.

"Look, I need to see—let's take it to the lighthouse together. I need to understand this better. I need to see it."

Eric considered. "Okay. He won't mind. We need to hurry. He hurts."

Immediately, he walked to the door, opened it and strode into the hall. David, suddenly giddy with excitement, followed, pulling the door closed behind him.

Thirty

Body House: 3:23 P.M.

Minnie watched David Masters and Eric Swenson until they had run nearly a third of the way to the lighthouse, then returned to Masters' office. She hadn't heard much of the conversation, thanks to that damned opera music, but it was something about dolls and that old story about the headless ghost. The retard was about out of his mind over it and Masters had caught his madness.

Gingerly, Minnie tried the door and, just as she'd suspected when she'd clandestinely watched them race from the room, the writer had forgotten to lock it.

It was about time! She tiptoed into the room, absently rubbing her hands together as she surveyed her surroundings. The music played on, rising and falling as a herd of female cows, probably wearing metal bras and horns on their heads, caterwauled in some foreign language. Minnie moved quickly to the open crate and bent over, peered into it, but saw nothing. "Damn!" Suddenly, she jumped as the caterwauling turned practically into screams.

"Damn!" she spat again, then went to the hi-fi and pushed a button. Nothing happened. She tried another, squinting to read the tiny print, to no avail. She needed her reading glasses, but didn't want to waste time digging them out of her purse back in the kitchen, so she just kept trying until, finally, the hollering ceased. "That's better," she muttered as she noticed a painting of a gas station hanging on the wall. She whistled air through her teeth. "Crazy writer."

She crossed to the file cabinet because she'd distinctly heard him open and close it while the music was low. "Damn!" It was locked. Glancing briefly at the bookshelves, hissing in disgust at some of the pornography there, she pulled one book down. It was titled *The Book of Erotic Wisdom.* "Filth!" She flipped a few pages, pausing to study a drawing of an Oriental couple doing *it.* The man's *thing* was the size of a tree stump, and it had veins. It was stuck in the woman's *thing,* which was stupid because nobody could take the pain of a *thing* that big. She turned the page and found a picture of a native carving of a fat, squatting woman with huge bosoms. A head was sticking out of her *thing.* "Disgusting!" These pictures were even worse than the ones in the stained glass and they proved to her that David Masters was a sick man and his daughter should be taken away from him.

She put the book back, and indulged in rubbing her hands together again before she picked up one called *Jung On Sex and Death.*

Several more obscene books later, she realized time was passing quickly and she approached the desk. The best stuff would be inside, and she tried several drawers, but they wouldn't open. The sick bastard had thought to lock them, just like he had the file cabinet.

"What are you hiding, David Masters?" She scanned the desk top and, near the computer monitor, she noticed a couple of plastic bags. "Um hmm."

Delighted, she picked up the first, but it was a filthy thing, full of red dust and a broken doll. That couldn't be what they were talking about, could it? She picked up the other bag, and gasped as she caught sight of the male figurine inside it. It was all in black, with jet hair and beard, and it seemed to glare at her. It had to be one of the dolls from Lizzie's collection—and that meant it was worth a fortune.

Faintly, she heard the front door open and, she was pretty sure, voices. She glanced around quickly. The music was off, the door was open, and she was in serious danger of being found here if she didn't get out of the room in a hurry. Rapidly, she lifted the skirt of her flowered dress and stuffed the doll in the front of her LadyQueen panties. If she did get caught, at least she'd have the doll to sell, and if she didn't, well, things disappeared in this house all the time. *He'll blame it on the ghosts.* Nobody with the morals of a man like David Masters deserved to own it anyway. She crossed to the hi-fi and stared hard at it. "Damn," she muttered as the voices drew closer. They might be close to this hall by now. She ran for the door and plowed straight into Eric Swenson. Behind him, David Masters stood glaring at her.

"I—I heard something," she sputtered. "I think it was a ghost or something. It was in here, it—"

"Minnie," the writer said with extreme calmness, "Write your hours down for the week and leave them on the kitchen table. I'll mail you your check."

"But—"

"Your services are no longer required." The fire blazing in his eyes belied the softness of his voice.

"That's not . . ." *Fair,* she was going to say, but something made her reconsider. In a hurt voice, she asked, "Don't you trust me?"

"No, I don't."

His voice was even quieter this time and she decided to get while the getting was good. She'd have her revenge later. With a sniff, she walked past them to write down her hours, plus a few more, to get her purse, and to leave. "Pervert bastard," she whispered under her breath. "Dirty pervert bastard."

August 14

Thirty-one

Office of Keith Shayrock, M.D.: 10:45 A.M.

"Would you like a glass of water, Mr. Masters?" The receptionist, a pleasantly plump fortyish blonde, gave David a sympathetic look. "You don't need to be nervous. Doctor's very nice."

"Oh, I'm not—" David stopped himself from saying more. If Shayrock hadn't told his nurse why he was here, then he shouldn't either. "I'm fine, thanks."

"Doctor will be ready for you in just a few minutes. He had an emergency ear infection he had to fit in."

David nodded sagely, picked up a dog-eared copy of *People,* and pretended to read. The office was located on the ground floor of a beautiful Stick Victorian, and it had a comfortable homey feel to it. But doctors' waiting rooms always made him nervous, even when he wasn't in one for health reasons, and true to form, his body was busy subjecting him to a typical anxiety attack. His hands and voice both trembled, ever so slightly, his mouth and throat were dry as dust, and he knew from experience that his complexion had most likely turned school paste white.

It was ludicrous. He'd been fine when he interviewed a warden in a state prison, a mortician in his parlor, a survivalist in his lair, even a serial killer in his cell. But give him a doctor in a medical office and he turned to putty.

Unless, of course, he was still reacting to the incident at

the lighthouse. Yes, maybe that was it. *Be honest, my boy. You can't blame more then a trace of this on yesterday. Face it, you're a hopeless neurotic.* He smiled slightly. At least that was preferable to being a hopeless schizophrenic. Some day, when he got enough nerve to really research the project, he'd exorcise his fears with a book about evil doctors.

For now, though, he turned his thoughts bask to yesterday's events. At the lighthouse, he'd seen something that he couldn't describe. It was both paranormal and metaphysical, part B-horror movie and part divine enlightenment. He turned the magazine page. What he had experienced was, he realized, beyond his comprehension.

The headless ghost, resplendently shocking, had stood in the open doorway, almost as if it was waiting for them. Eric had immediately gone to it, totally unafraid. David expected it to pass through the young man as Lizzie's wraith had done to him last month, but rather it embraced the young man, as if it were a real physical being. Then it let him go and when Eric stepped back, David saw that there was no blood on his clothing, though it oozed, wet and slick, on the phantom's shirt front.

Carefully, Eric had placed the doll's head in the entity's extended hand. The creature had stroked it with one finger, in a gesture very nearly tender, before closing its fist around the orb. David heard the sickening crunch of breaking china, saw blood drip from the ghost's fist onto the floor of the lighthouse, and watched the broken bits of glass pepper the red puddle on the floor.

It was then that thc most amazing thing happened. As he and Eric stood by, a swirling darkness appeared above the creature's neck. In awe, David saw it form into a primitive face, a shadowy suggestion of mouth and eyes and nose, then slowly, resolve itself into a perfect replica of the doll's features, with the same bushy brows and thick brown beard, the same captain's hat. The eyes, bright blue, focused on him. David would have sworn that they not only saw him, but that they held sparks of keen intelligence.

He'd never seen anything like it. The sailor's face was friendly, but sorrowful in a way that nearly overwhelmed

David with emotion. "Captain Wilder, I presume?" he asked softly.

In reply, the spirit doffed its hat with old-fashioned gallantry, then gestured for him to approach.

"Can't he come out of the lighthouse?" David whispered.

Eric shrugged. "He wants to talk to you. Go ahead."

David took a tentative step forward. The spirit waited. Finally he took another, then another, and then he was inside the bright and shadowy lighthouse. The phantom reached out and grasped his forearms, pulling him toward itself. Its touch was cool, but not unpleasantly so and, as David was drawn into its embrace, he was relieved to see that the uniform was now without blood.

He thought that the creature would ingest his energy, as Lizzie had done, but he was wrong. Instead, he saw pictures, fleeting images, sent from the captain's mind to his, images of a woman in green with flashing eyes and fiery hair, feelings of love, of sadness, sounds of laughter and tears; so much and so many that he thought he would faint within this whirlwind of emotion.

Then the phantom let go of him and the images drained away, but David retained the sights and sounds and he still felt the richness of the emotions of a man dead over three-quarters of a century.

"Mr. Masters? Are you all right?"

David's brain snapped back into gear as he took in the speaker's white jacket. Stethoscope arms hung around his neck, the business end in his pocket, like a chameleon on a leash. "I'm fine," David said as he rose. "Just gathering wool."

"Keith Shayrock," the man said, extending his hand.

"David Masters," he replied, taking the hand.

"Sorry about the wait," Shayrock told him as they shook hands.

"No problem," David told him. Shayrock was a young man, tall and lanky, handsome in an unusual way with his strong jaw, piercing green eyes, and thick carroty hair that he'd tried, not altogether successfully, to imprison in hair spray. When the man smiled, dimples appeared, making him look about twelve years old.

"Let's talk in my office."

Down the hall and past the exam rooms, Shayrock's office proved to be a sprawling masculine throwback to Victorian times. A brass lamp with a green glass shade illuminated the massive walnut desk, and bookshelves lined the wall behind it. Several duck decoys peeked out from among the books. Paintings of fishing boats and trawlers, simply and elegantly framed, ornamented the wall above a tufted leather couch on the left wall. The carpet was deep forest green and a humidor on the desk held half a dozen pipes. The room reeked of testosterone.

"Have a seat." Shayrock gestured at the leather chair in front of the desk as he moved to his own, behind it.

David sat. "Nice office."

"Thanks." Shayrock took a pipe and began filling it. "I'm fond of it." He lit the pipe and leaned back in his chair. "So what is it I can help you with?"

"I'm researching the Body House murders and Craig told me all the records, including your grandfather's, were destroyed."

"They were." Shayrock puffed his pipe. "So I probably can't help you much."

David nodded. "I was hoping to talk to you about the 1968 murders."

"Swenson would have the police reports, and the coroner's reports. That's more than I have."

"Yes. I was hoping for a more personal touch. I wanted your impressions, but . . ."

"I'm too young?" Shayrock stroked his chin. "My father was the doctor of record. He died five years ago."

"I'm sorry."

"But I saw the bodies," Shayrock added softly.

"You did?" David didn't bother to hide his surprise.

"I did. I was in the fifth grade at the time, but I watched my dad do the autopsies."

David felt his jaw drop. "You were, what, twelve years old?"

"Ten."

What kind of a sadist would bring a child into an autopsy room? "If I'd seen something like that at that age, I'd have ended up in therapy for life," he said slowly.

The doctor chuckled. "You don't understand. I *wanted* to be there. The only thing I ever wanted to be was a doctor. At first I had to beg him. Then he began teaching me. He'd quiz me as he worked. Sometimes he even let me assist."

David shook his head slowly. "I'm sorry. I just can't imagine a child *wanting* to see a dead body."

"Frankly, I preferred watching surgical procedures." Shayrock smiled nostalgically. "Though he wouldn't let me assist, of course."

"That's . . . incredible."

"What's so incredible about it?"

"Bodies are . . . disgusting. I'd lose it. All that blood. All those organs."

Shayrock twined his long fingers together on the desk blotter, his eyes twinkling with amusement. "The human body isn't disgusting. It's beautiful, inside and out. A work of art." He paused. "You know how you moved into that haunted house?"

"Yeah?"

"You couldn't get me to spend a night in that place for a million bucks. *I'd* end up in therapy for the rest of *my* life." He shrugged. "You know, different strokes."

"Point well made." David smiled. "So, what can you tell me about the bodies?"

"What do you want to know?"

"Craig mentioned that he was pretty sure the murders were very similar in style to the ones in 1915."

"Very likely, but I can't give you any solid facts. My father only knew what his father told him, and he was very young when Grandfather died. The 1915 murders and the 1968 killings were both done with, you might say, a certain Jack the Ripper ambiance."

"Does anything particularly stick out in your mind about the bodies you saw?"

"Yes. They were all killed within a one hour period. The

most interesting, professionally speaking, was one that had been operated on with almost surgical precision. It was a heavyset male, found on the dining room table. He had been eviscerated with great skill." Shayrock paused, studying David. "The intestines were strung on the chairs all around the table, like a garland. The victim's tongue had been removed—Dad found it in the victim's rectum. Is this too much for you?"

Obviously, Shayrock hadn't read any of his books. "No. It's right up my alley. So to speak. I'm only squeamish when it involves me personally. Please, go on."

"The scrotum had been opened and the testicles removed. The man's eyes were placed in the scrotal sack and the testicles were in the eye sockets. The penis, which showed signs of recent ejaculate, had been sliced in two, from tip to root."

David crossed his legs. "The victim was killed before he was mutilated, right?"

Shayrock, who had been staring at the ceiling as he recited the death report, looked at David in surprise. "Yes. How did you know?"

"It sounds crazy."

"I won't tell."

"Well, a friend of mine, a gifted psychic, has seen the apparition a number of times in the dining room. He usually describes it as crawling on its hands and knees along the table. It's a sloppy, fat male with brown hair and beard and baggy jeans that hang too low. He calls it "Buttcrack the Ghost" and it's evidently a pretty silly sight."

"You've described the man," the doctor said. "But how did you know he died before the injuries were inflicted?"

"If he had lived through the torture, chances are good that my friend would see something like you described. Something to kill the appetite. That trauma didn't happen, so it's not there to replay." David smiled crookedly. "Now you think I'm crazy."

"No." Shayrock chuckled. "I might, if you said *you'd* seen it, though. I doubt if that victim ever even knew he was in trouble. He had enough LSD in him to trip all of Red Cay and part of Pismo."

Nodding, David asked, "What about the body of the girl found in the downstairs bathroom? Was she tortured to death?"

"The psychic has seen her too, I take it?"

"Yes. Not a pretty sight."

"Of all the six people killed that day, she was the only one who died after torture instead of before. She was also the only female in the group. She was in the tub. Her body had been opened from the base of her neck to the pubic bone, and her heart had been torn—not cut—from her chest. Her fingers had been severed and one of her big toes." Shayrock grimaced. "Whoever did it had a black sense of humor because the toe had been stuck in the tub's faucet."

"What about the rest?"

"Her heart was in her mouth and her fingers were found in her vagina and rectum. Her eyes had been removed and set into her breasts. I can make a Xerox of the reports for you if you want. I, ah, also have the photographs on file, if you want to see them."

Despite himself, David felt ill. "Thanks." He didn't want to look at the photos, but knew he should, assuming they were reminiscent of the 1915 killings.

"Excuse me a moment." Shayrock rose and moved to a pair of tall oak file cabinets. He unlocked one and began rifling through it. "Aha." He took a thick manilla folder out and handed it to David. "Take a look at this, decide what you want copies of, and I'll be right back. There's something else you might like to see, but it's upstairs. In my house," he added. "I'll be back in five minutes."

"Thanks."

The doctor left, and David rather reluctantly opened the folder. The simple clinical descriptions of the atrocities were bad enough, but the photos were the stuff of nightmares. David flipped through them quickly, just so he could say he'd seen them, then returned to studying the descriptions which, he decided, were all he really needed.

Swags of intestines across doors and windows, genitals severed and switched with other organs, it was all there, all sick, and beyond the comprehension of a normal human. The sudden sound of the door opening practically sent him through the roof.

"Sorry, it took me a moment to find this." Shayrock placed a thick, antique photo album on the blotter. "Do you have any more questions about the 1968 murders?"

"Yes. Do you have any personal opinions on those killings?"

Shayrock sat down and rubbed his chin. "I suppose I do. First, the commune members were indulging in some sort of black magic."

"I didn't know that."

"It was kept out of the papers. They'd chalked circles and other symbols on the floor, we found a few dead chickens, some goats' horns, some crystals, stuff like that. The police thought that one of their own members did in the others, but they never found anyone. The commune had probably been indulging in their magic shortly before they were killed. And the most interesting aspect of all this is that whoever murdered them was not consistent in his methods. Some bodies were mutilated with surgical precision, others were hacked and torn. I had the feeling, even then, that the killer got frustrated for some reason."

"Fascinating," David said. "I really appreciate the information."

"You're welcome," Shayrock said, consulting his watch. "My next patient will be here in a few minutes and I want to show you this first." He opened the leather-bound photo album and turned it toward David. Black and white photos, slightly browned with age, covered the black paper pages and captions had carefully been penned in with white ink. "These photos date from about 1910 until 1920. There's my grandfather, Louis, with Robert Lee, the chief of police, in 1912."

Keith Shayrock was a chip off the old block. Same hair and build, same jawline. Robert Lee was a handsome man, also quite tall, with rather Nordic features. He looked slightly familiar. "Are the Lees and the Swensons related?"

Shayrock laughed. "Everybody's related around here, even if they don't acknowledge it. Robert Lee's only daughter, Sarah, married Charles Swenson in 1920." Eyes twinkling, he added, "Of course, many of our citizens have parents or grandparents who were conceived in Body House, but they won't admit that, either."

"Who's this? I can't make out the caption." Hiding his excitement, David pointed at a photo of Louis Shayrock with a portly, balding man with white whiskers.

"Let's see. I believe that's Harrison Cox. He was a public official. The Coxes have always been big in politics. As the story goes, he ran off with his secretary." Shayrock studied David. "You appear excited."

There was no real harm in talking about the dolls, he decided, and he wanted to give the doctor something in return for his information. "I've found some pieces from Lizzie Baudey's doll collection." He pointed at the photo of the mayor. "Including one of Harrison Cox."

Shayrock beamed with delight. "She made dolls of her customers, right?"

"Right."

The doctor chuckled, shaking his head. "If you want, I can come by with this album and we can try to identify some of the others. I've got to warn you, though, there are some old families here, particularly some of the Coxes, who think butter won't melt in their mouths. You can do some serious boat-rocking if you care to."

Judging by the eager expression on his face, Shayrock thought this was a grand idea, and David guessed that the Shayrocks and the Coxes still had problems. "That might be interesting," David said finally. "Though, I'd prefer to keep the collection a secret until it's all put together."

"Naturally. I've got an appointment now," the doctor said, checking his watch. "But I can come by a bit after five today, if you're not busy."

"Five is fine." David stood, shook Shayrock's hand. "See you later."

Thirty-two

Body House: 12:51 P.M.

Amber had spent the morning buying groceries, straightening the kitchen, and finishing up waxing the floors because she wanted to make absolutely sure that Dad wouldn't get frustrated and ask Minnie Willard to come back. If, as he'd said, they didn't stay here much longer, she could handle most of the housekeeping: the sacrifice would be worth it.

As she was rinsing out the mop for the final time, the phone rang, and she raced to catch it before the machine did. "Hello?" she asked breathlessly.

"Hi! It's me."

She felt a little thrill at the sound of Rick Feldspar's voice. "Hi, Rick. What's up?"

"Want to go to the movies tonight?" He paused. "Just you and me? You know, a real date?"

Yes, yes, yes, oh yes! "Um, that would be fun," she said, trying to sound cool. "I mean, I think I'm free." *Yes, yes, yes!*

"Great! Do you need to check with your dad or anything?"

"I'll check, but he won't mind."

"How about I pick you up at five and we'll go get pizza first. The show's at seven-thirty."

"What's playing?"

"The Rialto in Pismo Beach is this great old revival theater. They've got a double feature: *It Happened One Night* and

Ruggles of Red Gap." He hesitated. "Of course, if you'd rather see the new Schwarzenegger movie, we can do that."

Rick was perfect: he even liked the classics better than action movies. "Let's do the Rialto," she said warmly.

"See you tonight!"

Hanging up, she went to her dad's office door and knocked.

"It's open," he called, and she let herself in.

He had dragged all the crates that had contained clothes into the center of the room and now sat on a stool in the middle of them. "You haven't seen the ugly male doll in black, have you, kiddo?" he asked, looking up quickly.

"No. Is it missing?"

"Yeah." He scratched his head. "I can't figure it out. Yesterday, it was right here with the broken one."

"When did you see it last?"

"Let me think. It was on the desk when Eric came running in yelling, 'He wants his head.' "

Amber snickered at her dad's bad imitation. "I wish I'd been here."

He smiled. "Me too. Anyway, Eric got the false bottom open and we got out the dolls and then the head and . . ."

"And?"

"And we went to the lighthouse." His mouth set into a grim line. "And when we came back, Minnie was in here, snooping around."

"She took it, Dad," Amber stated without hesitation.

"She didn't have anything in her hands." He paused. "It's hard to believe she'd do something like that. Just because she's a gossip, it doesn't mean she's a thief."

"Come on, Daddy, grow up! She stuck it down her girdle or something. She's so fat, you'd never see it."

"I just can't believe it . . . But I've spent a whole hour looking for it and it's just plain gone."

"She's got it."

"I suppose," he said finally.

"Call Chief Swenson. Have her arrested."

"Gee, Amber, you're really gunning for her. Why is that?"

No way was she going to tell him about the rat lady's underwear rumor now. "She's a thief," she said simply, as she walked behind her Dad's chair and put her arms around his neck. "And she messed with my father." She kissed him on the cheek, then perched on the edge of the desk.

"I'll tell Craig it's missing, in case it shows up somewhere outside the house—"

"Like at Minnie's."

He gave her a look. "But I'm not going to accuse her of anything, at least not right now." He glanced over at his computer. "I don't need the hassle at this point in the book and, frankly, I'm not entirely sure she did take it."

"Why not? You don't think Eric did, do you?"

"Not in a million years. This house has a history of things appearing and disappearing. It might be here."

She couldn't argue with that. The cake of soap that belonged in the shower in the red bathroom upstairs had vanished three times now. Each time, it had turned up balanced on the bannister leading downstairs. It was an annoying and common phenomenon and it didn't mean much. "Okay, but I still think the rat lady's behind it." She grinned. "For the record."

"For the record." He glanced at the Felix the Cat clock wagging its tail against the wall. "No cheerleading practice today?"

"Oh, no, I forgot about practice!" She could still get there, almost on time, if she hurried.

"Forgot? *You?*" he teased. "That's not like you."

She smiled smugly. "I cleaned the house."

Her father raised his eyebrows in surprise. "Thanks, but why?"

"To celebrate the firing of Rat Woman. Dad, you heard the phone ring a few minutes ago?"

"Yes?"

"Can I go out with Rick Feldspar tonight?" Quickly, she told him their plans.

"Just be home by midnight," he said.

"You'll be here alone," she said doubtfully.

"I'm a big boy now, dear heart. I can take care of myself." He paused, then added, "Keith Shayrock's bringing an old photo album over." He told her about identifying the white-whiskered doll. "We're going to see if we can finger any more customers." He made a face at the nearest crate. "That is if I can figure out how to get these open and get at the dolls."

"Let me try." Without looking, she reached into the crate and started feeling around. An instant later, the bottom slid away and she gently lifted out half a dozen dolls, all wrapped in cloth like little mummies, and handed them to her dad. "I wish I could hang around and check them out with you," she said, opening the next crate.

"So cancel your date . . ."

Amber felt her jaw drop, but her dad only laughed.

"I'm joking, kiddo. You can see them later tonight or tomorrow." He stood, twisting his back to work out the stiffness. "Just show me how you do that magic on the catch, then you can go to practice."

She quickly opened another and handed him five more dolls. "It's easier if I just open them all for you, Dad. You're just not good at things like this."

Within five minutes, all the crates were open and twenty-eight more dolls lay on his desk. Her dad smiled. "What would I do without you?"

"You'd be helpless." She fixed him with her gaze. "Totally helpless. Is it okay if I take the truck?"

"Go ahead. You've earned it."

Thirty-three

Body House: 4:20 P.M.

Unwrapped, the dolls were exquisite works of art, and now that they were safely displayed behind the glass doors of one of the built-in wall cabinets in the parlor, David stood back, arms crossed, and happily studied his finds. He hadn't taken the time to undress any to see if they were Lizzie's or Christabel's work, though he suspected the latter because of the disturbing bulges he felt while handling the males. There were oddities on some of the dolls too—limbs were missing on some, tiny ropes and chains decorated others. On one scarlet-dressed female, a hand was missing and David noticed with some uneasiness that the stump was covered with a reddish substance similar to that on the doll of the headless Captain Wilder. On another doll, a small red hole defaced the center of the forehead. Several others had red lines drawn across their necks that were chillingly reminiscent of slashes on throats. Two had their hands and feet tied with twine.

He'd intended to begin removing the clothing to examine and catalog the dolls, but that was before he'd come across a large, age-yellowed envelope tied to the voluminous skirt of one doll.

He'd forced himself to ignore the envelope until the dolls were in the case since Dr. Shayrock was coming by, but it had been a real test of control. Now, he returned to his office and settled himself in his desk chair, opened the envelope, and withdrew a sheaf of brittle papers.

The handwriting was elegant, but spidery, revealing the advanced age of the writer. He glanced at Felix the Clock and hoped Shayrock would be late, then adjusted his desk lamp and began to read:

To Whom It May Concern:

If you are reading this letter, it means that you have found that which I have attempted to hide—the dolls of Christabel Baudey. I would have burned these creations of the devil, but to destroy them would mean disaster, for the living and the dead.

I am Naval Commodore Maxwell Patton, Retired, and I inherited this cursed house upon the passing of Elizabeth Baudey, my godchild. During her last tortured days on this earth, she explained many things to me and begged me to do as I have done with the dolls.

I must first tell you that, despite her profession, Elizabeth was a fine woman who gave the ladies who chose to work for her every advantage she could. She took in many young women who were otherwise homeless and she never forced any to work as ladies of pleasure. She found jobs in town for those who desired them, so that they might save enough to make their own way in the world. She let others do housekeeping and gardening in exchange for room and board and tuition fees while they bettered their education. Many of the ladies who worked as prostitutes later used their considerable earnings to finance new lives and careers for themselves.

Elizabeth did have a remarkable appreciation for the physical world, it is true, but she was also a fine, fine woman who never deserved to be cursed by that inhuman evil, Christabel.

When Ezra Wilder, the son of my good friend Rear Admiral Joseph Wilder, God rest his soul, agreed to detour his ship the *Golden Horde* to the island where Elizabeth and her child were reported to be living, to bring them to their inheritance, I was joyful. I did not know of the heartache and untimely death I would cause this fine young man.

I had not known if Elizabeth was even alive until she sent a letter to me some years ago, telling me of the hurricane that claimed her father and of her rescue from the water by a village voodoo practitioner. That letter, as well as the handful that followed over the next six years, claimed that she was happily married to that same priest—a man of mixed birth whose background is an utter mystery except for three facts: he had been educated for a time in England; he had come to this village claiming to be sent by the *loa,* the voodoo spirits of the land; and he was utterly, completely charming. Alarmingly so.

I met Christabel shortly after she and her mother arrived at Baudey House and was immediately struck by the girl's beauty, which surpassed even that of her mother. She took after her father, I am told, for she had raven-black hair, a milky complexion, and large, dark eyes that betrayed a trace of Asian blood. Her heart-shaped lips, full and red, were the only feature she had in common with her mother.

Christabel's beauty, as well as her attitude, was that of a grown woman, but where Elizabeth's soul came from heaven, her daughter's clearly came from hell.

She was expelled from school after school. At one, it was said she killed a small dog and ate its heart, raw; at another, she was caught in the act of raping another girl with a hairbrush. I don't know if these things happened, but I would not be at all surprised to find that they were true.

At thirteen, the girl suddenly blossomed into a full-grown woman, and by that time, Elizabeth was teaching her at home, and trying to keep her out of the business.

Prior to realizing the futility of her efforts to properly socialize her daughter, Elizabeth confided to me one day that she had instructed Christabel in the art of doll-making and that the girl excelled at the craft. Her mother had high hopes that, at last, the child would settle down into normalcy.

Elizabeth and Ezra Wilder had fallen in love and, at this time, Ezra proposed. Elizabeth accepted and plans were made to sell the house and move to Florida. Full of hope and joy, she told her daughter, who said she did not wish to move. Elizabeth refused to back down and, soon after, Christabel, who had begun behaving in a charming fashion, created a doll of Captain Wilder. She asked him sweetly for snips of his hair to make it more perfect, and he gladly gave her some.

Two weeks later, she twisted the head off the doll and, the next night, Ezra was found beheaded in the lighthouse. It was not a clean severing, but ragged and horrible, as if it had been twisted off by some great force.

Elizabeth was heartbroken, but found solace in her friends and in her own doll-making. Christabel began to insist on being allowed into the business, but Elizabeth refused and was appalled at the way men would look longingly at the girl as she passed by. She was even more appalled at the way Christabel returned their stares.

In her fourteenth year, Christabel began seducing men behind her mother's back. She liked to take them up to a small room on the third floor where no one would catch her, though once, Elizabeth walked into the room and found her daughter had imprisoned a man. She had tied him so that he could not escape and had whipped most of the skin off his back with a cat-o'-nine-tails. Christabel was furious with her mother for stopping her. The man later said, as did many of his fellows, that he was bewitched by Christabel and could refuse her nothing.

Elizabeth began to realize that Christabel, who had now created many dolls, complete with obscenely vile sexual anatomy, was evidently using them not only as black magic fetishes to control men—and women—causing them to perform perverse acts with her, but also to kill people. More customers, all sailors unknown in these parts, died mysteriously, as did one of the working ladies, a woman known to have argued with Christabel a short time before her death.

In 1915, Elizabeth discovered the exact secret of the

dolls. Christabel, who worshiped the goddess Erzuli, had voodoo powers that exceeded even her father's. She had learned the secret of soul stealing and was using it to increase her power and to insure that she had slaves to do her bidding.

What she did to the dolls to empower them, I do not know, but I do know, for Elizabeth told me, that they were created to store the souls of those she killed. These souls would remain chained to Christabel, and to the land here, for as long as the young woman held power.

Elizabeth suspected this horrible truth, but believed it was fact only when she found an effigy of herself. Horrified, she scratched the arm of the doll. At that instant, her own flesh-and-blood arm began to bleed profusely.

She confronted her daughter, who responded with gleeful threats: if Elizabeth continued to refuse to let her do as she pleased, then she would be sorry, very sorry indeed.

And so, before much time had passed, Elizabeth *was* sorry. One day a few weeks later, as Elizabeth rose from a chair, one of her ankles shattered—snapped, just like that. She fell to the floor, crying out in horrible pain, and her daughter entered the room holding her mother's effigy up so that Elizabeth could see the broken leg on the doll.

Then, Christabel laid the doll down and took a small silver nutcracker from her pocket. She placed the doll's other leg between its teeth. Slowly, she squeezed the handles together, and the pain of it was more than Elizabeth could bear. Finally, the porcelain cracked, as did her mother's other leg. Christabel seemed sorry the process was over so soon.

After that, she did as she pleased because Elizabeth was an invalid. Her legs would not heal properly, and she spent most of her time in a wheelchair, always in great pain. After a while, with effort, she could walk using a pair of canes.

In times past, Elizabeth had made use of the stone cellar beneath the house as a sort of opulent pleasure den where a man might be manacled in velvet and tickled with feathers, a sweet torture that many men desired. The chamber entrances were kept secret, the customers were blindfolded, and only the women knew how to open the doorways.

Though her employees were too frightened to say so, Elizabeth suspected that Christabel had turned the den into a true chamber of horrors, and was killing people down there. One day, she managed to go down and see for herself. Her daughter had done away with the feathers and velvet, turning the place into a hellish pit filled with iron manacles, a rack, stocks, and pillories that had perverted sexual uses that Elizabeth would not describe.

That evening, she secreted herself in a dark corner of the room and watched Christabel as she brought several men down and proceeded to degrade them in the most unimaginable ways. The men offered no protest. Rather, they seemed hypnotized by her, willing to let her do anything—*anything*—to them. Before she let each one go, she sliced his nipple with a small blade and sucked blood from the wound.

As the night progressed, Christabel seemed to Elizabeth almost to glow with a diabolical inner light. At last, she brought down a strong-willed working girl named Jenny. Jenny was in the same hypnotic state of thrall as the men had been and she willingly did as Christabel ordered, undressing and allowing herself to be manacled to an X-shaped torture device mounted on one wall.

After taking her pleasure with the poor girl, in ways so horrifying that even my blunt-spoken Elizabeth could not repeat them, Christabel produced a doll that was Jenny's perfect double.

She undressed it and, as she called upon her dark goddess Erzuli to accept her sacrifice, she plunged a hatpin into the doll's breast. The needle entered the effigy as if it were made of flesh rather than fired porcelain.

Imprisoned upon the cross, the real Jenny's eyes suddenly opened wide and she screamed in agony. For a few brief moments, a hole appeared in her left breast, just over her heart, a bleeding red wound, then, as Jenny's screams died and her breathing stuttered to a halt, the wound disappeared, fading to nothing as if it had never been there.

The doll, Elizabeth saw, had a single ruby drop of blood upon its breast. Christabel extended her tongue and licked it clean. She held it up and admired it, then put her nail to its belly and scratched it. Elizabeth almost cried out when she saw the blood well from the little china body. Christabel again licked it clean, then ran her hand over it while repeating an incantation. When she lifted her hand, the scratch was gone. She redressed the doll and locked it carefully away in a cabinet that contained other dolls, and though Elizabeth could not see them well enough to identify any, she suspected that they represented other missing people.

What the girl then did to Jenny's body was so vile, so foul, that Elizabeth would not speak of it, except to say that Christabel devoured poor Jenny's heart.

The next day, Elizabeth sent for me. It took me some weeks to arrive and when I did, Elizabeth seemed a ghost of her former self. Her physical and emotional pain showed in her eyes, in the way she held her mouth, drawn and tight, and occasionally in the timbre of her voice, yet she never complained.

At her insistence, I carried her outdoors and took her for a ride in her charming little one-horse surrey. She directed me to go to end of Byron's Finger, all the way to Widow's Peak, and even though it was obvious to me that each bump and rut in the path caused her more pain, she insisted we go on and would not speak of anything important until we sat looking out to sea, all alone, where we could not possibly be overheard.

It was then that she told me those things of which I have written here. Those things, and more. In the weeks that passed before I arrived, Lizzie found Christabel's book of spells and now knew exactly how the dolls worked.

Christabel could use them in the typical voodoo way to torture people who angered her, as she did by breaking

Elizabeth's legs. Then, when she tired of that, if she desired she could use them to kill the person and store the soul in the doll. The soul became her slave and each soul she acquired increased her power. According to her grimoire, there had to exist an effigy of Erzuli somewhere. It would be a squat, fecund-looking, primitive doll. This would be Christabel's own house should she lose her physical body during her transformation.

The transformation, as Elizabeth understood it, was a death and resurrection ritual similar to those in many countries and religions (such as those of our own Red Indians). Once she acquired enough souls—enough power—this ritual would allow Christabel to live eternally, always with her slaves to do her bidding.

Elizabeth believed that the only way to stop Christabel and to save the souls she had entrapped, was to *destroy both her daughter's physical body and the Erzuli doll.* Then she would only be a spirit, incapable of doing real harm or of controlling her fellow souls.

If her physical self but not the doll were destroyed, Christabel's spirit would be free to roam, returning to the doll as it pleased. The Erzuli doll would be her safe refuge, a place for her to go to restore her power by drawing it from the stolen souls stored in the other dolls.

If one of those other dolls was broken, totally smashed, the imprisoned soul would be free to manifest within Christabel's realm, though it could not leave as long as she remained, nor could it do anything she did not wish. If she did not want a soul to manifest in the house—such as, I believe, she wished for poor Ezra's spirit—it could not, even though in places it was not forbidden, anyone with a sensitivity to such things might perceive it.

Imprisoned in a doll, a soul manifested simply as a ghost, a chill breeze on a summer wind, something a few people sensed but not others.

Christabel, were her physical body destroyed, would be far more powerful than all of these poor spirits combined, and she would also be able to possess bodies for her own use. Elizabeth thought that as long as the Erzuli doll existed, if Christabel lost her own body and when she found one she wanted to keep, she could oust the rightful soul entirely. She had to be stopped.

With heavy heart, Elizabeth asked me to help her arrange for her daughter's assassination. I agreed. After delivering her safely back to Baudey House, I took my leave to prepare for what was to come.

In San Luis Obispo, I hired two men known to me to be trustworthy in their own ways, and we laid the plans. The next day, I took Elizabeth for another ride and, when we were alone, told her the plan. The two men would allow themselves to be lured into the dungeon and, once below, would dispatch first Christabel and then the Erzuli effigy. One of the other women would then have to release the latch and let the men free. Mariette Cantori, very young but very trusted by Elizabeth, agreed to do this. If the Erzuli doll was not in the dungeon, it would be upstairs in the locked case in Christabel's bedroom. In either case, it would all be over in one night. Christabel's torture chamber would become her tomb.

The night arrived and, honoring Elizabeth's wishes, I stayed away from the house. Prior to this night, Elizabeth instructed me as to her last will and testament, in case anything should happen to her, and also to the removal and storage of the dolls, should the assassination attempt fail. In that case, she asked me to leave this letter with the dolls, in case they should some day be found.

I spent the evening in Barnacle Bob's, whiling away the hours, wishing I could be there to help Elizabeth. But she insisted that bringing my presence to her daughter's attention could easily spell disaster for me. She might quickly fashion a doll—a simple cloth effigy might not satisfy her artistic eye, but it would hold my soul prisoner just as well as the ornate ones—and Elizabeth was adamant that I not let this happen.

At last, with dawn approaching, I rode out to Baudey House and found a scene of carnage so terrible that I, a veteran of three wars, nearly passed out. I saw no sign of Elizabeth or Christabel and so I went up to Christabel's bedroom in the west wing and examined the remaining dolls. Most of them were undamaged and I destroyed these immediately so that no souls would be trapped within. The damaged ones, almost all with drops of blood upon them, I knew held freshly harvested souls trapped within them. These are the dolls that you, my reader, now possess. The effigy of Elizabeth, thank God, was undamaged except for the broken legs. She, at least, had not been captured. Not knowing whether Christabel was still alive, I took this effigy with me to protect it.

Seeing no sign of the men I had hired, I went to the third floor, as Elizabeth had previously directed, and entered a room in the east wing, that overlooks the terrace. There, with heavy heart, I found the mutilated body of poor Mariette Cantori, obviously killed while trying to complete her mission. Nearby, I found the latch that opened the secret door to the dungeon.

Every part of the plan had gone awry, for there, as the door slid open, I saw *her.*

Christabel was on the stairs, and she must have been about to open the door herself. I believe I screamed like a woman, so horrified and surprised was I, for the girl was naked and covered in blood, drenched in it, reeking of death. Her hair was clotted with the stuff and it hung in red plaits over her bloody shoulders and breasts.

In her hand, she hold a heart. Looking at me with her brilliant dark eyes, she murmured foreign words and I realized she was casting her spell upon me.

I forced myself to look away, though I did not want to. I swear to you, dear reader, that I wanted her at that moment, both physically and with my heart, such was the magic that she used on me. I would have done anything for her, but something helped me fend her off, and now I believe that Elizabeth herself was my guardian angel: I shall tell you why in a moment.

Angry at my resistance, Christabel put the human heart to her mouth and bit into it. Strengthened by my guardian angel, I took that moment to draw my blade and throw it at the girl's eye. My aim was true and the dagger, a gift of the Navy for bravery in 1898 during the Spanish-American War, sank into her eye. Snarling like an animal, she tried to pull it out, but it had done its job and she toppled and fell down into the darkness beyond.

Filled with fear, I proceeded downstairs. Bodies were everywhere; bodies dead of torture, and worse. To my surprise, Elizabeth's body was not among them.

There, I also found a cabinet filled with more ensouled dolls, just as Elizabeth had described, though the Erzuli icon was not among them. But I could feel the cold presence of Christabel swirling around me, laughing, smelling so strongly of her favorite perfume, that accursed jasmine, that I nearly vomited.

Feeling that I might faint at any moment, repeatedly attacked by Christabel's spirit, I'm sorry to say that I left the dolls and hurried upstairs. I nailed the dungeon gateway closed, then entered the tower and blasted the other dungeon entrance with dynamite Elizabeth had placed there for that purpose. That entrance shall never be opened, and the well-hidden third floor passage shall be revealed only if you, my reader, decide to do so.

It was 7:00 A.M. when I was done and I hurried from the house after hiding the doll of Elizabeth safely in the wardrobe in her old second floor bedroom, also as she had instructed. (There are hiding places all over the house, in cabinets and furniture, and I often wonder just how many more dolls may be secreted in these places.)

As I made to leave, I noticed the surrey down by the lighthouse and, with heavy heart, I galloped toward it. I found a note from my goddaughter upon the empty seat. Elizabeth had escaped and taken her own life so that Christabel could not rule her in death. At the end of the note was a pointed message that surprised me. It said, "If my effigy is safe, I may have learned enough of the magic to be able to inhabit it in a manner similar to that in which my daughter intends to use the Erzuli figure. Though I could not be as strong as her, I vow to stay and protect you and those who follow from her evil influences. I shall do this until she is destroyed and until the souls already entrapped by her are freed. I shall stay until Ezra and I are united again, in death, if not in life."

And that was that. In due course, I inherited the house, as I knew I would, and I slept in Elizabeth's bedroom, which often smelled faintly of her favorite lavender sachet. I turned the place into a veterans' home, but Elizabeth was not strong enough to protect the entire house. Tragedy after tragedy befell us and many men told me of a succubus who visited them at night, though not many of them considered that part such a tragedy.

I often wished I had the sort of mind that could communicate with the spirits because I have often wondered if Elizabeth's strength might increase if the doll was destroyed. I dare not try, since it might just as well destroy her as empower her.

As I write this I make ready to depart. I closed the house a few months ago. Most of my boarders have died or moved away and my health is not what it once was. Though it distresses me to leave Elizabeth alone in this cursed house, I can stand the atmosphere here no longer. Surely, I tell myself, she understands.

I have failed to locate the Erzuli effigy, though I have tried and tried. The one place I did not search well was the dungeon, for I hadn't the heart to return to that hell hole after the brief search I conducted on the night I murdered Christabel.

If you, the finder of these notes, wish to remain here, (though I would not advise it), you must try to find the Erzuli icon and destroy it. It is the only way to weaken Christabel's hold on Baudey House and to release the innocent souls trapped within this place.

While you live within these walls, protect yourself at all times. Do not be seduced by the demon's wiles. Having failed to save the souls of Elizabeth, Ezra, and the others, I can only tell you now that, as long as I am living, and in the eternity thereafter, I will pray for those who are imprisoned and for those who would free them. May God have mercy on your soul.

Maxwell Patton, Commodore, U.S. Navy, Retired
5 September, 1921

A tapping on the window brought David back to the real world. Looking up, he saw Keith Shayrock staring in at him through the glass. He waved and, in a blue haze, tried to stand up and almost tripped over his own feet. His mind reeled from what he had read. He crossed to the file cabinet and, after a brief glance at the schematic Patton had made to show the location of the secret entry to the dungeon, locked the missive inside, then went to answer the door.

Thirty-four

Beings of Light Church: 8:23 P.M.

"Look, Minnie," that hussy Theo Pelinore said. She stood in front of the stained glass window of the Beings of Light Church, like she was a saint or something. *St. Hussy of the Open Thighs.* "You had it coming. You weren't careful. I told you to be careful, but you didn't listen, did you? You never listen because you're never quiet long enough to hear—"

"But he was *rude,* just so *rude.* He just pushed me out of his office like—like, just never mind what." Minnie's outrage washed over her, tightening her face, narrowing her eyes. "He has dirty books in there, books with people's *things* in them. He's wicked. Wicked and—"

"He's a perfectly fine man and he caught you going through his office, Minnie. You blew it. Why can't you admit it?" The hussy stared at her like she was trying to set fire to her with her eyes. "There's nothing you can do about it now."

"But you're paying me to watch him for you—"

"Not any more, and it's your own fault. He won't let you back in there, and I don't blame him."

Minnie stepped closer. "Hussy!"

Gleefully, Minnie saw that a fleck of her spit hit Theo's cheek. The hussy didn't wipe it away, but drew herself up to full height. "Be quiet, you dried up old twat."

Minnie lunged.

"Sisters, please," Reverend Alice soothed, inserting herself between them. "Please, this *is* a sacred place!"

Both women *hrumphed,* still glaring at each other.

"Any minute now, our members will start walking in," Reverend Alice said quickly. "You two can't be at each other's throats. After all, we did agree that the others shouldn't be told that Minnie's been monitoring the house for us, at least until we knew what type of spiritual aid the spirits within are craving."

Theo and Minnie stood like pit bulls, each waiting for the other to move. Minnie wanted to tear her throat out. How dare she call her *that* word. If she only knew what Minnie had in her purse, well, she'd be kissing her feet, just to see it.

"Alice," Theo said cooly, "We let Minnie back into the church with the understanding that she was working for us. Now that her work is over, I think we should ask her to leave. For good."

"I was a member here before you, you . . . you hussy! *I* was a member of the Inner Circle."

"Minnie, that was before we were truly organized, and the inner circle was nothing but a small group trying to put together an organization," Alice placated. "There's no more inner circle—we're not a secretive organization anymore. We've evolved. Now, we have a channeling circle and we do keep it closed so that those who channel Spiros are protected—that's the only reason we keep the circle closed." She paused, smiling. "I'm sure you understand."

Minnie nodded sourly.

Alice turned her gaze on Theo. "Theodora, everyone should be welcome here. After all, it is a church."

"In theory, yes," Theo said slowly. "But you know why she was ousted before, Alice. She twisted everything we said and made the town hate us. We can't function with her here." Theo crossed her arms with finality.

"Theo, I'm only proposing that we allow her to attend the open meetings on Sunday mornings, just as anyone else can. I know you did what you thought was best at the time, Theo, but now we're a *real* church, and no church can deny anyone the right to worship."

Theo didn't answer and Alice turned her gentle smile back on Minnie Willard. "You're welcome here Sunday mornings, Minnie. We just can't grant you membership in the channeling circle."

"But—"

"Tonight, we're having a channeling session, so you'll have to leave now."

"But I can tell them things—"

Theo drew herself to full height. "You just can't stomach the thought that there are secrets you don't know—"

"Wait." Alice put her hand on Theo's arm. "Anger won't help. Minnie, out of fifty-three faithful members, only a handful have earned their way into the channeling circle. Remember, we agreed you would report only to me or to Theo, so why don't you go on home? Tomorrow I'll call you and you can tell me everything you've found out about Body House."

"But I came here tonight to tell the Inner Circle." No matter what Reverend Alice claimed, Minnie *knew* the Inner Circle still existed.

Alice started to look like she was going to lose her temper too. "We're not an inner circle, or a secret cabal or anything like that, Minnie, so please don't call us that. It gives a false impression." Alice paused, looking at Theo. "Since her work at Body House is done, if Minnie wants to briefly address the group before we get started, I don't really see anything wrong with that, do you, Theo?"

"Alice, all she'll do is go on about books she believes to be pornographic, and—"

"I won't say a word about those filthy books that that pervert child molester has in his office. I have *information.*" She looked from Theo and Alice, her eyes narrowed and bright. "That's what you wanted, isn't it? Information?"

"Yes," Alice said slowly. "But—"

"If you don't want to hear it, then I'll tell Calla and she can write it up for the *Guardian.* They'll love it."

"You blackmailing, dried-up old cu—"

"Theo, hush," Alice ordered. "We'll hear what you have to say, Minnie."

At that moment, the door opened and four members of the channeling group strolled in. "Minnie," Alice said kindly, "There's the coffee pot, over in that corner. Why don't you sit down and relax a while. We'll call you into our meeting room in a few minutes."

With a *hrummph,* Minnie got herself a cup of coffee, with plenty of cream and sugar, then situated herself where she could keep an eye on everything. People had been treating her poorly, and she was going to do something about it. First that disgusting David Masters fired her—and she bet his slut of a daughter had something to do with it too—and now the Beings of Light were treating her like a pile of dog doody, going back on their promise to let her into the Inner Circle.

Minnie set her cup down and patted her purse. She had no intention of showing them the black-garbed doll she'd found—that was too good for the likes of them—but she did plan on telling them all about the broken doll that David Masters had, and about that crap the idiot Eric Swenson had yelled about the lighthouse ghost wanting its head. She was telling because she wanted to know who did the channeling, and she was bound and determined to find out, no matter what it took—and those New Age doo-doo heads would eat up what she had to say like frosting left in a bowl. Then they'd owe her and they'd have to let her in.

She was also going to tell them about the conversation she'd overheard between Masters and some Englishman. She hadn't meant to listen in, but she'd picked up the phone at the same precise moment as the Holy Hermit had in his precious office, so she couldn't put it back down until he hung up, could she? When the Beings of Light heard Jerry Romero was bringing his show to Red Cay, they'd be owing her all the more for the information. Why, they'd all be kissing her feet!

The meeting room door opened and Alice poked her head out. "Minnie? We're ready for you."

It's about time. Putting on her perkiest smile, Minnie went to meet with the Inner Circle.

Thirty-five

Body House: 10:55 P.M.

"Dad, I'm home!" Amber's voice startled David and he almost spilled the dregs of his scotch on the rocks on Keith Shayrock's photograph album.

"You're early, kiddo," he called as he set the items carefully aside, rose, and pulled on his white terry cloth robe.

"Rick had to be home at ten-thirty. Can I come in?"

"Hang on." He knotted the tie and crossed to the bedroom door, feeling distinctly drunk. Shayrock had not only brought the album, but a bottle of Dewar's as well, and they had spent the evening sipping and talking and examining the dolls. It had been the sort of evening that made David wish he smoked cigars. He unlocked the door, opened it, and his daughter swept in, her cheeks ruddy from the cool night wind, her eyes happy and sparkling.

"It was great," she said before he could ask. "Rick's really nice." She grinned. "You'd like him. He's really shy, too."

"Shy is good," he said, hoping his voice wasn't as slurred as his brain. He hadn't meant to have any more to drink after the doctor left, not so long ago, but the evening had been so enjoyable, he'd decided to have a nightcap.

"What's that?" Amber asked, pointing at the album.

Glad to have something to talk about, he related the details of the evening. He and Shayrock had identified a number of the dolls—Louis Shayrock, a true country M.D., had known everyone in town, from the poorest fisherman to Red Cay's elite, and he'd evidently taken great pleasure in collecting pictures of himself with his friends and patients. The album had proven to be a gold mine of information.

"Keith Shayrock's lent me the photos for a few days, so we can wait until tomorrow to do some more comparing," David said, yawning. "You'll get a kick out of it, though. Baudey House serviced nearly everyone in town—the mayor, a senator, a Presbyterian preacher." He flipped through the pages. "Look at this."

He waited while Amber studied the grainy photo of a fisherman and a pretty dark-haired young woman standing arm-in-arm in front of a trawler. "Peter Castle," she read, then gasped. "And Christabel Baudey. Dad, it's *her!*"

"It sure is. Does Castle look familiar to you?"

"Yeah, kinda. Think he was her boyfriend?"

"Very possibly."

She stared at the photo another minute, then looked at her dad. "He looks a lot like that ugly doll in the black clothes."

"Exactly my thoughts."

"You didn't find the doll, did you, Daddy?"

He shook his head. "No. Not a trace. It's making me crazy."

"Minnie has it," Amber said.

"You'll be happy to know that I let Craig Swenson know it's missing."

"Did you tell him Minnie took it?"

"No, but when he asked I said it was a distinct possibility."

"He *asked?*" She giggled with delight.

"Seems that other people she's cleaned house for have had a little problem with Minnie's sticky fingers at one time or another." He paused. "You can't repeat that."

"I know. But I love it when I'm right."

He smiled wearily. "Presumed right. Kiddo, your old man's bushed."

She grinned. "And bombed."

"Guilty."

"Well, maybe it'll help you sleep." Amber stood on her tiptoes and pecked his cheek. " 'Night, Daddy."

"Good night."

After she left, he relocked his door, flicked on his bedside light, removed his robe and slipped between the sheets, stretching luxuriously. Maybe Amber was right about the drink. He hoped so: he could certainly use the sleep.

Despite the alcohol, his mind refused to calm down: it wanted to rehash the things he'd learned tonight, wanted to move them around and create stories around them. *Face it, Masters, you want to write.*

He groaned, disgusted and pleased at the same time. When the urge came on by itself, he never fought it. Rising, he padded to the writing desk, sat down and turned on his laptop.

The screen glowed, blue and friendly, in the dimly-lit room, inviting him to add more words and, after a moment of hesitation, he put his fingers to the keys and the words began to flow, the way they always did after he'd reached mid-point.

Thirty-six

The Willard Residence: 11:55 P.M.

Mickey Willard snored so bad that the Willards not only had separate beds, but separate bedrooms. Even from here in the living room, Minnie could hear him sawing his logs and, as much as she loved the old cuss, sometimes she just wanted to put a pillow over his face and hold it there until he was out of his misery.

Shaking her head, she held up the doll and studied its mean little face. Wouldn't those New Agers have died if she'd shown them this? They'd been fascinated by the stories about the lighthouse ghost and the retard, that was for sure, and completely ga-ga over the fact that Jerry Romero was coming to Red Cay. The only bad thing that had happened was when Alice thanked her and escorted her out before the Inner Circle—no matter what those people said, that's what it was—started discussing her story. Dying to know what they'd said, she'd gone home and sat in front of the television with Mickey until he hit the hay around ten, just like always. After he disappeared, she took the doll from her purse.

He wouldn't approve of her find, she knew. He'd never approved of any of her others, either, even though she always assured him that they were things no one would miss. She had taken to telling him they were gifts, though that had backfired last year when that stuffed-shirt Lyle Worthy had reported to Chief Swenson that two of his Hummel figurines had turned up missing after Minnie had been there to clean. He had at least a hundred of the things, what did he care? *Selfish, spoiled creep!*

Chief Swenson had called on her, but she'd put the figurines away in the back of the breadbox where she stored waxed paper, plastic wrap, and tin foil. He didn't exactly accuse her of anything, but Mickey had walked in while they were talking, and, afterward, he took the little statues, wrapped them up, and mailed them anonymously back to Worthy.

It was nearly midnight and past time for bed. She hit the remote, turning off the television, and rose, holding the doll tightly in her hands, The feel of the bulge of the doll's *thing* under her fingers sent a little thrill through her belly and, if she wasn't so sick of Mickey's snoring, she might have stopped off in his bedroom.

Instead, she walked down the short hall to the tiny bathroom, where she set the doll on the counter while she brushed her teeth and rubbed cold cream into her face. The mean little face seemed to leer at her as she undressed, took her blue nylon nightgown from the hook on the door, and slipped it over her head. She finished getting ready and smiled at the doll. She especially liked the little cat-o'-nine-tails it held in its hand, despite the sharp little blades tipping it. "Let's go to bed, sailor," she whispered, turning off the light. The words made her titter and her face grew warm. In the darkness, she picked up the doll, again feeling the bulge against her fingers.

"Oh!" she exclaimed, thinking the *thing* moved under her touch. It couldn't have.

It moved again.

She let out a little yelp, and the doll slipped from her fingers, crashing with a porcelain crunch on the hard tile floor.

"Heck, heck, heck," she whispered.

As Minnie flicked the light on, the room suddenly felt very chilly and a faint odor of bay rum sifted through the air.

On the floor, the doll lay in pieces in a puddle of blood. "My goodness!" Minnie quickly began to examine her hands, thinking she must have cut herself on the whip when she dropped the effigy.

Then something clamped over her mouth, a massive hand as cold as death. Another hand, just as cold, yanked her backward. Frantically, she clawed at them, seeing the thick black hairs coating them, vaguely smelling bay rum like Ferd and Andy Cox wore. She felt the chill body as she was pulled against it, felt the huge erection straining against her backside.

The hand at her waist was removed, but the other was so strong she couldn't get away. The more she struggled, the harder it dug into the flesh around her mouth.

Then she heard the crack of a whip, a whip with many sharp tails.

Thirty-seven

Body House: 11:56 P.M.

The overwhelming, powerful odor of night-blooming jasmine suddenly assaulted David's nose. Alarmed, he turned in his chair, his work abruptly forgotten. The scotch glass—he'd decided to have one more nightcap—flew to the floor as his hand smacked against it, but he paid no attention.

He stared at the locked bedroom door as the room filled with bitter, freezing cold, and his gut turned as cold as the air as he saw the ball of darkness begin to form. The hairs on the back of his neck came to attention and he heard himself moan as he discerned the unmistakable stench of decay oozing through the jasmine.

He rose, tugging his robe more tightly around himself. The entity—*Christabel*— elongated into a rectangle, just as it had previously before it took human form, and it stood between him and the door.

Don't panic! He reached slowly behind himself and pulled the desk drawer open, never taking his eyes from the phantom as he felt for the bag of salt—old-fashioned ghost repellent—he'd secreted there. Throwing salt probably wouldn't work, he realized; Christabel had already crossed the line of salt he'd poured across the doorway weeks ago, but it was worth a try—and he didn't know what else to do.

As it had on that day in Amber's room, the darkness slowly formed into the shape of a human female, and details began to appear as he slipped his hand into the bag and withdrew a small handful of salt.

He took a step closer, staring at the ghost, at the beautiful black off-the-shoulder dress, at the flash of leg, at the long white hands. Slowly, his gaze rose past the breasts, up the graceful white neck, and finally, his bowels loose, he stared into the exquisite face of Christabel Baudey, saw the red bow of lips, the milk-white skin, and the piles of jet hair. A single red plume ornamented her hair.

He looked into her huge, flashing eyes, black as hell, black as heaven, and dropped the bag, felt the grains of salt sift down between his numb fingers.

David . . . David . . . Come to me.

The voice, spun of silk and silver, could not be resisted. He took a step forward, then another, and she did, too, and then her chill hands were on him, untying the robe, pushing it off his shoulders. It dropped, forgotten, to the floor.

He reached out to touch her, his whole body throbbing with unexplained desire for this creature. He couldn't think, he was all emotion, all desire, and he didn't question it.

He tried to take her hand, but she was without substance, except for the coldness. But she knew what he wanted, and took his. *She's trapped in a doll!* some boring part of his intellect told him. *If she wasn't, she'd kill you.*

She seemed to read his thoughts. *No, David.* Withdrawing her hand, she began to unfasten the black dress.

David, free me and I'll be yours . . . David. Free me and you can touch me, too.

A perfect rose-tipped breast appeared, then the other, as the gown slipped sensuously down her torso. He reached out to touch it, but his hand found only thick, cold air. *Masters, you want to hump a cold spot!* He told his intellect to shut up, and tried again, his whole body aching with desire.

David . . .

The gown dropped in a black puddle around her feet and he drank in the slope of her belly, the thick bush of pubic hair, the triangle of light shining through the juncture of her thighs just below her sex. Her legs were long and smooth.

He was rock hard and aching with a sweet pain beyond anything he'd ever felt before.

But he could only look. Then, she took his erection in her cold hand and led him to his bed. Obediently, he climbed on, vaguely aware of the covers slipping off the bed of their own accord, very aware of her as she climbed on top of him. Her center, rubbing against his abdomen, was a freezing flame, and he wanted her more than anything he'd ever wanted in his life.

David . . .

She pushed his hands above his head, showed him that she wanted him to hold onto the headboard.

Until I'm free, you can't touch me . . .

He grasped the wooden rail, shuddering with desire, watching her breasts as she moved above him, arranging his body to suit her.

The doll is in the dungeon, David. Free me and you can do whatever you want to me, David . . . David . . .

Suddenly, he was deep inside her, and she rode him like a horse, he bucking to meet her thrusts, his excitement unaffected by the coldness of her.

She threw her head back, mouth open, eyes slitted, and in his mind he heard that silk-silver voice cry out in orgasm, and then he was over the edge, screaming with his own release, letting go of the headrail, trying to pull her to him, finding only the cold.

You're mine, David . . .

Spent, he stared up at her, into the dark eyes that trapped him. Lust receding, his brain came to life and he felt the cold, and his own fear, enveloping him.

She laughed, her smile turning into a cruel twist, and she reached down and touched the seed that glistened in her pubic hairs.

I have a little bit of you, David. You're mine, and I'm yours forever if you find the doll. Find it and break it, and we'll be together forever . . .

The cry building in his throat broke free and he bucked, trying to throw her off him. She laughed again.

You're mine, all mine . . .

Then she began to disappear back into black smoke and, in a moment, she was nothing but a dark haze that traveled through his door as if it wasn't there.

"Oh, God." He rose, his legs trembling, his mind fighting to comprehend what had happened. Or hadn't happened. He yanked his robe on, suddenly aware that his groin was dry and pristine. He raced across to the bed and examined the sheets. He found one small drop of ejaculate, a tiny pearl, but no more.

I have a little bit of you, David. Her words played over and over in his mind as he went across the hall and washed. There was no reason to do so except that he felt soiled.

He could barely believe what had happened as he silently unlocked Amber's bedroom door and peered in. Seeing that she slept peacefully, he relocked it and returned to his own room, where he turned off the computer. Did he imagine it all or not? He'd been awake, though a little drunk . . . Briefly, he eyed the bottle of Dewar's. He could use one more drink to help him sleep.

It hasn't helped you sleep yet, old pal. Suddenly he remembered all the old parapsychology books with warnings about alcohol consumption in them. "It opens portals," said one book, "that put the drinker in dangerous positions when dealing with more negative hauntings."

He'd never paid the warnings much attention before, but, suddenly, he believed them, fully and completely; tonight was the first time he'd drunk alcohol in the house. "Christ." He picked up the Dewar's, took it across the hall, and poured it out in the sink. Tonight was the first and last time he would drink in Body House.

Back in bed, it took him a long time to go to sleep and, when he finally did, his dreams were full of Christabel Baudey. *You're mine,* she told him, over and over and over again.

August 15

Thirty-eight

Body House: 6:48 P.M.

David had allowed Amber to take the Bronco for the evening, suggesting that she and Kelly go to the movies in Pismo Beach, and he'd done it for a very selfish reason: he wanted to keep his date with Theo Pelinore a secret from his daughter.

The planned overnight at Kelly's had been moved to Body House because, as Kelly had said in her breathless way, "The bug man came and the whole place smells like Chem City." David only hoped that Amber was right in her assurances that she and her friend would be totally safe in her room.

The show would let out around eleven-thirty tonight, which meant Theo needed to be long gone by midnight, but that was fine by him. He didn't want to spend a whole night with her again; it was too exhausting, not to mention hazardous to his skin. Most especially, he did not want to spend it in Body House with her. Lord knew what could happen. Though last night's events seemed like a drunken dream now, he was still pretty sure that something significant had happened, and he was also sure he'd touched his last drop of alcohol for as long as he lived here.

He splashed on a little Drakkar, thinking, as he had all day, about the dungeon. Earlier, he'd gone briefly into the first floor tower and examined the floor, fascinated to find definite signs of a blast showing on the outer stones. There was a newer, rough area in the cement in a two-foot-diameter circle in the center of the floor, further backing up Commodore Patton's claim to have closed off an entrance to the cellar. Satisfied, David had left the tower room quickly, hating the cold, sad atmosphere of the place.

He'd considered going to the third floor entrance all day, but had held off, more loath to explore by himself than eager to find the Erzuli doll that contained Christabel Baudey's soul. Her promises to be his just weren't as riveting now as they had been last night, and he was also frightened: the legends about her being irresistible to men were certainly true and it would be foolhardy to go by himself. He'd either get Craig and Eric to explore with him, or he'd sit back and let Jerry Romero do the dirty work.

Or not. He still couldn't quite accept all that had happened.

He straightened his tie and shrugged on his jacket. Theo would be here at any moment to pick him up. She'd said *she* was taking *him* out this time, and wouldn't even tell him where they were going for dinner.

He finished up and left the room, closing the door behind him, moving quickly through the silent halls to the stairwell.

Just as he reached the first floor, the doorbell chimed.

She's here. His palms suddenly broke into a sweat and he stepped quickly into the downstairs bathroom and wiped them off before walking on to the front door. Just before he grasped the handle, the bell chimed again. *She's impatient tonight.* The thought made him smile nervously. *Theo's always impatient.* This was a new situation, being anxious about a date . . . knowing he was going to be expected to "put out." Though his penis found this a grand idea, his intellect just kept asking him if he'd ever made women he'd dated feel as much like meat as *he* did around Theo Pelinore. He found it rather disgusting, not to mention disquieting.

But you're a guy! his penis piped up, *You like disgusting!*

With that, he cleared his throat and pulled the front door open. "Theo, how nice to . . . see . . . you." The words died on his lips.

The woman who pushed her way into his house had frizzy orange hair, and the overbite of Mr. Ed. As she moved, all her joints seemed to travel loosely in a cacophony of pops and twitches worthy of a tap-dancing marionette.

She carried a ratty black bag slung over one shoulder, with a notebook sticking half out of it, and in one prehensile hand she clutched a beat-up camera. In the other, she held a microcassette player, its little red power indicator glowing a guilty red.

"David Masters, I've finally got you where I want you." Her slightly nasal tones wound down as if she were a languishing Southern belle and, as she moved farther past him toward the parlor, she followed the words with a sigh.

"Calla Willard, I presume?" His own voice sounded dry to him as he moved to head her off.

She maneuvered around him like the professional snoop he figured she was. *Like mother, like daughter.*

"Miss Willard, this isn't a good time." *The dolls!* Just around the corner, a whole hutch full of them awaited her camera and her questions. Quickly, he grabbed her elbow and propelled her forcibly around to face the front door.

"I only require a minute of your time," she objected. She sighed again.

"I don't have a minute," he replied smoothly. "I'm about to leave."

"But there's no car in your driveway." She cocked an eyebrow significantly.

"Astute of you to notice." David forced himself to smile ingratiatingly. "That must be why you're a reporter."

That remark stopped her with her mouth half open. She obviously couldn't tell whether he was serious or not. Calla gulped air like a guppie. "I—I've been trying to reach you since you moved here." She heaved another Southern sigh.

"As I said, I'm very busy now. I'm sorry, but you'll have to go, Miss Willard."

"But—"

"Perhaps we can chat for a moment at the dance next week," he added, determined to get rid of her before Theo arrived.

"But *I* write *books!*" she blurted. "My masterpiece is titled, *A Woman's Purple Onion,* and my mother said you'd read it if I brought it to you." She began to dig in her big black bag.

Outside, a horn beeped twice. *Theo!*

"Your mother lied to you," he said abruptly. *God, I can't believe I said that!* He resisted a fleeting urge to apologize. The horse-faced woman was beyond rude, beyond obnoxious, beyond foul. *She's worse than her mother!*

Calla Willard might have been a reporter, but she certainly wasn't unflappable, he thought as she did a few more guppie impressions. "My mother *what?"* she demanded.

He turned her to the door again and placed his hands firmly on her shoulders, marching her toward the threshold like a rusty tin soldier. "Nothing," he muttered. "Look, I'll be happy to talk to you at the dance."

He pushed the door open and saw Theo, elegant in a beige trench coat, belted and buttoned, with only a paisley scarf showing at the neck. Her hand was raised to ring the bell and she lowered it smoothly, smiling with those dark red lips.

"Mr. Masters," she said warmly, as her eyes traveled distastefully over the length and breadth of Calla Willard. "I'm so glad I caught you at home."

"Why, Miss Pelinore," David purred back. "It seems everyone in town is dropping in on me tonight."

Theo studied him for a brief moment, then her demeanor visibly changed. With a slight straightening of the shoulder and stiffening of her normally mobile lips, she turned from seductively casual to all-business in the time it took for Calla to sigh again.

"I apologize for just dropping in on you like this, but I was on my way down to San Luis Obispo, and I thought I'd see if you'd found that escrow paper we misplaced."

More than his penis was charmed by Theo now. "Yes, Theo, I have it. In my office."

Theo stepped through the doorway and smiled at Calla. "Just leaving, dear?" Her voice was filled with cat's claws.

David loved it. "Yes, she is." He led the reporter out the door and onto the porch. "Perhaps I'll see you at the dance, Miss Willard."

"Yes, dear," Theo called after her. "Have you found a date yet?"

Ignoring Theo, Calla abruptly turned a sharp-eyed glare on David. "You said my mother lied, Mr. Masters. Why did you say that?"

Because it was more polite than slugging you. "You misunderstood," he soothed. Theo's remark had struck him as a little too far below the belt. "I said your mother *tried. Tried* to talk me into reading your wonderful book, but I can't do it right now." He tried to look helpless—that usually worked for him. "I'm just very overworked right now."

Calla perked up like she'd swallowed a tab of Benzedrine. "If you need help, I can certainly come by and help you with your editing." She grinned, showing her equine overbite. "I'm a great editor. Why, I'll bet I could really improve your books with my talents. You know, you were a little sloppy with that last one—"

He'd been wrong about Theo's remark—it hadn't been nasty enough. "I have an editor." David forced himself to say this politely, despite the fact that he was now seeing several shades of red. *How dare she!* "But thank you for offering." He nearly choked on the words.

It worked. Calla smiled slightly. "I'd really like to do an *in-depth* interview." She wet her chapped lips and, sighing, fluttered her colorless lashes at him.

He barely kept himself from spontaneously recoiling at her attempt at flirtation. Talk about horrors! "We'll do that sometime." He smiled sickly. "An in-depth interview. Twenty or thirty minutes. We can sit down at the *Guardian* office—"

"Or here," she interrupted, sighing and fluttering.

"Sure," he said, crossing his fingers behind him for Theo to see.

"Great," Calla said, finally beginning to move of her own volition. "May I ask just one question? It'll only take a sec," she added before he could say no. "Where's your car?"

You nosy bitch! He considered telling her it was in his garage, then thought she might ask where that was. "My daughter's using it. A business associate is picking me up any minute now." He glanced at his wrist watch. "He's running a little late, in fact."

Calla nodded, apparently and at long last satisfied. "We'll be speaking soon," she informed him, then walked down the steps.

Just before he shut the door, she turned toward him. "Mr. Masters?"

"Yes, Miss Willard?"

"You called her Theo." She smirked, gargoylish in the dim porch light. "I heard you." With that, she walked off and climbed into a dented old Datsun. It belched smoke as she ground the ignition.

"Charming creature," Theo murmured in his ear as Calla Willard's car backfired and sputtered her away.

"If you like silverfish," David replied, feeling smooth and devilish. "So, business associate, where are we going this evening?" He began to pull the door shut.

"Don't," she told him as Calla's taillights disappeared into the evening mist. "We're just going down the steps to my trunk."

David raised an eyebrow.

"I brought a gourmet picnic," she explained. "When I saw Calla's car, I thought it would be best to leave it where it is was until she left."

"You're smooth," David said appreciatively. "Escrow papers, indeed."

"We'll have to come up with something new—you've been here too long now for that to work much longer." She tucked her hand under his elbow. "Shall we get our picnic?"

"Let's."

"You know," she said as they walked down to the car, "it's fairly warm out tonight. We could drive out to the lighthouse and spread a blanket. Dine under the stars. How does that sound? Romantic?" she added, her voice sultry.

And Captain Wilder can join us for dessert. "It's really cold out there on the point, Theo. If you want to do this outdoors, we could sit here, on the lawn, or up on the porch."

She appeared to be considering the plan.

"We'd have more privacy," he added.

She smiled and opened the trunk. "Privacy sounds nice. Let's take this inside." She handed him the basket.

Once they were back indoors, she spread the feast on his coffee table while he sat back and watched—at her insistence.

"You must be starving," he observed as she brought out a plate of rare roast beef and a tiny container of horseradish.

"Why do you say that?" she asked with a cock of her eyebrow.

"Well, you haven't even taken off your coat yet."

"I know." Her smile outdid the Mona Lisa's. "Look what I have." She held up a champagne bottle for his inspection. "Mumms."

"Oh, ah, well . . ."

"David, is something wrong?"

"Would you be offended if I passed? I don't drink—"

"But you did at the restaurant," she interrupted, a note of confusion in her voice.

"Yes, well . . ." He could say it was doctor's orders and go on about hypertensives, or he could tell her the truth.

"David?"

He decided on the truth. Some of it, anyway. "Last night I had a few drinks with a friend who stopped by. Later, after he left, I found that I was particularly susceptible to the phenomena present in the house."

She gave him a quizzical look. "You were nervous?"

"Well, I guess you could put it that way. Theo, the reason I can live in a house like this is that I'm not very, ah, psychic." He paused, searching for words that wouldn't offend her or set her off on a crystal-packing binge. "People come in a few basic types. Amber and I come from the same mould: not much happens, even here, unless another sort of person is present."

"One like me? A psychic person?" As she spoke she opened the champagne bottle, smiling in the face of his nervousness.

"Yes. That's a good example. Usually, it's pretty quiet around here, but last night was extremely difficult. My defenses were eaten away by the alcohol. I was susceptible."

She set the bottle on the table and put her hand on his knee, her eyes wide. "What happened?"

"Oh, nothing much," he lied. "Just more than I cared for in the middle of the night."

"Tell me!"

"The jasmine scent was terribly strong in my bedroom, that and the decay. The laughter was very loud to my ear and there were cold spots to deal with. Usually, my room is quiet." *Except for my friendly neighborhood succubus, of course.* "I want to keep it that way."

"You said nothing happened until your visitor left?"

"Yes. I had a nightcap—*or two*—before I went to bed and, earlier, we'd laid pretty heavily into the scotch."

"Well, David, if you'd had dinner and a bottle of wine, wouldn't the alcohol have worn off by the time you went to bed? Then nothing would have happened to your defenses?"

"Well . . ."

She took two champagne flutes from the basket. "Tell you what, we'll have this *before* dinner. That way, you'll be utterly sober two hours from now."

She had a point. Though the notion continued to nag him that letting Theo Pelinore, your basic cosmic ink blotter, drink in Body House might be trouble no matter what the circumstances, perhaps she was right: one bottle of champagne this early in the evening couldn't do much damage. Here, in the parlor, they could leave quickly if they needed to . . . "I don't know," he said finally.

She poured two glasses as if he hadn't declined, then stood and began to unbuckle the belt of her trenchcoat. "We'll do it backwards, David," she said, pulling the scarf carelessly from around her neck and letting it drift down across his lap. She began unbuttoning her coat. "We'll have dessert first."

Her transparent black nylons reached only halfway up her long, long thighs, leaving all the white skin above them framed in a lacy black garter belt and panties so small they didn't count. Her lush breasts were imprisoned in a matching underwire bra that pushed them so high that her nipples, rock hard, were entirely revealed.

"Do you like my outfit?" she asked.

"Breasts on the half-shell," he blurted, then his mouth went dry.

"I like that." Smiling again, she sat down close to him and handed him a champagne flute. "To us." She raised her glass and clinked it against his.

She'd positioned herself so he was looking at her eye-to-nipple. David took a healthy swallow of champagne. "To us."

For a moment, he thought he smelled the jasmine wafting around them, then he forgot about it in his excitement at the thought of touching a real, live woman.

Later, his back covered with a fresh set of scratches, and an with embarrassing stain on thc gray suede couch, they sat naked on the floor, leisurely nibbling the last of the cheese and meat. Theo had been right about the liquor. It was wearing off already and he never would have withstood her sadistic lovemaking without it.

He told her about the dolls and about identifying many of the house's customers and, when they finished eating and put everything away, he pulled his pants on—though she remained dressed only in garter belt, nylons, and spiked heels—and led her to the hutch displaying the dolls. She was very impressed and he basked in her ooh's and ah's for some moments.

"I'll bet Jerry Romero will die for these dolls, David," she said softly. "Even if you don't find the dungeon."

Shocked, he turned to face her. "How do you know about Romero?" he dcmanded.

"Why, I—"

"No one is supposed to know. No one!"

"Calm down, David. I won't tell."

He took a deep breath. "I don't want a circus here, Theo. I'm sorry if I sounded angry, but I don't want a circus. He's getting in and getting out and it's supposed to be very hush-hush. Please tell me how you found out."

"Minnie."

He felt his eyes roll. "Of course. But, how could she know? There's nothing on paper and I haven't said a word—"

"She listened in on a phone call, evidently," Theo said. "And she used the information to try to buy her way into our channeling group at Beings of Light. It didn't work, of course."

"She told the world," he stated glumly.

"Just the group, and none of us will tell."

"She's probably told the entire town by now. Damn." He shook his head. "Damn. That daughter of hers will be all over this place."

"I'll help you keep her—and everyone else—away. If you like, I'm sure my friends would be happy to guard the doors for you."

She was only offering since that meant she and her friends would get to be on hand, but it might be a good idea. "Let me think about it," he told her. A better idea would be to call Romero and try to reschedule. This late, it probably wouldn't work. He might have to take Theo up on her offer. "I'll let you know." He tried to smile and look into her eyes instead of at her breasts. "There's a photo of Christabel in Shayrock's album. Would you like to see it?"

"I'd love to."

"I'll go get it."

He turned, heading for the stairs, wanting a moment to compose himself, maybe a moment to give Gaylord a quick call and ask him to work on rescheduling, but halfway up the stairs, he realized Theo was right behind him. She smiled, holding her shoes in one hand.

"It would be better if you wait downstairs," he said.

"I'm sorry, David," she said, snuggling up to him. "I didn't want to be alone."

He'd grab the album and take her back downstairs, where things seemed safer. "Okay."

In his room, though, she immediately draped herself across his bed.

He smelled jasmine, faint but distinct. Pretending not to notice her pose, he grabbed the album from the desk. "Let's go downstairs. The light's better." The jasmine grew stronger.

"Oh, David." She stretched like a cat. "Just come over here and show me the picture of Christabel."

"I—"

"Now," she purred.

Gingerly, he sat on the edge of the bed and opened the album while trying to ignore her hands, which were draping themselves all over his chest. "Here she is."

Theo pulled herself around so that her face would have been in his lap if it weren't for the album. "Which one?"

"There." He pointed nervously. *Down, boy!* His penis wouldn't listen and insisted on straining against the heavy book. At least Theo couldn't see.

They stared at the photo. "She's pretty," Theo said finally. "But her boyfriend looks like a rough customer."

"Literally, probably." He studied the picture. "You're rather the same type, physically. As Christabel, I mean."

In response, she rose and took the book from his lap, placing it back on the desk. Slowly, she began to walk back toward him.

Suddenly, the air turned frigid and the jasmine and decay overwhelmed his senses. Theo smelled it too: she stopped in her tracks, her seductive expression giving way to open-eyed fear.

"What—?" she asked.

"Come on!" He jumped off the bed and grabbed her hand. "We've got to get out of here. Right now!"

As they arrived at the door, the dark pulsating mass emerged through it. David stepped back, dragging Theo, who'd turned to stone, with him. "Come on, Theo. I'm going to open the door and we're going to duck under that thing and run like hell, right out of the house."

"I—I—"

"On three. He reached around the mass and put his hand on the knob. "One." He turned the knob. "Two." He got ready to pull the door open. "Three!"

He yanked Theo forward and pulled on the door at the same time. His ears filled with Christabel's laughter. The door wouldn't open. He kept trying. *Mind over matter, mind over matter, mind over matter.*

Suddenly, Theo lurched and screamed. He looked around just in time to see the black orb disappear into her body.

"Oh shit," he said sincerely.

She looked at him with those big dark eyes. "David, you didn't do what I asked."

"What?"

She beckoned. "Come to Christabel, David." Then she laughed and he knew it was *her.*

Thirty-nine

Body House: 10:57 P.M.

"That slut!" Amber Masters slammed on the brakes just behind Theo Pelinore's car.

"Get a grip!" Kelly squeaked, hanging onto the dashboard. "Totaling her car isn't going to get rid of her!"

"It couldn't hurt," Amber muttered. She opened the Bronco's door and got out. "Come on," she urged. "Let's go get rid of her."

Kelly slung her knapsack over her shoulder and slowly got out of the truck. She knew her friend hated Theo Pelinore, but she'd never seen her like this before.

"Amber?" she ventured. "We're back early. Maybe we should go down to the diner and get hot chocolate. You know, kill an hour?"

Kelly had already been a little nervous about spending the night in the notorious Body House, even though Amber had assured her there was nothing to be afraid of, but she was really, really nervous about walking in on Amber's dad and Pelinore. The way Amber looked, she might barge right into his bedroom and catch them in the act.

"Maybe they're just having dinner or something, Amber," she said as the thought occurred to her.

Amber rolled her eyes. "Yeah, at eleven at night." Shaking her head, she spoke grimly. "Pelinore is trying to reel him in. She must've known I wasn't going to be here. But how?" She stared at the house, deep in thought.

"Maybe Minnie?"

"Nah, she's out of here. She wouldn't know."

"What about your dad? Wouldn't he tell her?"

Amber considered. "He might, I guess. He used to sneak around with his old girlfriend and not tell me because he knew I disapproved."

"Melanie?"

"No, the one before. Lorna, the stringbean from hell." She smiled smugly. "After they broke up, he even told me I'd been right all along. But does he remember that? No, of course not." She shook her head in disgust. "It's up to me to save him from her clutches, Kel, and that's just what I'm going to do. Come on."

She trudged toward the house and, hesitantly, Kelly followed. Near the porch, she thought she saw a dark man standing in the crisscrossing trellis shadows, but everybody teased her about what a chicken she was, so pulling her jacket closer around her, she quickly caught up with Amber and never looked back.

Forty

Body House: 10:57 P.M.

David awoke on the floor of the ballroom, his naked body aching, his head throbbing, his memory a wash of crazy images. Slowly, he sat up, rubbing his right temple. It was sore, as if he'd been hit. Staring down at his body, he was shocked to see the long scratches on his inner thighs, claw marks that came fearfully close to his groin.

"Oh, God," he whispered, seeing lipstick and abrasions on his privates.

The groan that rose from somewhere behind him made his hair stand on end.

"Theo!" he cried, turning too fast. "Theo!" Shakily, he got to his feet. He felt like he'd been run over by a steamroller as he approached her.

"David?" She was sprawled on her back, nude except for the garter belt and one ripped stocking.

It all came back in a rush and he stopped dead in his tracks, staring at her warily. "Theo?" he asked again, sniffing the air. He could smell Carnuba wax, but that was all, so he went to her and helped her to her feet.

"I don't—" she began.

Her makeup had smeared on her face, her mascara filling the normally invisible crow's feet at the corners of her eyes. He tried not to notice. "Christa—" he began, then halted, remembering Eric's warnings. "You were used by a paranormal entity. Do you remember what happened?"

"We had sex, here, on the floor, didn't we?"

"Yeah."

She stared at him, at the long scratches on his arms and legs and torso, at the bruises in the shapes of hand and fingerprints that were already forming on his flesh. "Did I do that?"

"Yes and no." He couldn't get over it. The woman had been possessed, truly possessed. That was another thing he'd never believed possible. Lizzie had passed through him, gathering his energy, and that, he almost understood. But possession. *My God.*

"David?"

"I'm sorry. Don't blame yourself for these." He indicated the scratches, and almost added, *don't blame yourself for most of them,* then thought better of it. "Let's get out of here and get dressed."

She nodded and, meek as a lamb, let him lead her from the room. In the hall, just outside the stained glass doors, he found his pants and gratefully slipped them on, though every movement was painful. He wished he could remember more, but it was all a blur of animal passions untempered by any sort of intellect. Whatever Christabel's powers were over men when she was alive, she certainly still possessed them now.

"Come on," he said, putting his arm around her. "Let's get your coat. We don't have much time before Amber gets back."

Halfway down the stairs, he heard Kelly Cox's voice. "Amber, you can't just go up there and barge in on them."

"Like hell I can't," his daughter replied.

Oh, shit! "Go back to my room and shut the door," David whispered. Immediately Theo turned and ran, obviously not as sore as he. Swallowing hard, he walked down the rest of the stairs, coming face-to-face with Amber in the thankfully dim hallway. Her face was set with a determination he remembered seeing on her mother's face years and years ago. Behind her, Kelly Cox fidgeted, obviously very unhappy.

"Had a picnic, Dad?" Amber asked smoothly.

She's your daughter, not your mother. Steeling himself, he smiled at her. "Yes, Theo brought a gourmet picnic basket over for dinner. We had a nice evening. Did you?"

She stared pointedly at his bare chest and feet. "I guess."

"We were just upstairs going through Dr. Shayrock's photo album," he said, even though he knew he owed her no explanations.

"We're going to my room," Amber said cooly. She passed him, then Kelly skittered by, mumbling, "Hi, Mr. Masters," in a tone that suggested Amber might shoot her if she said more.

Sighing, he grabbed Theo's coat and glanced around to make sure there were no more incriminating articles of clothing in sight. Thankfully, there weren't.

Quickly, he moved up the stairs and found his door locked, thank God. He knocked quietly. "It's me," he whispered, and Theo opened the door.

"We've got to get you out of here," he said as she donned the coat and belted it.

She nodded. "Guess you were right about the champagne. I'm sorry I didn't listen to you."

He shrugged—what could he say?—and led her to the door. He looked out to be sure the hall was clear, then led her down the stairs, pausing to pick up her shoes on the landing.

In the parlor, he helped her gather everything up and get it out to the car. She closed the trunk. "What happened, David? I don't understand."

"You were used," he said simply. "And so was I." Chastely, he kissed her cheek. "Good night."

Back upstairs, he showered and quickly got into bed. Past experience with ghostly phenomena told him there would be no more visits from Christabel tonight and, as he lay back against the pillows, he tried to remember, or at least reconstruct, the blur of the evening's events.

There had been more than mindless sex, and as he lay there, images drifted into his brain; images of Christabel—in Theo's body—putting him under her spell with promises of sexual pleasures beyond his wildest dreams if he would come with her to the secret stairway on the third floor and descend it with her to destroy the doll and set her free.

They'd left his bedroom and he clearly remembered following her down the hall. Just after they turned the corner to walk the corridor, he was almost certain, *something* had blocked their way, just outside the ballroom. Suddenly, he remembered catching the scent of lavender. *Lizzie.* Of course.

Try as he might, he couldn't remember any other details, except for the anger flashing in Theo's eyes when she—or rather, Christabel—grabbed him and pulled him into the ballroom. In the huge, empty room, she had attacked him, taking out her anger on his body, using him, clawing him, taking him over and over. Somehow, she had caused him to perform in a way men normally could not. *Voodoo.* That's all it could be, he told himself. The way he felt now, he never wanted to make love again.

I used to want sex all the time, but thanks to the Christabel Baudey Center for the Control of Fucking, I'll never have that craving again.

The ringing of the phone startled him just as he began to drift toward sleep. Quickly, he snatched the cordless from the bedside table and extended the antenna.

"David?" Static crackled on the line, but it didn't mask the urgency in Theo's voice.

"Theo? What's wrong?"

"I thought I should tell you—someone's prowling around on your grounds. He stepped out in front of my car as I was driving away. I nearly hit a tree when I swerved to miss him."

"What did he look like?"

"I couldn't see much. He was tall, broad-shouldered, I think, and dressed in dark clothes."

"Which way was he headed? Toward Widow's Peak or toward town?" He paused, wondering if Captain Wilder had left his lighthouse home.

"He was near the house, that's all I'm sure of. One minute he was there, the next, he'd just vanished into thin air."

The static worsened. "Thanks for letting me know, Theo. I'll call the police, get them to take a look around." Through a burst of interference, they said their goodnights.

"God," he whispered, hanging up. He rose and shrugged on his robe. He had no intention of calling the cops. He thought Theo, in her shaken state, had probably imagined the man—after all, she'd said he had simply vanished—but he thought he should check the locks downstairs.

Preternaturally silent, Body House seemed to be holding its breath as he moved through the hallways and down the stairs. Nothing creaked, nothing settled. He checked the back kitchen door, the hairs on his neck slowly rising.

The air felt cloyingly thick as he moved to the front door. *Body House is waiting for something.* Chilled, he put his hand out to check the lock, then jumped backward as someone on the other side rapped twice, loudly.

Jesus! He tried to see out, but the colored glass was too thick. Two more raps sent his adrenals into overdrive.

Grow up, Masters! Prowlers don't knock before entering! "Who's there?" he called.

No reply, except two more raps, closer together, more impatient.

He stepped back up to the door. "Who's there?"

Two raps, nothing more.

David hesitated, then the door latch started to jiggle, then rattle. The door itself shook under the force of whatever it was that was trying to break in.

"Shit!" he cried, remembering the broken hasp on the lighthouse door. The same someone—or something—that was responsible for that break-in was about to do the same to this door. *It's going to come in whether I open the door or not. Might as well . . .*

He twisted the lock and stepped back, wondering if he was going to lose control of any bodily functions. The rattling ceased as he glanced behind himself, hoping to spot a weapon, but there was nothing.

When he looked back and saw the latch depressing, he said a silent prayer. As the door slowly began to open, the silence of the house itself was broken as the ghostly pianist began to play.

Six inches, and he saw nothing, but he recognized the tune: "I'm Only a Bird in a Gilded Cage." Somehow that seemed very appropriate right now. The door suddenly swung wide open and a tall silhouette blocked the night behind it.

Time seemed to slow as the figure stepped forward into the light. David thought he was going to faint, then he saw who it was and still thought he might pass out.

"Captain Wilder!"

Appearing to hear its name, the ghost focused—*seemed* to focus, David corrected—on him. It stepped forward and reached for him. As shocking as this was, David, knowing this entity meant him no harm, felt ready to faint from relief as he waited to be engulfed in the massive arms.

It was as before. Wilder felt cool but solid, though when David tried to touch him, his hand moved through the ghost as if through cool water.

Then, also as before, the spirit began to send emotions, in visual form, into his brain. At first, they were like the ones sent previously—full of Lizzie and feelings of love and sadness. Then came a wash of hate and fear in the form of Christabel—and a chilling image of the dark sailor represented by the doll that had been stolen.

Relentlessly, Wilder pounded the images into David's mind, pounding until David couldn't tell Wilder's emotions from his own. There was a feeling of desperation behind it all, and when the image shifted into that of Body House itself, a blood-curdling sense of danger pervaded it. In front of the house, Lizzie appeared, eyes wide with fear, mouth open in a silent scream, and then, suddenly, the captain's hug became so tight that David could barely breathe and Lizzie's screaming, terrorized face metamorphosed into Amber's.

Horrified, David heard himself groan and then, superimposed over Amber, he saw the dark sailor, Peter Castle, and Christabel. Finally, he saw the image of Captain Wilder himself, and experienced a sense of protective watchfulness.

As the ghost of Ezra Wilder let him go, David's rubbery legs betrayed him. He stumbled and dropped to his knees, trying to catch his breath, as the ghost of Captain Wilder somberly turned and walked down the porch steps. The soft strains of "Gilded Cage" faded away.

Shakily, David got to his feet. After a moment he ran out

onto the porch and down the steps. At first, he couldn't see the long-dead captain, then he spotted the dark silhouette moving slowly toward the lighthouse.

The wind shifted and as he turned to go inside, he thought he saw another figure standing quietly among the Monterey pines just west of the house, but it was gone in an instant. David, who knew he wrote what he wrote because he had always seen shapes in shadows, paid it no more attention, but turned and went inside, locking the doors securely behind him before returning upstairs, vaguely wondering if the entire world had gone crazy. Or if it was just him.

Wilder had been trying to tell him something, David thought as he climbed into bed. He suspected it was a warning about the sailor, Peter Castle—perhaps the doll had been broken or was in danger of breaking, thus releasing the soul of the man.

David shivered, pulling the quilt up around his neck. If breaking the doll of the beneficent Ezra Wilder made *him* powerful enough to break locks, communicate, and physically interact with the living, what might the soul of Chistabel's black-hearted lover be capable of doing?

Finally, he considered the most disturbing part of Wilder's visit and the reason for his own rubbery legs. The spirit had projected to him the image of Amber and it was obviously a warning about her safety, but, beyond that, he wasn't sure of the implications.

Confused, David rubbed his temples and decided to dismiss the captain from his mind for the night. Further pondering would be useless—he was beyond exhaustion. In the morning, he'd consider it all again. *Maybe you're just losing your alleged mind, Masters.*

David reached over to turn off the bedside lamp, then changed his mind and left it on. *To keep away the ghosts.* He closed his eyes and fell immediately into a deep, fathomless sleep.

August 16

Forty-one

New York City: 6:05 P.M.

Melanie Lord stood in her tiny kitchen waiting impatiently for the microwave to finish zapping her Lean Cuisine. She was still rattled by David Masters' phone message, and still contemplating its meaning. She wanted to call him back, but he hadn't asked her to and, as a result, she'd spent all day today scrubbing down her apartment, which was what she did when she couldn't make up her mind about something. She and Ray had planned to go to the Museum of Modern Art, but she'd canceled on him, knowing she'd be rotten company.

"Five, four, three, two, one," she counted as the microwave finished cooking her dinner. Ray had whined about the cancellation and she didn't like that. He'd also been whining about his proposal, the one he'd given her to submit to Harry Rosenberg over at Dorner. *David,* she thought, *I wish I'd listened to you about mixing business and pleasure. Boy, were you ever right, you son of a bitch. You sweet son of a bitch.*

In the other room the phone rang, and she paused, straining to hear who was calling. Probably Ray, to ask her if he could come over for a quick fuck and a little pillow talk, which would consist of him telling her how he needed her to get him half a mil from Rosenberg. Hell, she'd be amazed if Harry even nibbled at the proposal: Ray Blaisdell had done it up trite and sloppy.

"Hi, Mel? It's Amber. I—"

"Amber!" Melanie dropped her potholder and raced into the livingroom, snagging the receiver off the hook so quickly that the phone tipped and fell. She caught it before it reached the ground, crying, "Hang on!" over the static invective of the answering machine.

"Sorry," she said, switching off the machine. "Amber, is that really you?"

"It's me." The teen laughed delightedly. "Miss me?"

"Miss you? How can you even ask me that?" The fact was that the sound of the girl's voice filled Melanie so completely with a mix of emotions—most of them wonderful—that she was fighting back tears. "I miss the *shit* out of you, girl! How are you?"

For the next half hour, Amber rattled on about cheer leading, her sort-of boyfriend, how her dad was going to get her a car, and about her costume for a local dance. Finally, she paused and Melanie knew that the real reason she'd called was about to be revealed.

"Dad misses you, Mel."

Music to my ears. "What makes you think that, Amber?"

"He's pining away. He needs you."

"Well," she admitted, "I miss him too. Sort of." *Like hell, sort of!* "But—"

"I overheard him talking to Georgie, Mel. He's really jealous of Blaisdell. I think he wants to kill him."

"He knows about Ray Blaisdell?" Melanie smiled to herself, mentally retracting all the bitchy things she'd ever thought about Georgie Gordon. *Bless you, Georgie, you matchmaking devil!*

"Uh huh. Are you in love with him?"

"With Ray?"

"Yeah, I mean, are you engaged or anything?" Amber asked tentatively.

Melanie laughed. "No, hon, Ray's nice, but he's just a friend." *And he looks good escorting me around town, but he's nothing but a big hunk of petulant meat, just like his nickname.*

"Good," Amber said. "Can you fly out next Saturday?"

"What?"

"You've got to come to the party."

"What party?"

"You know, the Come As You Were Dance. You have to! I've got a costume ready for you and everything. Dad's dressing as the sea captain who loved Lizzie Baudey. Do you know who she is?"

David had talked about Lizzie and her house for as long as she'd known him. "Yes, I do, but—"

"Listen, Mel, you look a lot like her and I've got her dress ready for you. You can make *such* an entrance, Mel. It'll be, like, symbolic. The reunited lovers. It'll be *so* cool. He'll just die when he sees you."

"I don't think it's really such a good idea," Melanie said as she flipped the pages of her calendar to the twenty-second. "I mean, doesn't he have a date or something?"

"Or *something*." Amber's tone hit new heights of sarcasm. "You've got to save him, Mel, before the Wicked Witch of the West gets him for good."

Oh, great, Amber wanted her to crash a party *and* a date. "Amber, I can't just waltz in there and—"

"I know, I know. You can go with Rick and me."

Oh, boy . . .

"She's a gold-digging slut, Mel. She'll kill him."

"Amber—"

"She's like Lorna."

Melanie's stomach twisted with delight, or fright, she couldn't tell which. She knew all about Lorna. "You must be exaggerating."

"Not one bit," Amber replied firmly.

"Amber, I'd like to come," *and I have the time,* "but I don't think it's a good idea. Not unless David invites me himself."

"Listen, I'm going to tell you the rest, but you can't tell Dad, okay?"

"Okay."

Melanie's emotions spun between disgust and protective anger as the teenager recounted how the housekeeper had spread the filthy rumor about Amber's and David's relationship and then how this bitch, this Pelinore woman, had handed the girl her dad's underwear in a bag. That was too much, way too much.

"You swear she did that, Amber? Swear to God?"

"Any god you want."

"You're not exaggerating to talk me into coming?"

"I'm telling you *everything,* the whole truth and nothing but." Amber sounded a little angry, a lot desperate. "It's humiliating. I couldn't let Dad know. I hate telling you, but if that's the only way I can convince you that he's in danger from that witch, Pelinore, then . . ." Her words trailed off. Amber was trying not to cry.

Melanie believed her, all her instincts fluttering up into a weird older sister or maternal thing that Amber had always brought out in her. The teenager was the one being attacked. *She needs me, she really needs me.* The thought filled her with joy. She'd take this Theo Pelinore by the tits and twist them off and when she was done, the bitch would never fuck with Amber Masters again. She'd see to that and she'd make sure David knew what was going on, one way or another. "Okay, Amber," she said. "I think I can get away for a few days."

The moment Amber hung up, Melanie phoned her travel agent and made reservations because she knew she'd chicken out otherwise. Seeing Amber was one thing, but seeing that bastard David was another.

She know full well that the adjectives she always stuck in front of his name were empty words that she used to keep herself from missing him, from feeling foolish for blowing their relationship. David had been her friend—her best friend—as well as her lover, and that had made losing him a bigger blow than she thought possible.

She'd been able to tell him things she never thought she could tell anyone, and no matter what, he accepted her. She missed that and wondered if he did too. And then there were all the unimportant conversations—they'd talk for hours on end and, afterward, neither could remember the topics, but it didn't matter because what had really happened was that they'd connected on another level— recharging each other's batteries, was what David had called it—and it left them as close or closer than making physical love.

She missed that, too. David had been a gentle, thoughtful lover, the rare man who understood that feminine arousal began in the brain, not the crotch. He had the patience of a saint. *A horny saint,* she corrected, smiling to herself. He knew how to tease and titillate her. Often, he'd begin in public, early in the day with whispered comments and looks that made her feel like the most desirable woman on earth so that, by the time they were alone, she'd be ready to rip his clothes off. And still, he'd make her wait, indulging his inherent hedonism, teasing himself as much as he teased her. He'd start by touching her hair, kissing her eyelids and cheekbones and ears and neck, smelling her and making little moans, noises of pleasure that drove her mad and made her feel as if she were a priceless work of art.

Slowly, he'd undress her, always looking and smelling and tasting, an expression on his face that made him look like a kid in a candy store, and when all her clothes were off, he would continue his foreplay, kissing her inner thighs, right up to the place where leg and pubis met, but no further. And finally, when she could stand it no longer, and she was at the point of begging him to let her touch him and taste him, he would. At the same time, he moved in, giving her orgasm after orgasm, always dragging just one more out of her than she expected and, when she'd finally make him lose control, his orgasm would be so overwhelming that, at first, she was afraid he was going to have a heart attack. His eyes would roll back in his head and, if Amber was around, she had to put her hand over his mouth to muffle his cries. After, he would fall back, exhausted, for about five minutes. Then he'd look at her and say, "I need a steak—rare," and they'd dress and go out and indulge their palates, all the while staring stupidly at each other and knowing they had better sex than anyone else in the world.

Ray Blaisdell's hunky smile as he whispered, "How about a blow job, Babe?" just couldn't compete.

David, I want you back. A tear escaped and she wiped it away roughly. There was no way he'd have her back. She knew that. When she saw him again, she'd have to maintain tight control over her emotions and not let herself hope. Too much.

Forty-two

The Willard Residence: 4:00 P.M.

Calla Willard arrived at her parents' home for supper precisely at four in the afternoon. Usually, she hated the weekly get-together—her mother never wanted to hear a thing she had to say—but today, as she rapped smartly on the door, she was eager to listen to all the tales her mother could tell about David Masters.

She rang the bell impatiently. Calla hadn't listened to much of what Minnie had said about the arrogant writer before, but now she was more than ready. After the shameful way he'd treated her the night before, she wanted to hear it all. Maybe, she thought, she'd gather all she could on the man and sell it to one of the national gossip magazines. She could see the headline now: "Horror Writer Is a Real Life Horror: His Housekeeper Tells All." She smiled, then knocked loudly again. "Mother?"

There was no answer and, puzzled, she walked around the side of the house and found that the truck and the car were both there. Inside the white frame cottage, the phone began to ring.

Calla tried to blow air out her nostrils but her nose was too stuffy—she was catching a cold. Going back to the front of the house, she withdrew the spare key from the fake rock under the geraniums, slipped it into the lock, and opened the door.

The phone had stopped ringing and the house seemed deserted. "Mother?" she called. "Dad?"

She moved quickly through the shadowed living room, and into the hall, not bothering to stop in the equally dark kitchen. Farther up the hall, the bathroom light burned. "Mom?"

She let a little yelp of shock escape when she saw the reddish powder and black material on the bathroom floor.

She stooped to examine it more closely and saw that the powder had spilled from the broken remains of a china doll. Goosebumps rose on her neck as she hurried from the room.

Her mother's room was empty but when she opened the door to her father's room, she recoiled.

The shadowed room was cold, so cold, and there was a stink of old-fashioned men's cologne—the kind Ferd and Andy Cox liked to wear—mixed with a horrible metallic odor that Calla didn't immediately recognize. "Dad?" She felt behind her for the light switch.

She screamed as light blossomed within the room, revealing a red wash of blood and her father's body on the bed . . . and in the rocking chair . . . and on the dressing table.

"Oh God, oh God, oh God," she whispered in unconscious litany. She began backing from the room, her eyes still fixed on the arms, the hands neatly folded as if in prayer, upon the dresser. "Oh God, oh God, oh God—"

Sudden pain shot across her back in a dozen places. Dimly, she heard a cracking sound, then a whistle, and again, she felt stinging pain. She screamed.

Her scream was cut short by a hand over her mouth; a hand far colder than ice.

Forty-three

The Willard Residence: 4:40 P.M.

Bea Broadside had been trying to phone Minnie Willard since early this morning and, as she puffed along Gull Street, she was supremely annoyed at her friend for not answering the phone, thereby forcing her to move her six-foot, two-hundred-twenty-pound body nearly two whole blocks from her house on such a warm day.

She finished her cigarette and tossed it into the road before lighting another. Corking it into her mouth, she patted her jet black hair—she'd had it done just this morning, in preparation for the upcoming Come As You Were Dance. She was going as Queen Nefertiti this year. Her acrylic nails, also done this morning, flashed redly in the afternoon sun, and she admired them as she walked along, thinking that her date would be very romantic once he saw them.

Of course, she still had to ask Ferd, but she was pretty sure he'd say yes after she took him in the back room of the Stop n' Shop and left his wrinkled little dingus covered with her Blazing Beauty Red lipstick. He'd sure said yes in a hurry last year, after she'd done the same thing.

And wouldn't Minnie like to know about that? Bea coughed and spat as the Willard home came into view. Minnie wouldn't get to hear about it, though, but what she would hear about—Lyle Worthy's involvement with a college boy from San Luis Obispo—would just curl her hair. Just curl it.

It was exactly the sort of thing Minnie loved. And she'd be absolutely green that Bea had found out about it first.

"Crap," she said, recognizing the car belonging to that whiny snip, Calla parked in front of the Willard cottage. Bea couldn't stand the girl, but she hadn't come this far to leave on account of her.

Steadfastly, she walked up the path to the front door, which she was surprised to see was open. As she drew near, a stranger came out, a tall man in black pants, boots, and pea coat. He had white, white skin and black whiskers and long hair under a black watchcap.

"Hello—" Bea began, but her words died on her lips. The man's eyes bored into hers with frightening intensity, and he was coming right at her.

Dropping her cigarette, Bea halted. The man raised his hands as if he were going to grab her. Bea flinched, but held her position—what could he do to her out here, in broad daylight? Besides, during her secret-to-this-day stint as a dancer at Girly A Go-Go—a topless club that was the biggest draw in San Luis Obispo in 1967 (wouldn't Minnie *adore* knowing that?)—she'd crushed more than one pair of nuts in self-defense.

His hands were huge and Bea was pretty sure he was going to grab her double D's. "Don't try it, asshole," she said evenly.

The man didn't seem to hear. Suddenly, his hands were on her and they were the coldest sons-of-bitches she'd ever encountered.

"You asked for it, fuckhead!" Bea shoved her knee into his crotch as hard as she could.

An instant later, she was flat on her ass, because her knee had gone right through him. *Right through!* Now the guy stood looking at her. He started to bend down.

"Get the hell away from me!" she hissed, baring her teeth and showing her red claws.

He paused, then had the audacity to make a face, a big ugly sneer, before walking *right through her.*

Stunned, Bea Broadside sat sprawled on the sidewalk, her insides chilled from the passage of the man—or *whatever* it was—through her body. Slowly, she rose and watched him walk down the street. "Son of a bitch," she whispered. "Son of a bitch."

"Damn you, Minnie," she added, as she grunted her way to her feet, "Damn you." This beat the crap out of her story about Lyle Worthy. Beat the living shit out of it.

"Minnie?" she called as she approached the open door and peered inside. "Minnie Willard! Where the hell are you?"

She waited a moment, listening to the silence in the darkened house and, slowly, goosebumps prickled up on her neck and arms. She told them to go to hell. "Minnie!" she yelled. "It's Bea and I'm coming in."

The instant she stepped through the doorway, she smelled the blood. She hesitated, her fingers on the wall switch. *You don't want to do this. Just turn around, march out of here and call the cops. That man—that thing—that knocked you over was up to no good and you know it. Call the frigging cops.*

But that was the coward's way out and Bea wasn't about to turn chicken at this stage of the game. She'd seen plenty in her time; she'd even found a dead body stuffed in an old freezer out back of the nightclub way back when. She could take it, whatever it was.

Her hand hit the switch and the living-room lights blossomed. "Hmmph." Everything looked normal and she took several more steps inside, then stopped cold. Sitting on top of the television was Calla Willard's scrawny little head. It still wore its stupid granny glasses and that I-tasted-shit expression.

Bea barely felt the urine streaming hotly down her leg. *Call the cops.* She turned to pick up the phone on the table next to Mickey's easy chair, but it was buried under a big pile of guts that trailed from the chair. Calla's headless body had been split from neck to twat and the ribcage looked like it had been pulled apart by monstrous hands.

"Fucking Jesus," Bea whispered, as she dug in her handbag for a cigarette. Shakily, she corked it in her mouth and lit it.

Knowing it couldn't get any worse than it was already, she puffed the butt, and forced herself to stare at the body. Bea prided herself on her self-control and, though she was feeling a little rocky, she decided to finish what she started.

She moved into the hall and entered the kitchen.

Most of Minnie appeared to be in the sink, though her flayed and gutted torso lay in the center of the kitchen table like an Easter ham. A blood-speckled pie—it looked like apple—sat next to it.

Black spots swam in front of Bea's eyes, but she denied them, forcing herself to go to the huge kitchen sink. The legs were severed at the joints, as were the arms, and they were piled up, hands and feet in the middle. Waves of blood-stained silver hair curled up from between the fingers, as if Minnie was trying to fix her hair. Minnie always liked to look nice.

A guffawing laugh escaped Bea's lips. *Good old Minnie, always has to look her best.* She laughed again, clamping her hand over her mouth to stop herself. *Don't lose it, Bea, or you'll never live it down. No hysterics for you.*

Dizzy and dry-mouthed, she decided she needed water, but the sink was out—that made her laugh again. She turned to the refrigerator and opened it. A half-gallon carton of milk sat in front and she grabbed it, opening the top. She opened her mouth wide and tilted her head back, taking huge gulps directly from the carton.

Suddenly, something large and slippery entered her mouth. She dropped the carton and tried to spit the thing out. Something attached to it tickled her chin.

A rat! There's a rat in my mouth!

Frantically, she clawed at the tail, yanking it forcefully out from between her lips.

Holding it by the tail, she forced herself to look at it. It wasn't a rat. It was an eyeball, with a cornflower blue iris.

Here's looking at you, Bea. That's what Minnie would probably say, if she had a mouth to say it with. *Here's looking at you, Bea.*

"Here's looking at *you,* Minnie!" Bea said, and with that, she started screaming.

Forty-four

Body House: 8:17 P.M.

"Next Friday?" David took his feet from his desk and stood so rapidly that he nearly pulled the phone off the desk. "Why the change of schedule?"

The call from Jerry Romero had taken David by surprise but the news that Romero wanted to do the program almost a week early changed his delight into panic, or annoyance, he wasn't sure which.

"I understand that the town's holding a reincarnation party next Friday night," Romero explained.

"The Come As You Were Dance," David said, wondering how the man had found out.

"Yeah, that's it. We thought we'd take some film, do a little on-the-spot interviewing. Local color. It all ties in with the show, after all."

"Yes," David said. "I suppose it does." The Romero Show people had probably been checking the local papers, he realized.

"Are you attending?" Romero asked.

"I believe so." *So much for mixing with the natives.*

"What are you wearing?"

David hated these kinds of questions.

"Just some old sailor suit I found in the attic."

"Does it have bloodstains on it?" Romero asked eagerly.

Despite himself, David chuckled, and warmed to Romero.

"No, but it does have a fascinating history, if I'm correct." He told Romero a little about the love affair between Lizzie Baudey and Ezra Wilder.

Romero asked him to repeat part of it, obviously trying to get it all down. "This is great," he said finally. "Just great. Who's your date, if I might ask?"

"A local woman, a real estate agent. It's nothing interesting, Jerry," he lied quickly. "We're just friends."

"Do you have a lady love?"

"There's someone on the East Coast," David said slowly. He wasn't even sure why he said it. Wishful thinking, he supposed. After all, Melanie had never called him back. *Of course, I didn't ask her to.*

"This woman," Romero began, "the real estate agent?"

"Yes?" David asked, relieved he wasn't going to quiz him about the East Coast woman.

"Would that be Theodora Pelinore?"

"Yes, that's her name." He felt sick. "How do you know of her?"

"She called this morning, talked to one of my location managers. That's how we found out about the reincarnation thing. She belongs to a church of some sort that goes in for New Age beliefs. Are you a member, David?"

He controlled his voice only with great effort. "No, I'm not, and I don't have any interest in it beyond the scholarly aspects. Also, I'm not involved with Miss Pelinore. It's merely a date of convenience."

Romero laughed knowingly and David wanted to shoot him, right after he shot Theo.

"As your agent told you, David, we'd like to film a seance in Body House. Miss Pelinore says she can help arrange that. I assume that's all right with you?"

Shit. That interfering— "I suppose, as long as it's well supervised. I can't have anyone other than your crew and her channeling group in the house, however." He wondered what the hell would happen with Theo and her seance harpies messing things up. *She should have learned her lesson when we were attacked by Christabel.* He wondered if she remembered too little to be afraid, or if her need for fame outweighed her fear.

"We'll get that set up for Saturday morning, if that's okay with you."

"Fine." He didn't want Romero to know how upset he really was. "Anything else I can do for you?"

"The dungeon—"

"Well, Jerry," he said, his stomach twisting into macramé, "as I told Gaylord, I don't think I can—"

"David, Miss Pelinore told me you've found the entrance."

That bitch! Amber, why don't I listen to you? Why don't I ever listen to you?

"David?"

He cleared his throat. "Miss Pelinore had no business telling you that," he said, then began to lie because he'd decided he wanted nothing, absolutely nothing, to do with that damned cellar—and he didn't want anyone else to have anything to do with it either. "I've examined the area in question and I've found absolutely no evidence to support any kind of secret passage there."

"Surely you don't mind if I take a look?" Romero asked smoothly. "I've found some pretty amazing treasures over the years. I've got a knack."

"The old reporter's nose," David said, trying not to sound too sarcastic. "I'll show you the room. You can look." He'd show him the dormer room on the wrong side of the terrace, he decided. If Theo had told him where it was located, that should hide it well enough, as long as he could keep her out of the act. But how? Suddenly, he had a plan.

"Jerry, if we did happen to find the dungeon, I wouldn't want half the town in my house. It could be dangerous. What do you say you film the seance Friday night—you can get the people to come over at midnight, still in their costumes—and Saturday, when it's just you, me, and the crew, we'll try to find it."

"I like the costume angle. Sure, we'll do it your way."

"Dad?"

Amber's voice through the office door startled him. "I'm

on the phone, kiddo," he called, putting his hand over the mouthpiece.

"It's really important."

"So's this." He removed his hand. "Sorry, Jerry."

"No problem."

"Dad, it's *really, really* important. Craig Swenson's here."

"Jerry, something's come up. Can I get back to you?"

"We're all set. We'll see you at your place Friday afternoon to go over the plans. Fourish?"

"Fourish," David confirmed as Amber called him again. "Good evening."

" 'Night."

He hung up and opened the office door. Amber's face was flushed, her eyes bright as she looked up at him.

"Dad, something—"

He bent and kissed her forehead. "I owe you an apology."

"You do?"

"You were right about Theo all along. I was too stupid to listen to you. Again."

"And now you're stuck going to the dance with the witch?"

"How'd you know about that?"

"Gee, Dad, I'm your daughter. You can't keep stuff like that from me. So, you gonna stand her up?"

"No, no, of course not. But you were right. Now, what's the ruckus out here?"

"The chief's here. He's in his uniform."

"He's at work?"

"Yeah, I guess. He wants to talk to you. Something happened. I don't know what."

The chief was pacing the width of the parlor as David and Amber entered.

"Craig?"

Swenson turned and David saw that his face looked pale and tired, not lively and ruddy like it usually did. "Amber?" Swenson said. "Maybe you should leave."

"Do I have to?"

"Not if your dad doesn't care."

"She can stay."

"The Willards are dead," Swenson said heavily.

"Both of them?" David asked, too surprised to think.

"All three of them." Craig shook his head. "Looks like Minnie and Mickey died some time in the early hours of yesterday morning. Calla, this afternoon. Perp was still in the house."

"How?"

Swenson glanced at Amber. "Murder. A real mess."

"Amber's okay," David reassured him.

"Sexual assault. All three of them. Savage beating with a whip, Shayrock thinks it was a cat-o'-nine-tails with metal tips. Then he chopped them up." Swenson turned a little green. "Chopped them into little bitty pieces."

"Do you know who did it?"

"That's why I'm here—"

"My dad wouldn't kill anybody in real life." Amber suddenly grabbed David's arm protectively. "He only does it in books, and if you think—"

"No, no, Amber, I'm not accusing your father."

Silently, David sent a prayer of thanks to whatever gods were looking out for him.

"We have a description of the perp and it doesn't make any sense, Amber. *That's* why I'm here. You got any whisky, Masters?"

"Not a drop. Coffee?"

"Decaf?"

"I'll get it," Amber said before he could ask. "But don't say anything good until I get back."

Craig sat down heavily on the couch and David eased onto the easy chair opposite. "What's going on?"

"Bea Broadside, who's about as big as a quarterback and twice as mean, is our witness. She was going up the walk when the perp exited. He reached for her and she says she tried to knee him in the groin. Says she hit nothing but cold air."

"Jesus."

"Joseph and Mary. Says he walked right through her. Not around her. Right through her. Says he felt real cold."

David said nothing.

"Shayrock says you have his photo album?"

David nodded.

"I need to borrow that picture you told me about on the phone yesterday. The one of Christabel and that nasty-looking sailor?"

"Sure, but why?"

"You said the doll you think Minnie might have taken was a ringer for the photo?"

"Absolutely. It's a man named Peter Castle. Evidently he was Christabel's main squeeze. Why? What does this have to do with the Willards?"

"I wish I knew. Everything, I think. Broadside's description of the perp was very detailed. It sounds like she saw this Castle guy. I want to show her a picture."

"I'll get it."

Amber returned with the coffee as David rose to get the photo from his bedroom. Before he reached the stairs, he heard her pumping the chief, who wasn't telling her anything.

He returned five minutes later to find Amber still trying to get Swenson to talk. "Kiddo, I forgot to tell you, Rick Feldspar called earlier this evening. He wants you to call him back."

"Oh!" She jumped to her feet. "Can I use the phone in your office?"

"Go ahead." After she was gone, David smiled. "I hope Rick's home." He extended the photo. "Here you go."

Craig looked at it, shaking his head. "I'll be damned." He paused. "I need to ask you a weird question."

"Shoot."

"What did you do with the doll of the headless sea captain?"

"Eric insisted on burying it by the lighthouse. The body and the head. He told you—"

"The captain wanted his head." Craig gave him a tired smile. "I can't believe I'm buying this shit."

"Frankly, I can't either. Myself, as well as you," David added.

"The captain wanted his head." Craig shook his head. "Eric says he's a lot easier on the eye now."

"He is." David hesitated, then decided to go on. "He visited last night."

"What?"

"Came to the door. Knocked." David briefly told him the major details.

"Well, if we're not all heading for the rubber room, then I'd guess your captain was warning you about this guy." Swenson tapped the photo. "I can't believe what's coming out of my mouth. Of course, I can't believe what I did this afternoon, either."

"What did you do?"

"I messed with the evidence," Swenson confessed as he unzipped his jacket and reached inside. He withdrew a large Ziploc baggie.

"I was the first one on the scene. Broadside gave me her description and I left her outside with my deputy. I found this in the bathroom."

He extended the bag to David, who gasped as he saw the broken doll representing Christabel's lover. "She did have it. I don't believe it."

"Neither will anyone else. I shouldn't have taken it, but I made a snap decision." He chuckled grimly. "I thought about the explanations and I snapped. There was a lot of that red powder around the doll—you said you wanted it analyzed, so now you're in luck. Anyway, after Broadside described the perp and said all that stuff about him being cold and walking through her, well . . . My best guess is that they were killed by a frigging ghost. If I put that in a report, it'd be my ass and my badge."

"Why did you ask about what I did with the other broken doll?"

"A hunch. Broadside claims the guy didn't walk very far, and I swear to Christ, twice since I've had this on me, I thought I saw somebody lurking nearby. Probably nerves, but . . . You said the captain came all the way to the house?"

"Yeah. But he didn't come in. I thought he'd want to."

"His sweetheart's haunting the upstairs, isn't that the story?"

David nodded.

"Was there anything in those journals about ghosts being tied to the dolls?"

"Not exactly, but they weren't really detailed. The souls are supposedly tied to the area—the grounds, whatever—until Christabel is destroyed. It would make sense that they'd be tied to the dolls."

"It would. Which leaves me in a hell of a quandary. I was going to leave this with you." He gestured at the doll. "But maybe I should take it back to the station."

"Take it out in the middle of nowhere. That's the only way we'll know it's safe." David told him. "Throw it off Widow's Peak."

Swenson smiled. "A fitting end." He rose and David walked him to the door. "Masters, you ever feel like you're losing your mind?"

"These days, most of the time."

"Me too. I'm going to drive out there, toss this damned thing, and get back to work. See you."

"Say hello to the captain for me."

Swenson turned and gave him a sick look, then went on out to his cruiser.

David stood on the porch and watched him do the job, then went back inside once the chief had safely driven past the house.

"Dad?" Amber appeared as he approached his office. "Are you sure it was Rick who called? He said he didn't."

"He was happy you called, right?"

"Yeah, but—"

"I'm starved, kiddo. You want to go out for a pizza?"

"You bet."

Standing there waiting for Amber to grab her purse, he felt old, so old. The house was draining the life from him in dribs and drabs, draining his creativity with demands from a reality so skewed that no one could deal with them. Away from the house, he'd ask Amber how she was holding up. He didn't have more than a quarter of *Mephisto Palace* left and he thought that once the Romero interview was done, closing up and renting a nice little place in Pismo might be just the thing to help him finish. He understood how Commodore Patton felt when he said he could no longer stay here. He understood all too well.

August 22

Forty-five

Body House: 5:48 P.M.

"It's going to be a pleasure to work with you, Mr. Romero."

Dragging his gaze up from the bodice of Theo Pelinore's nineteenth century gown, Jerry Romero, nearly as tan and rakishly dashing as he appeared on television, smiled, favoring her with the full extent of his dimples. "Call me Jerry. And don't worry about your identity as channeler being revealed, Theo." His dark Latin eyes, as famous as his dimples, returned to her platter of breasts. "Your secrets are safe with us."

I'll bet. Theo's bosom, David thought, would be the talk of the Come As You Were dance, and she knew it. And loved it. He wasn't jealous, just filled with a disgust that had been building for nearly a week, ever since he found out she'd told Romero everything she knew about Body House and its secrets. After David discovered this, he'd called her and tried to talk to her about it rationally, tried to get her to explain her actions, but she'd blithely brushed him off. In a way, it was the best thing that could have happened, because since then he'd made himself unavailable, holing up and working on *Mephisto Palace* like one of those proverbial fiends. He had put the finishing touches on the novel shortly before lunch today, and by now it was winging its way to New York.

All week, the house had been as quiet as a tomb: no sounds

of laughter or piano music, no smell of jasmine or rot, no cold spots. He hadn't even had any erotic dreams, at least none that he remembered.

The only sign of paranormal activity came during a brisk walk he'd taken out to Widow's Peak and back. He was fairly certain he'd caught sight of Captain Wilder high on the lighthouse catwalk, but the phantom wasn't there when he looked a second time and he would have chalked it up to his imagination if Eric hadn't reported seeing the captain several times.

David smiled to himself: if things remained as quiet as they were now, Jerry Romero would be very disappointed and David would be quite relieved.

In a way, though, the quiet of the house had been more disturbing than its usual tricks. In the last week or so, during the first truly quiet times, David had had the feeling that Body House was holding its breath, watching him and waiting. That feeling had increased tremendously over the last few days, but his utter involvement in the book had helped him to ignore the sensation most of the time. Several days ago, it had become harder to ignore when he'd realized that Eric, too, was having a reaction to the apparent calmness of the house. The young man had constantly found excuses not to work inside its walls. David couldn't get him to say much about it: Eric claimed only to be unsure of why he felt the way he did, and David decided be was telling the truth, mostly because he doubted that Eric was capable of lying.

The Willard murders were still the talk of Red Cay, and Romero, since arriving earlier this afternoon, had asked several questions about them, but seemed fairly uninterested, thank God. David had talked to Craig Swenson and Keith Shayrock enough in the past week to know that Craig's not-by-the-book actions had been a fortunate choice. The powder had turned out to consist of blood, *old* blood, and Shayrock had listened, skeptical but fascinated, as Swenson and David had haltingly revealed what they knew about the dolls.

That the chief of police and the town doctor were virtual conspirators with him in this insane circus, secretly tickled the hell out of David, and even as he smiled to himself, he felt slightly sorry for the well-respected men. If either of them could dig up any kind of rational explanation, he was sure they'd embrace it like a long lost love—and he didn't blame them: he wanted an explanation pretty badly himself. He'd always thought of supernatural horror as something that arose in daydreams and nightmares, fantastic thoughts born of facts and twisted to the imagination's wishes. It seemed to be the other way around now.

The townspeople, caught in the grip of the nightmare of the Willard murders, were quiet too. They spent the nights locking and relocking their doors as they reassured themselves that the four-man police force and three auxiliary officers patrolling Red Cay would catch the murderer, while on the docks, the fishermen scrutinized all the incoming boats, watching for the mysterious and bloodthirsty sailor in black.

If they only knew . . . But, fortunately, they didn't, because Bea Broadside had unknowingly cooperated with Craig Swenson's wish to cover up the paranormal aspects of the case. After a single bout of controlled hysteria at the scene of the crime, where she told police the supernatural aspects of the man in black, she had said no more about it, stoutly claiming that the horrible sight of the bodies had made her imagination run wild. Swenson, relieved, figured that the woman didn't want to be thought of as a nut any more than anyone else in this town—except, of course, he remarked to David, for the Beings of Light, who thrived on nuttiness.

Nuttiness is putting it nicely, David thought as he watched Theo eeling around Romero like a cat trying to con its owner into giving it a saucer of milk. When David had found out that Theo was a channeler—he'd been told an hour ago, only because he'd walked into the room as she was talking to Jerry Romero—all he wanted to do was say he was ill and get out of this evening's festivities.

It wasn't that he considered all channelers to be charlatans. He'd encountered two—both of whom preferred the old-fashioned term, "medium," primarily because they didn't want to be associated with the New Age movement—to whom he grudgingly gave some credence. Their groups were closed, and no amount of money could buy you in—attendance was by invitation only. Evidently, he passed the mediums' musters, because he'd been invited to both and, whatever it was these groups were hooking into—David suspected that it was Jung's Cosmic Consciousness with an anthropomorphic twist—it did nothing more than observe and suggest. Also, unlike Theo's "Spiros of Atlantis" and most of the other "channeled beings," neither of these requested that members of the group carry out specific tasks or worship them. They'd also made comments about his personal life that were so succinct and so secret that no one could possibly have known and that told him that if it wasn't the collective unconsciousness these mediums had hooked into, they were at least very telepathic and selfless individuals.

Not like Theo, who had told Romero about her alleged talents in order to get herself a little fame and glory on television. *Whatever she gets in Body House, she deserves,* he thought unkindly. On second thought, he hoped that the house remained quiet and she got absolutely zilch.

Romero was now busy planning shots with his camera people, and Theo Pelinore, unaccustomed to being ignored, stood nearby, her lower lip protruding in a way that David knew to be sulky, though it could also masquerade as a show of voluptuousness. Feeling David's gaze, she glanced at him, then quickly looked away when he failed to smile at her.

At least she wouldn't be hanging on his arm all evening, showing off her catch like a fisherman with a two-hundred-pound marlin—obviously, she'd found herself a bigger fish. *I've been thrown back.* David smiled with amusement. The glance a moment ago was only the second time she'd looked at him this evening. Instead, she'd trained her attention—as well as her frank, sexual gaze, wet lips, and amazing cleavage—completely on the richer and more famous Romero.

I should have listened to Amber. He'd known that all along, but his hormones had taken off with his common sense. Amber had also known all along, and just a little while ago, as she was leaving to dress at Kelly's, she couldn't resist giving him one I-told-you-so smirk. At least it had held a modicum of pity. She'd kissed his cheek and told him things would look up soon, then she was out the door. Now, as Romero's crew began to file out of the house, he watched Theo flirt and he knew Amber was right: things were looking up already.

"We're all set," Romero told David as the sound man left the house. "Okay if we follow you down into town?"

"No problem," David said. He waited for Romero to exit, Theo clutching his arm and looking at him like he was a piece of tenderloin. He followed, pausing to lock the door. Tonight at midnight, the Beings of Light Channeling Circle would be back, along with the film crew, and he wished he could do something about that. *Oh well.*

He adjusted his jacket and captain's hat—he'd taken them to a tailor and now they fit perfectly, but the itchiness of the wool wherever it touched his skin was driving him crazy. As he walked down the steps and got into the passenger side of Theo's Volvo, he wished he'd thought to wear long johns beneath the trousers.

They rode in uncomfortable silence, David's resentment and anger growing with each passing moment, but Theo was too busy watching Romero's van in the rear view mirror to pick up on his body language. Finally, ready to explode, he cleared his throat. "Remember that night when we ended up screwing in the ballroom?"

Surprised by his blunt words, she glanced at him. "Yes?"

"I assume you were only pretending to be possessed?" He'd chosen his words not for any truth they might hold, but for their cruelty and, though their harshness startled even him, they felt so good that he pressed on. "Isn't it true that you were aware of what you were doing the entire time?"

"Why, David," she purred, "how can you ask such a question?" If he'd riled her at all, she'd hidden it perfectly. "You saw her. She manifested as a dark cloud. Poor Christabel," she added with a sigh.

Poor Christabel, my ass. His need to explode dissipating back into distaste, he wasn't even tempted to voice his thoughts. Instead, he shrugged and they rode in silence until they arrived at the Moose Lodge's parking lot.

"Here we are," Theo said. She got out of the car, carefully lifting her full satin skirts to keep them from brushing the ground. Smiling, she turned, and bending to peer at him, asked, "Don't you think Jerry Romero is a darling man? I wonder . . . Do you know if he's married?"

David's worry about ending their sexual relationship while remaining on civil terms—a necessity in such a small town—had lessened slightly when Jerry Romero had appeared on the scene, but he'd assumed that she'd be back, ready to crawl into his bed and shred his flesh as soon as Romero left town. Her words now made him realize that either she was pathologically self-absorbed, or she'd already written him off. Getting out of the car and adjusting his sailing cap, he realized that for the first time, getting dumped wasn't devastating: it was a relief.

Forty-six

The Cox Residence: 6:28 P.M.

Melanie Lord, her red hair flying and her brain fried from driving around in circles in the *absolute* sticks, pulled the rental car to a screeching halt in front of the ranch house on the outskirts of Red Cay. She couldn't see a house number, but it was the only one that matched Amber's description: it had yellow paint and gingerbread trim. "This has to be the place."

Though there'd been nothing wrong with the map she'd picked up at the rental agency in Santa Barbara, Melanie had repeatedly gotten lost once she'd reached Red Cay because there was an amazing lack of street signs, and Amber had laughed when she'd asked for landmarks. "There's a cow on the corner of Mollejas and Las Cabezas."

California was a foreign land with foreign names and, if that wasn't bad enough, her plane had arrived an hour and a half late, adding to her frayed nerves. Then the car people had made her wait another twenty minutes while they prepared her vehicle. But, she told herself as she turned off the ignition, those mundane irritations had at least kept her from going nuts thinking about what might happen when she surprised David with her presence in a public place.

"Melanie!"

Startled, she looked up and saw Amber flying down the front walk. An instant later, she was yanking the car door open and dragging her from the car.

"I was afraid you chickened out!" Amber cried as she threw her arms around her.

"The plane was late, then I got lost," Melanie explained, returning the hug. "I'm sorry!"

Amber stepped back and surveyed her. "You're a mess."

"Thanks a lot." Melanie tried vainly to pat her windblown hair into place.

"Don't bother with that," Amber said as she touched her own hair, which was piled in waves on top of her head and held fast with old-fashioned pearl-encrusted combs. "It's really late and we have to get you ready!"

Within three minutes, Melanie found herself standing in the middle of Kelly Cox's room, dry-cleaner's bags in her hands, as the two girls slipped into their dresses. Amber wore a revealing black gown from early in the century and her friend, a completely sweet little airhead, wore a red dress from the same era.

"Cool, huh?" Kelly asked, as Amber grabbed another dry-cleaner's bag from the back of a chair and pulled it from the gown it protected.

Melanie nodded, raising her arms to let the girls slip a drop-dead-beautiful green dress over her head. She felt like a half-baked Cinderella. "Amber, has your dad seen that dress you're wearing?"

"No. It's a surprise." Amber blushed lightly and both girls giggled.

The gown made her look twenty-five years old. "He's in for a lot of surprises tonight," Melanie said darkly.

"I'm going to phone Jason and Rick," Kelly announced suddenly, "and tell them to get their tails over here now."

She left, shutting the door firmly behind her. "I knew she'd leave," Amber said blithely. "Let's do your hair. I wish it was longer," she added, brandishing a curling iron.

"Are you sure this is a good idea?" Melanie asked.

"Uh huh."

"What about this Theo woman? She's his date?"

"Daddy's only going with her because he said he would," Amber said through a mouthful of bobby pins. "He found out I was right."

"Still, she *is* his date. I shouldn't intrude in public."

"Don't sweat it. All she did while I was at the house this afternoon was flirt with Jerry Romero, right in front of Daddy. It was *so* embarrassing. She's got her tits trussed up like you wouldn't believe and she kept shoving them in Romero's face. Poor Daddy, he was humiliated. Believe me, he'll be overjoyed to see you."

"I hope you're right."

Kelly came back in. "They're on their way. Wow, Melanie, you look incredible." She walked to her dresser and brought over a tray of make-up.

Ordinarily, Melanie hated to be fussed with, but tonight it was a relief.

"There," Amber said, holding up an ostrich feather. "We'll just stick this in your hair and you'll be all set."

Five minutes later, Kelly finished making her up, and only pouted slightly when Melanie declined to have her modest cleavage highlighted with blush. The teen stepped back and examined her. "God," she whispered, "you look just like her."

"Like who?"

"You really do," Amber chimed in. "Oh, you'll look just *perfect* with Daddy."

Melanie rose and walked toward the full-length mirror on the back of the door. "Okay," she said impatiently. "Spill it. Who do I look like?"

"Lizzie Baudey," Amber said.

Melanie barely recognized herself. Her hair had been swept up in soft curls and tiny tendrils coiled down her neck. The feather wasn't garish, as she'd feared, but perfect, and the gown was beyond perfection. The emerald color matched her eyes and set off her red hair and pale complexion faultlessly. The gown's straight, off-the-shoulder bodice was made for her petite bustline and the skirt flowed sensuously down over her hips, caressing her legs and making the same soft swooshing sound as a satin and chiffon party dress she'd especially loved as a child. A bare flash of calf showed when she moved and, after Amber clipped small green bows to them, her soft black ballet-style pumps complimented the rest of the ensemble.

"Wait'll you see the painting," Kelly said. "You'll freak."
"Painting?"
"In Body House, there's a portrait of Lizzie hanging in the parlor. She's wearing your dress." Amber snickered. "Or you're wearing hers. Here, put these on." Amber handed her a pair of delicate marcasite-and-pearl drop earrings.
"Girls," called Kelly's mother. "Your dates are here."
Melanie heard herself giggling along with the teenagers and, for the first time, she was glad she'd come. If nothing else went right, at least she got to enjoy feeling like a kid again.

Forty-seven

Red Cay Beach: 6:50 P.M.

"Come on, Billy, we have to get to the Lodge. The party started an hour ago!"

Billy Galiano, dressed in a pirate costume from last Halloween, looked up from the tidepool. "Just a sec, Mom! I'm coming."

There was something in a plastic bag floating down there among the sea urchins and he intended to see what it was, even if it killed him. He climbed farther down into the rocky recesses and fished the bag from the water. "Gotcha!"

"Billy!"

"Coming!" He had to hurry because he was completely hidden by the rocks now and Mom would send Dad after him if he didn't reappear quickly.

Out of the corner of his eye, he saw something move on the rocks across from him. *Crab!* Delighted, he looked up, then caught his breath as he saw a mean-looking man with big black whiskers staring at him from his perch on the rocks across the tidepool. He couldn't have been there the whole time, could he? The man smiled, and he was so scary that Billy almost threw the bag at him.

"Billy! Now!"

The sound of his father's voice ended Billy's paralysis. He scrambled up the rocks and ran like crazy.

His mom and dad, dressed as Pilgrims, stood waiting for

him. Dad checked his watch as Billy appeared. "Get in the car, sport," he said. "Pronto."

Billy ran ahead of his parents, wanting to see what was in the bag before they caught up, but they were walking fast too, so he couldn't. They were always afraid of him finding bad things on the shore, like hypodermic needles and stuff, and they would probably make him throw away the bag, sight unseen, if they caught him with it. They'd been extra weird about all sorts of things ever since his best friend Matty Farmer fell out of the lighthouse last May. Thinking of Matty suddenly made him feel very sad.

"What were you doing down there, Billy?" Mom asked as she got in the car.

"Looking for shells," he said, climbing in the back seat. If he told them about the creepy man, his dad would have to go look and Billy didn't want that—he was way too scary, even for Dad.

"Did you find any?"

"A couple. I put 'em in a bag."

"Well, don't get the seat dirty."

"I won't."

As they drove, his parents started talking to each other about other parties and other costumes. Meanwhile, Billy carefully unzipped the plastic bag and was disappointed to find that it contained nothing but a stupid old broken doll. A guy doll, which was weird, because it sure as heck wasn't a G.I. Joe. Well, he thought, maybe Janise Radsum would like it. She loved dolls—just to collect, because, at ten, she said she was too old to actually play with them. She also once told him that she liked really old stuff, too. Antiques. She'd be at the party tonight, dressed as a princess, and he thought that if he gave her the doll, maybe she'd give him a kiss again, like she had in the coat closet at school. Then, maybe, he'd have enough nerve to ask her to dance with him.

Forty-eight

Red Cay Moose Lodge: 6:59 P.M.

David stood with Keith Shayrock and Craig Swenson in a secluded corner of the Moose Lodge. The huge room, festooned with balloons and crepe paper streamers, gave him the nostalgic feeling that he'd gone back in time to a high school dance. As he sipped watery, slightly alcoholic punch from his paper cup, he watched the small-town spectacle taking place all around them. He thought that the decorations, the costumed people, and the odd snatches of conversation he overheard, all belonged in a book.

"It can't happen," Shayrock said suddenly. Like David, Craig, and—from the looks of things—most of the town, the doctor had eschewed the advisories of the crystal-packers' channeling service, choosing instead to dress as his own grandfather, assuming, he had explained with a twinkle in his eye, that Louis Shayrock had been Jack the Ripper. A bloody plastic cleaver stuck not-so-subtly out of his ancient black medical bag, and if you looked closely, the fingers of a severed hand poked from the pocket of his English greatcoat. He looked every inch the mad doctor, right up to his incurably stubborn shock of carroty hair, which was already escaping from beneath his otherwise distinguished derby.

"It did happen," David said, scratching his wrist where the wool coat was irritating it. Shayrock had been saying "It can't happen" ever since they'd told him about the blood-filled dolls.

"Yeah," Swenson agreed. He wore an old-fashioned policeman's uniform that looked equally itchy and nearly as old as David's seaman's suit. He gave his ancient nightstick a quick twirl. "It happened."

"Something *else* happened," the doctor insisted. "What you two are describing is impossible. It doesn't work that way. If a doll was filled with fresh blood long ago and it was sealed tightly—and I mean airtight—and you broke it eighty years later, the blood could still be liquid. But it wouldn't be hot, like you described, Masters, unless the doll had been heated, and it wouldn't turn to powder in an hour. Blood clots." He paused thoughtfully. "However, if you broke open a doll that wasn't airtight, after eighty years, you'd probably have the powder, just like we found at the Willards'. I'd like to see the doll."

"That's impossible," Swenson said sourly.

"Why? Don't you have it? If I could examine it, I might be able to tell you something solid."

Sheepishly, the chief glanced at David. "It's gone," he said finally.

"Gone where?"

"Into the ocean."

"What?" Shayrock demanded.

Swenson was looking more and more embarrassed. "Tell him, Masters," he grunted.

"Minnie Willard stole the doll from my house. She took it home and somehow she broke it, thus releasing the spirit of Peter Castle, the man the doll represents. Castle killed the Willards—somehow."

"Voodoo?" Shayrock asked dryly.

"Shit," Swenson commented.

"He was Christabel's lover, so who knows?" David cleared his throat. "The chief took the doll."

"And I felt like I was being watched the whole time I had it," Swenson said. "So I took it to Masters here and we decided that the only way to get rid of Peter Castle was to get rid of the doll. So I threw it off Widow's Peak."

"And I thought you didn't have a superstitious bone in your body, Swenson," the doctor chided.

"Hell," Swenson grunted.

"Let's get back to the blood," Shayrock said. "Masters, are you sure it was warm?"

"Yes."

"Was the doll in the sun?"

"Hardly, my daughter was in the laundry room. She found it in a cupboard."

"Water pipes?"

"None in sight," David told him. "Amber said it was hot and it sprayed her, you know, like a vessel bursting. She said it got in her mouth and that it tasted like blood."

Shayrock shook his head, a tell-me-another-one look on his face. "So you didn't actually *see* any of this?"

"It had just happened. I walked in and found Amber screaming and covered with blood. Fresh blood." David suppressed an involuntary cringe. "She said it tasted like blood," he repeated.

"You're sure she's not pulling your leg?"

"I saw the results, material and emotional," David said grimly. "My daughter is not the hysterical sort."

"I'll vouch for that," Swenson added.

Something in the tone of their voices seemed to convince Shayrock that both the writer and the cop were deadly serious. He looked from one to the other, then shrugged helplessly. "Then I have no way of explaining it medically."

That was exactly what David had expected to hear, but the chief wasn't ready to accept David's voodooesque theories without a fight. "Could somebody have intentionally powdered the blood in the Willard residence?" the chief asked.

Shayrock took the derby off and scratched his head. Immediately, his hair sprang up like he'd stuck his finger in a light socket. "Someone could powder dried blood if they wanted."

"Hey Uncle Craig!" Eric Swenson, all cowboy from his Stetson to his boots, strolled up, an attractive blond woman in gingham and a bonnet on his arm. "Hey, Doc. David, this is my mom, Holly."

"It's a pleasure to meet you." David doffed his sailing cap.

"And you," she said, shaking his hand. "Eric speaks very highly of you."

"I speak highly of him."

Eric turned red. "David, you were worried about not having any fun because people'd be asking you for your autograph all night. But they're not. How come?"

"Eric," Holly began.

"It's all right," David said swiftly. "Eric doesn't mince words—that's one of the things I like about him." He paused. "Jerry Romero happened, Eric. He's here interviewing folks about their past lives."

"Are you angry?" the young man asked.

"No, I'm relieved. I get to talk to friends like your uncle and Dr. Shayrock—*we won't mention the topics covered, however*—and that's a lot more fun than answering that age-old question about where I find my ideas."

Though he was tired of public recognition, now that Romero and his minicam had stolen his thunder, not to mention his date,—*small loss*—David found that, despite his words, he was also slightly miffed at being ignored. He knew he should enjoy it, savor it in fact, but as the saying went, the grass was always greener.

"Isn't it awful about the Willards?" Holly Swenson asked, in a tone of voice that showed a distinct lack of sorrow. "Eric, would you like to dance with your old mother?" she asked as the enthusiastically mediocre Moose band struck up "Boogie Woogie Bugle Boy."

As the pair wandered off, Craig Swenson squinted in the direction of the punch table. "You said you wanted to talk to the twins, Masters. There they are."

"Twins?" David asked, confused.

"The Cox boys."

David, his book complete and his enchantment with Body House rapidly dying, had little desire any more to chat up Ferd and Andy, but he followed Craig's gaze, smiling as he studied the matched set of hawk-faced, dour-looking old men. They stood side by side, both dressed in buckskins and coonskin hats, their arms folded identically across their chests. "They don't look happy."

"They aren't." Craig chuckled. "Every year, both of them dress up as Davy Crockett, and then they fight over which one of them really was the king of the wild frontier."

"You're kidding." David paused. "Right?"

"Seems they went to the High Hooey Center and got themselves past life readings. Well, I guess that entity of Theo's got mixed up, what with the old boys looking so much alike, and thought they were the same person. They were both told they were Davy Crockett."

A large woman, unfortunately dressed as some sort of Egyptian royalty—maybe not Cleopatra, but something similar—joined the twins. A cigarette waggled in her mouth as she looked, from one to the other then, obviously unable to tell which was which, pushed between them and took both their arms.

Shayrock cleared his throat. "That's Bea Broadside."

"The woman who saw Peter Castle?" David asked quickly.

"The very one." Craig shook his head. "She won't talk, though. Took back every last word about the ghost walking through her." He raised his eyebrows. "Guess she's saner than you or me."

They people-watched a while longer. "I wonder where Amber could be," David said finally.

"I don't see much of the high school crowd in here yet," the chief said. "They all hang around outside, pretending we force them to come."

David nodded, chuckling. "They love the dance, but it's not cool to admit it."

"Right. They'll be in by nine—that's when they hold the costume contest," Swenson said as a couple dressed as Donald and Daisy Duck strolled by.

"Wonder if *they* got advice on their past lives from Spiros?" Shayrock commented dryly.

David shook his head. "Christly crystal-packers."

"You pissed at Theo?" Swenson asked, giving David a sidelong glance.

"Why do you ask?"

"She's your date, isn't she?" Swenson said. "That's what she was bragging about all over town."

David watched Theo as she clung to Romero's arm and whispered God-knew-what in his ear. "She's my date, but in name only. She called Romero and told him everything I asked her to keep to herself." He grimaced. "As a result, we're having a seance tonight. Jerry and the channelers."

"In Body House?" Shayrock asked.

"Yep."

"Theo's always been a social-climbing bitch," the doctor commented. "Excuse the language, but the word is precisely chosen."

David suspected the doctor had also been climbed and tossed at one time or another.

"You worried about letting them do it?" Swenson asked. "The seance, I mean?"

"A little. I don't really think anything will happen with a camera rolling. That goes against your basic haunted house rules."

"That house breaks a lot of rules, Masters. You want me to come out tonight? I have a few things to do first, but I could make it out there by half past midnight or so."

"Chief, I'd appreciate it greatly. You, too, Doc, if you want."

"No thanks. I get nervous when my night light burns out." Shayrock set his empty cup down on the table. "Excuse me." He wandered into the crowd and a moment later David spotted him dancing the Tennessee Waltz with Holly Swenson. Eric stood at the edge of the dance floor and watched them, a smile on his face. A moment later, a young woman whom David had seen working in Greenaway's twirled the handsome young man onto the dance floor.

"I think I might be getting a new brother-in-law," Swenson said. "Doc's been stuck on Holly forever, but he's too damn shy to do anything about it until lately." He chuckled. "Guess he'd be a brother-in-law-in-law." Swenson tapped David's arm and nodded toward the entry doors. "That's Billy Galiano and his parents."

"The boy who survived the accident last May? I'd like to talk to him."

"Not a good idea. His parents have become very protective of him and I understand he's in therapy. I wouldn't say anything if I were you."

Reluctantly, David nodded. The boy, dressed as a pirate with an eye patch, tri-cornered hat, and fake mustaches, was carrying something under his arm, and he made a bee-line across the room to a little pink fairy princess. Solemnly, he handed her a dark object. She accepted it with equal solemnity, then both children looked around. Finally, they walked over to the folding chairs lining the opposite wall, and she set his gift and her little rose-colored purse down on a vacant chair. A moment later, the kids were out on the dance floor, the boy looking as if he'd died and gone to heaven. His lady love looked equally happy. *Better lay off the punch,* David told himself, realizing there were tears of sappiness in his eyes, *or you'll have to give up horror and write romances instead.*

Forty-nine

Red Cay Moose Lodge: 7:12 P.M.

Theo Pelinore wished Jerry Romero would stop interviewing the local yokels for a few minutes and pay attention to her, but he kept going from person to person, smiling, asking questions, and giving instructions to his three-man crew in between.

She didn't feel very bad about ignoring David Masters in favor of the darkly handsome telejournalist. David was nice, but he lacked the fire she so desired, and when he did heat up, she usually felt like she was a substitute for someone else, probably that Melanie creature that that spoiled brat Amber kept throwing in her face.

She'd thought there was hope for a passionate relationship with David when they'd encountered the spirit of Christabel last week. David had been caught, for a few brief moments, in the passion that surrounded the spirit, though he soon regained himself and tried to drive it away. *Coward!* He couldn't let himself go. Theo, on the other hand, sensed that Christabel was her kindred spirit, for the ghost possessed a passion and appetite for pleasure that matched her own. She had welcomed the girl's spirit into her body, much as she welcomed Spiros each week.

The experience had frightened her in some ways—Christabel was stronger than she—but she didn't resist and soon found that she could share her body with the spirit, retaining full consciousness, and could feel many times over the depth of passion that she herself so needed.

Tonight in the car, Theo had been a little irritated when David had accused her of pretending her possession, but then she realized that he'd only been trying to hurt her. She smiled to herself, pleased that she could arouse jealousy in the man.

She glanced at Jerry, who was speaking animatedly with Gary Morris. The mayor of Red Cay was dressed as Sherlock Holmes and his wife stood next to him, her eyes twinkling with merriment behind her Dr. Watson mustache. Last year they'd shown up in Civil War costumes—a Union officer and a nurse—and had won the costume contest. The only reason they'd won—Theo had expected the grand prize and was still a little miffed—was because Mary had been the officer and Gary the nurse and, evidently, the town had loved the sight of their mayor in drag.

Romero was laughing at something the couple had said and Theo, bored stiff, looked around just in time to see the Galiano boy hand something to his little schoolmate, the daughter of the Radsum couple who had bought the Cape Cod two-story out at the end of Cottage Street. The girl carefully set the something down, then took the boy's hand and led him onto the dance floor. *Puppy love. How tiresome.* Theo sighed, wondering what the boy had given her to get her to dance with him.

Jerry was still talking as she saw that redneck cop, Swenson, and David standing in a corner. David was watching the kids dance and looked positively diabetic over them. *No wonder he has no passion—he's nothing but a romantic.* Theo didn't have time for things like that, things that took away from the zest and reality of life and replaced them with false dreams.

"Excuse me," she said to Jerry, who didn't even reply. Casually, she crossed the room, stopping to chat with friends and acquaintances along the way. Finally, she made it to the chair where the Radsum girl's belongings had been placed. Using her wide courtesan's skirt to bump the pink plastic purse off the dark object below, she bent to retrieve the purse, taking her sweet time so that she could examine the object.

It was a doll. A broken doll, obviously from the Baudey collection. It was slightly damp and sandy, as if he'd fished it out of the sea.

Furtively, she glanced around. No one was watching. As she placed the purse on the chair, she slipped the doll into a vast pocket hidden beneath the apron of her skirt. Then, utterly pleased with herself, she wandered to the punch table where a stranger, a tall man in black seaman's clothes, smiled at her from behind a black beard. His eyes were fierce and passionate, and Theo felt a thrill travel down through her belly to nest warmly in her crotch. The crop of a short black cat-o'-nine-tails poked out from beneath his arm.

He didn't say a word, just handed her a cup of punch, then turned and disappeared into the crowd. Her fingers tingled where his chilled hand had touched hers and, unconsciously, she put them to her lips. They tasted of salt water and smelled of bay rum.

Fifty

Red Cay Moose Lodge: 7:25 P.M.

"David Masters," Jerry Romero said as he pushed the microphone into David's face, "why would the most popular horror writer in this country—or any country, for that matter—choose to live in a sleepy little town like Red Cay?"

The camera lights blinded him, but David smiled and answered Romero's questions, one after another, with as much aplomb as he could muster. Gaylord had warned him that Romero was known for his refusal to edit out embarrassing gaffes—he considered others' mistakes to be the meatiest part of an interview. In fact, it was more likely that Romero would edit out his best answers and keep the ones that David bungled.

At least the questions Romero threw at him now were fairly easy to give Teflon answers to—how he liked Red Cay, if he believed in reincarnation, how his daughter was getting along. The hard questions would come tomorrow, at Body House.

Romero launched into a brief introduction to Body House itself, then said, "David, I know there's a fascinating—and romantic—story behind the sea captain's uniform you're wearing this evening. Would you care to tell us about it?" He paused, turning to his assistant. "Make sure we cut in a shot of the portrait of Lizzie Baudey at the right moment when we put this together, maybe an overlay with David so it looks good and ripe." He turned back to David, saying. "Sorry, didn't want to forget that," then pushed the microphone back into his face. "Go ahead."

Glancing at the door once more, hoping to see his daughter, David began recounting the romance of Lizzie Baudey and Ezra Wilder, embellishing upon it the way he did in his new novel. Soon, he was completely caught up in the telling of the tale, which was really no surprise: as the weeks had passed, it had become his favorite tale and the most important aspect of *Mephisto Palace.*

He could barely see past the camera lights, but as the tale drew to a close he realized that a large, silent crowd had gathered to listen, and he thought fondly that perhaps the love story, not the flashy journalist, had caused the intense quiet.

"And, to this very day," he finished softly, "Lizzie, as beautiful as ever with her red hair and emerald-green gown dyed to match her eyes, is imprisoned within the walls of the old stone mansion on Byron's Finger. Here, she awaits her beloved Ezra's return while, only a few hundred feet away, Captain Wilder forever walks the spiral staircase of the old lighthouse."

A tear sprang to his eye and, unashamed, he wiped it away. "For eighty years, the murdered lovers have been so condemned, and through all those years, their hearts have been heavy with the aching sorrow which only those who have known and lost their one true love can ever understand."

"What a story, folks," Romero said, his voice shaking with feigned emotion. "What a story. And David is dressed in the very uniform that the good captain wore while he courted his beloved Lizzie." He wiped an equally fake tear from his cheek. "Perhaps later in tonight's program we'll get a glimpse of one, or both, of the ghostly lovers."

At that moment, the crowd began to applaud and the lighting technician and minicam operator swiveled to pan over the audience, leaving David blinking away spots as his vision returned. He began to scan the audience for Amber, but only managed to briefly lock eyes with Theo Pelinore, who didn't even bother to disguise the look of contempt on her face. *She probably laughed when Bambi's mother died.*

The applause began to die down, then it grew again, louder

than ever. Suddenly, people were parting, making a path to let someone through. Romero glanced at David, obviously wondering if he knew what was going on. David gave him a barely perceptible shrug, which the journalist acknowledged with a nod before he moved forward to greet whoever it was. A few feet into the crowd Romero halted, his crew with him, then they all began to move backward as the person or persons advanced.

From where he stood, David could see nothing but the backs of Romero and his men. Then the crew swung to one side and Romero to the other, revealing the woman in green.

"Lizzie?" he whispered, uncomprehendingly. For an instant, he thought he was seeing her ghost.

Her smile trembled on her lips and Romero was pattering on and on, but David heard none of it, aware only of the vision before him.

Melanie? No, it can't be! She wore Lizzie's dress, the one from the portrait, and her hair, caressed by a green ostrich feather, was piled on top of her head, though a few fiery tendrils dared to kiss her neck. Her green eyes were luminous, and her skin pale, though there was a high flush on her cheeks and across her breasts that David recognized, a characteristic blush that appeared on Melanie Lord whenever she was embarrassed—or had an orgasm.

"Melanie?" he asked, his throat dry, his voice a bare rasp. *It can't be, she's in New York. It's someone Romero planted to look like Lizzie. It's theatrics. Don't fall for it.*

But then she spoke. "David?"

"My God," he gasped. "My God, it *is* you! What are you doing here?"

She hesitated, obviously unsure of his reaction, which made sense, since he didn't quite know what he was feeling.

"Amber?" he asked.

Melanie's nod was barely perceptible. "I'm sorry—" She faltered, glancing at Romero and his camera. "I didn't mean to intrude . . ."

And then he knew his feelings. "Mel," he said, Stepping toward her.

Instantly she was within the circle of his arms and he forgot everything else as he swept her up, finding her lips as her gentle, warm hands pushed into his hair, toppling his captain's cap to the floor. He drank in the scent of her skin and hair, tasted her lips, and explored the silky smooth feel of her shoulders and neck with his fingertips. "Melanie."

And then the world inserted itself between them in the person of Jerry Romero, who was gushing on about how famous author David Masters had obviously thought he'd lost *his* one true love, folks, but here she is, and if poor star-crossed lovers Lizzie and Ezra are looking on—

David and Melanie sprang apart, Melanie's skin flushed with embarrassment, his own face burning.

Romero asked them a few questions and they both answered noncommittally, professionally, without meeting each other's eyes.

"How did you happen to be here tonight to surprise David?" Romero asked Melanie.

"It was Amber's idea," she said, and Romero bit into that like a pit bull, calling for David's daughter to join them.

Amber finally came forward, pushed by her giggling friends, and David gasped again as he saw what she wore—the filmy black dress, the red lipstick, the provocative hairstyle.

She couldn't know that she wore the very dress that Christabel had appeared in on the day she materialized to fight with Lizzie.

Despite his swimming head, David finished the interview fairly smoothly, helped by Theo Pelinore's hateful glare. Though it was primarily directed at Melanie, it kept a little part of him grounded. Mel, too, was well aware of it and holding her own with a look of breezy disdain that indicated that she considered Theo as important as a fly on the wall.

After Romero wandered off, Melanie and David stayed close together, though they were unable to exchange two words due to the press of people that continually gathered around them. Occasionally, David caught Theo's scowl and every time he did, the urge to protect Melanie from the witch—Amber had named her correctly—nearly overpowered him. He did nothing, however, since the woman was again attached to Romero and showed no sign of letting go for a little petty vengeance.

Between the mindless chatter and Theo's freezing gaze, he also managed to keep an eye on his daughter. He wanted to send her home to change her clothes, but decided it was more trouble than it was worth. Besides, her date, Rick Feldspar, seemed to be keeping his hands to himself, and simultaneously guarding her from the approaches of other boys.

So David did nothing but maintain. The costume contest gave him a brief respite, and when he and Melanie won without even entering, he felt like they'd been named King and Queen of the prom. It felt good and that helped him enjoy, rather than endure, the next couple of hours of socializing. Finally, around eleven, he and Melanie had a few moments alone, and he filled her in on the plans for the rest of the evening.

"You don't sound too happy about this seance business," she said.

"I'm not."

After their initial scramble into each other's arms, he'd felt painfully awkward with Melanie. Perhaps she felt the same, because instead of talking about their relationship, she began asking him questions about Body House. Gratefully, he answered them and soon, as they discussed the phenomena, the awkwardness disappeared.

They slipped away at eleven-thirty to walk down to the beach—a two-minute hike—and once they were totally alone, David told her not only all about Theo Pelinore, but also about the seeming possession, as well as the wet dreams, the apparent succubus visits, and the fight between the ghosts of the mother and daughter. Mel listened intently, without judgment, just as she always had, and he felt as if the biggest weight in the world had been lifted from his shoulders. Finally, he had Melanie to talk to again. He'd missed that more than anything.

"It's almost midnight," she said, checking her watch under the glare of a yellow sodium light. "Should we be getting back?"

"Unfortunately, yes. But let's walk nice and slow."

She smiled at him and, as they strolled back, she told him about her affair with Meat Blaisdell, and about a short fling with a minor editor at Knoll Books. "David," she said, pausing as they neared the lodge's doorway. "You were right, and I apologize."

"What was I right about?"

"You can't mix business and pleasure. Ever. I guess I had to learn it the hard way."

"Well, I learned it the hard way too," he admitted, "but I was probably a self-righteous prick about it. You know, preaching at you when you wanted me to leave Georgie, instead of telling you about my experiences. I apologize too."

"I'm glad I don't represent you, David," she said softly. "Then I couldn't do this." She stood on her tiptoes and brushed her lips chastely against his cheek.

Pleased and surprised, he nearly grabbed her for a more serious kiss, but still he felt slightly unsure of himself, perhaps because they'd talked about sex with other people—*other things, for Christ's sake*—as if they were old friends, platonic friends, and nothing more. *Slow and easy,* he cautioned himself. *Don't rush it.*

Silently, they stood in the open doors a moment, and watched the party-goers. Vainly, David squinted in an attempt to recognize the strange dark-clothed, bewhiskered man Theo was dancing with. He looked vaguely familiar, even at this distance, and for some reason this disturbed him. *Probably just some High Hooey artist in costume,* he decided, returning his attention to Melanie.

As he studied her, he regretted that they might have hurt each other too much in the past to again attempt any kind of relationship beyond a platonic level. But at least, he consoled himself as they reentered the hall, he had his best friend back.

August 23

Fifty-one

Parking Lot of Red Cay Moose Lodge: 12:00 A.M.

"Chief Swenson?"

At the sound of the child's voice, Craig turned and saw the Radsum girl—Janise, he recalled—waving at him from the window of her parents' car. They were just getting ready to pull out of their parking space.

Craig walked over, tipping his hat. "What can I do for you, young lady?"

"Oh, Chief, it's nothing," Mrs. Radsum said quickly.

"Just a misunderstanding, I'm sure," added the girl's father.

"I saw her do it!" Janise insisted vehemently.

Both parents looked mortified. "Janise, we'll get you another doll," her mother said.

"But it's wrong! She stole it, and Billy gave it to me, and I don't *want* another doll, I want the one Billy gave me."

"Honey, you said it was broken—"

"I don't care!" insisted the fairy princess.

Alarm bells going off in his head, Craig lifted his left hand, signaling the parents to be quiet. "Janise, what kind of doll did Billy give you?"

"It was real old and it was a boy doll. It was ugly and there was a big crack in it, but I really liked it."

"What did it look like?"

"He had dark hair and a little beard and, you know what,

he even had eyebrows made out of real hair. He was like glass."

"China?"

"Yes, Chief Swenson. Like china."

Shit! It couldn't be. "And Billy gave it to you?"

"Yes."

"Where did Billy get it?"

"He found it in one of the tidepools."

God help us, Peter Castle's back. Hiding his agitation, Craig merely nodded and asked mildly, "Who took your doll, princess?"

"The lady we bought our house from."

"I just can't believe that Miss Pelinore would do something like that, honey," her father said.

"Me either," chimed in her mother.

But I can. Craig cleared his throat. "I'm going to be seeing her in a little while. I'll ask her about it—"

"Oh, no, please," said Mrs. Radsum.

"I'll be diplomatic," Craig promised.

"She stole it! I saw her do it."

"Maybe it belongs to her," Craig said gently. He wasn't defending Theo Pelinore, he was stopping embarrassing questions. "Maybe she lost it and when she saw it, she didn't even think about anything but getting it back."

The little girl nodded without much enthusiasm, though her parents made up for it. "If she stole it, I mean *really* stole it?"

"Yes?"

"Will you punish her?"

"I sure will, Janise. I'll call you in a day or two, okay?"

"Okay."

"Evening, folks."

He walked back to the cruiser, his mind racing. He was so tired, he had intended to beg off the Romero thing at Body House, but now he had to get out there. Eric was still inside the lodge talking with Holly and Doc Shayrock. Craig had to collect him, then stop by the station to take care of some business. He wouldn't get to the finger until twelve-thirty, at the earliest, but at least he'd get there. Masters had to be told about the reappearance of the doll.

Fifty-two

Body House: 12:09 A.M.

"I really wish you'd gone back to Kelly's like we'd agreed, kiddo."

Amber pulled past Romero's van and a half dozen other cars, including Pelinore's, and parked, then, taking the keys from the ignition, she tossed them to her father. "Oh, Dad, don't be such a worrywart! I wouldn't miss this for the world." She glanced back as Melanie nosed her rental car in next to the Bronco. Her dad had said virtually nothing about Melanie's appearance during the ride back to the house, preferring to talk about the costumes and the small-town gossip. She figured he was either really pissed at them for going behind his back, or he really wanted to be but wasn't. She couldn't stand not knowing any longer. She swallowed, and asked brightly, "Aren't you glad Mel's here?"

"You shouldn't have—" he began, then paused. "But I'm glad you did."

She grinned, amazed he'd admit it. "You should listen to me more often."

"Don't get cocky."

Melanie tapped her keys on the glass before Amber could reply, which was just as well—she didn't want to push her good luck. Instead, she opened the door and jumped down to the ground. Leaning against the hood to wait for her dad and

Mel, she stared at the brightly lit house as it played peek-a-boo behind the whispery curtains of fog.

Kelly, Rick, and Justin, along with some of the other kids, were at the pizza parlor right now and she really wished she were with them, but she wouldn't have enjoyed it because she was too worried about her dad, Melanie, and that witch, Pelinore. Maybe if she'd paid more attention this evening, she would have known he and Mel were getting along and then she could have gone, but she'd been having too much fun dancing with Rick to notice.

Dad and Melanie were talking quietly on the other side of the car and, furtively, she watched them, hoping they'd get romantic. But so far, nothing.

She turned her attention back to the house. When she'd told her dad she wasn't afraid, it wasn't exactly true, but to be honest, she was more afraid of what Pelinore might do than what might happen in the house—she really doubted that anything would happen anyway. Dad always maintained that pointing a camera in the direction of a spook guaranteed a lack of ghostly activity, and usually he was right. Also, although she tried to be cool about it, having Jerry Romero and his television crew here was really exciting and she didn't want to miss it.

"You sure you want to do this, kiddo?" her dad asked as he and Mel joined her. "You can take the Bronco and go back to Kelly's."

She hesitated, briefly tempted, then shook her head. "I want to watch Pelinore make an ass out of herself."

He smiled slowly. "Well, I wouldn't want to deprive you of that. Just promise me you'll stick close. Don't go upstairs by yourself." He glanced at Melanie. "That goes for you, too. I'll give you the grand tour tomorrow."

"I can't even go up to my room?" Amber asked. *Boy, he's really nervous!*

"No."

"Really?" Mild fear trilled down her spine as she realized he wasn't just nervous—he was scared. "Why?"

"Nothing will happen at the seance," he explained. "I can

almost guarantee it. But all the energy downstairs may stir things up in other parts of the house. Places that are off-camera."

"We'll stick to you like glue," Melanie said. "Right, Amber?"

"Right."

A moment later they stood in the foyer of Body House, watching the chaotic activity of the film crew and the channeling group. Romero stood in the middle of the parlor, directing the placement of standing spotlights and the setting up of a round folding table, which was being positioned under the portrait of Lizzie Baudey. Pelinore stood beside him looking and sounding like a regal bitch as she instructed her scurrying little crystal-packers to do this or that for her. Finally, as a red tablecloth was thrown over the table, Romero looked over and saw them.

"David, we were wondering where you were!" Romero strode enthusiastically over and pumped his hand, then kissed Melanie and Amber on their cheeks. "Amber, I didn't think you were going to join us!"

Amber felt herself blushing. Looking at her fingers, she said softly, "I can have pizza any time, but it's not every day I get to see my dad expose a con artist."

Melanie cleared her throat, obviously trying to hide a snicker, but David, standing just behind her, put his hand on her shoulder and gave it a little warning squeeze.

Jerry Romero had lit up like a Christmas tree. He turned to David. "You don't believe Ms. Pelinore is a true psychic, then?"

"Let's just say that I prefer to reserve judgment on these things until I see it for myself."

"But you *are* going to attempt to expose her?" Romero persisted.

"I'm not going to do anything but observe."

"Besides," Melanie said smoothly, "I think Ms. Pelinore is perfectly capable of exposing herself without David's help."

Romero stopped cold, his expression briefly blank, then a slow smile spread across his face. "I believe you might be right, Miss Lord."

"Jerry!"

He glanced around. "Yeah?"

"We're ready."

Romero smiled. "We've got a seat for you in the circle, David, and you ladies can watch from the couch there, by the cameraman."

"I don't—"

"You're the star, David, you've got to be in the seance."

Amber stood on her tiptoes and whispered in his ear, "It'll really piss off Pelinore, Dad."

He gave her a reproving look, but told Romero he'd do it and followed him to the table, where they seated him right next to Pelinore.

Melanie and Amber got comfortable on the couch. "Good shot," Amber whispered, referring to Mel's remark about Pelinore.

"Thanks." Melanie took the feather from her hair and ran her fingers over it. "So, I never saw that woman who was spreading rumors about you. Was she at the party?"

"Oh. Oh, God, you didn't hear, did you?"

"Hear what?"

"She was killed. Chopped up into little bits."

"I heard people talking about some murders. She was one of the victims?" Melanie asked, shocked.

Amber nodded.

"Have they caught the murderer?"

"No. They aren't going to either, if Dad's right."

"What do you mean?"

"Did he tell you about the dolls?"

"Yes . . ." Melanie answered slowly.

"Did he tell you about Peter Castle?"

"The name's familiar, but I'm not sure. We only had a few minutes to talk."

"He was Christabel's lover—"

Melanie nodded. "Yes, he told me."

"Did he tell you Minnie Willard stole the doll?"

"No."

Quickly, Amber filled her in. "So that's why they can't catch the killer. He's already dead."

Melanie stared at her. "And you believe this?"
"Heck, the chief of police believes it."
"You're joking."
Amber shook her head. "No kidding. He even went out to the end of Widow's Peak and threw the doll into the ocean so that the ghost of Peter Castle wouldn't hang around town and kill somebody else."
"Your father's persuasive, but I can't believe he's talked a cop into believing—"
"Oh, well, after Chief Swenson saw the headless sea captain in the lighthouse, he was pretty easy to convince."
"Slow down." Melanie set the feather aside. "The story about the ghost in the lighthouse is famous, and your dad told me about the romance between the captain and Lizzie. But I didn't know anyone had seen his ghost."
"Oh, yeah. Eric, that's the chief's nephew, he's always been able to see him. After the doll broke, we *all* saw him. God, Mel, it was *so* gross! But then Eric found his head and he and Dad broke it and buried the doll right there in the lighthouse, where the captain hangs out. He's pretty handsome now that he's got his face back."
"You've lost me, Amber. You and David will have to tell me more after these people clear out. It's just too fantastic." She grinned. "Especially the part about the chief of police buying into all of this."
"Well, Dad told me that he's going to be here tonight, so you can ask him yourself."
"Quiet, everybody!" called a gravel-voiced crewman. "We're going to roll."
Romero, who had been bent over Pelinore giving her last-minute instructions—or staring at her tits—rose and seated himself in an empty chair directly across from her. "Ready," he called.
Amber settled comfortably on the couch and turned her attention to the seance table.
"And five, four, three, two, one," called the crewman. "And action."
The lights were slowly dimmed until the glass-encased votive candles flickered eerily on the table, underlighting the

faces of the sitters. Except for her dad, Romero, and Pelinore, Amber didn't know any of the rest of them, though she was pretty sure that the youngest, a sandy-haired man in his early twenties, was a grocery clerk in Greenaway's. For some reason, that struck her as funny.

"Everyone please join hands," Pelinore ordered imperiously. She waited for her sitters to comply, then continued on in the same tone. "Tonight, I will attempt to contact some of the spirits inhabiting this house, and perhaps send them into the light, but to do so I shall need everyone's cooperation. You must remain silent until the spirit indicates it is ready to answer questions, and you must remain seated. I will first call upon my guide, Spiros, and Reverend Alice will ask him certain questions before we go on." She looked at David and then at Romero. "Spiros is a benevolent teacher who lived thousands of years ago on the lost continent of Atlantis. He is here to offer us his wisdom and guidance and he presents no danger to anyone here. But—" She arched her eyebrows meaningfully. "But the poor misguided spirits within these walls may be very dangerous until we convince them we're their friends and want to help them."

Give me a break! Amber and Mel exchanged a roll of the eyes.

Theo was still yammering away, as if she were queen of the universe. "I must insist that, no matter what you see or hear, you do not break the circle. Keep your hands firmly grasped and on the table at all times. If the chain is broken, I, as your channel, am in great bodily danger."

Break it! Break it! Amber glanced at Melanie and barely contained a giggle. They both knew that the main reason a charlatan psychic didn't want a circle broken was to ensure that she could perform her under-the-table hocus pocus with less chance of getting caught in the act.

Pelinore closed her eyes and took a deep breath. "Spiros, are you here?" A long moment passed, then her eyelids snapped open, her posture turned from relaxed to rigid, and she examined the others with bird-like intensity.

"I am Spiros," she said, "and may you all be blessed."

If E.T. were from India, he'd sound just like her. Amber

clamped her hand over her mouth and didn't dare look at Melanie.

"I have a question, Spiros," said a tiny middle-aged woman.

Theo cocked her head as if she were ready to snag a worm with her beak. "Sister Alice, ask your question."

"Tonight, Sister Theodora is going to try to release the spirits trapped in this house. I ask you to protect everyone here and to give us your blessing. In return we give you, as always, our eternal faith and devotion."

Gag me. Amber tried not to fidget, wishing Pelinore would get on with the show.

"As always, I am with you."

"Can you give us insight into the nature of the spirits trapped here?" Alice asked.

"They are legion—"

Suddenly, the spotlight nearest Romero blazed so brightly that the sitters' skin looked paper white. An instant later, it exploded. Romero cringed but stayed put as sparkling bits of shattered glass fell into his hair.

"Did you get that?" he called as one of his crew raced to the lamp.

"Got it," called the man at the main camera.

The minicam operator came around the table and focused on Romero.

"Folks, things are starting to happen here. One of our lights has just exploded and now the room seems to be filling with some exotic flower scent."

Amber jumped as something touched her arm, but it was only Melanie, staring at her questioningly. Amber leaned over and whispered in her ear. "Christabel's here." Melanie nodded and took her hand.

"Beware!" Theo called in the Spiros voice. "There is danger here!"

POP! Another light exploded, then three more, the sounds mixing with screams from several of the sitters and Romero's frantic cries of "Did you get that? Did you get that?"

The revolting odor of decayed flesh began to underlie the jasmine, stronger than Amber had ever smelled it before, and as the final bulb exploded, she heard Romero doing a blow-by-blow, Pelinore doing Spiros, someone sobbing and someone else retching, all that behind her own breathing, which was loudest of all.

Melanie's hand gripped hers like iron. "What—" she began to whisper, then stopped, as Christabel's laughter rang through the house.

"Jesus, did you get that?" Romero screamed.

"Not registering," called the crewman.

"Keep rolling!" Romero ordered as the crew scurried.

"Not enough light, but we're rolling!" called the camera operator.

"Fix the damn lamps!"

"We're working on it, Jer," called the gravelly-voiced one. "Ted, turn on the overheads!"

"They're not working! Mr. Masters, where's the fusebox?"

"In the kitchen." David started to rise, barely visible in the flickering candlelight.

"Don't break the circle!" Alice ordered.

"I'll show you!" Amber called out. She rose, Melanie with her, Ted following them as she headed toward the doorway that led to the dining room and through the kitchen.

Suddenly, something cold and invisible slammed into her, and she fell backward, toppling Melanie and the crewman like dominoes.

"Amber!" cried her dad.

"We're okay, Dad!" she called, scrambling to her feet. As she helped Melanie up, Ted moved past them, his arms out in front of him. He reached the doorway and flinched back. "It's there," he said in a shaky voice. "It won't let us through."

"Nonsense." Romero rose.

"Don't break the circle!" Alice ordered.

Romero glanced at her as he pulled his hands free. "We've got something *real* here, lady."

Amber watched as Romero, followed by her Dad, ran toward them.

The telejournalist, still talking into his mike, approached them. "What did it feel like?" he asked Amber.

"David!" Melanie said as he put one arm around her and the other around his daughter.

"Can you tell me what it felt like?" Romero persisted.

"Feel it for yourself," David said, leading Amber and Melanie back to the couch with him.

"Hold this." Romero handed the wireless mike to Ted, then put his hands out. "Jesus," he whispered. "That's cold." He took the mike, said something into it, then called his minicam operator over, refusing to listen to his protests that it was too dark to get anything on tape.

An instant later, he backed up, than ran forward, barreling into the doorway. He yelled as he was thrown halfway across the room to crash into a side chair, face first.

"You okay, Jerry?" Ted bent over him.

Romero sat up, hands cupping his nose. "I think it's broken."

"You want to go to the emergency room, boss?" Ted asked hopefully.

"No. David, are there Band-Aids in the bathroom?"

"Medicine cabinet."

"I'll be right back."

The moment Romero left the room, the air became sodden with the stench of jasmine and decay.

"Look!" Amber said, as a blackness partially occluded the candlelight.

"Christabel," whispered David.

The dark mass moved toward Pelinore and then her face was veiled with the blackness.

Pelinore started to scream, but then it turned into a laugh, Christabel's laugh, rising higher and higher.

Body House's lights came to life and the horrible odors disappeared at the same moment that Jerry Romero, a Band-Aid across his nose, reappeared.

"What's going on?" he asked, staring at the disheveled group. "Are we rolling?"

"Rolling," confirmed the gravel-man as Ted handed Romero his mike.

"Folks, what we're seeing here tonight confirms Body House's infamous reputation and—"

"David, why did it stop?" Melanie asked softly as Romero talked on. "Not that I'm complaining."

"I'm not sure."

"Christabel's in Pelinore," Amber whispered.

"Maybe," he allowed. "But look at her. Does she look possessed to you?"

Pelinore was smiling and nodding and answering Romero's questions.

"I guess she looks normal," Amber said finally.

As they watched, Pelinore turned and said something to the channeling group, most of whom still looked pretty green. After a moment, they rose en masse and filed from the table. While Pelinore lingered, talking to Romero, Reverend Alice approached, pale and shaken, her crystal-packers in tow.

"Mr. Masters, thank you for having us at your—" she hesitated, "ah, at your home tonight."

"My pleasure," he said smoothly.

Alice only nodded, and they all high-tailed it for the door. A moment later, engines hummed to life and several sets of headlights played against the stained glass as the New Agers turned their cars around and drove off.

"Guess they couldn't take it, huh, Dad?"

"Kiddo, I wasn't sure *I* could take it." He shook his head and gave them a helpless smile. "Will you ladies excuse me a moment? I want to get Theo out of here and have a word with Romero about tomorrow."

Fifty-three

Body House: 12:43 A.M.

"David, hello," Theo said warmly as the novelist joined her and Jerry Romero by the seance table.

Masters studied her suspiciously before returning her greeting and she wondered if, despite the lack of lighting, he'd seen Christabel join with her.

Of course he did! Christabel told her impatiently.

The woman who called herself Theo thought she was in charge, but, in truth, she was little more than an interesting detail in Christabel's mind. She certainly appreciated the woman's strong, voluptuous body and she was amused by her arrogance and lusting, selfish nature, weak though it was. Because of Theo's infatuation with her and her willingness to be used, Christabel had so far allowed her to think she was a partner in this, just as she had that night in the ballroom. A cooperative victim did much to strengthen her powers, which was what was necessary at the moment: the theatrics she'd displayed during that farce of a seance had drained her and she would need all her strength to complete her plans.

"Quite a show," Romero was saying to Masters.

"Yes, it was," the writer agreed. "Think you got any of it on tape?"

"I hope so. I was just telling Ms. Pelinore here that she's quite a talented channeler."

David nodded. "Speaking of which, Theo, the rest of your group has left."

"I know—I dismissed them. They were rather shaken by the evening's events."

David gave her a plastic smile. "I assume you're on your way out now, too?"

"I didn't realize we were in a hurry to leave." She smiled disarmingly.

"We're tired," he said coolly. "We'd like to get some sleep." He turned his gaze on Romero. "You're intending to be back bright and early, aren't you?"

The man nodded. "We've got spare lights with us, so we'll be back by nine A.M."

"How's your nose?" Masters asked.

His civility to Romero infuriated Theo, and Christabel had to exert her influence to keep her serenely smiling.

"I got lucky this time," Romero said, peeling off the Band-Aid. "Just a cut and a bruise, I think." He cocked his head. "So, are you actually going to sleep here tonight?"

David glanced at Theo before answering. "We haven't decided yet. We might go to a hotel."

"That's what I'd do," Romero commented as his crew began carrying their equipment out. "We were going to leave the big camera here, but given what happened earlier . . ."

"Good idea," David said. Before you leave, I'd like to speak with you in private for just a moment."

He wants to talk to him behind my back, Theo thought.

Of course he does. This woman was stupid, Christabel realized. She'd done one brilliant thing and that was to take the doll of Peter Castle. It was still hidden in her skirts and Christabel could feel the presence of her former lover all around. It drove her mad. She wanted to set him free, but as soon as Theo had walked in and she'd sensed Peter was here, she'd performed a hurried spell to force him back in the broken doll, at least until she could take care of him permanently.

Peter had always been . . . impetuous, and he was powerful enough himself that it drained her to keep him under control. Yet those were the very reasons she adored him—his lust for physical pleasure and for blood nearly equalled her own.

That, along with his anger, was why she couldn't allow him any freedom, let alone place him in another man's body. It would be much too dangerous, even after her own body was reanimated—something Mama hadn't known about until that final night—and she'd regained the full power that went with it. No, she would have to destroy Peter's soul as she had his body, and content herself with other men. Even Peter's anger excited her and she regretted having replaced his tongue with his genitals—if she hadn't gotten so carried away she might risk it—but he would never forgive her that final humiliation.

Theo, find out if anyone else is coming here tonight.

"I'm surprised Craig and Eric didn't come tonight," Theo said, right on cue.

"They intended to be here, but the chief had some things to do first."

"Do you think they're still coming?"

Don't sound so eager! Christabel ordered.

"I don't know. Why?"

"Well, I'd hate to see them drive all the way out here for nothing."

Masters shot her another funny look. "It's not that far. Besides, they've already missed the fireworks."

As Theo talked and flirted, Christabel waited in the recesses of her mind and watched her move in the myriad of parlor mirrors, admiring the body with its lush full curves and graceful posture.She was glad to use it instead of the one she'd intended—Amber's—both because it was so much more sensual and because the girl's resistance, especially since Mama was protecting her, would cost Christabel a great deal of strength.

Locked away in the cellar were the things she needed to reanimate her own body—her physical remains, dolls filled with souls and blood, and the Erzuli doll.

She'd fashioned Erzuli as a sacred repository for her soul and for her power, a place from which she could complete the ritual of death and revival that perfect, everlasting reanimation required. But instead it had become her prison, because Mama had found out how to use it against her. One of her whores, Mariette Cantori, was from the islands and possessed a little knowledge. She'd showed Mama how to remove the goddess Erzuli's influence from the doll and how to trap Christabel's soul in Erzuli after her body's death and before its revival. And that much, her mother had accomplished.

But her mother was a coward. If she wasn't, Christabel's body would be dust and she no more than a simple ghost, unable to do more than flicker a light or send a whiff of jasmine through the house. Since Mama couldn't bring herself to finish what she'd started by destroying her daughter's physical body, however, Christabel retained much of her strength. But because the Erzuli icon remained intact, she was still its prisoner, unable to travel out of the confines of the house, and unable to draw upon her whole power. She could not even materialize as Peter Castle had done as long as she was tied to the doll.

But now, that would all change. To attain life, she needed to properly prepare her old body and to break the Erzuli doll. She would need to use Theo's body to accomplish these things: only after the doll was broken would she be able to reenter her own body. What Mama hadn't known when she'd cast her simple confinement spell was that Christabel was powerful enough to possess another's body and force her to do her will, which meant the possessed—Theo—would prepare Christabel's corpse and break the icon for her. Once that was accomplished, she would no longer need Theo's body, for she could perform the rest of the procedures herself.

Mama, she thought, *you stupid, sentimental woman.* Mama had failed to destroy her only because she couldn't bring herself to face a little blood. Instead, after capturing and imprisoning Christabel's soul in the doll, she'd locked the lifeless corpse, undamaged, away in an old steamer trunk. *Mama, you're so weak!*

But she was, Christabel had to admit, a smart woman. Mama had lain in wait for her in the dungeon and after Christabel had gorged to build her new power by murdering everyone in the house, with Peter's gleeful help, they'd come downstairs. He'd thought they were going down to use the victims shackled there to give him the same power and eternal life she intended for herself.

She'd told him that she wanted to reanimate him first and his gullibility had been his fatal error. Willingly, he'd let her strap him to the ritual table and had watched as she'd killed the others shackled about the room. She'd done it slowly, sending the souls into the imprisoning dolls with great love and care. Finally, they were all dead except for Peter, and it wasn't until she stood over him with her sharp curved knife that he began to suspect that her promise of everlasting life was a lie. When she flicked the knife across his nipple, severing it, then placed the bit of pink flesh in her mouth and swallowed it, his eyes had grown wide with shock, though he had refused to show any sign of pain. He was a strong man, Peter Castle.

Then, she brought out a perfect porcelain replica of him and wordlessly showed it to him. He knew then that he was destined to spend eternity as her slave, yet still she saw no fear in his eyes, only fury and hatred. His reaction infuriated her, and she gave him a slow, lingering death. During his torture, he swore vengeance against her over and over, until she was forced to cut out his tongue. As he watched, she'd replaced it with his penis. The memory stirred excitement within her which translated to long forgotten physical pleasure as Theo's body unconsciously reacted.

Soon, she would be whole again, and able to experience sensual pleasures fully and completely, rather than muted as she did in her spirit form, or vicariously through another's body. That knowledge made her impatient to begin.

She would require two more things after reanimation was complete. She needed a pure female heart, ripped still beating from its victim. This would be presented to the true goddess Erzuli as thanks for her blessings. The other thing she needed was fresh blood to bathe her body in. The reanimation ritual itself required only the blood stored in the dolls locked in the dungeon, but to complete the cycle, to baptize her new body in the name of Erzuli, she needed to bathe in gallons of fresh, warm, blood. Only then would her body be completely restored to full power, vigor and beauty. Only then would she be invincible. For this, she needed the blood of half a dozen people, preferably more. The people here, now, could provide enough.

She could do it tonight, she realized, her excitement growing. It would be safer than waiting until tomorrow, when others could show up at an inopportune moment. Tonight, all she had to worry about were Eric Swenson and his uncle, and she wasn't really concerned about them: if they showed up tonight, they would supply more of the blood she required. One could never have too much blood . . .

Quickly, she conveyed her wishes to keep the people here, in the house.

Theo vocalized them perfectly. "Before you leave, Jerry," she said casually, "would you be interested in getting a sneak preview of the dungeon tonight?"

Masters' jaw dropped as Romero turned to her. "Are you serious?"

"She doesn't know where—" Masters began, not bothering to hide his indignation.

"Yes, I do, David," she purred. "Remember, you showed me the entrance the same night we explored the ballroom?"

He didn't reply. Either he didn't want to make a scene, or he couldn't remember enough of that night to know if she was lying or not—Christabel suspected it was the latter.

"Well, Jerry," Theo continued, with a warm smile. "I was just thinking, you've already got your equipment here, and we probably won't be disturbed tonight." She chuckled softly. "You know how word leaks out about these things—tomorrow morning half the town might be here."

"Theo—" Masters began.

She patted his arm. "As David will confirm, examining the room now would be wise—the ghostly activity is almost assuredly over for the night."

Romero considered. "You know, I really want to get some of that activity on tape, so I'd rather film tomorrow, but I think going down for a preliminary check while it's quiet would be a good idea. What do you say, David?"

Masters glared at Theo. "I'm not sure it's such a good idea."

"Wouldn't it be safer, as Theo mentioned, to go down while the ghosts are resting up?"

"Well, possibly . . ."

"You coming, Jerry?" called the deep voiced crewman.

"You guys go on to the hotel. I'm going to stay a while."

You can't let them leave. I need them.

"Maybe they should bring their equipment downstairs tonight, Jerry," Theo said.

"We'll film tomorrow. Can I get a ride back into town with you, Theo?"

"Of course."

Enraged, Christabel nearly squashed the woman's personality down at that moment, then suddenly decided that it would be easier to manipulate fewer people. She could at least get downstairs and break her tie to the doll, and tomorrow, she could collect the rest of her blood donors.

The crew left, shutting the door behind them. "David," Romero began, "we won't do this tonight, if you don't want to. You said you were tired . . ."

"May I be frank?" Masters asked, glowering at Theo.

"Of course."

"I had intended to tell you this in private, but Ms. Pelinore has forced my hand. I have no intention of allowing her to accompany us into the cellar." He cleared his throat. "Frankly, I didn't want her here at all due to the nature of her, ah, talents."

Theo shrugged at Romero, giving him a tiny *I-don't-understand-him-either* smile.

"I don't understand," the journalist said lightly.

"She's too open to the influences here. Too suggestible." He stared directly at her. "She's a danger to herself and to others because she's very easy to manipulate."

"How dare—"

Be quiet! Christabel ordered.

Romero paused. "Theo is easy to manipulate? She seems like an unusually strong woman to me."

"Looks can be deceiving," Melanie Lord said as she and Amber joined the group in the foyer.

Christabel stopped Theo's hand from coming up to strike

the petite redhead. *You'll have your revenge later.* Like a faithful dog, she instantly acquiesced. "I promise you, nothing will happen tonight," she said calmly. "So, whether or not what David and his . . . this woman say holds even a crumb of truth, doesn't matter."

"Hell," Masters said lightly. "Hell, go ahead." He shrugged and said, more to himself than anyone else, "Might as well let people who want to go down there go and check it out first." He put his arm around his daughter. "We'll wait here."

"You're sure?" Romero asked.

"Yes." Masters crossed to one of the cabinets and withdrew a pair of flashlights. "Don't be too long, though."

As Theo and Romero started up the staircase, she put her hand through the crook of the reporter's arm. Though Christabel had continually reassured her that she was perfectly safe, she sensed that the spirit was not confiding everything to her. There was a sense of urgency about the things Christabel directed her to do that frightened her, though not enough to make her hesitate.

Romero's voice, pattering small talk, sounded slightly nervous as they reached the second floor landing and turned onto the third. She responded by hugging his arm more closely and acting as nonchalantly as she could manage, but as they approached the dormer room, her stomach filled with butterflies. She came to a halt at the door, surprised to see that David had replaced the phallic door latch with a locking doorknob.

"Is this it?" Jerry asked, his hand on the knob.

"This is it," she replied, sure it was locked.

Don't worry, Christabel whispered in her mind.

Romero turned the knob and the door swung open. Theo turned on the light and saw that except for the new knob, the room hadn't been touched.

Let me use your body now.

It was almost a relief to have Christabel take over for her and, fascinated, she watched herself adroitly touch a latch hidden on the inside wall of an empty bookcase. A three-inch square of wood slid smoothly away, revealing a chain pull.

She hooked her finger into it and exerted a minimum of pressure.

Romero yelped and jumped backward as part of the oak floor slid away. Cold, dry air, slightly sweet and rotten, wafted up as Romero shined his light into the hole, revealing a seemingly endless flight of spiral stairs.

Nervously, Theo stared down into the near-darkness.

Don't be afraid, Christabel soothed. *I'm going to leave you for a few minutes.*

No!

Only a few minutes. Nothing will harm you. Start down the stairs. Go slowly, it's easy to fall. By the time you reach the cellar, I'll have rejoined you.

Are you sure, Christabel?

Don't worry. I won't let anything happen to you.

Theo swallowed and smiled tremulously at Romero. "Shall we?" she asked. Christabel's presence—a fleet, cold zephyr—left her, and she felt somehow incomplete.

Fifty-four

Body House: 1:10 A.M.

"I can't believe you let them go down there," Amber said as soon as Pelinore and Romero were out of sight.

"Me either," Melanie added.

"I guess I shouldn't have, but what the heck, they both signed liability waivers." He chuckled sickly. "I wanted Theo out of my sight and giving permission seemed like the quickest short-term answer."

"What are we going to do if they don't come out?" his daughter asked as the three walked over to the couch and sat down.

"You've got me, kiddo." Since the moment they'd left the room he'd regretted his decision to let them go, and now her question doubled his misgivings.

Vaguely, he heard the thrum of an engine, then headlights flashed through the window.

Amber hopped up and peeked out, then turned back to David and Melanie. "They're hee-erre," she sang as she went to open the door.

"Who's here?" Melanie asked.

"The cavalry, I assume." Despite all of the goings-on tonight, David hadn't been able to take his mind off Melanie's heart-shaped face, off her green eyes, off the laughter that lived in her voice. He wanted to take her hand, but still unsure, he refrained. "Craig and Eric Swenson were going to come by to watch the fun, but Craig had some things to do first. I didn't think he was going to make it. Fortunately," he added as he heard the men's voices, "I was wrong."

"Craig Swenson's the police chief, right?"

"Right."

"He seemed like a good guy," Melanie added as they rose to greet the newcomers.

"Chief, Eric, you remember Melanie Lord?" David asked as they joined them in the parlor.

"Of course." Swenson looked from Melanie to the portrait of Lizzie and gave a low whistle. "Sure she's not your grandmother?" he asked.

"It's the clothes," Melanie said, shaking his hand, then Eric's.

Everyone sat down. "So, we missed the show," Swenson stated. "Was it a bust?"

"Only Pelinore was a bust," Amber said dryly.

David didn't even try to hide his amusement. "It was quite a performance," he said, but before he could begin to tell them about the seance, Eric interrupted.

"Where's Miss Pelinore? She's still here, isn't she?"

Melanie was staring at him in amazement and Amber said, matter-of-factly, "Eric's a real psychic, not like that witch Pelinore."

"Yes, she's still here. So's Romero." David said. "They're looking for the dungeon."

"You're letting them wander around—" Swenson began.

"They bulldozed him," Melanie explained.

"Nothing's likely to happen tonight," David went on, feeling horribly sheepish, "and Romero wanted to see what he was in for."

"That's right . . ." Craig said slowly. "You found the secret passage . . ."

"Thanks to Patton's letters, I know where it's *supposed* to be. I have a schematic of the latch. But, frankly, I haven't had any desire to check it out."

"Did you give the schematic to Romero?" Swenson asked.

"No." David paused. "Theo says I showed her, that night that she was possessed by Christabel."

Craig cracked his knuckles. "Yeah, I think you said you don't remember much about it?"

"No, I don't." And he'd revealed even less of it to Swenson, primarily because it was just too embarrassing to retell. "All things considered, I guess it's likely that I told her. Christabel *was* trying to get us into that dormer room . . ." His stomach did a slow, nauseating flip as he realized that he'd seen the dark misty form the specter favored enter Theo tonight—but that he hadn't seen it come out again. *It was dark,* he told himself. *And just because a ghost usually takes a particular form, that doesn't mean it* has *to. It might be invisible, or it might look like something else.*

"David," Eric said.

He looked up, saw the young man's pale face, saw the terror in his eyes. "What's wrong, Eric?"

"We have to get them out of there."

"We've never had more than one incident occur at a time, Eric," he said gently. "We had major phenomena here tonight. If I didn't think Christabel's going to have to rest up before performing again, I'd never have let them go down." He looked at the others. "Maybe this seance was a good thing, after all. It should still be safe around here tomorrow."

"She wants you to think that," Eric said bluntly.

"Theo?" Melanie asked.

Eric shook his head. "No. The other."

"Christabel," David said. He ignored Eric's warning look, but his stomach was growing sicker and sicker. *The boy's right,* his guts insisted. *He's right.* Telling his misgivings to shut up, he said, "Let's give them a little while. I'm sure they'll be back soon. The locking mechanism probably doesn't even work."

Melanie and Amber had been speaking quietly to each other, and now they stood up. "Dad, we're going up to my room for a minute. I want to show Mel Lizzie's doll."

"I'm not so sure you two ought to go wandering off by yourselves," David said.

"We'll be right back, Daddy. You said yourself nothing's going to happen."

That was true. "Okay, but hurry back down and don't go anywhere else."

Amber rolled her eyes. "We won't." She turned to Melanie. "Come on, Mel."

As they walked away, he heard Amber tell Melanie that her dad was a worrywart. Melanie's gentle laughter trailed down the stairs.

"So, tell us about the seance," Craig said. "And Theo's big bust," he added, his face deadpan.

Fifty-five

Body House: 1:25 A.M.

"I can't wait to see the whole place," Melanie told Amber as they approached her room. "This house is like a museum."

Amber laughed. "It's weird, anyway. Here's my room," she added, her hand on the knob.

They entered the room, and Melanie was surprised by the strong scent of lavender which permeated it. Amber glanced at her, then said calmly, "That's just Lizzie. I guess she wants us to know she's here." She opened a beautiful oak wardrobe, then knelt in front of it, her hands inside, fiddling with something Melanie couldn't see.

"This is Lizzie," Amber said, rising to show Melanie the doll she held carefully in her hands.

"She's beautiful," Melanie said.

Suddenly, the air turned chill and Lizzie's lavender fragrance was overwhelmed by the sickly sweet odor of jasmine and decay.

"God!" Amber cried, pulling the doll protectively against her. "No! Get away!"

It looked as though Amber was fighting with herself, as if her hands and arms wanted to throw the doll, while the rest of her wanted to keep it safe.

She looked at Melanie with wide eyes. "Help me!"

Before Melanie could respond, the maniacal sound of Christabel's laughter filled the room and the doll flew from

Amber's arms. The girl screamed as it crashed against the wall with a sound like breaking dishes.

"No!" Amber cried again. "No!"

Melanie grabbed her. "Come on!" she ordered over the sound of Christabel's laughter. "We've got to get out of here!" The putrid odor of decay was so strong now that Melanie had to fight down the urge to retch. "Come on!"

A dark cloud swirled into existence in front of the open door, blocking it. As Melanie watched, it took shape, forming quickly into the image of a young, dark-haired woman. "Christabel," Melanie said softly.

Abruptly, Amber was yanked from Melanie's grasp. She landed at the feet of the spirit's now faded, flickering image.

"Amber!"

The girl moaned.

The ghost laughed, the sound echoing in Melanie's head. Then it spoke and, though its mouth didn't move, she heard every insane word. *You can't hide from me now, Mama. I broke your little house. Your little doll house.* Again, the terrible laughter rang out.

"Lizzie," Amber whispered. "Lizzie, where are you?"

Melanie barely detected the lavender scent beneath Christabel's overwhelming stench. "She's here."

It doesn't matter if she's here—she can't help you anymore. Christabel laughed maniacally. *You can't hide from me, Mama. Get out of this house, or I'll destroy you!*

The lavender, like a cool breeze, descended upon Melanie, and faintly, she heard Lizzie's desperate voice in her head. *She'll kill her, she'll kill Amber! Stop her!*

Stunned, Melanie thought one word: *How.*

Her body lies in the dungeon, Lizzie explained. *Destroy it. Cut it up, or burn it.* Melanie could feel Lizzie's agony as if it were her own. *She cannot reenter her own body until the Erzuli doll is broken. She will try to do this herself while possessing the body of another. Once it is broken, she will immediately move into her body and then she will be too strong for anyone to fight and all those imprisoned in the dolls will be her slaves for eternity.*

You must not let her break the doll. You *must do it*—you

must take control, because you must destroy her body and *her soul. It's the only way to free the others and make this place safe.*

You interfering bitch! another voice screamed in Melanie's head. *When will you learn you can't stop me, Mama?*

Christabel's laughter rang in Melanie's ears and she looked up to see that the spirit's image, though still soft and translucent, had lost its flicker. It was already regaining some of the energy it had used during its attack.

I must go now. I will try to help you. Remember. Remember . . . Lizzie's words faded away.

Christabel, her expression so evil that Melanie could barely look at her, was nearly solid now. Slowly, she moved forward, her feet floating right through Amber. The girl, nearly unconscious, shivered and made a tiny mewling sound as the spirit moved through her, toward Melanie.

I hope you're not foolish enough to listen to my mother. You can't stop me. No one can. You're going to die, bitch, and I'll have your heart for my breakfast!

Suddenly, laughter filled the air and the spirit raced toward her so quickly that Melanie had no time to move. The last thing she felt was something that felt like a cold sheet of ice slamming her down to the floor.

Fifty-six

Body House: 1:42 A.M.

She left the red-haired woman who was dressed like Mama on the floor and entered Amber's body. Though the girl gave little resistance, forcing her to rise and walk to the third floor was difficult because Christabel had expended so much energy already this evening.

There was no time now for recuperation, but what she had just accomplished had been well worth it. By planting the notion in Amber's head to show Mama's doll to the other woman, she had finally gained access to it, effectively destroying her mother's power to fight her. Mama knew it, too—that had been obvious by the way she'd fled after making her small, pitiful attempt to communicate. Later, if she continued to stay in the house, Christabel would seek her out and drain her down until she became nothing more than a cool breeze.

She had also decided to procure Amber now, since it was imperative that she have her for the sacrifice. As she reached the third floor and turned toward the dormer room, she felt relief. As soon as Christabel had her safely in the room, she would leave the girl there and have Theo carry her down and put her in bondage.

Soon, the others would follow, but by then she would be ready to trap them, and since Eric and his uncle had shown up, she would have enough bodies to completely finish the reanimation ritual tonight. There would be no more waiting!

She used Amber's hand to close the dormer room's door, then left the girl's body, laughing as she watched it fall to the floor. She looked forward to the not-too-distant moment when she would tear the girl's beating heart from her chest with her own reanimated hands, a process that would give her almost as much pleasure as slipping back into her own body again.

Fifty-seven

Body House: 1:59 A.M.

"We need to go upstairs," Eric said suddenly. "Something's happening."

"With Theo?" Swenson asked.

Eric shook his head. "It's Amber, I think."

David leapt to his feet and ran for the stairs, vaguely aware of Swenson and Eric behind him.

"Amber!" he shouted as he made the landing. "Melanie!" Turning the corner, he saw that Amber's door was open and her light was on. "Amber!" *It's okay, everything's okay—they've only been gone fifteen minutes!* "Amber! Melanie!"

"David?" It was Melanie's voice, soft and uncertain.

He tore into the room and rushed to help her as she pushed herself up off the floor. "Melanie."

Dazed and disheveled, she looked at him with little comprehension as he helped her to Amber's desk chair.

"What happened?" asked Craig Swenson.

"Where's Amber?" David added.

She looked from man to man but didn't answer.

"Christabel's been here," Eric said from behind them.

"Yes," Melanie said, understanding coming back into her eyes. "Christabel. She hit me."

"Hit you?" Swenson repeated.

"A psychic slug," Melanie said dryly. "She hit Amber, too. Amber?" Frantically, she looked around. "Where is she?"

"You don't know?"

She shook her head. "She was here."

"Okay, tell us what happened," the chief said gently.

Melanie took a deep breath and exhaled noisily. "Amber was showing me the doll. We could smell lavender, and she said Lizzie was here, but then that horrible odor drowned it out, and something—Christabel, I guess—made her throw the doll."

David followed her gaze across the room and saw the shattered, but bloodless, effigy of Lizzie lying there.

"Christabel materialized. We saw her. She knocked Amber down, and then I could sense Lizzie again. She sort of got on me." Shocked, she looked into David's eyes. "She can't protect Amber anymore, David. She told me Christabel will kill her." She rubbed her forehead. "Oh, God, I remember now."

Quickly, she told the men what Lizzie had said they had to do to stop Christabel and save Amber. "She must have taken her away somehow."

"She can possess," David said. He turned to Eric. "You and Melanie stay here. Craig and I are going downstairs. We'll be right back with flashlights."

Swenson followed him out, silent until they reached the first floor and David pulled two small flashlights from the parlor cabinet. Then he shook his head. "Those won't last ten minutes. Bring them for spares and come with me."

He led David out to the cruiser and took two huge fluorescent lights from the trunk, and his revolver, twelve-gauge shotgun and billy club from the cab. "You know how to shoot?"

David shook his head.

"Damn, Eric can't either. Guess you can figure this out though." He handed him the billy club, then replaced the rifle in its rack, withdrew his holster, and fastened it around his waist. He slipped the handgun into it with practiced ease. "Let's go."

"I don't think a gun's going to stop what we're after," David said as they dashed into the house.

"Can't hurt."

David couldn't argue.

Melanie and Eric came out of Amber's room as they approached. He handed one of the smaller flashlights to Eric then turned to give the other to Melanie. Suddenly, he halted. *You idiot!* In his worry over his daughter, he'd forgotten to get Mel out of there. "You've got to leave. Come on, I'll see you safely out."

"I'm not going anywhere," she replied sternly, "except into that damned dungeon. Give me the light. And the nightstick."

David knew what her tone of voice meant, so he didn't waste time arguing with her. "Let's go," he said grimly.

He felt only the barest trace of fear as they entered the dormer room, and he was relieved that it felt empty and undaunted. "Damn," he said as he studied the bookcase that Patton's notes said contained the hidden latch.

"What's wrong?" Swenson hissed.

"I should have brought the schematic. I don't remember how it works . . ." His words trailed off as he caught a faint whiff of lavender. "Lizzie?"

The scent strengthened and then he sensed, more than saw, a slight turbulence in the air, like heat waves undulating above a desert highway. Slowly, it approached, then paused, hovering a foot from him. "Lizzie," he said softly. "Help me."

She moved onto him like a cool, fresh breeze, and then he felt her in his mind, shared her sorrows over her failure to first redeem, then her failure to destroy, her own daughter. And he knew her fears for Amber's safety, which were so like his own.

Let me use your hands, she ordered. At first, he didn't think he could let go enough, but somehow he did and, a moment later, he watched as she directed his fingers to the proper places. Suddenly, the opening in the floor slid open on the cool, rancid darkness below, and then Lizzie vanished.

Find the trunk and destroy her body. Destroy the doll. The looks on the others' faces revealed that they, too, had heard the words.

Fifty-eight

Body House: 2:17 A.M.

They were coming now, but Christabel was not yet ready for them. Perched in Theo's mind, she urged her host to move quickly. The woman was enjoying her task—tying Amber Masters to the table that would become her sacrificial altar—and was lingering over it. Normally, Christabel would have approved, but not now.

"What the hell do you think you're doing?" Jerry Romero yelled again. He'd been yelling from the moment he'd laid eyes on the skeletal corpses scattered around the room. To get him out of the way, they'd quickly tied his hands then pushed him down and trapped his legs in a set of stocks located in a shadowy corner about ten feet away from Amber. Theo glanced back at him.

Ignore him! Hurry! Christabel urged as she sensed the trap door four stories above them slide open. *Hurry!* She suspected enough of her strength had returned to allow her to take over Theo's body instead of relying on the woman's cooperation, but she didn't dare waste it, not now. *You can have your fun with Amber later,* she promised Theo. *We need to open the cabinets now.*

Far above, the stairs creaked.

Everything had taken longer than Christabel had planned. The ancient candles in the wall sconces had to be lit, as well as the brazier that now glowed red not far from a massive wooden chair that sported heavy metal manacles. In the brazier was what remained of the doll of Peter Castle. With sorrow, she had removed the power from his spirit and then sent it away.

It had also taken longer than expected to get the girl downstairs. She had come to before Theo could make it back up to the dormer room and Christabel had to knock Amber senseless again to stop her flailing and screaming—the girl was a fighter. It had also taken twice as long as she expected for Theo to carry Amber downstairs into the dungeon since Christabel didn't want to waste her energy giving Theo a boost, and the woman was not as strong as she appeared to be. Then, when she'd finally laid her on the table, its built-in leather straps came apart in her hands and they'd spent more precious time finding enough good rope with which to tie her down.

"Done," Theo said as she finished the last knot.

Go to the cabinets on the short wall. Open them for me.

Theo crossed the huge room quickly, apparently unaffected by the sight of the corpses manacled to the torture devices scattered about the room. In fact, Christabel realized with amusement, Theo was in a mild state of sexual excitement, especially now, after tying up the girl.

Three of the walls were of natural, unpainted stone, but the last was fitted with wooden cabinets. The steamer trunk containing Christabel's corpse was hidden in one of the huge lower cabinets, while the upper ones contained the ensouled dolls and the Erzuli figure. She needed Theo's hands to retrieve all these things, but after that, the woman would be useless. Well, perhaps not totally useless. Once Christabel was in her own body again, she thought it might be pleasant to play with the woman a little. Perhaps she would stretch her on the rack until her beautiful skin tore and her shoulders and hips left their sockets. To make this woman scream would be as great a pleasure as it would be to watch her flesh as it grew taut, stretched, and finally, tore. Then, after she'd had her fun, she would suspend her from the ceiling over a brass tub and cut her throat, just as she would do with the others. But not yet.

"It's locked," Theo said.

Christabel directed her to the place where the keys should be, but Mama must have taken them long ago. *Break the lock!*

"How?"

Use the branding iron from the brazier and break it! Quickly!

Fifty-nine

Body House: 2:28 A.M.

"What was that?" Melanie whispered.

"Sounds like somebody's trying to break down a door," Craig Swenson replied softly. His hand rested on the butt of his .38 and, as they neared the dungeon, the hairs on the back of his neck stood up and saluted. He wondered if the others felt as apprehensive as he did.

The spiral stairs seemed to go on forever and the blackness had quickly become claustrophobic. *Give me a hit-and-run,* Craig thought, *Give me a shoplifter or a drunk. Give me anything but this.*

Masters, in the lead, halted and turned off his flashlight. Immediately, Craig did the same. The cold, foul darkness threatened to consume them.

"Do you see it?" Masters whispered. "The light down there?"

After a moment he discerned the tiny moving shadows in the flickering light far below. "Candles," Craig whispered.

"Yeah." Masters turned his light back on and adjusted the hood to mute it. He shined it directly at the stairs. "Let's try to sneak up on them."

Craig didn't think that was too much of a possibility, since the stairs creaked and groaned almost constantly, but he didn't say so. If this Christabel was like every other supernatural creature he'd ever read about, she'd know exactly what they were up to anyway. "Okay, everybody," he hissed. "Go slow. If we're attacked from below, drop so that I've got a clear shot."

"Uncle Craig," Eric said gently, "You can't shoot a ghost."

"I can try."

"I don't know how it works," David murmured, "but if she's got her old body up and running, that gun just might save our butts."

"Amen," Melanie said softly.

Sixty

Body House: 2:34 A.M.

"It won't open!" Theo cried frantically. She hit the heavy lock again. "It won't open!"

They're coming. Christabel could sense the warmth of their bodies, could perceive their fear and anger. Ordinarily, she would have savored this moment, but she had no time now. *Theo!* she ordered. *Do as I say!* She directed her to open one of the lower cabinet doors, an unlocked one, and there, just as she remembered, were several red velvet bedspreads. *Take two of them and cover Romero and Amber! Do it now! Hurry!*

Thanks to the dry air, the cloth was intact and Theo swiftly covered the still-unconscious Amber, but Romero started to yell when she approached him. "Shall I knock him out?"

"Yes, quickly."

"Please, no. No!"

After she delivered a rabbit punch to Romero's temple, the man groaned, then slumped. Theo studied him a moment, pinching his cheek hard to make sure he was really out, then threw the cloth over him.

We haven't much time. Until we're rid of them, you're going to have to do everything I tell you, exactly as I tell you, Theo. Can you do that?

"Of course."

Can you kill for me if you have to?

"I'll do anything for you."

That was what Christabel wanted to hear. She didn't want to use up more energy than she had to, and Theo's cooperation made all things possible. After sensing the pleasure the woman took in restraining Romero and Amber, she knew that Theo's promise wasn't empty: this woman, at least while she was under her influence, was perfectly capable of killing, and enjoying it.

They're almost here. We'll have to open the cabinets later. Here's what I want you to do now . . .

Sixty-one

Body House: 2:35 A.M.

The dungeon looked like it belonged in a horror novel. David stepped off the staircase and into the shadows of the arched stone doorway that led into the huge room beyond.

The room appeared to be deserted now, but candles, perhaps fifty of them, flickered in high wall sconces, casting golden light that shifted maniacally throughout the closer portions of the huge room and chasing shadows into the darkness at the far end. Throughout the dungeon loomed the darkly ominous silhouettes of tables, stocks, pillories, and man-sized crosses, all instruments of torture, some with metal manacles hanging from them. He squinted, thinking that the lines weren't clean enough. He realized that there were bodies on some of them.

They were thin, still corpses of the missing victims from the 1915 massacre, and though David had been virtually certain they were down here, the sight, even at this distance, shocked him.

He stared hard, aware that Melanie and the Swensons had joined him and were doing the same. Toward the far end of the room, he could see coals glowing red in a waist-high brazier of some sort, and beyond that were several more torture devices, two of which were shrouded.

He turned, startled, when someone tapped him on the shoulder. It was Craig Swenson, his gun drawn and pointed into the air.

Silently, he gestured at David to let him pass. He did so, nodding as Swenson made it clear that he wanted him to remain where he was and wanted Eric and Melanie to stay farther back in the shadows. Heart racing, David nodded.

Swenson edged into the archway, his back against the cold stones, gun straight up. He paused then turned, peering along the inside wall, first toward David, then behind himself. David sent him a questioning look; he answered with a shrug.

Swenson moved into the center of the arch, paused, then took two solid steps into the dungeon. He stopped, his legs braced apart.

"Come out with your hands up!"

His words echoed hollowly in the silent room.

They waited one beat, two.

"Chief Swenson?" answered Theo Pelinore in a trembling voice.

"Theo?" Swenson called. "Are you alone?"

"Yes."

David thought her voice was coming from somewhere in the darkness back beyond the glowing brazier. He stepped forward, ignoring Swenson's dirty look. "Where's my daughter?"

"I—I don't know."

Swenson cleared his throat. "I want you to come out slowly, Theo. We'll take you out of here."

"I can't." She was almost sobbing, and David thought the sound was utterly unnatural. "My ankle . . . I think it's broken."

Swenson glanced back at David and murmured, "Stay here."

"It's a trick—" David began.

But Swenson ignored him, turning and walking farther into the room. "Where are you?"

"I—I don't know. You sound closer, though."

"Okay, keep talking." Craig moved into the center of the room, listening for Theo's voice.

"It's a trap," Melanie hissed in David's ear.

Swenson passed the brazier, moving forward into the darkness.

"I think you're very close," Theo said.

Another sound, a small moan, followed her words. It didn't sound like Theo, it sounded like . . .

"Amber!" he yelled.

Swenson's head swiveled toward David, then Theo Pelinore leapt out of the darkness, brandishing a thin club of some sort, and threw herself on him. They fell, scuffling, to the floor.

"Daddy?"

Amber's muffled voice broke David's paralysis and he ran into the room, Eric and Melanie right behind him.

"Amber? Where are you?" David called as Eric raced to help his uncle.

"I don't know. I'm under something."

David caught movement under the shroud on the table at the rear.

They ran to the table and yanked the cover off.

"Daddy!" Her eyes were wild with relief.

"Are you okay?" Melanie whispered as she pushed tangles of blond hair from the girl's face.

Amber nodded as David began working on the ropes.

Someone cried out in pain and David glanced toward the Swensons. One of them was down, but the other was locked in combat with Theo Pelinore, who seemed to possess preternatural strength. He needed to get over there and help.

"She's not just Pelinore," Amber said, as if she had read his mind. "Christabel's in her."

David nodded, digging in his pocket for his jackknife as Melanie started working on one of the heavy knots securing Amber's legs. "Here!" He gave Mel the knife and ran across the room.

Eric lay on the floor, holding his head and groaning. David paused, seeing the blood in his hair. Suddenly, a gunshot blasted in his ears. Deafened, he looked up and was appalled to see Craig Swenson backing slowly away from Theo. She had the gun, but at least no one appeared to have been hurt.

"Shit," Swenson said.

She laughed Christabel's laugh, and motioned toward David

and Eric with the gun. "Okay, Chief, go stand over there with your friends." Slowly, Swenson backed toward them.

Theo kept the gun trained on them as she moved through the room toward Amber. David turned slowly, and saw that the heavy velvet was again covering Amber. There was no sign of Melanie and he prayed Theo hadn't noticed her.

Before reaching Amber, Theo paused at the shape under the other velvet spread. She didn't bother to look beneath it; instead she poked it, hard, with the muzzle of the gun. There was no response, and that seemed to satisfy her. *She must have Jerry Romero under there.*

Giving David a knowing smile, she proceeded to Amber's table and pulled the cloth down to reveal his daughter's face. She appeared to be unconscious. "Here's your little girl, David," she purred as she lifted Amber's head by the hair to let him see better. "You were looking for her, weren't you?" She let go of the hair and Amber's head dropped back to the table. David cringed, but Amber showed no reaction and, thank God, Theo moved away without checking her bonds.

"Where's your slut, David?" she asked as she moved toward them.

He said nothing.

"Answer me!"

"Melanie's gone. I sent her away."

Theo smirked. "Too bad. I would have liked to have known her better." She laughed obscenely as she came to a halt by a tall pillory. A skeleton stood trapped by its head and hands, its mummified skin stretched tightly over its emaciated body and its long brown hair in tangles around its eyeless, screaming face. It wore only a faded purple corset and a gold heart-shaped locket around its neck.

Theo tapped its collar bone. "This is Colette," she said. "She was very pretty in her day." She pushed the skeleton out of the device and it fell, skin cracking, into a pile of bones on the floor. "Come here, David."

He didn't move.

"Don't be obstinate. We have to keep you out of trouble."

"No. Theo, listen to me. You're possessed. You can fight her, you can force her out of your body."

She stared coldly at him. "What makes you think I *want* to fight her, David?"

"She's tricking you, Theo. She's using you." David paused. "She doesn't have the Erzuli doll yet, does she?"

Theo glared at him. "Get over here now!"

"Once she has it, she won't need you anymore. She'll put you in one of these too. Then she'll kill you, just like she did Colette."

Keeping the revolver ready, Theo stepped up to a portion of stone wall where ancient whips and blades were hung. She took a knife, a nasty one with a slightly curved eight-inch blade, from its holder, then moved back to stand over Amber. "If you don't get in the pillory *now,* David, I'll remove your lovely daughter's little finger. If you *still* refuse, I'll remove another. Ten fingers, ten toes, then a hand, a foot . . ." She smiled, pure evil, as she flicked the knife through the air. "Don't worry, David. The brazier's all ready, so I'll be able to cauterize her wounds. I promise you, David, I won't kill her." She paused. "So, what's it going to be?"

Out of options, he put his wrists and neck in the contraption she'd indicated and waited while she dropped the top and flipped the latch. "Good choice, David. Now, you, Chief, I want you to pick up your nephew and put him on that table near the brazier."

Glowering and grunting, Swenson finally managed to put Eric over his shoulder, fireman style. David watched out of the corner of his eye as the chief pushed an old set of bones onto the floor, then laid the nearly comatose boy carefully down on the table. Finished, he remained where he was, his hand resting gently on his nephew's shoulder.

Sixty-two

Body House: 2:51 A.M.

He stood by Eric, knowing the boy had a concussion, at least; knowing he had to get him to a hospital, and wondering if he—or the others—would be alive long enough to do so.

Swenson's mind had been reeling from the moment he'd first looked into this chamber of horrors, and when Theo Pelinore came at him with that poker or branding iron or whatever the hell it was, she'd knocked him off balance easily, then fought him with the strength of a woman possessed. Which he supposed she was.

He'd thought they had her when Eric jumped in, but an instant later, she'd grabbed her iron rod and bashed the side of his head. The boy went down, but Craig kept fighting.

And then, the most unforgivable thing of all had happened: Theo Pelinore had wrested his revolver from him.

He glanced left and right. Now, here they all were: in bondage, hurt or held at gunpoint. The way things looked right now, he thought as he stared down the barrel of his own gun, Melanie was their only chance—and she was going to have to have God's own luck just to stay alive herself.

"Chief, come here." Theo beckoned him toward her. Slowly he moved forward, stopping a few feet from her, wondering what she was going to do now.

"You see the cabinets behind me?"

"Yes?"

"Two of them are locked—the tall one behind me and the very large one below." Keeping the gun trained on him, she used her other hand to extract a long bobby pin from her hair. She tossed it to him and he caught it by reflex.

"Pick the locks."

"I don't know how to—"

"Don't play stupid, Chief. Remember, you've picked locks for Theo—for me—several times. The last time was just over a year ago, when the seller forgot to leave me a key for that split-level on Gull Street."

She had him there. "Which one first?"

She pointed at the bottom door. "That one."

Obediently, he took the pin and squatted in front of the lock. The wood and hinges were heavy, but the lock was old and simple, the sort that required nothing more than a special skeleton key. He had it open in fifteen seconds.

"Now, Chief, do you see a blue steamer trunk in there?"

"Yes."

"Pull it out for me, very, very carefully."

The trunk moved more easily than he expected and he had it out in a moment, surprised to see two lengths of chain wrapped around it and secured with a padlock.

"Jimmy it," Theo ordered.

The padlock took longer, and when it finally opened, he was sweating profusely despite the chill in the room. He looked up and came face-to-face with his gun.

"Now," Theo said, "I want you to listen very carefully. You are going to open the trunk and you are going to treat what lies inside it as if it were a king's treasure. If you don't, I'll start paring your nephew's toes and fingers. Go ahead, open it."

He flipped the brass latches and slowly pushed the arched lid open. The stench of jasmine and bodily decay rose in a putrid, choking cloud, and when he saw the body, it took every ounce of control in his possession to stop the dizzingly black swirl that spiraled through his brain.

His head spun and he pushed himself away. "My God," he whispered. "My God."

She lay curled in a fetal position, her raven hair swirling down over her white shoulders and black gown. Despite the odor, which reminded him of a two-weeks dead body he'd had the misfortune to discover in the trunk of a car abandoned by the beach several summers ago, there were no visible signs of decay. Long black lashes edging the closed eyelids emphasized the unnatural pallor of her skin. There was a fragility about her that made her look more like one of her porcelain dolls than a woman of flesh-and-blood.

"Lift her out of the trunk," Theo ordered softly. "Go ahead, she won't break."

He took a deep breath and held it as he scooped the body into his arms. It lay cold and limp in his grasp and was not desiccated, as he'd expected, but heavy with muscle and, judging by the blue traceries in the forearms, blood. The head had tilted back and he searched for a pulse in the neck, but saw none.

Theo moved to an empty table near the cabinets. "Put her here," she directed. "Be careful."

He gave up holding his breath as he placed her on the table, and was again nearly overwhelmed by the noxious, sweet odors.

"Okay, stay where you are." Theo, standing across the table from him, lovingly straightened the old-fashioned black gown Christabel wore. She lingered a moment, gently touching one cold cheek, then combing her fingers through a tangle in the thick black hair.

"Alright, Chief," she said a moment later. "Open the other lock."

He walked back to the cabinets and worked on the keyhole that held two tall upper doors together until it yielded.

Various vials and bottles of oils and powders lined the upper shelf, while the lower contained dolls, male and female. "These dolls all contain souls," Theo said softly. She pointed at one. "See? It's sweet Colette. Now, Chief, I want you to carefully take them down and set them on that tray next to my body."

There were eight of them, and each seemed to stare at him

accusingly as he laid them on the tray. Dazed, he stared back. Nothing seemed real anymore.

"There's one more, Chief."

Slowly, he returned to the cabinet. "I don't see it."

"In the far left corner."

His hand closed over a cool, rough object and he drew it out. It was nothing like the porcelain dolls. Instead it was a primitive female figure made of red clay. It squatted, as if giving birth, and its gaping vagina and jutting breasts were obscenely exaggerated. *Erzuli.*

"Give it to me." Theo moved closer and held out her free hand.

He made no move until she cocked his gun, then reluctantly he handed it over.

Holding the icon protectively against her bosom, Theo gave him an ugly grin. "I have one more job for you, Chief, before we put you with your friends."

He said nothing, but continued to watch her, hoping her guard would drop so that he could make a move for his gun, though so far she'd left him no openings.

"Over here, Chief." She walked him back to Christabel's body and the tray of dolls, then gave him another leering smile. "You should be honored, you know. I could truss you up like I did the others, but instead, I'm going to let you help me."

Stonily, he stared at her as she moved to the opposite side of Christabel's body. Keeping her eye and the gun trained on him, she set Erzuli near it, then reached down and gently opened the corpse's mouth.

"Now then, Chief, we're going to begin reanimating my body. Pick up a doll. Any one will do."

He did, without even looking at it.

"Good. Now, being very careful not to spill any blood, snap its head off."

He heard Jerry Romero begin to moan somewhere in the shadows.

"Do it."

Taking the doll in both hands, he exerted pressure on the neck. For a moment he didn't think it would give, but all of a sudden it snapped off cleanly. Hot blood oozed over his hands and a sudden blast of energy swirled around him, then flew across the room to a mummified body manacled high on a wall. The ghost took form—it was a well-dressed male—and seemed to superimpose itself over the hanging bones. Faintly, as he watched it writhe, Swenson imagined he could hear its screams.

"Don't spill the blood!" Theo screamed, grabbing the doll from his hand. "I told you not to spill it!"

She poured the blood—the doll contained at least a cup of it—into the corpse's mouth. Though he didn't see it swallow, it obviously went down smoothly.

"Now," she ordered, "do the same with the rest of them."

Clutching Erzuli, Theo watched critically as he snapped and poured doll after doll. Each broken doll produced an imprisoned spirit that instinctively sought out its skeletal remains.

When he was done, the only traces of blood were the thin trickles of scarlet that ran from the corners of Christabel's mouth. All around them, the long-dead corpses seemed to writhe in their bonds.

"Look at her, Chief," Theo murmured as she touched a finger to a drop of blood on the body's lips. "Do you see the beginnings of life?" She put her fingertip in her mouth and sucked off the blood.

There was a subtle difference in the body's appearance now. The flesh, though still deathly white, appeared somehow less fragile, less like porcelain. The lips showed a trace of color. A chill ran down Swenson's spine as he detected the faintest of pulse beats in the long, pale neck.

"She's nearly ready," Theo spoke Christabel's thoughts, without knowing they weren't her own. "It's been so long." She laughed with delight. "So long."

Sixty-three

Body House: 3:33 A.M.

Melanie, hidden beneath Amber's table, winced and massaged a charley horse out of her calf as she watched Theo Pelinore and Craig Swenson from between the folds of the velvet cloth.

She had to do something soon, or they'd all be dead, but she still didn't know what. What if she did something stupid and got them all killed? *If you don't do anything, they're already dead. Whatever you do, it's better than sitting on your ass!*

Above her, the table creaked as Amber shifted slightly. Melanie had cut three of the bindings and was halfway through the last ankle rope when she had to hide, hoping that Theo hadn't realized she was there.

Squatting under the stifling velvet, Melanie absently stroked David's now-folded jackknife. Its four-inch blade was reasonably sharp, and now, as she saw Craig Swenson, and Theo behind him with the gun, slowly approaching a set of arm and leg manacles set into a portion of wall not ten feet from where she crouched, she silently opened the knife. Lizzie's instructions had been very specific: destroy the body, then destroy the doll. *How?* The body in question lay on a table halfway across the room, and the Erzuli figure was tightly clutched in Theo's hands, only a few feet away. Though she wasn't sure, she suspected that as soon as Swenson was trussed up, Theo would break the doll, unleashing Christabel's full power. She couldn't let that happen. *How?* she thought again. All the woman had to do was throw it or drop it and that would be that. *There has to be a way.*

"Put them on," Theo told Swenson as she gestured at the manacles.

"What if I don't?" Craig asked, staring directly at Melanie's hiding place.

"We'll kill you."

Carefully, Melanie raised the velvet so Craig could see her.

"You're going to kill me anyway," he countered.

Melanie held up three fingers, then made a fist, waited a brief second, then put one finger back up. *On three, Craig, on three!* she thought.

Theo laughed. "If you don't cooperate, your death will be harder. But Eric will die first and that will take a very long time. You'll watch him die and I'll slice off your eyelids so you can't look away. You don't want that, do you?"

Melanie put the second finger up. Her other hand clenched the knife handle tightly.

"You're bluffing, Theo," Craig said.

"You think so?" Theo cocked the gun.

Melanie held up her third finger just as Theo pulled the trigger, and as she moved out from beneath the table, knife up, time slowed down. In the instant it took her to propel herself four feet, she heard Craig gasp, saw blood spray from his thigh before he grasped it, and heard Theo say, "I never bluff."

Then Melanie grabbed Theo's leg and plunged her knife into the thickest part of the calf muscle. Theo screamed and dropped the gun as she tried to kick her away. Craig dropped heavily to the ground.

Time sped up as she clung to the woman's leg, aware of nothing now except that she was twisting the blade deeper into the flesh, yanking it back and forth, mangling muscle and tendon and ligament with a ferocity she'd never known she possessed.

Suddenly, Theo's hands were in her hair, pulling, tearing, clawing for her face. Melanie withdrew the knife and plunged it in again, behind the knee this time. She sliced sideways, feeling hot blood spray across her face as she sliced through an artery and sawed into a tough ligament.

Theo's red-enameled claws raked down her forehead, searching for her eyes.

Then the gun went off again.

The claws dug harder for an instant, then let go as Theo fell. Melanie rolled left as the woman landed, staring at her with huge dark eyes. A red hole gaped in the center of her forehead and, as Melanie pushed herself away, she saw that the back of Theo Pelinore's head was gone. She closed her eyes. *I won't be sick. I won't be sick.*

"Christ, that's the first time I've ever shot anyone," Swenson rasped as he stared at the body.

"You had to," Melanie heard herself say dully.

"Yeah, in the line of duty." The chief laughed humorlessly. "Guess it's true about possession being nine points of the law."

When she didn't comment, he asked, "You okay?"

Fighting down the bile in her throat, she lifted her head so she wouldn't see what lay on the floor in front of her, then opened her eyes and saw Craig sitting propped against the wall, still holding the gun.

"What the hell's going on?" Jerry Romero demanded from beneath the velvet spread.

"I'm okay," Melanie told Craig. Staring at his bleeding leg, she began ripping a long wide ruffle from her dress. Then she stopped cold. "My God, the doll!"

Craig shook his head. "It's okay. She's still hanging onto it. Look."

"I'll take your word for it," Melanie said grimly. She finished ripping the ruffle, tossed it to Swenson, then rose shakily to her feet, turning so that she wouldn't have to look at the dead woman. Behind her, Amber sat up and pushed the heavy velvet off. "Mel, can I have the knife a minute?"

"Yeah, hon, here, let me."

"No, I can do it. Get Daddy out of that thing."

"Yeah," David called.

"God, David!" She turned and saw him, saw that he'd seen

everything. "God, David, I'm sorry—" Guiltily, she gave Amber the knife and went to him.

"That was a nice piece of work," he said as she released the latch and lifted the stock's crosspiece.

"Thanks, I guess."

David rubbed his neck. "Swenson, are you okay?"

"What the hell's going on?" came Romero's muffled demand.

"Hang on another minute, Jerry," Melanie called.

"I'll live," Craig told David as he tied the green satin bandage in a tight knot. "One of you'd better grab that voodoo doll," he added. Slowly, grunting and wincing, he got to his feet. "I've gotta check on Eric. Gotta' get him to a hospital."

"I'll check him," Melanie said. "You stay put."

"I thought I was going to suffocate under that thing," Amber remarked as Melanie crossed the room. *Thank God she's okay,* Melanie thought as she placed her palm on Eric's pale forehead. It was clammy with sweat.

She bent over him. "Eric, can you hear me?"

His eyes moved beneath the lids and she said his name again. This time, they opened, but his gaze seemed slightly unfocused.

"I have a headache," he said.

"How many?" she asked, holding up four fingers.

"Four."

She took his hand and squeezed it. "Don't try to get up. We'll get you out of here in a few minutes."

"Okay."

She turned and rejoined the others. "He's going to be fine," she told Craig, who sat holding his leg.

"Good," Amber said. She stood close to her father, secure under his arm. In his other hand he cradled the Erzuli doll.

"Want me to take that?" Melanie asked, gratefully noticing that the velvet spread had been draped over Theo Pelinore's body.

"Thanks," he said as she carefully took the effigy.

"What now?" she asked.

"We finish what we started," he replied.

"Do you think we should get Craig and Eric out of here first?"

"We *should,* but we don't have the time or strength," he replied. "Getting those big guys up that spiral staircase by ourselves doesn't sound too promising. Besides," he added, grimacing, "what we have to do won't take long."

Melanie followed his gaze to the table where Christabel's body lay. Her stomach flopped. "What do we have to do?" she asked, "To destroy it?"

"Would somebody please get me out of here?" Jerry Romero pleaded.

"Sorry," Swenson said.

David started to withdraw his arm from Amber, but Melanie stepped forward quickly. "I'll get him." She'd seen enough blood for one night. Jerry Romero could help David with the burning or dismembering or whatever it was he was going to do.

She grasped the edge of the velvet to pull it up. "I'll have you out of there in a jif, Mr. Romer—"

"Christ!" yelled Craig Swenson.

Startled, she let go of the material and whirled, nearly dropping the Erzuli doll in her surprise.

Amber stood behind her father, clutching his hair with one hand, and with the other, holding the open jackknife hard against his exposed throat. A thin ribbon of blood oozed down his neck.

Her eyes, cold chips of ice, bored into Melanie's. "Bring me the doll."

"Don't do it." Craig held his revolver trained on the girl.

Christabel's chill laughter bubbled from Amber's mouth. "What are you going to do, Chief? Shoot an innocent little girl?"

Swenson lowered the gun.

"Now, sweetie, if you want your loverboy back in one piece, you just bring that doll to me."

Her mind racing, Melanie took one tentative step forward.

"That's right," Amber said, "But you'd better move faster. This knife is slipping." She laughed harshly.

David made a strangled sound as the bloody trail on his neck widened.

"Okay, okay." *Oh, God, what do I do? She's going to kill him. She's going to kill us all!* Melanie took a slow step. If she dropped the Erzuli figure, it would break and that would mean that Christabel might abandon Amber and race into her own body. But what would happen then? Would she be so powerful that they'd have no chance against her? *What do I do, oh God, what do I do?*

God didn't answer, but Lizzie did. A faint swirl of lavender perfume wafted into Melanie's nose and something cool touched her cheek.

Help me, Lizzie! Help me!

And then Lizzie joined her, as she'd joined David to show him how to work the secret latch upstairs. She moved onto Melanie and, for one brief moment, she felt all of Lizzie's guilt and pain, all of her sorrow. Then it was all swept away as the spirit directed her attention to the collection of knives, whips, and other instruments of torture that hung on the wall adjacent to the cabinets. It was perhaps twenty feet away.

The scythe, Lizzie whispered in her mind. *Do you see the scythe?*

Yes. It hung like a crescent moon between two thin fencing swords. It had a heavy wooden handle and the blade was a graceful and deadly two-foot half-circle of polished steel.

"Give me the doll!" Amber said in deadly tones.

Melanie took another step. *Tell me what to do!*

You must do what I could not. Sadness edged Lizzie's thought.

Tell me!

You must behead her . . .

Oh, God.

It's the only way.

Tell me.

You must break Erzuli and surprise my daughter. Throw it at her, very hard, so that she tries to catch it. I think that's your best chance to save your beloved from her knife. But make sure she can't catch it. Throw it high. It must *break!*

The instant it breaks, Christabel will enter her body and

she'll have incredible power. You won't be able to fight her, none of you will.

The instant you throw the doll, run and take the scythe and do it! Don't hesitate! Behead her! Finish it, dear God, finish it!

Lizzie left as suddenly as she had come. Melanie glanced at the scythe. *No, don't think about it. You won't be able to do it.* God, she doubted that she could do it anyway!

"I guess you want me to kill him!" Amber said.

"No . . . No, please," Melanie said quickly. "No. I'll give you the doll. Here—"

In a wink, she drew her arm back and flung it with all her might. Amber instantly let go of David and dropped the knife as she reflexively reached for the doll.

RUN!

Lizzie's voice resounded in her ears and Melanie was off, racing for the weapon, hearing the pottery shatter as the icon struck the wall, hearing David scream her name as she grabbed the scythe's handle and yanked. It wouldn't come loose. Frantically, she pulled on it again and it came free.

It seemed to weigh nothing as she ran with it held above her head, time trickling once more.

Christabel sat up on the table and looked at her. "You can't do it," she spat, and then she began laughing—a sound infinitely more horrible now than it had ever been before.

Melanie froze. Lavender scent swirled through her as Lizzie rejoined her. *GO!* she screamed in her brain. *GO NOW!* Something forced her to take a step, to raise the scythe a little higher. *FOR GOD'S SAKE, DO IT!*

She covered the ten remaining feet in a half-dozen running steps, refusing to hear Christabel's laughter, swinging the weapon back as she ran, as if it were a baseball bat. "Baseball," she whispered. "I'm playing baseball."

The laughter did not stop until Melanie brought the scythe around in a perfectly controlled arc. Shocked, Christabel started to raise her hands to her face, but by the time they arrived, her head was rolling across the floor, the eyes still full of surprise, the mouth open in amazement.

They're free now, all of them. You did it. Lizzie, still with her, was full of joy and sadness.

We did it, Melanie returned as she sensed Lizzie leaving her. *We did it together.*

Christabel's body slowly began to slide to the floor. She watched it, feeling no horror, only relief.

"Melanie!"

She turned at the sound of David's voice, but stayed where she was, waiting as he came to her, Amber right behind him. She vaguely noticed that the ghosts that had clung to their tortured corpses were gone—were free—and she thought she might be smiling, though she wasn't really sure.

"Melanie!" David said, holding out his arms. The cut on his neck, she realized now, was very small. She was glad.

She started to lift her hands to his, then realized that she still held the bloody scythe.

David stared at the weapon. "You're amazing, Melanie."

She shook her head, letting him take the scythe from her, watching as he hooked the weapon through the neck hole of a pillory. That struck her as funny and she allowed a tiny hysterical giggle to escape. "No, not amazing," she said, as more giggles came. "But after I tell you how I did it, you're never going to want to watch baseball again." She collapsed against him, giving in to the release of laughter and tears. Around them, the scent of lavender still lingered.

"Will somebody *please* let me out of here!" Jerry Romero cried plaintively.

Sixty-four

Body House: 4:34 A.M.

"Are you sure you don't want me to drive you?'

"No, Dad, I'm fine." Amber, dressed in a sweatshirt and jeans, a backpack slung over one shoulder, gave David a kiss on the cheek. "I called Kelly and she's expecting me. I just want to get out of here, you know?"

"I know, I know. But do you really feel like driving yourself?"

"Are you afraid I'm going to wreck the Bronco, Dad?"

He smiled weakly. "No, kiddo, but—"

Melanie smiled to herself as she watched David fuss over his daughter. She could tell that Amber was trying very hard not to show how irritated she was at being treated like a child, and Melanie thought it was the most wonderful thing in the world, getting to watch those two bicker and fuss with each other.

So much had happened in the hour since she'd hit a home run with Christabel's head—she couldn't think of it in any other way and the thought made a crazy giggle try to bubble out even now, but she stifled it without David and Amber hearing, thank God. It seemed like years had gone by.

They'd had to answer a few official questions as soon as the police arrived, but fortunately, they worked for Craig, who had cut things short by explaining that he'd be overseeing the details of the reports and investigation himself in the morning.

At that, Dr. Shayrock, a tall wiry guy who looked to Melanie like he should still be in school, gave Craig a severe look, but the chief had merely called him an old mother hen and assured everyone that no flesh wound was going to keep him from being at work on time.

Melanie was glad she'd seen Craig handle the man because the minute the paramedics loaded up the Swensons—they and the doctor having assured the others that Eric was in no real danger—the doctor was all over Melanie, who was still suffering from giggling fits as baseball pun after baseball pun popped into her head. Having seen Craig's firm tactics, she did the same. "Doctor, I'm working out my trauma," she'd explained as the realization that if Christabel had had two heads, it would have been a double header made her start giggling again. "If you stop me from dealing with it now, I'll just have to later."

Reluctantly, he left her alone, though he insisted on giving her a supply of tranquilizers. And the truth was, she was glad he did—later, she'd be happy to pop a couple and go to sleep for a century or two. But for now, she wanted to be fully alert.

After that, things had moved even more quickly. Jerry Romero had to be dealt with. He had complained bitterly about missing "the show," and hadn't let up until David promised him he could come back tomorrow and film whatever he damn well pleased. Still, the man wouldn't leave, until Amber, who seemed to have fared better than anyone, told him about the doctor's photo album with its picture of Christabel. Romero immediately chatted up Shayrock, who was flattered and pleased and took the man home with him.

Now, Melanie saw Amber walking her way. She stood up, her legs still a little shaky.

"No, Mel, don't get up."

"I already did." She walked into Amber's extended arms and traded a long, warm hug.

"Thanks for coming," the teen said finally. She glanced at David, who had joined them sometime during the embrace. "She saved our bacon, didn't she, Dad? We wouldn't have made it without her." She winked at Melanie as she spoke.

Bless your matchmaking little heart, Amber, but you don't understand: if he doesn't love me anymore, nothing I do will make him love me again.

"Yeah, kiddo, she sure did." As he spoke, he gazed steadily at Melanie.

"Oh, you would have been fine without me." She smiled weakly, butterflies shooting through her stomach as she wondered how she should read his look.

"Kelly's waiting for me," Amber said. "I'd better go." She paused. "Are you guys going to stay here or what?" She hesitated. "I mean, it's so creepy and all. Maybe you should go to a hotel."

"We'll see, kiddo. I'll phone you in the morning and we'll decide where to meet." David was grinning at his daughter's not-so-subtle hints and Melanie took that as a good sign, although, when he glanced at her, she was careful to keep her expression neutral.

"Where all three of us will meet, right?" Amber asked.

"Sure."

"Good." She gave her dad one more hug. "Don't call before noon, okay?'

"Okay."

The moment Amber shut the door behind her, Melanie's heart started to pound. She walked over to the cabinet containing the dolls. "Do you suppose that there were souls in these, too, David?"

"Yes." He joined her. Taking a small key from his pocket, he unlocked the cabinet and extracted one of the dolls, a pretty blonde in a yellow dress. "I wonder . . ." he said and began undoing the dress. "This one, like most of these, just had a little pinhole in its breast. I assume that means the woman she represented would have had a heart attack when Christabel shoved the pin in."

"Yes, that makes sense," Melanie said softly. Having him so near, made her want to hug him, as she impulsively had when they'd first seen one another at the party. But he might not like it. *Go slow,* she cautioned herself. *Let him make the first move . . . If he's going to make one at all.*

"There," he said, exposing the doll's torso. "The little hole is gone. See?"

She studied the smooth china. "Yes. What does it mean?"

"I think that if we looked, we'd find that all the dolls 'wounds' have disappeared and that it happened when the souls were released."

"What a lovely thought," she said. Suddenly, lavender wafted around them. "Lizzie's here."

"Maybe she's waiting to see us out," David said gently. "After all, she's the hostess." He paused awkwardly. "Are you going to a hotel?"

"Why?"

"Uh, well, I thought I'd rent a room. I don't want to stay here either, quite frankly." His smile was a little crooked. "I think Lizzie would appreciate it if we'd hurry up and leave so she can too."

Melanie felt like crying. *Do you want to share a room with me, David? Do you want to see if we've still got it?* She couldn't bring herself to say the words. Lavender swirled into her nostrils, and for one brief instant, Lizzie was in her mind, but she said nothing. *Just passing through,* Melanie thought. "It'll be dawn soon." Her words surprised her.

"Yes, it will." David smiled and the way the skin around his tired eyes crinkled sent a little worm of pleasure through her.

"I've never seen dawn on thE West Coast," she said. "Are you up for a walk?"

He looked surprised, then chuckled. "Sure. But dawn's not spectacular here. Sunset is. Maybe tonight . . ." His words trailed off. "Let's walk out to Widow's Peak. To the lighthouse."

He held the door for her and, as she stepped onto the veranda, Lizzie's scent followed them, though when they started down the stairs, she knew that the spirit of Lizzie Baudey had remained behind.

Sixty-five

Widow's Peak: 4:59 A.M.

David stood with Melanie at the westernmost tip of Widow's Peak and listened to the cry of a gull, a forlorn melody to accompany the soft, insistent cadence of the waves as they crashed against the rocks below. Behind them, the eastern sky had just begun to show the first pale glimmerings of dawn, but here, night continued its dark rule.

David thought that the full moon looked like a huge gold coin, a pirate's ransom, as it hung low over the ocean and cast its shimmering reflections against the dark water. A single fishing boat, a dot of yellow light lazily riding the waves, lay at anchor just outside the bay. To the north, Red Cay, with its criss-cross of street lights, appeared to be nothing more than a child's miniature toy town.

All these things served only to deepen David's melancholy, to strengthen his fear that he had lived through this night only to some day die a lonely old man, bereft of love, without the woman who was standing silently beside him.

"It's beautiful here, isn't it?" Melanie spoke in the same soft tone she'd used ever since she'd gained control over her hysterics down in Body House's dungeon.

"Yes. Beautiful." David didn't know how to read her, and afraid of doing or saying the wrong thing, thus assuring his lonesome fate, he said no more, but continued to stand there and look out to sea, hoping that she wanted him as much as he wanted her, but fearing that she did not. When Amber had encouraged them to go to a hotel, David had smiled at Melanie, but she'd looked cool and unimpressed. That left him afraid to try again. Her icy expression was bad enough: to actually hear her reject him was too much right now.

He wondered if the old wounds ran too deep to allow them to try again. He wanted to ask her, but it seemed futile if he was too afraid of her answer. Maybe, he thought, that meant he was fooling himself in thinking *he* wanted to try.

"Are you going to stay here?" she asked finally. "In Red Cay?"

"No, not here. The view's great," he added lightly, "but I've had just about all I can take of Body House. I was sort of thinking about looking for a place in Connecticut. Something nice. You know, less than a dozen rooms, central air, a pool, no ghosts."

She glanced at him, amused, and, he thought, interested. "Really? Why Connecticut?"

"It's an easy commute to the city," he explained. "I miss Manhattan." He saw the corner of her mouth crook briefly in a tiny smile, and took a chance. "I miss *you.*"

"I miss you, too." She stared at the water. "But . . ."

"I know." He examined his fingers intently. "But we can still be friends."

"Friends," she sadly. "Just friends."

He didn't know what she meant and was afraid to ask for fear the answer was not the one he wanted.

They studied the sea for a long time.

"Lizzie's still in there," she said finally. "In the house. All the others, the ones Christabel had trapped, they left. But Lizzie didn't."

"I think she was waiting for us," David said.

"Then why didn't she leave when we did?" Melanie asked in that same soft, sad voice. "She stayed on the veranda."

"I don't know. Maybe she's gone now. Maybe she's got unfinished business."

"It's cold out here," Melanie said, moving closer to him.

He slipped his arm around her. "Do you think Lizzie and

her captain will find each other now?" A cool breeze eddied around them, fluffing Melanie's hair and tickling his ears.

"I hope so." As he spoke, he turned to face her, determined to ask his question at last—that she had moved closer to him and now cuddled into his arm, gave him the courage. But he stopped short as he detected a vague movement of shadows against the pale lighthouse wall. "Look," he whispered.

She followed his gaze. "What is it?" she murmured.

"I think it's the answer to your question." He took her hand, and as they walked slowly toward the tower, he knew he was right. Drawing nearer, he could see the shadows take on form, but no substance. The spirits of the long-lost lovers stood facing one another. Ezra Wilder, free now of Christabel's curse, had lost the solidity he'd acquired when his doll was broken.

"Dear God," Melanie whispered. "She was waiting for us to leave so she could find her captain. Do you think we should leave? They probably want privacy."

"No," David said. "Let's wait a moment."

They halted a few feet from the spirits, who were caught up in one another, and seemed unaware of them.

Lizzie, the green of her dress barely discernable in the dim gray light of dawn, tilted her face toward her captain and, slowly, Ezra lifted his hand to touch her cheek.

But his fingers merely brushed through her image. Her face sad, Lizzie tried to take his hand, but neither one could seem to touch the other. Longingly, they gazed at one another.

"David?" Melanie murmured. "Do you think we could—"

"Yes. Come on."

Hand in hand, they approached the ghostly lovers. The spirits, lost in their own world, didn't seem aware of them until Melanie reached out to Lizzie, letting her fingers drift into the cool, ghostly energy. The spirits studied them for a long moment, then looked back at one another. Ezra smiled gently at the luminous face of his beloved.

And then they joined with the living couple and, as Ezra slipped into his body and mind like a cool sea breeze, David felt hot tears of joy, his own and the captain's, spring to his eyes.

Slowly, he lifted his hand to touch Melanie's radiant face, marveling anew at the feel of her soft, smooth skin, then bending to kiss away the hot tear that fled down her cheek.

Mingled images shot through his brain, memories of himself and Melanie in other times, and the captain's memories of Lizzie, clothed in different times and places, yet identical in their joy and longing. In their love.

Trembling, he moved his lips to hers and, as they embraced, all thought fell away in a fire of emotion, in a blaze of love requited. Eighty years or a few months, they felt the same bittersweet, rapturous joy.

At last, David sensed that the captain was ready to depart. He and Melanie parted, though they still held hands and, as the spirits moved away from them, the living couple stared into one another's eyes, speaking without words, as they had done so often in times past.

A swirl of lavender drew their attention and they turned to see Lizzie Baudey and Ezra Wilder watching them with pleasure on their faces and, as he drew Melanie closer to him, he knew that he and Melanie had been Lizzie's unfinished business. Lizzie and Ezra's time on earth was complete now, and as he watched them, they became more and more transparent, fading away until they were only flickers. It seemed sad, in a way, to see them go, though there was only joy on their faces as they disappeared.

The first low rays of sunlight were shooting through the pines near the lighthouse as David turned to Melanie, pulling her closer and looking into her emerald eyes. "I once found my one true love," he told her softly, "but I didn't know it. I was foolish and I lost her."

She brushed a lock of hair from his eyes then ran her finger down over his cheek and across his lips. "Funny," she said, just before he kissed her, "the same thing happened to me."

ABOUT THE AUTHOR

Tamara Thorne lives with her family in California. She is the author of four horror novels published by Pinnacle Books: HAUNTED, MOONFALL, ETERNITY, and CANDLE BAY. Tamara loves hearing from readers; you may write to her c/o Pinnacle Books. Please include a self-addressed, stamped envelope if you wish to receive a response.